Mystery Car
Carlson, P. M.
Deathwind : a Marty Hopkins
 mystery

DEATHWIND

Further Titles by P M Carlson

DEATHWIND

P. M. Carlson

This first world edition published in Great Britain 2004 by
SEVERN HOUSE PUBLISHERS LTD of
9–15 High Street, Sutton, Surrey SM1 1DF.
This first world edition published in the USA 2005 by
SEVERN HOUSE PUBLISHERS INC of
595 Madison Avenue, New York, N.Y. 10022.

British Library Cataloguing in Publication Data

Carlson, P. M.
    Deathwind. - (The Marty Hopkins mysteries)
    1.   Hopkins, Marty (Fictitious character) - Fiction
    2.   Police - Indiana - Fiction
    3.   Detective and mystery stories
    I.   Title
    813.5'4 [F]

    ISBN 0-7278-6175-1

Typeset by Palimpsest Book Production Ltd.,
Polmont, Stirlingshire, Scotland.
Printed and bound in Great Britain by
MPG Books Ltd., Bodmin, Cornwall.

Acknowledgements

I want to thank Kay Williams, Al Ashforth, Robert Knightly, Joanna Wolper, Ralph Gardner, and especially Major David W. Toumey—Chief Deputy, Monroe County Sheriff's Department—for sharing their insight and expertise. Errors remaining are mine and not theirs.

One

Summer clings in southern Indiana. As harvest time approaches in a drought year, the trees, still dry and rustling, struggle to set nuts. Spindly late tomatoes and early apples fleck the exhausted countryside with crimson. Grainfields are sparse and brown. So the humidity of a late invasion of Gulf air from the south is welcome, and causes farmers and gardeners to look skyward hopefully for signs of rain, and fearfully for signs of storms.

To the north, polar air is massing, preparing for its wintry slide over the limestone knobs and hills. Yet for a time the warm southern air holds on, like a jealous parent reluctant to release a child to the future. Refusing to retreat, every now and then it pushes back as though it were springtime instead of fall, as though it had a chance of prevailing against the cycling seasons. The sun continues to beat down, heating grass and thistle, soil and stone. Warmed by the warm earth, the sticky surface air rises to higher, chillier realms to form clouds. Churning and roiling in place, energized by high dry winds from the southwest whipping across its top, a massive storm cloud builds, dark and heavy as an anvil. On the earth's surface, creatures hold their breath in the electric stillness, knowing that in this titanic standoff the only result can be titanic violence: explosions of lightning, raging thunder, hailstorms.

Even tornadoes.

The first time the phone rang was a false alarm. Its shrill jangle jolted Marty Hopkins full awake. Four fifteen, said her bedside radio alarm. A major catastrophe, she thought, a pile-up on the highway or some boozed-up Rambo type trying to gun down everybody who'd ever crossed him. Or maybe it was— Her hand hesitated over the receiver, but she picked up before the third ring. "Deputy Hopkins," she said crisply.

"Hopkins! Nice name you've got there!"

Shoot. Marty took a deep breath. "Brad, it's four o'clock in the

1

morning. We'll be talking with the lawyers this afternoon, right? So there's no reason to talk to each other now."

"Listen up, Marty. I've figured out what your problem is. You've always had these fantasies, you know? A little out of touch?"

Yeah, right, thought Marty, like thinking somehow you and I could make a go of marriage. Aloud she said, "Brad, it's better if we don't—"

He ignored her and pushed on. "Well, your little fantasy about taking away my home and my kid—"

"Your what? What are you talking about?" Was he drinking? She listened for bar noises, but there was nothing in the background.

"—that fantasy won't work, hear? It won't work. I'll never let you do that! Swear to God, sometimes I think I don't know you at all. You've turned into this selfish bitch. Used to be, you cared about your family. Now you're in this dream world, thinking you can cheat, turn my kid against me, walk all over my life—"

"Yeah, right, you're an abused spouse, all right! Why can't you—"

"Stop it!" screamed a voice on the downstairs extension, a young voice. "This is so dumb! You're wrecking everything!"

Shoot. Marty's hand clenched on the receiver.

Brad said, "Chrissie, honey, you're right. Your mother's trying to have everything her way again. She won't listen."

"Look, let's everybody cool off, okay?" Marty said. "Brad, it's not fair to Chrissie to drag her her into this. We can talk about it at the meeting this afternoon. Or— Are you calling because you can't come?"

"Yeah, you'd like that, wouldn't you? Me here in Tennessee, so you can have things totally your way? No sir, I'll be there. I'm packing right now. You'll be sorry you ever started this stupid thing!"

"We'll discuss it this afternoon, okay?"

She was talking to air. He'd hung up.

Marty replaced the receiver with a shaky hand and ran her fingers through her curls. What did he want? For years he'd spent more time away than here, looking in one state after another for his big break in broadcasting. Meanwhile Marty got a good job in the sheriff's department, made friends, fixed up the old house her mother had left her, and comforted him time after time when he'd come home bruised by another failure. Each time they had less to say to each other, less in common. She'd ended up weeping alone after every visit last year, mourning the dreams that could never come

2

true. When she'd filed for divorce last month she'd thought it would just make things official, let them both get on with their lives. But he was fighting it as though there was something to fight about.

She pushed her toes into the pink slippers he'd brought her from Chicago four years ago. Wrapping her terrycloth robe around her, she headed for the stairs. Aunt Vonnie, her platinum-blond hair in rollers, met her in the upstairs hall. "What's going on? Emergency call?"

"Just Brad."

"At this hour? Lord have mercy! He's trying to torture you, isn't he?"

"He's upset, Aunt Vonnie."

"Upset!" Aunt Vonnie snorted. "You shouldn't ever have gotten involved with him. Your mother always said he'd cause you grief."

It was twice as irritating that Aunt Vonnie was right. Marty's mother had complained a lot about Brad. To Marty it had seemed like clinging, her widowed mother, full of dreams cut short by her husband's death, asking Marty to fulfill them. Marty had had dreams of her own. Maybe her mother had seen Brad more clearly. But right now Marty didn't need any second-hand I-told-you-sos. She said as evenly as she could, "Look, this is between Brad and me, all right? No need for you to get into it. Or my mother."

"Your mother cried like a baby when you married that man! And you're crazy if you think it's just the two of you, girl! What about your daughter?"

It was like a knife in her heart. Marty snapped, "I know! *My* daughter! Not yours!" But at the flash of hurt in the older woman's eyes, Marty put her hand on her aunt's soft forearm. "I'm sorry, Aunt Vonnie. I know you care about Chrissie and me. But I've got enough problems today, right now, without having to hear about what my mother thought twelve years ago." Marty turned and started downstairs.

"Yeah?" Aunt Vonnie's voice floated down after her. "Your mother makes a lot more sense than you do, young lady!"

Old grump. Marty glanced across the dark living room as she passed the door on her way to the kitchen. She could see out the window. It was a starless night, inky black except for the porch light on the next house a quarter mile away. Then she caught a glimpse of movement in the room. It was Chrissie, hunkered down in the dark, staring out the window. Marty went in, flopped on to the couch, and switched on the lamp.

Chrissie didn't turn. She was eleven now, with dark curls and a

3

thin back that was rigid under the frayed black T-shirt she wore as pajamas. It was one her father had brought her from New York. Yessiree, Marty thought, great new life we're starting, kid, wearing the T-shirts and slippers he brought us. She said, "I know it's rough now, Chrissie. I wish things could be easier. But we'll get through it."

Chrissie swung around and glared at Marty. Her little-girl arms and legs were lengthening and she looked knobby-kneed and coltish, brown from the summer outdoors and decorated with a bandage on one shin. Her face, Marty thought, was beautiful, even though her eyes, as dark as Brad's, were red-rimmed now and blazing with scorn. Chrissie exclaimed, "You've turned into a selfish bitch!"

It wasn't the first time she'd said that but it stung even so. Chrissie was so angry about the divorce. Could she be right? Would it be best for her to try to make it up with Brad, move to Tennessee, give up her job, her house, everything she'd worked for over the last few years?

But Brad had broken so many promises already.

Marty said gently, "Honey, Daddy's just upset. Things won't be that different, really, once this is over. We'll both take care of you."

"You're wrecking everything!" Chrissie ran across the room and up the stairs.

Marty rested her face in her hands for a moment, then switched off the light and dragged herself back to bed.

The next phone call came half an hour later.

It was not a false alarm.

Five A.M. Sheriff Wes Cochran replaced the gold plastic receiver of the bank's space-age phone. Good, he thought, Hopkins would be here within minutes. She'd turned out to be a damn good deputy despite his early misgivings. Wes took off his Stetson, smoothed back his sleep-rumpled silver hair, and turned back to look at what he didn't want to see.

The body was a woman's. Early thirties, decently dressed in a blueish dress. Turquoise, his wife might call it. The high-heeled shoes were turquoise too, and the silky scarf around the neck had a blurry-looking pink and turquoise design, real artistic. It was damp. So was her face, her lipstick faded and her eye make-up streaky, just a touch of turquoise remaining on the closed lids. Her hair was a tumble of blond curls, and you had to look close to see the brown roots. Dangling silver earrings, silver bracelet.

No visible blood. No visible cuts or bruises.

4

She had a nice figure, Wes thought. Well-nourished Caucasian, Doc's report would say, meaning not too skinny, a nice womanly figure. She looked pink and healthy except for the death-slackness of her face. Fit, took care of herself, dressed well. What the hell was she doing dead on the gold carpet of the Montgomery State Bank lobby?

And what a lobby. Airy high white ceilings, tall round-top windows, starless September night beyond. You could fly a crop-duster around this lobby. Down here at human level, the golden-oak counters were faced with rugged Gothic-grade limestone, pitted with dime-sized fossils and air pockets. Wealth, solidity, the building murmured to its visitors, even at five o'clock in the morning. Gold-colored placards listed the current interest rates and winked bright with each flash from the police photographer's camera. Gold-colored carpet squished under their thick-soled official shoes.

Wes cleared his throat. "What do you think, Doc?"

Doc Altman adjusted his John Lennon glasses and glanced up at Wes's six-four. "I already told you. She's dead."

"Yeah, our mysterious caller said she was dying."

The coroner blinked at Wes reproachfully. "Hey, I'm supposed to wait for the state evidence technicians, and they haven't even arrived yet. And Kev's still making his pretty pictures."

"Yeah, well, he doesn't have to make them works of art," Wes grumbled. He turned away from the coroner toward the only civilian in the room. "Ed?"

"What can I do, Sheriff?" Ed Powers was a short, slim man in a gray suit, gray necktie, and neatly clipped gray fringe around his bald spot. He was vice-president of Montgomery State Bank and reminded Wes of a gray squirrel. A squirrel with a good barber. Wes knew Ed as off-and-on chairman of the United Way, occasional speaker at Kiwanis meetings, and umpire for Little League games. Pillar of the community. Someone had called Ed half an hour ago, saying there was a woman dying in the bank and hanging up quickly. Ed had called Wes directly, not going through 911, because he figured it might just be a prank. But whatever it was, Ed wanted official company just in case. Discreet official company. Well, for pillars of the community like Ed, elected officials got up in the middle of the night. Wes had agreed to meet him in the parking lot, hung up, and cursed. At this hour he wished the other guy had won the election for sheriff.

"You say her name was Stephanie Stollnitz?" Wes asked Ed now, looking at his notepad.

"That's right. One of our tellers."

"What can you tell me about her?"

"She's worked for us a couple of years. Reliable enough. Came from up north somewhere, Muncie, I think. Lived alone—divorced, I understand."

"Do you have her address?"

"It'll be on the computer."

"Did she have any medical problems that you know of?" Wes was aware of the solid thumping of his own heart. Not giving out on him, not at the moment.

"Never heard of any."

"Any other kind of problems?"

"Not that I know of. She did the work well enough. Maybe she talked to the other tellers. I wasn't aware of any problems but that means zip."

Ed was right. If Stephanie Stollnitz had had medical problems or other secrets, she wouldn't tell a vice-president. She'd tell her coworkers.

There was a screech of brakes in the parking lot. Wes glanced out the glass doors. It was Marty Hopkins, arriving at top speed, as usual. He looked over at the coroner. Kev the photographer had paused and Doc Altman was kneeling by the body now, not moving it before the state crime technicians arrived, but unable to resist peeking under the artistic scarf. No marks on the neck.

Wes turned back to greet his deputy. "Hopkins, good. We've got some work to do."

"Yes sir." She looked tired but her gray eyes were alert, taking in the scene.

Wes said, "Ed, Deputy Hopkins will be on this too. Mr. Powers is vice-president of the bank, Hopkins."

They murmured their glad-to-meet-yous and Wes went on, "We'll need a list of the other tellers."

Ed nodded. "Yes. I can get you her personnel file too."

"Can you look that up now?"

"Sure thing." Ed Powers seemed pleased to have a task other than hovering nervously around the edge of the scene. "I'll use one of the computers on the second floor. Stay out of your way."

"I'll come with you," Wes decided. Hopkins could stick around to help Doc Altman. At this lonely hour, with no clear idea of how the woman had died and his own mortality prickling under his skin, he too was pleased to have a task.

6

Two

Coral Turley hopped out of Hoyt's black BMW. Her Doc Martens boots squished some wild mint next to the asphalt driveway of their rented farmhouse, sending a whiff of fragrance into the air. The night was warm but starless, its inkiness accentuated by the lone porchlight they'd left on. Cicadas sang in the poplars. The summery scents and sounds brought a rush of sadness to Coral. A few months ago she would have danced with joy to be back in Nichols County. But then a few months ago she wouldn't have been wearing boots and torn fishnet stockings to show off her long dancer's legs. A few months ago she wouldn't have had this tattoo on her arm or nightmares about brutal wooden clubs every night. A few months ago she'd only been fifteen.

It was like a great steel shutter had clanged down to black out her past. That meant nowhere to go but the future. *Love is the light but its sun sets too* ... Coral was determined to create a bright future if she had to personally drag up the sun from behind the hills.

She ran up the steps of the farmhouse and into the kitchen. Duke was already there drinking coffee, his deceptively mild eyes watching her. Coral repressed a shiver and asked, "Who called?" The phone message light was blinking.

Duke shrugged. "Play it."

She punched the button to listen while she got herself a beer.

A male voice said, "Hoyt! Things are getting tense. Get your girlfriend over to the farm real soon."

Shit. Coral rewound the machine, used the bathroom, and went out on the porch. She heard Hoyt giggling in the car. Bastard, he was doing a line of coke. But at least he'd stayed clean to drive.

"Hoyt, c'mon in," she called.

Hoyt Heller climbed out of the car, grinning in the light from the porch. Black jeans and boots, no shirt, suspenders flopping around his narrow hips. He reached up toward the porch for her. His hand was tattooed with a skull that sprouted long, sinuous stems and leaves. They wound along his arm to bloom in an obscenely beautiful flower on his biceps. That flower had always fascinated her. She'd asked for one like it on her arm, but hers seemed flat and boring next to Hoyt's.

Hoyt said, "Hey, babe, come down here."

Coral shrugged and descended the steps. "Got another call from Mr. X," she said. "Who is he, anyway?"

"Some friend of Duke's. What did he want, for you to visit the farm? You don't have to stay more than a couple minutes. But that's why we're here."

"I know." But Coral felt uneasy at the thought of seeing her lovely mother's vast vegetable gardens, the orchards, the bright riot of autumn flowers against the house, her old room with the red poppy wallpaper. Her father too, small and wiry in his bright shirts, quietly repairing some machine, only his eyes anxious. But hell, she'd have to do it sometime. "Tomorrow we have to do the video-taping in Louisville. How about day after tomorrow?"

"Okay. Day after tomorrow." Hoyt pushed a long curly lock from his eyes. He had thin silver earrings in both ears. He draped an arm over Coral's shoulders and flashed his bright grin at her. "Still can't believe you came from a geek fruit stand, babe."

"It's a big business, Hoyt, not just a fruit stand! Anyway, your dad's a geek dentist."

"Sure." He spread his arms. "That's why I started thinking about embracing the darkness. I mean, what's darker than a visit to the dentist? Dentists, death—what's the diff?"

"Sounds like a new song," Coral giggled. She jumped on to the porch, brandished an invisible guitar, and sang, "'What's the diff, what's the diff? Whatever happens you end up stiff!'"

She gave a little hip wiggle and he lunged laughing against the edge of the porch, embracing her around the knees. "C'mon down, now, gorgeous, you're getting me horny."

"Duke's in there."

"Yeah, I can see his big car. I'll tell him to move out tomorrow. So how about right here, babe?"

Coral hated the scratchiness of weeds and pebbles on her bare skin, and hated to think of Duke coming out to discover them. She looked around and her eye fell on the underground storm shelter across the yard next to the driveway, a weathered door set flat in the scrubby grass. "I've got a better idea," she said.

"What?"

"Plunge into the depths!" She wriggled free and ran toward the shelter.

8

It took a moment to raise the door, another moment to climb down into the little underground space. There was a bench and a kerosene lamp. "Hey, got your lighter?" she asked.

"Yeah." He struck a light and looked around the tiny cement-lined room. "What is this?"

"Tornado shelter."

Delighted, he lit the lamp, singing, "Baby, love is the light but its sun sets too, and all I can see is the wind of death, the wind with dark on its breath." He placed the lamp on a shelf. The little space glowed.

Coral could remember several times at home when they'd had to run out to their similar shelter and huddle together in the tiny underground room. That was exciting, that edge of fear. She'd felt half relieved and half disappointed when the danger passed and they emerged to an intact world. Once they'd driven toward Evansville to see where a twister had actually touched down. It was awesome, the flattened sheds and great snapped tree stumps and wide-strewn debris. *The wind with dark on its breath . . .*

Ever since then Coral had felt safer underground.

Hoyt asked, "Hey, think we'll have a tornado?"

"It's real late in the year. They mostly come in spring and summer."

"It's still warm. Man, that'd be great! A tornado!"

He was from California and didn't understand. Coral said, "No thanks."

"Hey, babe, ill wind could blow some good," said Hoyt cheerfully. "Great visuals."

Well, that was true. Hoyt was a bastard but he knew the business. She watched him stretch, his lean muscles shimmering in the lamplight. When he did that on stage thousands of girls squealed in delight. Some day Coral would write the right song and they'd let her sing it, and she'd make the guys howl just as loud for her.

Hoyt was tugging at her T-shirt. "Hey, Coral, quit daydreaming. Time to get naked."

Never cross him when he was on coke. Just get it over with. Coral unzipped her black leather shorts.

Wes Cochran hitched up his gunbelt. "Okay, Hopkins, you take notes for us while Doc finishes his examination. I'll be upstairs with Ed."

"Yes sir." Hopkins crossed the lobby toward the body. She looked tired to Wes, with shadows under her gray eyes, a sag to

9

her shoulders. But at this hour, Wes figured he didn't look all that bushy-tailed himself.

He followed Ed Powers, who did look surprisingly bright-eyed, to the west side of the bank lobby and out the double glass doors to the entry corridor. Ceilings were lower in this part of the building, two floors of normal rooms stacked to equal the soaring height of the bank lobby. Mortgages and loans, second floor, proclaimed the gold placard by the elevator they entered. The second floor was more like a mezzanine, with rounded arches overlooking the lobby. Ed unlocked a corner office. Lots of windows here, looking out on the windy night. Wes could see the Burger King next door, the Rockland Mall across the highway and the Dunning city limits sign. If this bank had been built across the highway the dead woman would be a Dunning Police Department problem instead of his. No such luck.

The city was asleep, darker than this well-lit highway intersection. Floodlights near the bank lit the swaying foundation plantings, the drive-in banking bays, and part of the parking lot, shining on the sheriff's and coroner's vehicles parked helter-skelter and glinting on occasional plastic bags and papers that skipped by on the wind. At the far end of the drive-in bays, the big Montgomery State Bank sign was on, proudly identifying the building to the few cars and pickups that passed on the highway.

Ed Powers switched on his computer and puzzled over the menu. "I'm a little rusty. Usually have one of the girls do it," he apologized. "Oh, okay, here we go." The printer began to whine and spit out Stephanie's record. Wes took the paper and read it.

Stephanie Abbott Stollnitz was thirty-four, the record stated, hired in November two years ago. She'd been a retail clerk in a Muncie K-mart a couple years before that. Her references were Muncie references. She was divorced, didn't say who from. No children. Work ratings satisfactory, a couple of small raises. She'd lived at an apartment at 411 Maple Street in Dunning. Wasn't that Gus Johnson's place? Wes seemed to remember Gus mentioning a renter at one of the church suppers.

Ed handed Wes a second paper. "Employee list?" Wes asked.

"That's right."

They were interrupted by a middle-aged man in a dark-blue uniform with a square gold badge. "Sir, the state evidence technicians are here." He was in thickening middle-age, baggy-eyed, nervous around the mouth.

"Good," said Ed Powers, adding, "Our night watchman."

10

Was recognized the man as a retired Dunning city cop. "Hiya, Glenn," he said. "What can you tell us?"

"Not much. I'm real sorry. I came by according to the usual schedule, every two hours."

"When was the last time?"

"An hour and a half ago. And she wasn't down there then. Nobody was in any of the bank areas, sir."

"Yeah," Wes agreed. "I didn't see any broken windows or jimmied doors. You say the bank areas. Are there other areas?"

"The bank rents out offices on the third floor," Glenn said.

Ed pointed to the list Wes held. "The tenants are listed under the row of asterisks."

"What are they? Lawyers?"

"Lawyers, an accountant, a dentist."

"I may want to talk to them. Any of them work late?"

Glenn shrugged. "Yeah, but I don't check inside their offices, only the bank offices. Cleaning guy was here at eight twenty, and I could see lights in the accountant's office too, and his car was in the lot. At ten twenty I didn't see anyone, same thing the next three times I checked."

"Ed, did Stephanie work late last night?"

"I thought I saw her leave around five." He frowned. "When did it happen?"

"We don't know yet. Doc's working on it. Who cleans for you?"

"Greene Cleaning Service."

Wes wrote it down. "Okay. Can you guys tell me about bank security?

"Well, the vault and safe-deposit boxes are in a small basement area. Very secure. It's blasted into bedrock. You take the elevator down but a senior employee has to unlock the two sets of doors. That's before you get to the safe door. The computer files are secure too. We have a series of passwords, and—"

"Don't need to know about the computers now, Ed," Wes said. "Stephanie didn't get in here on a floppy disk."

"No. I see. You mean physical access. Well, besides the locks, Glenn checks every couple hours, as he said."

"Why don't you walk me through? Show me how people get in and out after hours?"

The tour was straightforward enough. From the parking lot, big glass doors led into the entry corridor, with the elevators and some small offices on the left, a back door at the far end, and on the right a second set of glass doors to the main bank lobby, now crawling

11

with busy state crime technicians. There were two sets of safety stairs with fire doors at the bottom, but they set off alarms if opened. No alarms had gone off. In any case, Stephanie had the key to the inner doors to the bank. Ed explained, "The tenants upstairs have keys to the entry but not to the bank. We let our employees have keys after a six-month trial period. Of course we instruct all of them to keep it to themselves, and we change the locks twice a year."

Wes asked, "Glenn, you ever had any trouble before this?"

"Not really. A couple times I had to chase off a carful of drunks in the lot. Once they were using the bank sign for target practice."

Ed said earnestly, "There's no special reason to guard this building more than any other business that has computers. You probably get more burglaries at a 7–11."

Wes nodded. "Yeah. Or liquor stores. The bad guys know banks keep it locked away pretty well. Still, we'd better take a look."

The elevator took them to the basement. The vault was locked, undamaged. Other rooms were filled with heating pipes, plumbing, electrical boxes. A quick scan didn't reveal any problems. Wes said, "Looks secure."

Glenn said eagerly, "It is. She got in with a key, I'm sure of it."

Ed nodded. "We work hard to make our bank dependable and safe."

Why hadn't it been safe for Stephanie? Well, maybe it had been. Probably the danger had come from inside her, something that could have hit anywhere, some disease that Doc would find at autopsy. Heart or something. Wes knew how sneaky hearts could be. He'd been inches from death himself a couple of years ago. He told the vice-president, "Sure, we'll keep it in perspective. A lot depends on the coroner's findings. We'll want to talk to her coworkers in any case. We'll be discreet, of course."

"Yeah. Thanks."

Wes left the banker and the security guard by the doors and joined Hopkins and Doc Altman across the lobby. The technicians had turned the body over to Doc, and he was finishing his first inspection. Wes asked, "What do you say, Doc?"

"Nothing!" There was a glint of anticipation behind those spectacles, Wes could have sworn. "No marks, no signs of disease externally. Not like those chopped-up folks you brought me last year. I'll have to do a bunch of tests on this one."

"But Doc wants us to treat it as suspicious," Hopkins reported.

"Absolutely," Doc confirmed.

Wes adjusted his gunbelt and frowned. "Yeah, we haven't found out yet why she was here. But even if someone saw something, they won't be around now. Most places have closed. Nearest all-night place is that drugstore across the street in the Rockland Mall, right? Hopkins, go ask if they saw anything. And canvass this building first thing in the morning."

"Yes sir."

She headed for the door. Wes would get Mason to help her on the canvass, unless Doc came up with an explanation first. He turned to the doctor. "Doc, if you can get us a time of death, it'll help a whole lot."

"Can't be very exact yet," Doc said. "We don't want to go poking thermometers in until we've swabbed for signs of sexual attack. But off the top of my head I'd say after midnight."

"And it's probably just a stroke or something anyway, right?"

Doc snapped his notebook shut. "Could be. But why here? Right now let's see what the state evidence boys have to say. Then I can get her out of here and take a closer look."

But the state crime technicians too had found nothing obvious.

Three

The Eagle squinted at the dawn sky. Humid today, rain by after-noon for sure. Maybe storms. He'd seen a TV show last weekend about storm chasers, guys who hunted tornadoes in their scientific vans or, better yet, pilots who flew into the eyes of hurri-canes. Shit, that was exciting to think about. Your plane buffeted and rattled by the shearing winds in the eye wall and then, wham! Utter peace in the eye of the hurricane, no winds, blue skies. And then, to get out of the eye, another trip through the churning chaos of the great storm. Shit, what an achievement that would be! That'd make people take notice. They'd quit trying to push you around.

They'd quit anyway. He'd see to that. He had his ways. He wasn't called the Eagle for nothing.

He lifted the Thunderbolt carefully and moved it into the building's shadows. If she'd only listened it wouldn't have gone this far. But shit, women were so willful. No matter how much you loved them they kept their secrets, went their own ways. And now, truth was, he couldn't see any other way out.

Last night wasn't the end, he knew that. But it was a good beginning. Might flush out the others.

Wiping his hands on a rag, he emerged into the parking lot once more and looked east toward the pink-tinged horizon. He'd wanted to fly ever since he could remember. A pilot, soaring above all the others, lord of the skies. That's what he should have been. Instead he felt choked, as though he couldn't breathe in this earthbound job. He yearned for the vast airy reaches above.

Early gray light spilled through the glass entry doors of the Montgomery State Bank. Nearly three hours had passed since the sheriff's call had dragged Marty from her bed, and the crime scene technicians had finished the fingerprinting and vacuuming up of dust and hairs and photographing and other preliminaries. Stephanie's car, located on the bank side of the next-door Burger King parking lot, had been impounded, and her body had been shipped off to Doc Altman's lab. Marty had interviewed the drugstore clerks across the street—they'd seen nothing, but had given her a list of their few customers. Finally the technicians had released the crime scene to Ed Powers, who'd personally brushed off the counters and tables to rid them of the taint of cop action.

When the Burger King opened Marty and the sheriff grabbed breakfast there, coffee and pancakes on plastic, and learned from Mandy the waitress that she hadn't noticed anything unusual the night before. Then young Betty Burke from the *Nichols County News* buttonholed them with questions about Stephanie Stollnitz's death. After dealing with her, the sheriff sent Marty back to the bank to work with Deputy Bobby Mason interviewing the bank employees and tenants while memories were fresh.

Now Mason followed Marty into the bank elevator and punched the third-floor button. Marty leaned back against the elevator wall, careful not to bump her Stetson, and studied Mason. At eight thirty in the morning his round young face was tired, bags under his eyes. She probably looked worse, after her interrupted sleep. But there was work to do. Most of the Montgomery State Bank tellers wouldn't arrive until nine, so they were starting with the offices on the third floor, supposedly in full swing already.

"We've got what, four offices up here?" Mason asked.

Marty didn't have to consult her notes. "That's right. Dr. Singh,

14

Wayne Bertram the CPA, and two law firms. Porter, Price and Taylor, and Hansen and Yeager."

"I've met Porter and Taylor in court. Tell you what," Mason added as the doors slid open to reveal the low-ceilinged hall. "I'll do the right side of the hall, you do the left. Okay?"

"Wait," Marty said. But Mason was already disappearing through the Porter, Price and Taylor door. Shoot. She'd rather do the right side. Too late now. She stepped into Dr. Singh's dental office.

Marty and her daughter went to Dr. Benton in downtown Dunning but this office had the same feel to it. It was done in cheery but soothing blues and greens, and cheery but soothing music was playing in the background. On the white walls, handsome art-exhibit posters showed how high-class it all was. But the one patient seated there, a young man in an Indiana State T-shirt, looked neither cheery nor soothed. Maybe it was because the effect was ruined by the stacks of leaflets with full-color photographic warnings about rotting teeth and receding gums. Or because the music didn't quite cover the whine of some machine or other in the back office. Marty approached the receptionist.

"Yes, can I help you?" the woman asked nervously. She looked faintly exotic, small, olive-skinned and dressed in a green silk blouse. Her thick dark hair was pulled back into a dignified coil.

"Yes, ma'am. I'm Deputy Hopkins. I'd like to ask you a few questions about yesterday afternoon and last night. How late were you here yesterday?"

"Until about six." The woman didn't have an accent, although Marty had half expected one.

"Is that later than usual?"

"No, we regularly schedule people after working hours."

"So you and the doctor were both here until after six?"

"Yes, maybe twenty after." Her lustrous dark eyes were still worried. "Excuse me, is this about poor Stephanie?"

News traveled fast. Marty said, "Yes, ma'am. May I have your name, please?

"Nora Singh."

"You're a relation of Dr. Singh?"

"Yes, his wife."

The grisly whine of the machine in the back room stopped. Marty asked, "Okay, ma'am, did you and your husband leave the building together?"

"Yes. Our assistant left at five, and we did the last two patients and then cleaned up."

"I'll need the names of the assistant and the patients."

Nora Singh hesitated, but then wrote the names on a card and handed them to Marty. The assistant was Tim Post's daughter, but she didn't know the two patients. Marty asked, "Now, when you and Dr. Singh left, you went down in the elevator and then through the hall to the back door?"

"Yes. We were hurrying because we were meeting friends to see a movie at seven."

A pink-complexioned old man came out of the back office, smiling with half his mouth. "Hey, Doc, you didn't hurt me half as much as you thought!" he said to the short dark man in a hospital-green jacket who followed him. "When I was a boy, old Doc Baker pretty near cracked my head open pulling a wisdom tooth."

The doctor smiled. "We've got better anesthetics now, Mr. Avery. Here, you can give Nora your check." He stepped around the old man and extended a hand toward Marty. "Hello, I'm Dr. Singh."

She shook hands. The doctor was neat and pleasant, an inch shorter than her own five-seven. "I'm Deputy Hopkins, and I'm asking about the woman who died last night. I understand you left the building after six yesterday."

"Yes, between six fifteen and six thirty. We had to hurry to get to Bloomington for a seven o'clock movie."

"Did you see anyone else?"

"There were several people still in the building," Dr. Singh said.

Old Mr. Avery was listening, bright-eyed. Nora handed him a receipt, waved him toward the door, and said, "There was a man in a visored cap who came out of the Hansen and Yeager offices and rode down the elevator with us. There were a few people still working in the bank too."

"Was Stephanie there?" Marty asked.

"Stephanie?" asked Dr. Singh.

Nora Singh was shaking her head. "No, she wasn't. I know her because we bank here and there are nameplates for the tellers. I think both men we saw in the bank were managers."

"Okay, we'll talk to them. Is there anything else you can tell us?"

Dr. Singh shook his head. "Everything seemed normal."

"Well, let us know if you think of anything."

She went out into the hall. Bobby Mason was nowhere to be seen. She stared irresolutely at the Hansen and Yeager door. C'mon, Hopkins, get it over with. Marty took off her Stetson, finger-combed her curly hair, replaced the hat firmly, and marched through the

16

gold-lettered door that read "Hansen and Yeager, Attorneys at Law."

"Hi, Debra, how you doing?" she asked.

Debra was a perky young woman with highlighted hair, a salmon-pink dress and matching lips and fingernails. She was hanging up her white jacket in the closet on the left wall. She looked around, surprised. "Marty Hopkins! I didn't recognize you for a minute."

"Yeah, this uniform is a good disguise." The office was a pleasant one, with plush gray carpet, oak furniture, seascapes on the walls, and she'd spent too many rotten hours here already. Marty took a deep breath and got down to business. "Debra, I'm here to ask some questions about Stephanie Stollnitz."

"Oh, God, yes, that's so awful!" Debra dropped her tote bag on the closet floor, carpeted like the office but grooved by the weight of objects that had been left there, and turned back to Marty, clasping her hands and frowning. "I can't believe it!"

"Did you know Stephanie?"

"Not real well. I mean, I went to a couple of lunches they gave downstairs, like a shower for Linda's baby, and Stephanie was there too. And when she first started work she came by a couple of times."

"You mean to say hello?"

"No, on business. Gordon was finishing some paperwork for her on her divorce."

Chip Hansen came out of the door to the right of the closet, his blond hair wind-tossed, his thick pleasant features frowning at some papers in his hand. He looked rumpled but fit, as though he'd already run ten miles this morning. Probably had. "Debra, send this— Oh my, Marty, is there a problem?"

"Nothing you can bill me for this time," Marty said.

"Oh, of course, it's about poor Stephanie Stollnitz. How can we help?"

Chip was forty, a nice guy with a nice family, but he was representing Marty in her divorce and just seeing him reminded her of the meeting this afternoon, the first where she and Chip would face Brad and his lawyer. Brad was threatening to take her house, to take her daughter. She stared at her notebook and tried to concentrate on Stephanie Stollnitz. "Okay, I'd like you to tell me about yesterday afternoon. What time did you leave?"

"Yesterday? I had to get Chuckie to a football game, so it wasn't real late. Five thirty or so. Gordon was still here with a client." Chip bounced over to the door to the left of the closet, rapped, and stuck his head in. "Gordon! Come on out when you get off the phone."

17

Marty asked, "Who else was here?"

"Debra? Had you left?" Chip asked.

"I left at five," Debra said. "Everyone was gone except you and Gordon and that man."

"What man?" asked Gordon Yeager, emerging from his office. He was in his forties, Chip Hansen's age, but in many respects he was Chip's opposite: his sad eyes were dark instead of blue, his hair was thinning instead of wavy blond, and you'd never suspect this paunchy guy of running ten miles. Like Chip he wore a striped tie, shirtsleeves, and dark suit trousers. He stuck out his hand to Marty. "Hi, Marty Hopkins, how're you doing?"

"Fine, thanks, Mr. Yeager. I'm trying to find out about the woman who died here last night. Stephanie Stollnitz. You did some work for her, right?"

"God, poor Stephanie. Yeah, I helped her file a couple of papers two years ago. Routine stuff for her divorce." Gordon Yeager's mournful eyes blinked. "What happened to her? Do you know?"

"We're waiting for the coroner's report, sir. Did she happen to tell you if she had a medical condition of some kind?"

"No, why would she tell me?"

"You were helping with her divorce. I thought it might be relevant to getting alimony or something."

Chip laughed. "You're right, everything's relevant in a divorce."

Gordon smiled briefly. "Even so, she didn't say anything to me about a medical condition. Does the coroner think that was the problem?"

"We're waiting for the report, sir," Marty said patiently. "Can you tell us anything about her divorce?"

"C'mon, Marty, that's privileged information, most of it."

"Even after she's dead?"

Yeager winced. "Hey, I'm not trying to be difficult. I'll tell you everything I can. But it won't be much, because I didn't do that much. The actual divorce was handled by an attorney in Muncie, guy named Phil Wilson."

"I'd appreciate the information, sir. Maybe you could give me Wilson's phone number too."

"Okay."

"Now, back to yesterday evening. What time did you leave the building?"

"Last night? Well, let's see." Gordon Yeager frowned. "My last client—"

"Andy Ragg!" exclaimed Debra. "That's who it was."

18

Yeager ignored her. "That client left about six fifteen. I stayed on for a few minutes clearing up some paperwork. I left maybe six thirty, quarter to seven."

"Did you see anyone in the building as you left?"

"The janitor was working in Bertram's office across the hall. I could hear the vacuum cleaner. I didn't notice anyone else, but of course if they were in an office with the door closed—" He shrugged.

"Yeah. You didn't see Stephanie Stollnitz?"

Gordon Yeager shook his head. "Nope. But I had some errands to do on the way home, picking up clothes at the cleaner's and so forth, so I was checking my book as I went out."

Marty closed her notebook. "Okay. If any of you think of anything, let me know."

"Sure thing. See you later, Marty," Chip said.

See you later. How could such friendly words carry such a threat? Marty said, "Right," and fled.

Mason emerged from the accountant's office a moment later. Marty took a deep breath and asked, "Anything?"

Mason jerked a thumb at the office behind him. "This guy, Wayne Bertram, said he left around seven thirty. Said everyone was gone except the janitor. Definitely didn't see any women."

"How about Porter Price?"

"They left earlier, around six. Something about dining at the country club."

"Same with these offices," Marty reported. "The dentists left about the same time as Yeager's last client, maybe twenty after six, and Yeager left less than half an hour later. No one saw Stephanie Stollnitz then. Guess we'd better track down the janitor. But I sure wish we knew what killed her."

Four

Jake Shaw parked his battered Toyota in the Burger King lot next to a gray Lincoln Town Car. Ohio plates. He unfolded his creaky legs, climbed out, and pushed back his Pacers cap to squint at the morning sky. Beyond the low wooded hills to the southwest, the

19

few clouds didn't look threatening. In twenty-six years of working for the *Nichols County News* he'd done his share of weather stories, but despite the hailstorm in Posey County last week, this didn't look like much. Too bad. He needed to find a story. That young whippersnapper Betty Burke had lucked into the big story today. She'd been on her way to the *News* when she'd spotted the coroner's van pulling out of the Montgomery State Bank lot, and was already writing up her interview with Sheriff Cochran by the time Jake arrived at eight. He'd worked the wire service for a couple hours and then had taken a break to get some coffee and keep his eyes open for something newsworthy.

And, he figured, he might as well have his coffee here next door to the Montgomery State Bank, where he might overhear something interesting from cops or bank workers. Of course Burke would probably get the main byline, but it wouldn't hurt to keep his ears open, at least until he thought of a story of his own.

"Hi, Mandy," he greeted the fortyish waitress. Mandy had dark hair in a ponytail, dimples as well as crow's feet, and was just plump enough to look cuddly but not fat. Jake considered her an asset to Burger King.

"Hey, Jake." She swabbed off a hunk of the counter and poured coffee without asking. "How's it going?"

"Can't complain. Hear there was some excitement at the bank."

"There sure was!" Mandy regaled him with the story he already knew from Betty Burke's report. He nodded and sipped his coffee, glancing around the restaurant. Not many people. Deputy Mason was having a cuppa at a booth, but he was doing paperwork and didn't look like a man who wanted to be disturbed. There was a family at another booth, a couple of oldtimers down the counter to his left, and a stranger two seats to his right.

"It's a real shame," Mandy concluded.

"It sure is. Probably good for business, though."

Mandy snorted. "Nothing's good for business this year. With the drought plus all the layoffs, nobody's spending anything anywhere."

"Yeah. Know what you mean."

"So what do you want? Piece of pie or something?"

Jake liked pie but preferred to get Melva Dodd's homemade beauties from Reiner's Bakery, especially the blueberry or the peanut butter flavors. He made a sad face at Mandy. "No, I'm not a big spender this year either."

"I'll take some pie," said the stranger to Jake's right. He wore a mustache and a longsleeved green polo shirt.

20

"Apple or cherry?" Mandy asked.

"Cherry," the stranger said. While Mandy fetched his pie he looked back at Jake. "How 'bout those Colts?" he asked.

"Yeah, they're doing okay. Managed to cream the Oilers last night," Jake said.

"Yeah. Say, are there any golf courses around here?"

"Golf?" Mandy asked, plunking down the stranger's pie. "There's the municipal course out northeast of town."

Jake studied the stranger. He was thickset, muscular, and had gentle brown eyes behind his aviator glasses. Jake figured the polo shirt and the shoes were expensive. Definitely not from K-mart. He said, "Or if you want something a little more elegant, you could try Asphodel Springs."

"The municipal course isn't so pricey," Mandy said.

"Asphodel Springs? That resort?" the stranger asked Jake.

"You could call it that. Swimming pool, golf course, tennis courts, café, bar, fancy restaurant. Well, I mean fancy for these parts. It's off Route 852. Just head for Paoli and follow the signs."

"Thanks."

The man put a ten on the counter and left. Mandy picked it up and gazed after him. "Asphodel Springs," she said. "Big spender."

"Yeah. I figured that would appeal to a guy with tassels on his shoes." Jake pushed a five toward Mandy.

"Guess you figured right." She made change for Jake and, shamed by the stranger, he also left too much on the counter.

But the conversation had given Jake an idea. They hadn't done a story on tourism for a while. Maybe it was time to talk to motels and restaurants in the area, find out how the businesses were getting through the economic slump. Might even get a short series out of it.

And next time, maybe he'd be the one to spot the coroner's van first.

Despite his creaky knees, Jake returned to his old Toyota with a bounce in his step.

Stephanie's landlady was swimming at the Senior Center but would be back soon, her husband said, so Marty decided to find out what the janitor had to say. She turned the nose of the cruiser toward the fading September hills east of Dunning.

Even though it was Tom Turley she wanted to interview, most of Marty's childhood memories of White Oak Farm were of his wife Dee, one of Aunt Vonnie's best friends. Bright-haired Dee

21

Reiner, Nichols County Harvest Queen several years running, had first married a Meade from the farm next door and inherited the combined rich and fertile acres when her husband died. She reigned radiantly over teeming gardens of tomatoes and huge glowing pumpkins, over rippling golden grainfields, over acres of rustling cornstalks higher than the youthful Marty's head. Dee was a skilled businesswoman, organizing the Harvest Festival each year as well as county-wide fundraisers for fire departments, churches, and other charities. Just this spring, Marty remembered, Dee had raised money for an operation for little Teddy Paul, whose parents didn't have health insurance when their two-year-old was struck with a tumor.

Even nearing sixty, she was handsome. She kept her hair blond and braided into a coronet and was fit and hard-working, never afraid of sweat or dirt, never afraid of anything. Marty's earliest memories, misted by nostalgia, involved tables laden with corn on the cob, ham and chicken, tender peas and beans, fresh bread and homemade strawberry jam, and heavenly pies—rhubarb in spring, peach or blueberry in summer, apple or pumpkin in the fall. Little Marty had helped Dee garden, collect eggs, feed the horses. One memory snapshot: Dee lifting her to the saddle of a tall chestnut-colored horse. Marty remembered the excitement tinged with terror at being so high and so at the mercy of an alien creature. Tough, wiry Tom Turley, back from the war and farming his home place over on Gate Road, had been visiting the beautiful widow Meade and suggested gruffly, "Isn't Marty kind of small for that horse, Dee?"

"She'll catch on, she's smart," Dee had told him, and murmured to Marty, "Tom's sweet but he's better with tractors than horses. Now, you hold the reins in your right hand like this." As Dee taught the use of reins and legs, Marty's terror gave way to a sense of power, of communication with a friendly animal intellect, of transformation into something immense and much more powerful than a rambunctious eight-year-old girl.

Another snapshot, this one clear and brutal, from when she was twelve: Dee's kitchen, Aunt Vonnie and Melva Dodd embracing Marty's mother, who was weeping helplessly. Marty was staring from across the room, and Dee knelt before her and said, "Honey, you've got to be strong now to help your mother. You'll stay with me this week so she can go do the things that have to be done."

Marty stood stiff and terrified and demanded, "Will someone please tell me what's going on?"

Her mother turned her tearstreaked face from her comforters to look at her. "Honey, your father . . . his car . . ." and bowed her head again.

"What about his goddamn car?" Marty screamed.

And none of those good Methodist women told her not to swear. Instead Dee hugged her and murmured, "His goddamn car crashed into a tree, honey. We've lost him," and Marty's unyielding indignant twelve-year-old body finally relaxed into sobs against Dee's motherly shoulder.

Not long after that Marty and her mother had moved to Bloomington because the jobs were better there, but they still visited Nichols County from time to time. Marty had finished high school and gone to IU for two years, but a handsome man full of handsome dreams had interrupted things. She'd married Brad because Chrissie was on the way. Dee too had married by then, loyal Tom Turley who'd been courting her for years. According to Aunt Vonnie, Dee's sister Melva hadn't approved of Tom. "He's such a shrimp," she complained to anyone who'd listen. "Dee just married him so she'd have someone to fix the tractors."

But, Aunt Vonnie reported, Dee had just laughed. "He fixed more than that, little sister! He gave me Coral." And it was true. Little Coral was about four years older than Chrissie, born when her mother was in her early forties. Another memory snapshot from a holiday visit to Aunt Vonnie: the Cedars of Lebanon Methodist Church social hall, the Christmas pageant. Dee was still radiantly beautiful, still the logical person to sing Mary's Christmas lullabies to the Christ Child. But the show-stopper had been Dee's real-life child. Little Coral Turley, six or seven years old, played the angel, and she transformed the bedsheet gown and cardboard wings into something ethereal. Her youthful voice was surprisingly strong and true and pure, her tumble of jonquil-yellow ringlets and huge eyes were mesmerizing. In the Annunciation scene the two sang together, the child-angel urging the woman Mary to assent to transformation, to tragedy, to divinity. It seemed to Marty that everyone in the church hall was awed, though afterward they said only, "Hey, Dee and little Coral did a real good job, didn't they?" Tom and Dee had made sure the girl got top-class music and dance lessons, taking her to Bloomington every week for years.

Yet Marty hadn't been completely surprised when, at the end of school last spring, she'd run away, breaking her mother's heart. Dee, frantic, got the sheriff's department and everyone else to mount a major search, but Coral had soon contacted her parents, said she'd

23

joined a rock band and was fine, so they'd called it off. The girl hadn't yet come back.

Marty hadn't seen Dee since then, she realized. And hadn't Aunt Vonnie said Dee was ailing?

It was odd to see how barren Dee's fields were this year. The whole county had been struck by the summer drought, and Marty was used to the sparse crops, but somehow she had expected Dee's place to be immune. No such luck. There were only a few tired vines in fields where beans and pumpkins usually flourished. But they were keeping up appearances. As Marty turned on to the county highway that passed White Oak Farm, she saw the glint of the greenhouse roofs. Tom had put those up for Dee, moonlighting after his work at Greene Cleaning Service. There was a new orange roof on the store and a shiny sign reading "White Oak Farm."

Marty parked the cruiser in the lot by the store. A gaunt old woman with long dirty-silver hair caught at the nape of her neck shuffled along the walk toward the house. Marty glanced at her and did a double take. "Dee?" she called.

The woman turned dull eyes toward her. "Hello," she said.

Could this be the vibrant woman of Marty's youthful memories? "Are you sick, Dee?" Marty blurted.

Dee brightened a little. "Marty, honey! Have you heard anything?"

Marty gave her a hug. "About what?"

"About Coral."

"No, ma'am. I thought you told us you'd heard from her and didn't need us searching any more."

"Yes. Yes, that's right." The light went out of her eyes again. "I don't know what I did wrong. I wanted her to go to college, to have a future."

"Dee, you look sick."

"Honey, I had two miscarriages, lost those babies before they were born. Now Coral is lost too. I'm tired of the world."

"Is there anything I can do to help?"

"Only God can restore what I've lost."

"But she's doing okay, right? Dee, don't just quit!"

Marty hugged her again, and flashed on another memory from three or four summers ago. Marty, back in Nichols County and already in this job, was working security for a disabled veteran's benefit, a talent show at the Rockland Mall. As usual, Dee had organized the benefit, finding a huge white tent and yards of patriotic bunting, spreading tables with delicious donated baked goods for sale, setting up a little stage with big speakers and lights for the local dancers and singers and accordion players. Coral, age thirteen, had organized some of her girlfriends into a band. Marty had been standing near the main entrance of the tent and remembered it well—the big-eyed girl with carefully beribboned golden ringlets, wearing skinny black jeans and a blouse of sky-blue ruffles. She sang a Patsy Cline song with such strength and assurance that she seemed a clear winner, but partway through she raised her hand high, and the band switched to a throbbing rock beat. Coral looked impishly at the judges. "I just want you to know our band can do more than country. Here's a Lily Pistols song, 'Embrace the Darkness.'" And with one dramatic gesture she stripped off her ruffled blouse and hair ribbon, revealing a black leather vest crossed with chains. The audience gasped. Marty glanced at Dee over by the baked goods. Next to her Tom looked like thunder but Dee ignored him, absorbed in watching the performance, her expression half apprehensive, half delighted. Coral shook her hair violently until it stood out wild as a dandelion, then took a seductive, aggressive step toward the judges. "Hug me baby, yeah hug me tight, embrace the darkness with me tonight," she brayed into the mike, and the squealing, thudding heavy-metal rhythms of the song shook the mall. Instant generational wars: older folks clapped their hands to their ears, everyone under twenty began to dance. The judges gave the prize to a tap-dancer.

God, though Marty, Chrissie's going to be that age in a year.

Dee was not weeping, not responding at all to Marty's embrace, so she gave up for the moment and said, "Dee, let me know if there's anything I can do. Uh—where's Tom?"

Dee waved her hand toward the warehouse-like building behind them. "He's in the store," she said without interest, and resumed her shuffle toward the house.

Marty looked after her a moment, then pushed open the door and greeted the small bony-faced man in a sunny yellow shirt who was sitting behind the cash register. Tom Turley was short, wiry, and weatherbeaten, and in his bright shirt he reminded Marty of a nervous jockey, trying to control forces he didn't fully understand.

"Hi, Marty." Tom glanced up and then down again at his project, a blue and white machine that sat on skids.

"What're you doing?" Marty asked.

"Trying to fix this blasted greenhouse heater before the frost comes."

Marty glanced around the store as she approached. They'd remodeled since spring—computerized cash registers and bright orange

25

counters. A couple of customers were inspecting the array of last year's White Oak Farm preserves and pickles. In the back, elegant new bins divided the area into five short aisles. But the fresh produce in the bins looked scanty this year. Even the potatoes were puny from the drought. Marty said, "It's your other job I want to ask about. You manage Greene Cleaning Service, right?"

"Yeah." He glanced up again warily.

"They tell me you do Montgomery State Bank."

"Yeah."

"Did you clean it last night?"

"I usually do, but last night I was supervising a special job out at the Rockland Mall, cleaning that restaurant that had a grease fire. Jimmy Corson did the bank."

"Jumbo Jim?" She'd gone to grade school with big Jimmy Corson.

"That's right. What's going on?" Tom asked.

"We're investigating the death of a young woman. A teller at the bank."

There was genuine shock in Tom's round brown eyes. "God! God, what happened?"

"That's what we're trying to find out. I want to know if Jimmy maybe saw something."

He shook his head. "I can't believe it! A teller, you say?"

"Did you know any of the tellers?"

"Not really. Different hours. How did she die? I mean—was it natural?"

"Tom, we don't have any answers yet, that's why we're asking questions. What's the routine when you guys clean the bank?"

He took a deep breath, steadied his voice. "Well, they prefer after hours. When I do it I usually get there around six, finish cleaning about eight thirty. I ask Jimmy to do the same."

"Do you clean in any particular order?"

"Usually we start on the bank floor because they close first. Work our way upstairs to the smaller offices. People stay late there sometimes."

"Have you noticed anything out of the ordinary at the bank in the last few days?"

"Everything seemed normal there Friday. That's the last time I stopped by."

"Okay. I'll talk to Jimmy."

"He works days at Brock Lumber."

"Thanks. Let me know if anything occurs to you." She closed her notebook and added, "Tom, is Dee okay?"

26

"Okay? Dee?" He gave a harsh laugh. "She's been like the walking dead for months."

"Is she sick?"

"Doctor says it's a depression. Dee says it's because Coral is gone. Dammit, the girl's sixteen, she's been threatening to leave home for a couple of years! The kid was starting to run wild but Dee wouldn't rein her in. I keep telling Dee, this was bound to happen." Tom shrugged. "At least we know where she is now."

"But she did leave real suddenly. Must have been a shock."

"Yeah, but Dee seemed okay for a while. Worried, yeah, but full of energy, calling everybody, looking everywhere, asking a lot of questions. She even found time for the fundraiser to save the little Paul boy. But after that she went into a slump. And I've done every damn thing I can think of, but she hasn't been herself since."

Marty felt for Tom. Working two jobs, trying to get ahead, to take control of his life, but his daughter runs away, his crops fail, his wife plunges into depression. Marty said, "But you hear from Coral, right? She's okay?"

"She's okay, says she's getting rich and famous, and she doesn't want to come back to Mama." Tom shrugged and picked up his screwdriver. "Kid's selfish, always has been."

"Well, most teenagers are," Marty said, thinking of the battles ahead with Chrissie. She added hopefully, "She'll get over it eventually. Listen, I'm sorry Dee feels so bad. Can I do anything for her?"

"Can't think of anything I haven't done."

"Yeah. Makes it real hard for you too."

"I'm getting along," he said edgily.

"Yeah, but this year, with the drought and everything—"

"So life is tough sometimes. You learn that on a farm." He stabbed at the greenhouse heater with his screwdriver.

"Yeah. See you later, Tom."

Marty pushed open the door. Yes, you did learn that on a farm. So why was Dee taking it so hard?

But when she thought of how she'd feel if Chrissie disappeared, suddenly Dee's reaction didn't seem so extreme.

Five

Sullen and stubborn, the humid southern air clamped down on the drought-weary limestone hills, refusing to yield to the cold pressing in from the northwest. Along the front a clash was building. And high overhead, the dry winds from the southwest were picking up speed, energizing the turmoil in the upper air. Meteorologists looked at their charts of southern Indiana with quickened interest.

But at earth level it was merely hot, hazy, and oppressive.

Marty took off her Stetson and wiped her damp brow before ringing the doorbell. 411 Maple Street in Dunning was a one-and-a-half story white clapboard with forest-green shutters and three little gabled dormer windows across the front punctuating the sloping gray roof.

"Hi there, Marty." Gus Johnson opened the door at her ring. He was a raw-boned, gray-haired man with blue eyes and a long Scandinavian face. He reminded Marty of a pale John Wayne who turned pink in the sun instead of tan.

"Hi, Mr. Johnson, how you doing?"

"Too sticky today for me. But lordy, this is a shock about Steffie. What happened to her?" He waved Marty into a green-carpeted hall about eight feet square. On the right-hand wall was a big framed photo of Waikiki, on the left an arch that led into the neatly kept living room, pink-walled, bright with floral-patterned pillows. Straight ahead, a flight of stairs led up to a plain white door.

Clara Johnson, younger and spryer than her husband but also gray-haired, blue-eyed, and rosy from the sun, emerged from the kitchen. "Hi, Marty honey. I never thought you'd be here, you know, officially!"

"Yeah, I'm sorry about that, Mrs. Johnson." The Johnsons were members of Cedars of Lebanon Methodist, like Marty, and Clara Johnson and Aunt Vonnie often served on church supper committees or altar flower committees together.

"Steffie seemed fine last night," Clara said.

"You saw her last night? When?"

"Only for a minute, right after work. Then she said she was going shopping at the mall, and left," Clara said.

"What happened to her, exactly?" Gus asked again.

"We don't know yet, Mr. Johnson. The doctors will let us know. No marks on her, so it probably wasn't violent."

"It wasn't?"

"Nothing obvious, anyway. You sound surprised, sir."

"Well, I just thought . . . you know, her husband. Clay Stollnitz."

Clara offered, "She said Clay told her he'd kill her if he caught her fooling around."

"Have you met her husband?"

"No. But poor Steffie mentioned a couple of times that she was glad to be in a different town."

Didn't always help, Marty knew. She said, "Yes sir, we'll check on him."

Gus Johnson picked up a nine-by-twelve manila envelope from a console under the Waikiki photograph. "And she gave us this. Asked us to keep it in a safe place." He handed it to Marty.

"May I look?"

"Yeah, sure! I'm giving it to you. I figure the sheriff's is a safe place to keep it."

Marty pulled the papers half out of the envelope and riffled through them. Divorce papers, a record of Clay Stollnitz's abuses, orders of protection, and so forth. He'd been a bad 'un, all right. The medical reports included a broken collarbone, concussions, lots of bruises.

The body had had no marks. Maybe there was a concussion Doc Altmann had missed. Though Doc didn't often miss things.

She slid the papers back into the envelope. "Yeah, thanks, these could be real helpful," Marty said.

"You said it wasn't violent," Clara said, a catch in her voice. "I'm glad. Steffie was a sweet gal."

"That she was." Gus nodded. "You'll let us know when you hear what happened?"

"Yes sir. Now, can I take a quick look around her apartment?"

"Sure thing."

"I'll take you up," Clara said, starting up the steps. "Gus's knees aren't what they used to be. I tell him he should come swimming with me at the senior center, but he's too lazy."

"Lazy!" Gus snorted. "Just don't feel like paddling around with a bunch of old biddies."

29

Clara paused on the stairs to shake her head at him fondly. "Can't reason with him at all."

Marty followed her. "She used the same entrance as you?"

"Yes. She told me once she liked that. Funny thing, the last people that rented it moved out 'cause they said they wanted more privacy. But Steffie was real sweet and friendly." Clara jiggled the key in the lock and the door swung open. They stepped inside and Clara added in a lower tone, "Don't tell Gus, but I think she meant for us to guard her."

"Guard her?" Marty couldn't quite visualize creaky old Gus in hand-to-hand combat. Still, they could probably dial 911 as quick as anyone.

"Because we'd know if that husband came to see her." Clara's blue eyes widened in emphasis of the importance of what she was saying. "He never did."

"Who did come to see her?"

"She had a few girl friends over sometimes. Never any men except for that Mary Jo's husband. Steffie was a real nice girl."

So having men friends made you not-nice in Clara's eyes? Clara and Aunt Vonnie would have fits if they knew Marty, still undivorced, had been seeing Romey Dennis. Marty felt a familiar surge of guilt but pressed it back down. Do the job, Hopkins. Who cares what Clara's definition of nice is? Do you really want to be nice?

The door they'd come through, at the top of the stairs, led into the upstairs hall. There were three more doors. The first was a closet where three coats hung next to a stack of still-unpacked moving cartons. Marty untaped the top one, marked "Ceramics." Sure enough, ceramic figurines and ashtrays in bright colors still nestled in their bed of foam peanuts. The other boxes were marked "Books" and "Wine glasses." Check them later.

Marty went through the door that led toward the front of the house and found herself in a long room painted off-white and enlivened by fuchsia and purple flowerpots and pillows. Following the angle of the roof, the low ceiling sloped down to merge with the wall. The three bright window alcoves were filled with plants. "She's got a green thumb," Clara Johnson said.

Marty crossed to the low bookcase that divided a sitting area from the sleeping end of the room. The bookcase, like the sofa and bedspread, was white. A plump little lamp with a fuchsia-colored shade squatted on it. There were three photos in white frames. She picked them up to look more closely. One was of a middle-aged man with curly receding hair and warm eyes.

"That's her father," Clara Johnson volunteered. "Mr. Abbott. Lives in Muncie but he was here visiting her just a couple days ago."

Marty set it down and tried not to think about what Mr. Abbott was feeling at the death of his daughter. If anything ever happened to Chrissie— Cut it out, Hopkins, she told herself fiercely. Getting emotional won't help Steffie or her father.

She ignored the sad knot in her belly and asked, "Were they on good terms?"

"Seemed to be. He's the quiet type, but Steffie chattered away to him."

Marty picked up the second photo. "And this is her sister or something?" A blond young woman with her father's warm eyes. She held a toddler, a little boy in OshKosh overalls. Behind them a dark-haired young man beamed proudly.

Clara Johnson nodded. "Her name is Jocelyn, and the little boy is Todd Junior. They live in California somewhere."

The third photo was of a high-school cheerleading squad. Marty squinted at it carefully. Stephanie was second from the end, a radiant smile on her face. Marty was glad Stephanie had had something to be proud of, something to remember besides the marriage that had gone so wrong. She thought sometimes that was why Romey attracted her so much, because he'd known her when she was ten years old and the star of the peewee basketball team and ready to conquer the whole damn world. Glory days.

Marty set the photo down and pulled a few books from the case. Accounting, business courses—Stephanie apparently wanted to be more than a bank teller. Self-help books, *Women Who Love Too Much*, *Divorce Handbook for Women*. Marty too owned a few books like that. There were some modern romances too, with covers featuring gorgeous women at computers, taking notes at fashion shows, running a television camera. One was in a cop's uniform. All of the women were being eyed lustfully by equally gorgeous men. One looked like Brad, but none of them looked like Romey Dennis, who was much more fun.

There was a television with the current *TV Guide* sitting on top, and a bedside table with two drawers. Tissues, mail-order catalogs, a couple more romances, a nail file, a bottle of Tylenol, and a package of birth-control pills. Interesting. As she slid it into an evidence bag Marty saw that Stephanie had written "September" on the package.

The closet held a small collection of dresses, suits, jeans, and blouses. A hanging vinyl sweater case held sweaters and T-shirts, and a good-sized collection of shoes and boots were lined up on the closet floor. A tennis racket in a green canvas case leaned in the back corner against another unpacked moving carton labeled "Frisbees, balls, etc." "When did Stephanie move in?" Marty asked.

"She's been here a year and a half. Lived in Muncie before."

Looked like Steffie didn't go out for sports any more.

"Have you found anything?" Clara asked. She was hovering by the bookcase in the middle of the room.

"Nothing unusual. Let's look at the other room, okay?"

The back room was similar to the front, except that one end had been remodelled to accommodate a bathroom and a kitchenette, so the main part of the room was almost square except for the sloping ceiling. It held a maple table with lime-green place mats. A few white-and-purple dishes, enough for a solitary breakfast, were stacked in the sink. The refrigerator contained a half-full bottle of wine in addition to the standard fruit juices, eggs, leftover tuna salad, and so forth. "You said she never had a man visit her," Marty said. "Did anyone ever pick her up for a date?"

"Sometimes she went out to parties, or to church activities. You know, the singles group? She'd go bowling or square dancing with them. But it always seemed to be in a group."

Marty nodded and headed for the desk against the wall. Bills, mostly paid. Last year's Christmas cards with a rubber band around them, check those later. A deep drawer of files, including one thick one on her divorce. Marty glanced through it. Mostly it was duplicates of what was in the manila envelope Gus had given her downstairs, but there was one extra item, a recent scrawled note. Stephanie had kept it clipped to its envelope, postmarked Muncie, which was addressed in the same hand to a Muncie street address and forwarded here. The note said, "Darling bitch, you won't get away."

Marty added the note to the manila envelope and stepped into the bathroom. Stephanie's apartment had been very orderly, even her closets, but here dirty clothes overflowed a hamper, used towels lay on the floor, makeup was jumbled on the vanity top. The crowded medicine cabinet contained more makeup, shampoos, hair coloring and styling gels, toothpaste, and several prescription bottles. Marty placed the medications carefully in evidence bags. Painkillers, anti-depressants, cough medicine, antihistamine, an empty antibiotic bottle. Most had been prescribed last year by Muncie doctors and filled by Muncie pharmacies, but the last two, both anti-depressants, had been prescribed by Dr. Cage. His office was out by the hospital, Marty thought. The drugstore that filled the prescription was out there too.

"I'm taking these for the coroner to check," she explained to the Johnsons as she signed a receipt. "Just in case they might have contributed somehow."

"Like a drug interaction, you mean?" Clara nodded wisely. "I never thought of that."

Like a drug interaction, yeah, or like suicide. *Darling bitch, you won't get away.* Marty walked through warm sticky air to her cruiser. As she turned the ignition and clicked on the air conditioning, she glanced back at the house. What lethal problems had lurked under that sheltering gray roof with the perky dormer windows? Stephanie thought she'd found a safe harbor, the entrance guarded by the two observant Johnsons. Marty's impression, vague in the particulars, was of a woman determined to build a new life but still running scared from a violent man, still afraid to build new friendships except in the safe environments of church groups or the workplace.

Then there were the birth-control pills. Did they mean a secret affair, hidden from her landlords and friends? Of course some women took them to stay regular, and maybe that's all it was. If not—

Clara's words came back: "Clay said he'd kill her if he caught her fooling around."

Stephanie's divorce had become final eight months ago, but the "darling bitch" note had been postmarked only two weeks ago.

Shoot. Couldn't you ever get free?

Six

When the Eagle slowed for the red light he heard the screaming. You had to keep working, putting food on the table, but sometimes it was hard because of the screaming.

The rush of air on wings could block it out, the crash of thunder. He'd been good with the planes, the best, said the pilots. He'd spotted that cracked turbine after two others had pronounced it sound, and that's when they started calling him Eagle-Eye. One pilot had bought him a drink and told him stories of war, of dropping pretty fire on to the rolling green land below.

"Yeah," a drunken infantryman had said. "Real pretty. Lost my buddy that way, one of you guys dropping a pretty bomb. You're blind up there, you know? You've never seen the goddamn war!"

"Hey, I'm sorry, but we just follow orders."

The drunk said, "I heard my buddy screaming. You didn't."

The Eagle could hear the screaming, the rush of air and the screaming of the small creatures snatched from their safe burrows by the talons of vengeance. King of the air, king of the clouds, king of the thunder, king of death and revenge.

The pilot had turned back to the bar and ordered another. He muttered to the Eagle, "Goddamn grunts expect everything to be perfect. Well, what do they expect when they're out of position? They want us to give up, go home, get punished? Maybe hit by lightning? Christ, they think war happens without casualties?"

"Yeah," the Eagle had said. "You have to keep going anyway."

The light turned green.

Marty signed over Stephanie's medications to the coroner's office, then called in from her cruiser. Adams was on dispatch today. "Why don't you take your lunch break?" he suggested. "Nothing much coming in here, and the sheriff's at the high school giving his anti-drug talk. Check back in half an hour."

"Okay." Marty keyed off and sat for a moment, weighing the virtues of the Three Bears versus Pete's Tavern for lunch. Nothing sounded very good. On impulse she headed out State 37 to Dennis Rent-All. She slowed as she approached but saw no black Taurus among the half-dozen cars and pickups parked in the broad asphalt lot. She continued along the highway. Not at the Pebble Creek Diner either. She took a left on Gate Road. A BMW, California plates, was pulling out of Joe Matthews's old place as she passed, two laughing teenagers inside. They didn't look old enough to have the kind of money a BMW implied. But shoot, she was on break. Let someone else pull them over for questioning. Maybe it was okay. California kids probably had more money than Indiana kids. She noted the license number and drove another half-mile through the rolling limestone hills, forested with tulip trees, maples, sassafras, all drooping from the summer's drought. Crops fared even worse than trees in this thin soil, and fields that had once been plowed had eroded, bare limestone showing among the thistles and grasses like an old woman's wispy-haired skull.

The mailbox said "Dennis" in black capitals. Surrounded by woods, a well-watered lawn with a carved limestone birdbath fronted a small one-story brick house. She drove around back, tucking the cruiser into the niche by the add-on kitchen, out of sight of the road. She left her Stetson on the seat, took a look at herself in the rearview mirror, and combed her curls back with her fingers. Then she walked past the black Taurus to the back corner of the lot. The air was summery, warm and humid. A leafy grapevine laden with bunches of reddening grapes climbed the trellis that shielded a trailer.

Brown-bearded Romey Dennis stood in the doorway grinning at her. "Hey, all right! This is a nice surprise. I heard Coach Cochran doing his sheriff thing on the radio about a murder at the bank. Figured I wouldn't see you for a couple of weeks."

Marty stopped in her tracks. "Did he say murder? When did he say that?"

"Nah. Sorry, that's just me and the media jumping to conclusions," Romey said. He was wearing a wine-red Dennis Rent-All polo shirt. Must be on break, like her. He went on, "Coach said it was a routine investigation but he couldn't rule out this or that. Of course the reporter billed it as a possible homicide. Must be a slow news day."

"Yeah, gotta get up the body count or Dunning will never be able to compete with New York or L.A." Marty grinned at Romey and walked past him into the trailer. He'd bought it used and brightened it with posters of the countries he'd visited.

35

Romey closed the door before he kissed her. "Mm," Marty said, throwing both arms and a leg around him and kissing back.

"Hey Marty."

"Yeah?"

"Is that a gun or are you just glad to see me?"

She dissolved in giggles. "Cut it out, you goofus! You know I've only got about fifteen minutes."

"Yep. I gotta get back too. But maybe tonight . . ." He kissed her forehead. The fragrance of spices hung in the air.

"What're you fixing? Something smells good."

"Want some?" Romey took down another Greek-design plate. In his bedroom he'd hung a couple of real Greek plates on the wall alongside a photograph of his mother, plates saved from the fire that had killed her. He also kept his small gold-colored trophy there, the one the Stonies had given him the year he'd been captain. He called it his loving cup and kept condoms in it.

Marty dragged her thoughts back from their raunchy detour and sat down at the built-in dinette table. He was spooning something yellow and something green over fluffy rice. She said, "Yes, I want some. What is it?"

"Chicken curry and spinach shaag."

"You got enough?"

"Sure. I picked up enough for four meals. Want a Coke?"

"Yeah, thanks. Mm, this is terrific!" She forked some more into her mouth.

Romey popped a can for her and grinned at her as he sat down. "You always did lay into food like a starvin' yaller dog."

"Did not!" she mumbled around a mouthful of curry.

"Did so! Remember when we played the Little Pistons? Coach Cochran passed around a bag of apples in the station wagon afterward and you ate half?"

She'd been ten, the best girl player on their peewee basketball team, and those damn apples had given her a huge stomachache. Marty looked haughtily at Romey. "Well, these days I'm a perfect lady."

"These days you're a starvin' yaller dog. But hell, so'm I." He attacked his own plate.

"This is yummy. Where'd you get it?"

"I was up in Bloomington yesterday."

"It's really good." She didn't ask what he was doing in Bloomington. Her friend Dawn thought he had a girlfriend there. He said he was taking a course at IU. All Marty knew for sure was that last year when this childhood buddy had returned to the county, she'd found something a lot deeper and more complicated than an old friendship. It was too soon to know what. How could she think about the future when the present was so damn confusing?

But hey, Hopkins, he sure brightens the present.

For a moment they ate in silence, and her thoughts returned to Stephanie. *Darling bitch.* When she glanced up she found Romey studying her. His eyes were a clear brown that reminded her of brandy. He asked, "Can you talk about it?"

She pushed a curl from her forehead and swallowed some beer. "Don't know what to say. No obvious marks on the body. The thing is, she has a rotten ex-husband, used to beat up on her. Still writes her nasty notes."

"But no marks on the body?"

"See, she had some pills prescribed. Anti-depressants."

"And you're wondering if maybe she took too many, because of her ex?"

"She's been divorced eight months. But two weeks ago he sent her a note. Said she wouldn't get away."

"I see." He covered her hand with his. "You're worried about what Brad might do?"

"Not exactly. I mean, he's never been violent toward me. But yeah, I could see him writing notes like that. For years. God, Romey, why can't guys be reasonable?"

"What do you mean? We're reasonable as hell. We're not allowed to cry when we get hurt, so we get mad instead. Isn't that reasonable?" A bitter sorrow flickered in his eyes. "Of course it kind of warps our point of view. Makes for good football players and soldiers, but it's hell on the rest of life."

"Women feel like beating up on people sometimes. At least I do."

"But you usually cry instead, right?"

"Well, usually. But not always."

"I suppose women can get warped the other way, crying when they should be yelling and stomping." He lifted the hand he was holding and kissed her fingertips. There was a twinkle in his eye. "I'm glad you're not a warped woman."

She grinned back. "Sorry, Romey. I'm as warped as they come."

"Really? Can I look?" He started to unbutton her shirt.

She punched him fondly in the shoulder. "You've seen it all, goofus. Listen, I gotta go. Thanks for lunch."

Kissing him good-bye took a few minutes. Afterward in the cruiser she puzzled over him for a moment. This wasn't like the adolescent swooniness she remembered from early days with Brad. Instead, Romey seemed to awaken something deep and rowdy in her, a belly-laughing, shaggy-haired Marty who could nail thirty baskets in a row and be U.S. President in her spare time. It was scary. She wasn't sure she wanted more of Romey in her life.

On the other hand, she sure as hell didn't want less.

Marty made good time back to the station, and had a couple of minutes to drop in to see Aunt Vonnie. Reiner's Bakery was just across the courthouse square.

"Hi, Aunt Vonnie, Melva. Hi, Laurie."

"Hi there." Aunt Vonnie was counting chocolate chip cookies into a bag for Laurie Yeager. Laurie was in her thirties but looked younger, a healthy freckled girl-next-door like a youthful Doris Day. Marty's friend Dawn at the Unisex Salon said her blond and artfully tousled hair wasn't natural, that she had it done at some fancy place in Louisville, but it looked real enough to Marty. Aunt Vonnie closed the bag and handed the cookies to Laurie. "There you go. Three-fifty."

"Thanks, Vonnie." Laurie dumped the contents of her billfold on the counter, bills and receipts and racetrack tickets, and picked out four dollars to hand to Melva Dodd at the cash register. As she stuffed the papers back in she eyed Marty with interest. "Is there any news about that poor girl in Gordon's building, Marty? The radio said murder, but when I called Gordon, he said they didn't know how she'd died."

"He's right, we don't know. Anytime it's mysterious the reporters make it sound like the end of the world."

"They doing an autopsy?" Laurie asked.

"Yeah, that's routine when there's a question. They'll probably be able to tell us soon."

"I didn't recognize her name," Melva Dodd said, handing Laurie her change.

"She only moved here a couple years ago," Marty explained. "Lived in that apartment the Johnsons have. She came to our church sometimes. Went out with the singles group."

Aunt Vonnie shook her head. "That church is getting so big now, can't keep track of all the folks."

"That's the truth," said Melva Dodd. She was in her fifties like Aunt Vonnie, with a sturdy figure verging on plumpness and a beehive of an unlikely blond shade. "That's why things are falling apart today.

It's not love your neighbor, it's rob your neighbor. Kill your neighbor."

Marty said, "She wasn't robbed. Might have been something natural, a stroke or something."

"Well, natural things can kill you too," Laurie said. "TV is full of diseases. And did you see the midnight movie last night? About a tornado? I was alone and it scared me to death."

Aunt Vonnie said, "Well, we know that wasn't the girl's problem."

"Thank God," Laurie repeated. "Well, I'll see you all soon." She left to the tinkle of the bell.

Melva turned to Marty now, her sad eyes brightening with interest. "Is it true that it happened in Montgomery State Bank?"

"That's right. But we don't know what happened yet."

Aunt Vonnie asked, "Have you talked to Tom? Melva's brother-in-law? His company has the cleaning contract."

"Yeah. He sent Jimmy Corson to clean the bank last night, so I'm going to check with Jimmy. Melva, Dee looked really sick. Is she getting better at all?"

Melva Dodd had been born a Reiner, and had taken over the family bakery when her parents died because her brother was a career Marine and her sister Dee preferred farm life. She shrugged. "Doctor says it takes time. I think if her daughter would come back she'd do better."

"Where is Coral? Do you know?"

"Touring with a rock group. She doesn't want to come back." Melva shook her head. "The girl always loved music, said she wanted to have a singing career. But Dee always encouraged her. The kid had no call to run off like that."

Aunt Vonnie snorted. "Teenagers! No brains, no heart."

"Hey, come on, Aunt Vonnie, we're going to have one of our own before long," Marty said. "Listen, the reason I came by is to say I might be late for dinner."

Her aunt looked mournful. "By now I know you might be late any night. Crazy job you picked out."

"Not my job this time. I've got that meeting with the lawyers this afternoon."

"Oh, I remember." Aunt Vonnie put tired hands on her hips and flexed her back, then gave Marty a weary look. "Well, get that bastard out of your hair, and maybe we'll get some—"

Marty's portable radio crackled. She keyed on and identified herself, "Nichols County Three twenty-one."

"Three twenty-one, four-year-old kid missing from 406 Shepard Road west of the intersection with State 37. What's your location?"

Marty jumped for the door. "Couple steps away from you. I'll get right on it, ten-four." As the glass door closed behind her she caught a glimpse of Aunt Vonnie shrugging at Melva. It was true, this job was hell on social graces.

A few seconds later she was racing to the scene.

Seven

A hundred and twenty miles north, in an office at Hoosier Heating and Air Conditioning in Muncie, Len Abbott stared blankly at the numbers before him and tried to remember what he was supposed to be doing. Checking the estimate for the new heating system at Russell's hardware store. Not that they'd get the job anyway. Russell's cousin ran a rival heating business. Helped to have relatives.

Relatives. God. Len ran a nervous hand through his thinning curly hair. Steffie. No, it couldn't have really happened.

Just two days ago she'd been bubbling to him happily about her apartment, and it was true, with the plants in those windows and the bright colors she'd used, it was full of cheeriness.

Len's fist hit the desk. This was ridiculous. When the Muncie police had visited him just after lunch, to tell him that his daughter had died, he'd protested. "I just saw her two days ago! She was fine!" But they'd insisted, and told him gently that her boss had identified her and there was no need for Len to go immediately to Dunning where the body lay, but as next of kin he'd have to take care of the burial.

"How did she die?" he'd asked.

"Sorry, sir, we don't have that information."

He couldn't believe she was really dead. He'd tried to go back to work, thinking it would distract his dismal thoughts, but the opposite was happening. He was thinking about the new life Steffie thought she'd built for herself in southern Indiana. He was wondering if that bastard Stollnitz had found her somehow. He was wondering if the sheriff down there even knew to ask about Stollnitz.

Len fumbled in his bottom drawer for the bourbon and refilled the glass on his desk.

How the hell could they not know how she died? Were they keeping it from him, trying to spare his feelings or something? Or were they just incompetent, out there in the boonies?

Or maybe she wasn't really dead. Maybe this was all a horrible mistake. A computer glitch.

He thought about taking some time off, driving down to see what the real story was. But that would require telling his boss what the police said had happened. He had a lot of work to complete before he could take time off. And he couldn't face telling his boss. That would be like admitting that the cops were right, that Steffie really was dead. And she just couldn't be.

Whatever had happened, Stollnitz should suffer.

Len took another sip of bourbon. Maybe when he finished this estimate he'd give that sheriff a call.

Jake had heard a police broadcast about a missing child but when he got there it turned out to be nothing the *Nichols County News* would be interested in, just a kid in a friend's secret clubhouse that he hadn't told Mommy about. Afterward Jake decided to go to Asphodel Springs to get some preliminary interviewing on his tourism story. Fiscarelli, his editor, who sported aviator glasses, a goatee, and a pot belly, liked story ideas to be practically written before he okayed them. Asphodel Springs, a nineteenth-century resort built around sulphur springs and now enjoying a good regional reputation, would be a good place to start.

If he hadn't been thinking about the resort where he'd sent the Ohio man with the mustache and tasseled loafers, he might not have noticed the gray Lincoln with Ohio plates. It was parked in the lot outside Big Blue Liquor. That was odd, because Big Blue was two blocks away from the nearest business section. Its location had been grandfathered in when they rezoned Dunning ten years ago, and the resulting cheap overhead meant it could give good discounts. So it was popular with people who lived here, but a stranger in town would have had to pass up three liquor stores near the main inter-section and dive into the dusty back streets of Dunning to find it. Well, the guy was good at asking questions, so maybe some gas station attendant had told him.

Jake headed southeast toward Asphodel Springs and turned his mind to the questions Fiscarelli would want answered.

Marty had hoped to change into her civvies before her meeting with Brad and the lawyers, but by the time she'd found the little boy whose frantic mother thought he'd run away when he was actually playing in a buddy's treehouse, and then talked briefly to the sheriff about the lack of progress in the Stephanie Stollnitz case, she didn't have time to change. Feeling decidedly unspiffy in her rumpled uniform, she stopped to fix her makeup and brush her hair in a McDonald's restroom. What the hell, Hopkins, she thought, looking herself in the eye. This is who you are. Changing to your Sunday best won't fool anybody. No telling what he wants to fight about today anyway: your house, your job, your erratic hours, your kid.

His kid too.

Damn. Quit fretting about it.

Marty jammed her hairbrush back into her kit and drove the two blocks to the Montgomery State Bank building. She was a few minutes early, and Brad's red Mazda was not yet in the lot. Upstairs, she greeted Debra for the second time that day.

"Oh, hi, Mrs. Hopkins. I'm glad you're early."

"Why? Does Chip want to see me?" He'd already briefed her about what to expect at this first official meeting: character assassination, mostly, he'd warned.

"No, Mr. Hansen's on long distance, but Mr. Yeager wanted to speak to you." She pushed a button with a salmon-pink fingernail and spoke into her receiver. A moment later Gordon Yeager stuck his balding head out of his office door.

"I've got that information for you. Come on in for a minute," he said, holding the door for her. Gordon looked tired. He was in shirtsleeves, his striped tie loosened. Red suspenders pulled his suit trousers halfway up his little paunch. He let the door close behind her and began rustling through the piles of paper on the big oak desk that dominated the center of the room.

Marty glanced around the office. The door where she stood was one of three in this wall. The others, louvered oak, must be closets backed up to the big closet in Debra's office. The wall on Marty's right was lined with oak file cabinets topped with matching bookcases full of sober-looking law books, a few out of place, piled helter-skelter at the ends of the rows. Straight across from her, the window wall looked out on the parking lot and the Burger King next door, but Gordon had angled the vertical blinds to cut out most of the view. A long, dusty-looking heating grille ran below the window. On the left wall, above a coffee-table grouping of a brown leather sofa and chairs, Gordon's diplomas flanked a photo of Spring Mill Park with the redbuds in bloom. Like the big desk, the coffee table was jumbled with books and papers, and a Sprite can lay on its side, still dripping on to a big wet spot on the carpet.

It was too late, but Marty grabbed it anyway and righted the can.

Gordon straightened from the desk, his soft, intelligent face puzzled. His eyes fell on the wet carpet and he exclaimed, "Oh hell! Thanks, Marty." He joined her and took the Sprite can. Then he spotted some papers on the coffee table and brightened. "Here we are! I didn't want it to get lost on my desk. The Muncie lawyer's number is on top."

"Thanks." Marty glanced through the papers, glad they weren't wet. A lot of this stuff, including the phone number, was in the file Stephanie had left with her landlords. But there were a few additional papers. Besides, you didn't want to tell a $150-an-hour guy that he'd been wasting his time. "We'll get back to you if we have more questions."

"Do you know yet what happened to her?" Gordon looked genuinely concerned.

"Not yet. I just spoke to the sheriff, and he says there's no report yet from the lab."

"Do you think it was a medical problem?"

"That's what they're checking on. It takes a while."

"Yeah." Gordon shrugged. "I only saw her a couple of times, but she seemed a real nice person."

"Yeah, we're hearing that from everyone. Thanks again."

Marty stepped back into the reception area. Debra was saying brightly, "Mr. Hansen will be out in a minute, and Mrs. Hopkins— oh, here she is."

There were two men standing before Debra's desk, but Marty's unwilling eyes were pulled to one as though magnetized. Six feet, handsome as sin, wearing a red-striped shirt, jeans, and snakeskin boots. He had a mustache and dark hair that flopped across his forehead. She couldn't meet his sad dark eyes.

"Hi, Brad," she muttered, and cleared her throat.

Wes Cochran shifted the phone to his other ear. "I'm sorry, Mr. Abbott. The medical report isn't in yet, so we don't know."

"Look, Sheriff, if it's Steffie, it's not going to be a medical problem. Steffie was a healthy girl. She must have got hit on the head, or she fell down the stairs—you say she was indoors?"

"That's right, sir. The doctor will let us know what happened. He's checking all those things."

It had taken a while to convince Abbott that the body had been

43

definitely identified as his daughter's. Now his disbelief was focused on Wes's inability to tell him what had happened. "God, I can't believe this idiocy!" Abbott exclaimed. Wes could hear the rage in the man's voice. He also knew it was covering up grief and helplessness. He knew because he'd felt the same way once.

"We should be getting a report tomorrow morning," he said. "If you want, I can call you and tell you the findings."

Abbott said, "Yeah. Yeah, I'd like that. But the main thing is for you to track down her ex-husband. Believe me, that's where you should be looking."

"Yes sir. Do you have personal knowledge of where Mr. Stollnitz was last night?"

"Personal? God, no! After he beat up Steffie that last time I told him to stay away from her and from me too, 'cause I couldn't promise him I wouldn't shoot him. But I saw him lurking around my business a couple times after she moved. I think he was trying to figure out her address. She says he mailed a couple of things to her old address and they got forwarded."

"Yeah. It's always bad news when a guy gets obsessed that way. Did she mention anything to you that makes you think he'd found out where she lived?"

"No. I just saw her two days ago and she seemed to think he was forgetting her. But I wouldn't be too sure of that. Dammit, I never wanted her to move! I would've taken care of her."

"Yes sir. Look, I'm sure you've told all this to the Muncie police."

"I sure have."

"But I'll call and give them a nudge. Make sure they're checking this guy's every move. And I'll call tomorrow to tell you what the medical examination showed."

"Thanks."

Wes hung up and looked sadly at the receiver for a moment.

Eight

"Hello, Mrs. Hopkins." Max Colman, Brad's lawyer, was from Bloomington. He was looking suave as usual with his blow-dried dark hair, gray suit, and red tie. You could almost see the "Esquire" after his name. Marty had given police testimony in a couple of civil cases he'd argued down here in Nichols County. Colman had won both cases, she remembered uneasily.

"Hi, Mr. Colman."

Colman's eyes swept her analytically, taking in the sheriff's uniform and probably her exhausted face as well. All at once Marty felt grubby, unattractive, incompetent. Lousy wife, lousy mother, selfish bitch.

Cut it out, Hopkins, she told herself fiercely. Just get through this. One step at a time.

Chip Hansen bounced out of his office. "Hey, Max, how you doing? Hi, Marty. Mr. Hopkins. Come on in. We won't need the conference room yet, I don't think." He waved at his open door to indicate that Colman and Brad should enter. "They say it's going to rain tonight, but we'll be out of here sooner than that. Marty, wait a second." He stopped her from following the others into his office and pulled her aside. In a low tone he said, "Remember what we talked about last week. They'll try to make you look bad. Don't get emotional. Just stay calm."

"Okay." She took a deep breath and went in. Chip's office was a mirror image of Gordon's, but much neater.

Colman had placed his briefcase on the coffee table. "So what do you think about the Pacers this year, Chip?" he asked.

"I've seen better, but they've got a chance," Chip said, closing the door. He patted the end of the leather sofa for Marty and she sat uneasily on the front edge.

"Man, they better have a chance," Brad said. The men had remained standing. "I've got a few bucks riding on them. Those no-brains in Tennessee don't know bad from good basketball."

They wanted to talk basketball? Well, okay. Marty said, "The

Pacers may get some trouble this year. I like the Hornets too."

Colman looked down at her, surprised, then seemed to register the fact that anyone associated with Sheriff Cochran, who'd twice been on the state championship team, would know basketball even if female. He said dismissively, "Well, let's get this show on the road." He pulled one of the chairs at the end of the coffee table around to face Marty directly and sat down. Brad pulled the other chair into place next to him, and Chip sat on the sofa.

Colman pulled some papers from his briefcase, saying, "As you know, my client denies that the marriage is irretrievably broken. Therefore today we are concerned only with temporary arrangements."

Marty sought Brad's eyes, but they remained stonily fixed on the papers in his lawyer's hand. She tried to explain, "Brad, the thing is, you've only been home about ten weeks out of the last two years. This is just to make it official."

He looked up angrily. "*I've* been home, Marty. Home is Tennessee now. *You're* the one who won't stick with the family!"

"Brad, no! That's not—"

Chip interrupted her. "Let's hear what Mr. Colman has to say."

Colman continued, "My client points out that Mrs. Hopkins refused to accompany him on a family move to Tennessee that was required by his employment, and that she has withheld his child from him and refused all his reasonable attempts to reunite the family."

Marty was furious. "Family move? What kind of bull—"

"Let him finish!" Chip said to her sharply, but it was the glint of triumph in Colman's eyes that told her she'd blundered. Don't get upset, Chip had told her, they're trying to make you look bad. Stay cool. She bit her lower lip.

Colman went on, "Until the family is reunited, my client demands full joint physical custody of his daughter, who is to spend fifty percent of her time with him and fifty percent with your client."

Impossible, Marty wanted to exclaim. Chrissie was in school! How could she spend half her time in another state? But she stayed quiet as Colman continued.

"Travel costs, of course, will be borne by your client. My client also demands equitable distribution of property and an equitable division of child support. Court costs and attorney's fees to be paid by your client." Colman looked up from his paper and added drily, "If this is acceptable to your client, we can draw up the papers and get out of here."

46

"Not a chance!" said Marty.

Chip said calmly, "Let's go over it point by point."

"But it's not acceptable," Marty said, trying to sound reasonable. "I want you to know that up front."

Brad leaned forward, his magnetic dark eyes hurt and angry. "What do you mean? It's fair, isn't it? Half and half?"

"God, of course it's not fair! How can Chrissie—"

Brad threw up his hands and leaned back, addressing Colman. "You see what I'm up against? She lives in this fantasy world where half and half isn't fair! Swear to God, it's like talking to a Martian sometimes!"

"Who's in a fantasy world? How can Chrissie go to school if—"

Chip stopped her again. "I think we'd better start with the property."

"Good idea," Colman agreed.

"Half and half, like I say," Brad said. "It's only temporary anyway."

Chip said, "You do understand that my client owns her house, having inherited it from her mother."

"Her mother?" Colman shot an angry glance at Brad, and Marty realized that her husband had neglected to give his lawyer all the relevant facts.

Chip seemed to realize it too. He handed some papers to Colman. "Yes, the house is outside the settlement."

"But what about all the work I did on it?" Brad demanded.

"What work?" Marty asked.

"Years of work! Like last summer I helped paint, right? And whenever I could, I fixed it up. Cleaned out drains, cut back weeds."

"Yeah, ten weeks out of the last two years! Who do you think was doing that stuff when you weren't around? Me! And I painted ninety-five percent of that house!"

"I was out there trying to earn a living for you and my kid, just like we agreed!" Brad exclaimed.

"And I was here, and I really was earning a living for all three of us!" Marty said hotly.

"Yeah, in your precious dead-end job!"

Colman had recovered from his momentary setback and said smoothly, "Well, there's plenty of time to get this straightened out. We'll have to see good evidence before we accept your claim that the house is not part of the settlement, of course. In any case, even if Mrs. Hopkins does own the house—and we are not granting that—but even supposing she does, the court will take that into

47

account when making an equitable settlement. My client contributed significantly to the value of the house and is entitled to credit for that."

"We'll also have to see good evidence of his contribution. What other property are we talking about?" Chip asked.

"Furniture."

"Yeah! We bought most of the furniture after we were married," Brad said.

Marty had a sudden vision of her house stripped to the bare walls. Chip glanced at his papers and said, "Don't forget the vehicles and the electronic equipment."

Brad smashed a fist on the table. "See what I mean? She's trying to get my car too! And my stereo! She doesn't give a damn that it's how I earn a living!"

Marty said, "And don't forget the record collection."

Brad went very quiet. Chip turned over a couple of papers. "I don't see a record collection listed, Max."

"Early Elvis phonograph records. Worth more every year, he told me." Marty could remember borrowing from her mother to pay the heat bills one winter because Brad had found an especially desirable set of records. Now she felt as though she'd finally scored a point.

But she felt guilty when she heard the pain in Brad's voice. "Marty, I can't believe you'd sink that low! What use would you have for those records?"

"Oh, Brad, I'll be reasonable. Don't worry about—"

"We're talking about equitable distribution," Chip put in brusquely. "Mr. Hopkins may be able to keep all the records as long as my client gets an equitable share of total jointly held property."

It was just a game, Marty realized. Bluff the other side, scare them into making concessions, trade this for that. Brad's beloved Elvis records, her furniture, his Mazda, her family home, all just playing pieces in a grotesque game. How had all their love and laughter and bright hopes for a future together rotted into this?

"Let's talk about custody," Chip said. "Your client's suggestion would require Chrissie to change schools frequently. That's not in the best interests of the child."

"We've got great schools in our part of Tennessee, and Chrissie already has friends that she's made in the neighborhood. I'm willing to take her more than half the time, if that's the only problem," Brad said.

Marty's fists clenched. "Brad, what is this? After years of ignoring her, all of a sudden you want to be a full-time dad? Her friends are here in Nichols County and you know it!"

"Not my choice, Marty! You've never been willing to share. Now I want Chrissie with me. You can come too, that's been the deal for two years, only you won't listen. I want our family together!"

Not true. Not any of it. Marty said in a tight voice, "Well, after all these years I think she should stay with the people who raised her and in the school she knows." Brad looked at her, so much pain and sorrow in his dark eyes that for an instant she wanted to hug him, tell him everything would be okay, rescue him again from the choices he'd made.

She'd tried to rescue him, over and over, for years. She'd failed. That's what she was trying to get away from, she reminded herself. But her voice was softer as she said, "Brad, look, I'm not saying you're a bad father or anything. I want her to see you a lot. But she's got to live with me!"

Brad shook his head sadly. "I didn't want to bring this up in front of other people, Marty, but you force me. You're not a fit mother any more! You put your job ahead of everything, plus I know you've been cheating on me. I don't want Chrissie to live with that kind of moral example any more."

His words gored her soul. She sat speechless, and it was Chip who jumped in to say, "My client is obviously a fit parent, and any court would find her so."

"Do we need this guy?" Brad addressed Colman. "Didn't you say we could hire a mediator and work things out for less money?"

"That's true." Colman smiled at Marty. "Mr. Hansen and I would go over the agreement at the end, but going to a mediator might save you some money, if that's important to you."

Chip said, "My client will consider it, of course, but at this meeting she has counsel. And Max, it seems to me as though your client's unfounded accusations are proving our contention that the marriage is irretrievably broken."

"See what I mean?" Brad addressed Colman again. "He twists everything! I've been working like a dog to get this family back together!"

"It's clear that custody won't be settled today," Chip said. His cheerfulness hurt, but at least it reminded her that it was all a game. "Okay, you mentioned holidays. What about those?"

"See, I'm trying to be fair," Brad said. "Like Chrissie should spend Thanksgiving with you, and Christmas with me."

"And next year, the other way around?" Marty asked, her wounded heart contracting at the thought of Christmas without her daughter.

"There won't be a next year. We'll be back together as soon as you get over your craziness," Brad said.

Stay cool, Hopkins, it's a game. Marty said carefully, "Well, in that case you won't mind making it alternating years. I can agree to that."

Brad frowned, but Colman muttered something to him and he said, "Okay. But it won't come to that."

"This is all just temporary," Chip pointed out. "And it's good to have agreement on something before we see the court officers."

But even though the meeting went on for thirty minutes more, at the end they'd agreed on only that one thing, the alternate holidays for Chrissie. When the other two left, Chip nodded, saying it had been very instructive, and told her to come in tomorrow to discuss things.

Marty made it to the cruiser before she started to sob.

Nine

Coral Turley gasped and jerked awake, staring fearfully into the midnight blackness. Her nightmare shuddered, the looming figures disintegrating, the menacing club melting to nothingness. Coral sat up and hugged her knees, still shivering, still cold with sweat. The nightmares seemed to come more often now that she was back in Nichols County. She thought she'd closed off her past, built herself a space bubble to guard against the horrors, where she could live alone and untroubled by attacks and betrayals. But here, unbidden memories of her girlhood, of laughter and song with her mother and friends, of grainfields and orchards and flowering meadows, came slipping through the cracks of her defenses. And behind the comforting memories crept other, darker thoughts. *The meadow was warm, the blossoms alight when I reached for you, but the deathwind blew . . .*

She'd do what she had to do and get out again. Get on with the future.

But right now she didn't dare sleep. The night was humid and ominous and those ugly dreams would come again. Hoyt had nightmares too and claimed that was why he did so much coke, but she knew a better way. She pushed her toes into her slippers and wiped the tears from her face. She'd work on some lyrics. That was part of the future, and a solace now.

Wednesday morning was cloudy, warm, and damp. Wes could see another shower peppering the puddles on the asphalt of the courthouse square across from his office window. He hollered at the telephone in his hand, "Doc? Speak up! This connection is rotten. Probably routed us via Timbuktu."

"Okay, I'll shout!" Doc's voice was a little louder. "But it's all right this direction. *You* don't have to yell. You're perforating my eardrums. Okay, now, time of death: not long before we found her. Body temp wasn't much below normal. Say two thirty, three thirty A.M."

"Okay! Got it!" Wes scribbled it down.

"Don't yell. Now, we checked for signs of violence—strangulation, concussion, et cetera. Nothing. Also no sign of sexual activity, consensual or otherwise. Also no sign so far of an overdose of any of the prescription drugs she took. Ditto the common poisons, but the toxicologist is doing more tests. Slight elevation of carbon monoxide, but that's common in smokers. No sign of the common medical problems like stroke, tumor, dadada."

"What?" Wes shouted.

"Ouch. No sign of stroke. Got that?"

"Yeah." Wes remembered not to shout.

"No sign of tumor. No sign of aneurysm. No needle marks. Look, I'll send a preliminary written report, but I'm waiting for more lab tests. Interesting case. Bottom line for you is, we still don't know cause of death." Doc's faint shout sounded cheerful.

Wes placed a foot on the scarred front edge of his desk and shoved back his chair a few inches. "What's your guess, Doc?"

"Right now, I don't even have enough evidence to guess."

"Forced choice?"

"Heart disease. Hers looks healthy but sometimes there's hidden neurological damage. I'll get another doctor to take a look too, but right now, I don't want to rule anything out."

"Including homicide?"

"Homicide, suicide, natural causes—who knows? This is a real interesting case. What about your end? Any special direction you want me to investigate?"

51

"An abusive ex-husband," Wes said.

"Hmmm. Nobody swatted her around recently. The lab's still checking those drugs. Maybe he's a pharmacist or something."

"Yeah, or maybe a South American with unknown poisons," Wes grumbled. "We're checking on him. He lives in Muncie, so I'm calling the department there to see if they've learned anything."

"Hope you get a better connection."

Wes hung up and turned to his waiting deputies. "No cause of death yet," he said.

"Shoot." Marty Hopkins sighed and leaned back against the door-jamb. She looked worn out today, Wes thought, her gray eyes troubled and her forehead taut with tension. She always looked tense when that no-good husband visited. But it didn't seem to interfere with her work. She asked, "What about time of death?"

"He says two thirty to three thirty A.M."

"So we saw her right after?"

"Yeah. I remember thinking she looked almost alive. Anyway, Doc's ruled out some obvious things but more tests have to be done. He said to check if the ex is a pharmacist. The father called yesterday, claimed she had no special medical conditions and told us it had to be the abusive ex-husband. But the guy lives in Muncie and wasn't supposed to know where she'd moved. Mason, I'm going to call Muncie again. I want you to liaise with the department there. Hopkins, did you get through to Greene Cleaning Service?"

"Yes sir. The manager told me that the guy who was on Tuesday night is Jimmy Corson. Works days at Brock Lumber."

"Oh, yeah. Jumbo Jim. Check him out, Hopkins. But first track down some of her girlfriends. They're more likely to know about medical conditions than her dad."

But none of Steffie's friends had heard her say anything about a medical condition. "She was real private," said big, elegant Mary Jo. "Friendly, but didn't talk much about herself. Not even that husband. Just said he'd been abusive and she wanted to forget all about it."

So Marty hadn't learned much by lunchtime. It was nearing noon when she parked the cruiser at the curb near Dunning Elementary. She picked up her daughter's pink slicker from the backseat. Brad had stayed with a friend overnight so he could take Chrissie out for dinner and some video games, and this morning he'd taken her to McDonald's for breakfast and on to school before starting back to Memphis. Characteristically, he'd forgotten to check the weather report. The morning showers had passed but thunderstorms were predicted this afternoon. At the moment the sky was clear, the sun beating down, hot little breezes curling by. More like June than September. Marty walked across a corner of the playground to stand by the basketball hoop.

Twenty years ago young Marty LaForte had been a student here, a sassy tomboy who was the pride of her father and Coach Cochran, but often the despair of her mother and her teachers. She could remember once telling her parents about a new play Coach had taught them. It required some complicated faking to get her opponent off-balance and herself in the clear to pop in her favorite jump shot. Her red-headed dad had twinkled at her. "Can't wait to see it on the court," he'd said, ruffling her curls.

Her mother's lovely gray eyes were troubled. "Marty, you know you can't always solve problems that way."

"What do you mean?"

"Well, seems to me all this competition is teaching you kids to mislead people, to be physical—see, maybe that works when you're all the same size, but the boys are going to outgrow you in a few years, honey. You should be learning how to discuss things. How to get along with people."

"Marie, for chrissake!" her dad exploded. "You learn how to get along on a team! How to stick up for your buddies! That's getting along!"

"Rusty, she's a girl!" her mother snapped. "A couple more years and nobody's going to want her on a team! You expect her to play for the Pacers or something? Is that fair, to give her dreams like that? Mrs. Braun says she spent most of her math class Friday throwing paper wads into the wastebasket whenever her back was turned!"

"Is that true, honey?" her father asked.

Marty glared back defiantly. "I won forty cents off Bud Gifford."

"Good lord, Marty!" her mother wailed. But her father was beaming his approval.

"Look, you guys, it's only a game!" Disgusted with grown-up squabbling, the young Marty had stomped off.

The older Marty sighed and leaned against the support post. Who'd been right? Her dad, surely. She'd tried taking her mother's advice when all her girlfriends began telling her the same thing. Sport LaForte, they'd called her, and said she'd never attract a boy. So she'd given up basketball, except for a couple of girls' teams— boring—and learned to use makeup and joined a sorority. Sure

53

enough, along had come handsome, talented Brad Hopkins, full of dreams, and needing her to make them come true. Except they hadn't. To support herself and her daughter, and often Brad, she'd turned back to her childhood love of action and teamwork and asked Wes Cochran for this job in law enforcement. She loved it. Once again she was on Coach Cochran's team.

So her dad must have been right. Although, to be fair, her mother had never approved of Brad either. "So he needs you?" she'd asked, unimpressed. "That doesn't mean you need him." There'd been no pleasing her, Marty thought crossly.

The bell sounded for lunch. Children erupted from the doors of the school, racing past her on to the playground, ignoring the oppressive weather. She tensed a little, scrutinizing the youthful mob, and then relaxed when Chrissie burst out, shouting to a friend. Her daughter was wearing flowered leggings, a yellow T-shirt, and bright daffodil earrings. She stopped suddenly halfway down the steps when she spied the cruiser. She glanced around, spotted her mother, then murmured something to her friend and marched down alone to confront Marty. There was thunder on her face.

"What are you doing here?" Chrissie demanded.

"Hey, take it easy, kid! I just brought your slicker. They say it's going to rain again this afternoon."

Chrissie glowered at her wordlessly.

"Why, you're welcome, Chrissie. Always glad to do favors for pleasant people. I was even thinking of giving you these M and Ms."

Chrissie took the package and stared at it with disgust. "Ma, you are so transparent!"

"What do you mean? What is it, Chrissie?"

"You don't trust him, do you? You came to check to make sure he dropped me off this morning! You think he'll kidnap me or something! Well, *you're* the one who's keeping me trapped! God, this is so embarrassing!"

Marty bit back a reply. She could see tears in Chrissie's eyes, held at bay only by the anger. Marty wanted to hug her, or slap her, or something. She held out the slicker and said, "I'm sorry, Chrissie. Really, I was just bringing your slicker."

"Well, I'd rather get wet!" Chrissie pushed it away and flounced off into the crowd of students.

Marty went back to the cruiser, tossed the pink slicker into the trunk, and headed for the highway that led south from Dunning. She could feel the sting of tears in her eyes too. Chrissie was right.

54

She *did* fear a kidnapping. She *was* checking up on Brad. What kind of a monster mom was she turning into?

He'd seemed so unreasonable at the meeting. But he'd always brought Chrissie back as agreed.

She had to try to trust him a little, or she'd push her daughter away.

C'mon, Hopkins, chin up, she told herself. All is not lost. At least the kid kept the M&Ms.

Marty wasn't supposed to see Chip Hansen until late afternoon, but worry was eating her up. She had to know where she stood. She radioed in that she was going on lunch break and went to Chip's office instead. She was in luck. Chip's twelve o'clock appointment had left early.

"Marty, take it easy!" Chip said. "That stuff they were talking about yesterday won't happen. They just want to scare you. They think you'll give up more if you think they can get all that. They can't."

"It sounded like they thought it was fair."

"We don't care what they think, we care what the judge will think. Let me double-check a couple of things. You want custody of your daughter, your house, and a fair share of the assets. Right?"

"Yeah. I don't even care about the support payments, but you said I should ask for them anyway."

"Right. We're asking for support so we'll have something to bargain with."

Her whole life had turned into bargaining chips. "God, I hate this," she said.

"You'll survive. Okay, next question. Can your husband prove he worked on the house, or contributed money to it?"

"Prove?"

"Receipts from plumbers or lumberyards or electric bills?"

"No, of course not. I paid all that stuff. I've got the receipts with my tax records."

"Way to go! Get them together, we'll need them. The other thing—" His blue eyes met hers, then slid away. "Okay, I'm not trying to tell you how to run your life or anything. But whatever your husband was hinting about with that line about cheating, it'd be best if he couldn't back it up with photos or witnesses if we have to go to court."

"I don't see how he could—" Marty began uncomfortably. There were guys in the department who were always making suggestive comments and would love something new to tease her about, so

55

she and Romey had been real careful. She hadn't even told her friend Dawn—though Dawn was a shrewd guesser. Shoot.

"If there is something, I better know, so they won't spring it on me," Chip said.

"I'll tell you if I think of anything," Marty said. Of course Chip was right, but hell, she saw him and his family every week at the supermarket, at ball games. It would be so awkward if she told him. Besides, there was no way anyone could know. Was there?

It made her mad. She asked, "Doesn't that kind of threat work both ways? Why couldn't I find out more about what he's been up to with Tiffany and Amy in Tennessee?"

Chip sighed. "You could. But it wouldn't be the same, Marty, you know that. In this county we'll probably end up with Judge Fischer or Judge Schmidt, and both of them have a high regard for the sanctity of motherhood. Means mothers have to be saints. You're already questionable in their eyes because of the full-time job."

"They'd rather have me on welfare? I was for a few months, you know, when Chrissie was a baby and Brad wasn't earning anything."

"Were you? That's good. That's good," Chip said happily, making a note. "You've worked your way off welfare. The judge'll like that."

"On that other thing, do you want me to find out about Tiffany and Amy, or not?"

"If your husband's fooling around, it just counts as boys-will-be-boys," Chip shrugged. Her anger must have blazed in her face because he held up a palm and added, "Take it easy, now. We all know there's a double standard. I'm not telling you what to do, I'm just reminding you how things are."

"Yeah." He was right. Marty folded her rage away and took a deep breath. "Okay. I'll get those house repair receipts together."

"That's the spirit." He held the door for her. "Don't worry, Marty, we'll do fine."

She stopped at the Burger King next door for a hamburger and fries to go, then, between munches, called the station to say she was back on duty, and if nothing more urgent had come up she'd roll on out to Brock Lumber and talk to Jimmy Corson about the Stollnitz case. "Go ahead," Adams told her.

Marty keyed off and headed for the lumberyard.

Ten

For miles around Nichols County, invisible powers prepared for war.

Moist tropical air still reigned in the region, circling slowly over the Ohio River valley, even edging northward a little. But to the northwest a mass of cold Canadian air was trying to push in, bearing the autumn's chill and encouraged by a powerful jet stream speeding west to east.

Below the jet stream raced a strong dry wind from the southwest, energized by the jet stream and shearing across the top of the moister air below. On the bottom layer, the tropical air, assailed from so many directions, did not yield. It stood stubbornly at bay, pawed the ground, prepared for a titanic clash.

Beaming through this invisible battle, the sun shone benignly on Nichols County, but its effect was not so kind. Dee Turley, a wide-brimmed straw hat hiding her gray-blond hair and shading her sorrowful eyes, walked restlessly across the field Tom had planted, and paused to touch a spindly, fruitless pumpkin vine. Its leaves seemed warm, breathing the moisture of the morning's showers back into the sluggish air. She squinted at the hazy blue sky with the wisdom of countless years of raising crops. No clouds. And yet there was an uneasiness in the lethargic air, like the imperceptibly lighter breathing of a great beast about to awaken.

The sun continued to beat down on Dee's shoulders, and on the earth; and the earth continued to heat the slow moist air.

Dee shivered and smiled a mirthless smile.

Jake Shaw poured himself another shot of coffee from the *News* communal pot and returned to the computer he shared with half the staff reporters. Every year it seemed to take more caffeine to keep him alert. Just gettin' on, maybe. Or maybe he was bored in a burg where nothing much ever happened. Who could get excited about the story he was working on now, an update on last summer's high bacteria count in the water supply, long since solved? His editor,

Fiscarelli, had been noncommittal about Jake's economic-slump series, suggesting he get a couple more good interviews, and meanwhile why didn't he find out if the Water Corporation had cleared up those violations? Boring, thought Jake, but of course he did it.

Only interesting thing today was the weather. He'd turned the office TV to the weather channel and muted it. The little yellow letters crawling across the bottom of the screen announced severe thunderstorms on the way. Rain at last. With luck a couple of trees would blow down across the highway and he could get some photos.

Jake took a sip of coffee. Seemed thin. Had someone substituted decaf? He scowled suspiciously across the room at young Betty Burke, who was on the phone with the sheriff, trying to pump up her damn story about the woman who'd died at the bank. But Betty's mug had a tea-bag tag hanging from it, some herbal concoction she favored. Surely even Betty wouldn't stoop so low as to water down a man's coffee.

Well, he'd better get on the phone himself. Jake dialed Indianapolis to get a statement on the Nichols County water violations from the state Environmental Management folks, and stifled a yawn.

The Eagle squinted at the hazy blue sky. Thunderstorms coming. There was a feel in the air, an uneasiness. Or maybe it was in the blood, a kind of acid building up, burning in the veins. And then the Thunderbolt acted and there was triumph, release. You had to ignore the screaming, sure, had to fly right through the screaming. Things never went exactly as planned, especially when there were women involved. Same as piloting a plane through the rushing winds into the quiet heart of the storm. And the glorious thing was how well the Thunderbolt had worked, and could work again.

One more time, one more. And then, somehow, two more.

Brock Lumber was three miles south of town, where the Orleans road joined the highway. Virgil Brock sent Marty past the paint and plumbing supplies and ready-made doors and fiberglass insulation to the back door. She crossed the blacktopped yard, following the whine of a saw into a big warehouse-like shed. Sweet-smelling stacks of pine and fir and cedar shingles perfumed the heavy air. In a cloud of sawdust, big Jimmy Corson was trimming some oak molding, watched by one of the local carpenters. Marty remembered both of them from grade school. Jimmy was rightly focused on the spinning blade, so Marty said, "Hi, Cal. What're you working on?"

"Remodeling Denton's law office. How 'bout you?" They both had to raise their voices.

"I'm here to talk to Jimmy about his other job."

"Oh, yeah, nights he's a janitor, right? At the bank where that gal died?"

"That's what I want to ask about."

Jimmy Corson turned off the saw, and in the ringing silence Marty said, "You guys go ahead and finish. Let Cal get back to work. Your boss knows I'm here, Jimmy."

Cal and Jimmy loaded the cut molding into the battered blue pickup parked by the shed door. Then Jimmy ambled back, removing his work gloves and swiping a hand across his dusty forehead. "Man, sure is warm for September," he said.

"Yeah. Must be in the eighties." Marty looked him over as she pulled her notebook from her belt. Jimmy Corson was wearing a navy blue workshirt, faded blue jeans, and work boots. He was a big guy, about six-two, heavyset and jowly, with thinning hair and a red complexion. He'd been a couple of years ahead of her in school, and she remembered his friends teasing him about always having pie in his lunchbox. Jumbo Jim, they'd called him. Probably wanted the pie themselves.

"What can I do for you?" Jimmy asked.

"Well, I'm here to ask about Tuesday night. They tell me you were working for Greene's that night at Montgomery State Bank."

"Oh, yeah. Wondered if you guys wanted to talk to me."

"Why? Did you see something?"

"Naw, that's the thing. Been racking my brains but I didn't notice anything funny. Would of called right away if I thought of anything."

Maybe he would have called, maybe not. It was hard to imagine big, friendly Jumbo Jim having anything criminal to hide. On the other hand, a guy who had to work two jobs might be open to a bribe to keep his mouth shut. Marty said, "Well, why don't you just talk me through. What time did you get there?"

"It was the only place I did Tuesday. I got there around six or six fifteen. Started on the ground floor and worked up, same as always. Finished the top floor about eight thirty."

"What kind of work were you doing? Vacuuming?"

"Yeah, usual stuff. Emptying the wastebaskets, wiping the counters, cleaning the restrooms."

"Was there anything unusual about the first floor?"

"The bank lobby? Nothing. I been thinking on it, and everything that was there is always there."

"What do you mean, everything that was there?"

"Like the tellers have this little closet where they keep umbrellas and sweaters and things. I vacuumed in there. I vacuum all the closets. But I didn't see anything strange."

So nobody had been lurking in a closet, at least not while Jimmy was there. Marty flipped to the next page. "You finished the first floor when, about seven?"

"Or a quarter of. Generally I get the two bank floors done by seven or seven fifteen. The third floor takes longer because it's all cut up into those offices."

"Yeah, I understand. Did you see anything unusual on the second or third floors?"

Jimmy shook his jowly head. "Nothing."

"What about people? Who'd you see?"

"Well, a bunch of folks were still there when I arrived. Always are. They mostly left during the first hour. I saw them taking the elevators."

"So after the first hour, who was left?"

"Nobody on the bank floors. On the third floor the accountant was still there. When I unlocked his door and went in for the waste-baskets he was behind the counter doing paperwork. He went out to get himself a Coke from the machine, then went back in after I finished cleaning."

"What about the law offices?"

"I saw Mr. Yeager leaving while I was cleaning the first floor. Nobody was in the law offices when I got to the third floor. All locked up. The dentist too. Only the accountant, like I said."

That confirmed what they'd all said. But something prickled in Marty's memory. Laurie Yeager, that was it, at the bakery, mentioning something about Gordon coming in after midnight. Was it that night? She'd better check back with Laurie and Gordon. She made a note and asked Jimmy, "Did you go down to the first floor again?"

"Sure, taking trash down and bringing up paper towels and toilet paper. Made three or four trips. But I didn't go back into the bank lobby, if that's what you mean."

"Could you see into the lobby?"

"Yeah, the front part of it. The security lights were on. But I was mostly by the back door on those trips, and you have to go right up to the glass doors to see the whole lobby." He frowned. "Was the poor gal there?"

60

"That's what we're trying to find out. Here's her picture. Do you remember seeing her Tuesday night?"

Jimmy's ruddy face rumpled in thought. "No," he said at last. "I remember seeing her a couple times. But not on Tuesday night."

"She drove a two-year-old Civic, white."

"Don't remember."

"We found it parked behind the bank, near the dumpsters."

"Well, there was nothing like that around when I was there. See, my van was parked right there by the dumpsters too. When I first got there, there were a few cars in the lot still, but when I left they were all gone except for a green Buick."

The accountant's car, probably. Marty looked back over her notes. "Well, I think we've covered everything for now. Thanks, Jimmy."

His jowly face was sad. "Wish I could of helped more."

"This helps. Sometimes the only way to find out when it happened is to find out when it didn't happen. But give us a ring if you think of anything."

She climbed back into the cruiser, flipped on the air conditioner, and sat musing for a moment while the car cooled off. They'd better double-check the dentist's whereabouts, and Gordon Yeager's. But Jimmy's account didn't narrow things down much, not if he was telling the truth. There were still six hours between eight thirty, when Jimmy had left, and two thirty, the earliest Stephanie could have died, according to Doc Altman.

What had she been doing for those six hours?

Why, and when, had she returned to the bank?

At the shift change Wes said, "Her father says the Stollnitz woman was healthy and it must have been the ex-husband. Blond football-player type, is all the description we've got. And we're still waiting on the coroner for cause of death. You got anything to add before you take off, Hopkins?"

"No sir, you covered it. We can use information about what she was doing the night she died."

"Okay," Wes went on to his four-to-midnight deputies. "Only other thing is the weather. Severe thunderstorms predicted. There's going to be civilians out there doing stupid things, skidding their cars off the road and trying to move fallen electric lines and so forth. That's all. Go do the job."

Four-to-midnight headed out, and Hopkins' shift started for home. "Good-bye, sir," she said.

"See you at the church supper, Hopkins." Wes returned to his office and a stack of paperwork from the county attorney, mostly dealing with the jail plumbing repair project. It'd be good to get out of here and go to the church supper. Make no mistake, the church supper was work too, part of the job. A good way to stay in touch with the folks, pick up the first rumblings about mysterious broken windows at a rural crossroads, or some new teenage fad like huffing Toluol or rollerblading down Highway 37. Things that if you caught them early, you'd maybe avoid big trouble later. So the church supper was a useful couple of hours for Wes, and pleasant too because of the array of everyone's tastiest dishes.

He scrawled his approval on the first of the plumbing repair papers and picked up the next.

Eleven

Four thirty P.M. Len Abbott had had a real bad day at work after a sleepless night. He'd been so slow today that shortly after lunch he'd had to confess to his boss about Stephanie. "Get outta here, man," Thompson said, and cleared his throat. "Go do what you gotta do for her."

Len wanted to say that working helped, that he needed the distraction, but he'd been so slow he couldn't pretend he was really working. So he said, "Thanks," and went home. Maybe he could grab a nap.

But images of his dead daughter still flashed in his mind and he couldn't sleep. Dr. Hayes had prescribed SomnoTabs for him. He'd tried a couple last night, but now he eyed the bottle suspiciously. If they didn't put him out, he could have nightmares, the kind where you couldn't quite wake up but struggled in a drugged twilight to escape, and couldn't. And maybe he didn't want to sleep at all, he thought as he popped a beer. That talk with the Nichols County sheriff had got him too worked up. Ever since, he'd been trying to think of what more he could say to show them her murdering ex-husband had done it. He'd checked three times with the Muncie police, but they'd said in their kindest way that you couldn't rush these things, that Nichols County had already contacted them and the departments were cooperating fully, but they didn't even know the cause of death yet. Meanwhile the murdering bastard was running around free as a bird, probably destroying evidence, that's why they couldn't figure out how he'd done it.

Dammit, how had he done it?

Len had tried to warn Steffie not to marry the bastard. He'd tried.

Len looked at the bottle of pills. But he didn't want to sleep. He felt like committing a murder himself. No—death was too easy. Torture was what Clay Stollnitz deserved, years of torture, like what he'd done to Steffie.

He got himself another beer, flipped on the TV, and decided to try Joss again. He dialed California for the eighth time, or was it the hundred and eighth? Joss's chipper voice came on the answering machine as usual. Len had left cautious messages earlier—call your father, it's important—but Joss hadn't called. How could sweet Steffie's sister be such a bitch? The hell with trying to break it to her gently. Len's jaw clenched and when the tone came he shouted at the receiver, "Clay Stollnitz murdered your sister, Miss Busy Bee. Call Barker's Funeral Home if you give a damn."

He slammed down the phone, chugged his beer, and glanced at the TV, chattering to itself in the corner. A newscaster, blond hair stiff around her animated face, was talking about the weather and the little inset graphic was an eye-catching picture of a tornado. Violent storms predicted in the southern part of the state, she said, especially Dubois, Martin, Orange, Nichols, and Lawrence counties. Nichols County! Hell!

Len put his shoes back on and ran for the car. The phone started ringing as he reached the door to the garage and he paused, hand on the knob, wondering if it was Joss. But so what if it was? He'd worked disasters and knew that in a major storm Steffie would be the farthest thing from anyone's mind. He had to make sure she didn't get lost in the confusion.

Len gassed up at a self-service Mobil on Highway 3 and headed south.

"God. You look like a fucking dweeb," Hoyt said with a glance at Coral. He was standing behind Skell, who was slouched at the keyboard, doodling with a song Coral had been writing all afternoon. Duke was lounging on the sofa, smoking. He hadn't hurt her for months but he still gave her the creeps.

"Naw, this is cutting-edge fashion in these parts," Coral said.

63

She was in torn blue jeans and a pink T-shirt. She'd traded her Doc Martens for sandals because it was so hot today.

"Wrong! Lily Pistols is cutting edge in all parts." Hoyt held up an admonishing finger, but was more interested in the song and the strange dark chords pulsing from Skell's fingers. Hoyt squinted at Coral's scribbled words and sang, "You're just a withered columbine, just a fleeting butterfly, just a waning summer love."

Hell. Coral had hoped to sing this one herself. She'd written it for a female voice, a heartbroken female voice. But now Skell and Hoyt were changing it, and she had to admit that the glowering chords and the raspy edge in Hoyt's voice gave the song a different appeal. Greedy slobs. But their albums sold. At least Hoyt was using her songs. "Deathwind," she'd written that, and he'd given her a couple of solo lines in it besides the backup job. She didn't have the contacts to go it alone, not yet. So what the hell, she'd write another song. She was teeming with songs, good songs, and Hoyt was burned out. She'd get her chance.

Plus she couldn't get Hoyt and Skell mad at her because one glimpse of what Duke was willing to do for them was one glimpse too many.

She brushed her hair fluffy, no spikes or corkscrews for this visit. Dweeb time, Hoyt was right. The other two finished the song and Skell and Duke said they were going to Bloomington to meet the others in the band and score some coke. Hoyt said he'd stay at the farm and Coral called, "You know I'm taking the BMW."

"It's okay, I wanna work on this. I don't need wheels."

"I won't be long." Coral fastened her waist pack. It held her car keys and her brand-new California driver's license. She yelled, "Hasta la vista," and ran out to the BMW.

It was five thirty as she followed Duke's gray car to the highway, where she turned the other direction, toward White Oak Farm. Dee had cut her off, so what the hell did they have to say to each other now? Why did they want her to go home for a visit? Coral had work to do. A life to live. Yeah, and sleepless nights to get through, and nightmares. Why, why hadn't Dee called back?

Too late to worry about that now. She'd just let Dee know she was doing great and leave. She didn't need Dee any more, she'd just be her own damn mother. She was on her own. So why were her eyes stinging? She ignored them and focused on the song that was taking form in her mind. On my own, all alone, hear me moan, don't telephone . . . She liked that. A tune, a beat, pulsed with the words in her head. She'd write it down when she got back. All about how oppressive life was, and family and friends, and how it was better to be queen of the bones.

Queen of the bones. Funny how her mind jerked her around sometimes. Really she was starting to feel really alive, full of songs and pain. This was going to be much better than raising pumpkins and barley and winning some talent contest or other and marrying a farmer, things her mother dreamed for her.

Coral had bought into those dreams too when she was a kid. Around here, if you could sing and dance and play the piano, they talked about your chances of winning the beauty pageants, because once a long time ago, ten years maybe, that Mary Ruth Butcher had gone from Miss Nichols County to Miss Indiana. For that matter, Dee herself had been Harvest Festival Queen in her younger days, but that was no big deal, that was like a county fair. Now her mother pretty much ran the whole festival. Said she preferred the business side to the show side anyway.

Oh, Dee, why didn't you call back? Were you so angry?

Well, two can be angry.

Come to think of it, wasn't the Harvest Festival supposed to be this month? How come nobody was advertising it?

Actually it didn't look like much of a harvest. The fields, most of them, were barren, and the grass looked tired and brown even though it had rained this morning. Coral scanned the countryside uneasily. The trees were still in leaf but they looked exhausted. It all had a November, almost wintry look, even while the heat and humidity said summer. Weird.

The air was weird too. Something so very sad about it. Over there in the southwest a big cloud was building. No rain, and overhead the sky was blue, but everything felt sad and creepy.

Including White Oak Farm. Coral pulled into the driveway. A Jeep and a white van, back doors opened so she could glimpse the power mower, greenhouse heater, and other farm equipment inside, sat in the store parking lot next to a maroon Mercury Sable. She looked across at her childhood home, white and graceful on the sloping lawn. Behind it the grove of white oaks stood silently in the slow-moving air. Coral couldn't deal with it yet and parked near the store instead, a long low building stretched between the road and the greenhouses, a big sign saying "White Oak Farm" edging the new orange roofline. She pushed open the aluminum screen door and stepped in. For an instant she was overwhelmed. The scent of apples and vegetables and the tinkly sound of the bell over her head struck at her very center, bouncing her into the past, to where

65

her memories had no words, just feelings. Why didn't you call back? Coral squeezed her eyes shut. It had only been a few months. It was just that she'd changed so much.

She opened her eyes and saw her father gazing at her. He was behind the cash register, wearing a bright orange shirt, and his face had a cautious smile. "My God. Little Coral at last," he said softly.

Not so little, she wanted to say. Hell, she was as tall as he was. But she didn't feel like getting into hassles right now. She wanted to get this thing with her mother over. So she gave Tom a casual hug and asked, "Is my mom around?"

"Yeah. Yeah, she's around. Coral, are you doing okay?"

"Sure. I'm doing great, Tom."

"Really?"

Tom was hard to get to know even if he was her father. He doted on Coral's handsome, independent mother and usually sided with her, although sometimes he'd spoken up for Coral when she wanted a later curfew or money for a special trip. So Coral merely answered, "Yeah, really, things are great."

"You're back for a while now?"

"No. I'm not staying here. I'm renting the old Matthews place just for a month. I'm with Hoyt. That's where I belong now, Tom. This is just a visit, okay?"

He looked dazed, as though he couldn't understand how anyone could prefer another place. She asked again, "So where's Dee?"

Tom roused himself. "Out walking somewhere. She's been real restless this afternoon. Like she was expecting something."

The only two customers, women with beehives like Aunt Melva's, were pushing their shopping carts up to the cash register. Coral said, "Hey, Tom, I'll go look for her, okay? Think she's outside?"

"Last time I saw her she was headed for her horses."

Coral started for the door. One of the two women said, "My goodness! Is it little Coral? Are you back, honey?"

"No, ma'am, just passing through," Coral said, and ran out into the moist and eerie heat.

Chrissie was still miffed at Marty. "See? It hasn't rained at all," she said from the backseat in an I-told-you-so tone.

Marty pointed through the cruiser window to the southwest. "But they've got a severe thunderstorm watch. See that cloud coming?"

"Oh, Ma, that's so totally far away!" Chrissie flounced back in disgust.

Aunt Vonnie, on the front seat next to Marty, frowned at the cloud. "Looks like a big one, all right."

"Well, the church has lightning rods. We'll be okay." Marty pulled into the Cedars of Lebanon parking lot and opened her door. She was wearing a summery blouse in tones of wheat and poppy-red, but the air was so steamy she wished she'd worn a skirt instead of jeans. Maybe the rain would cool things off.

Her daughter went streaking off instantly to look for her friend Janie, no doubt to complain about her unreasonable mother. Marty saw that Chrissie had left the pink slicker on the backseat and gave up. Clearly she'd rather get soaked than wear it. Marty grabbed her shoulder bag, heavy from the gun she carried there when she was off-duty, and picked up her rain jacket and Aunt Vonnie's creamed chicken casserole covered with aluminum foil. She fell into step beside Aunt Vonnie and headed for the church basement dining hall.

It was still a quarter to six, but there were a lot of people there already. Marty scanned the crowd surreptitiously as she placed Aunt Vonnie's casserole among the main dishes. Next to her in a gauzy tangerine-colored top, Dawn Arnold bobbed her mass of ash-blond curls as she simultaneously arranged her pan of chili, grabbed at Joey Jr., her towheaded three-year-old, who was trying to get to the dessert table, and told Marty the gossip from the beauty shop. "Alice Rowe told me she was so upset at Carson's drinking last week, she about hit him with a frying pan," Dawn reported. Alice was tiny, her husband Carson Rowe was huge. Marty hoped there wouldn't be a domestic violence call from them.

A moment later Romey Dennis came in the door at the other end of the room. He greeted people and paused to talk to a couple of them, but it took only seconds for his eyes to find Marty's.

She looked down at the aluminum foil she was removing from the casserole and gave Dawn a mechanical reply. Despite her distractions, Dawn looked at Marty sharply. "What's up, kiddo? Problems?"

"Divorce problems. Tell you later, okay?" Marty pounced on Joey Jr. and said, "Come on, bozo, let your mom fix her chili. We'll go see if anybody put any monsters on the bulletin board." She led him away from the dessert table. She could feel Dawn's eyes following her.

At the piano a group of teens launched into a rock version of "O Worship the King All Glorious Above." Against a heavy bass rhythm they sang, "His chariots of wrath the deep thunderclouds form, and dark is His path on the wings of the storm." Pastor Kemble, a good sport, began to clap in time.

Marty and Joey Jr. found no monsters on the bulletin board, but there was a big purple cut-out of Barney the dinosaur with a schedule of the church school activities, and she and the little boy were discussing them when Romey appeared beside them. Blue plaid shirt, sleeves rolled up. Shoot. Just a glimpse of his forearm, a whiff of his spicy aftershave, and her willful skin and tongue ached to feel him, taste him. Was it the same for him? His clear brown gaze was warm on her, but his words were casual. "Hi, Marty Hopkins."

She played casual too. "Hi. You know Joey Jr., don't you? Dawn and Joe's kid?"

"Sure I do. How ya doing, Joey Jr. ?"

The little blond boy looked away from the purple dinosaur only for an instant. "Fine. You know what Barney did today?" He launched into a rambling account of a song about wind and rain.

Marty took advantage of the childish chatter to murmur to Romey, "Chip Hansen says we should cool it."

A frown doused the happy glint in his eyes. "Thought that's what we were doing already."

It was true. They'd been damn cautious. Marty for one could have done with a lot more laughing, raunchy times with Romey. She steeled herself and struggled on. "Yeah, but Chip says if the wrong thing gets into the record I could lose Chrissie."

"I see. The bad mother thing. Hell." He leaned down toward the child. "Hey, Joey Jr., that's exciting! What did Barney do next? Was there a storm?"

"Yeah, a big storm! And Barney got an umbrella, and—" The three-year-old was off again.

"I'm sorry, Romey," Marty murmured lamely.

"Yeah," Romey said curtly. He scooped up the boy. "My turn, Joey Jr. I'll tell you a story."

"Does it have monsters?"

"Yeah, sort of. Except in this story the weird one is the hero. He's this magical guy named Dion and he'd been away for almost twenty years, and he was trying to sail back to where his lady was waiting. But the owners of the boat turned out to be pirates and lawyers and such. They said, hey, let's keep this guy from getting where he wants to go! We'll take him somewhere else so he'll get lost!"

"Yuck!" said Joey Jr.

"Yuck," Romey repeated. "But Dion didn't want to get lost. He

68

wanted to return to his lady because they were sad without each other. So he did some magic. He turned the oars of the boat into snakes so the pirates couldn't row, and he made vines grow up the mast and the rigging so they couldn't sail. And he made really loud music until the air was ringing."

"Really really loud?"

"Even louder than that wrath of God hymn they're singing right now. And he turned himself into a lion and roared, and the pirates and lawyers were so scared they jumped off the boat into the ocean and turned into dolphins."

Marty stifled a grin at the thought of Max Colman Esq. as a dolphin. Romey cocked his head at her and said, "We don't know exactly how Dion got back to his lady, but we do know he refused to get lost."

"Is that a real story?" asked Joey Jr.

"Yeah, it's as real as most stories." Romey put the little boy down. "Look, here's your mom."

"Hi, Romey," Dawn said. "Joey Jr. bothering you?"

"Course not. We were trading yarns, man to man."

"About a magic guy. He turned into a lion," Joey Jr. explained.

"Wow." Dawn grinned at her son. "But the pastor's getting ready to say grace."

It was true. The impromptu rock hymn had ended and Kemble was testing the microphone. Marty said, "We better get into line now."

"I want to say hi to some people. See you later, Marty, Dawn," Romey said easily.

"Are you going away?" Joey Jr. asked him.

"No, not far. I'll just go over there and turn myself into a lion."

The little boy giggled and Romey sauntered off. Dawn said, "He's a funny guy."

"Yeah," Marty agreed. But she didn't feel much like laughing.

Twelve

The humid tropical air stroked the limestone hills like an unwelcome lover, sliding across the sparse grain fields and tickling the brown-edged leaves in the orchards. It circled sluggishly in place, sucking heat and energy from the sun-warmed earth and sending it aloft in moist updrafts. Chillier air from the northwest pressed in, and a young giant of a cloud formed, piling up turbulent masses of condensing mist and charging the droplets and ice crystals with electricity.

A high dry wind from the southwest streamed by, and above the growing thunderhead, the jet stream ripped across from the west at two hundred miles an hour. Between the clashing layers the air began to boil, turning over and over like a long horizontal row of ball bearings or a vast invisible log rolling in the sky.

Seething with winds, water droplets, ice crystals and lightning, the new cloud sought to climb farther, but the racing winds aloft held firm as a pot lid, forcing it to spread out horizontally along its airy ceiling. From a few miles away the new storm cloud looked like a massive flat-bottomed anvil, rain-free but charged with crackling inner energy. Within it, powerful updrafts and downdrafts clashed and sheared. Lightning flashed continually. Meteorologists began to speak of it as a supercell. Behind it to the southwest, a row of thunderclouds was building, like a parade of attendants to some vast majesty.

In the seething heart of the cloud, the chief updraft hit the rolling horizontal tube of air and began to lift, so that one section of the tube was raised while the trailing end sank and the gigantic airy log was tipped toward the upright, spinning around an axis that was now nearly vertical instead of horizontal.

Far below, the sun-warmed earth heated more moist air and sent it pushing skyward. The atmospheric pressure dropped. In the oppressive quiet Dee Turley turned from her horses and started up the hill toward her white oak grove. Her practiced eye measured the stately thunderhead that led the line of advancing clouds. It already blotted out the southwest third of the sky.

Dee stretched her arms wide, welcoming the storm as an old friend, as dark mate to her despairing soul.

Wes had finally finished the plumbing repair paperwork and was heading for his cruiser. He'd be late for the church supper and the yummiest things would be gone, but these days Doc Hendricks had him eating lean anyway, so maybe it was safer to be late. There'd be less temptation. He'd said good-bye to Foley, the dispatcher, and had his hand on the door when Foley exclaimed, "Sir!"

"Yeah?"

"Just this minute, sir. Tornado warning."

Wes turned back. "Warning? You sure? They only just called a watch half an hour ago."

"Warning, sir."

"Damn. Check with the Dunning cops, Foley, and call all the troops." Where was Shirley? She'd be at the church supper. Good, that was a public shelter area. He wanted to rip over there and make sure she was okay, but he had a job to do here. Wes tossed his Stetson onto a desk and joined Foley at the radio.

Coral let the White Oak Farm store door slam behind her. God, she didn't want to do this. Her mother would holler or cry, as though it was Coral's fault, and Coral would holler back and be upset for hours and feel like a little kid. But Hoyt and Duke said she had to do it. Anyway, meeting Tom had been okay just now, no fireworks. Not that there ever were with Tom. He was easygoing, bottled up his feelings, hated fights.

Better get it over with.

The horses, she remembered, were usually pastured below the hill that rose behind the house. From the hill she'd also be able to see if her mother was in the vegetable gardens or the cornfields, or at the edge of the orchards. Might as well check the main green-house too. She entered the huge glass building. Except for a few potted chrysanthemums it was almost empty. Clean pots and plastic trays were stacked against the wall, waiting to be filled with spring seedlings. Above the slatted wooden platforms that would be covered with trays of baby plants come April, the pipes that sprinkled the young vegetables and flowers looked lonely, skeletal. One of the pipe joints dripped water slowly, like tears. Tom had stacked some glass near the greenhouse heater at the back, and when she looked up she saw that they'd lost a few window panes. He'd probably fix them after the harvest rush was over.

71

Not that there seemed to be much of a rush this year.

Coral went out the back of the greenhouse and started around the grassy hill. She could see her mother's three chestnut-colored horses now across the white board fence. They were restless today, their nostrils flaring, their ears swivelling edgily as they stamped and pranced. She saw one of the outdoor cats streaking toward the house. It disappeared into the bushes around the foundation.

She rounded the flank of the hill and stopped in astonishment. Was that her mother, that ragged old woman standing halfway up the slope? What had happened to Dee? She held a straw hat in her hand, and the late slanting sunlight struck sparks from her unkempt silver-blond hair. She was staring toward the southwest. Coral followed her gaze. Wow, that was some cloud sliding toward them across the sky, dense, gray, wedge-shaped, almost flat on the bottom, except for a ragged, slowly turning bulge. Even as she watched, the cloud spread over the sinking sun and the afternoon light turned an eerie green.

With a flourish of her hat, Dee bowed to the cloud.

What the hell was going on? Uneasily, Coral cleared her throat. "Hey, Dee!"

Dee turned. Her mother seemed as faded as the brown-edged leaves, gaunt, ancient. She wore no makeup, and her blue shirt was stained and missing a button. Coral thought, my mother is dead, and a wave of desolation washed over her. Then Dee saw Coral and a smile lit her face. "Coral! Oh, God, Coral!" She raced to her daughter and hugged her close. For a moment, everything was as it had been. Swaying in her mother's arms, Coral felt safe and beautiful and innocent again.

Then Dee added, "Baby, I'm so glad you're back home. So glad!"

Coral struggled back to herself through cottony layers of love and warmth and pushed Dee away. She had to get a couple of things straight. "Dee, look," she said firmly. "I'm not a baby. And I'm not back, not really. How the hell can you expect me to be back?"

"What do you mean, you're not back? Didn't you come to finish school? I mean, you can do the wonderful things you want to, but you're my daughter, Coral. Everything will always be the same between you and me."

"Nothing will ever be the same!" Coral cried, wishing she'd worn her Lily Pistols outfit instead of this wimpy pink thing, wishing her mother didn't look so ill. "And school is irrelevant now. I'm different, Dee. A whole lot different."

Dee shook her head. "But we're mother and daughter, however we might change. Don't you see? How can you be different?"

72

"Because now I'm queen of the bones, that's how!" Coral drew back a step. "Ma, let's get one thing straight. I belong with the band now. Okay, I was miserable at first, but now—"

Dee looked confused. "You were miserable?"

"Miserable?" Coral burst out. "I was in hell! And you did nothing for me! Nothing!"

Dee's anguish was palpable too. "Honey, I didn't know where you were! Why didn't you—"

"Oh, yeah, blame it on me!"

"Honey, I searched and searched!"

"Could have fooled me."

"Okay. I failed, honey, but now you're here. It's over."

"Over? You want to just forget it?"

"No, Coral, I can't forget it, ever. I was in hell too."

"You're right. We can't forget, because now I belong with them."

Dee glanced back toward the lowering clouds. Coral grabbed her arms. "Dee, look at me! Did you hear what I said? I'm leaving right now if you don't understand. So listen!"

Dee asked fearfully, "Where would you go?"

Coral rolled her eyes. "With the band! That's what I just said! Dee, listen, it was terrible at first. But I got through the awful days, no thanks to you, and—"

"I was trying, honey! I was—"

"Don't pretend, Ma, they told me you were mad. You want to make up now, okay, but I won't come back."

Dee stared at her, puzzlement in her glorious eyes. Coral explained, "See, if I gave it up and came back I'd feel, you know, smothered here."

"Smothered?" Dee pushed her tangled hair from her forehead.

"Ma, here you run everything. You're like a genius with growing things, and organizing things, and that's what you should be doing, okay? But I'm not you! My thing is music. That's why Hoyt wants me. Maybe not at first, but now that he's heard my songs he says I have big-time talent, okay? And I love it, and that's what I'm going to do, and if you try to make me into some goddamn Little Hoosier Miss I'll split!"

Dee's voice was shaky. "I thought . . . honey, I don't know what happened to you, but I love you! You know I'd give you the world!"

Coral pushed back a strand of hair and realized she was mimicking her mother's gesture. "Yeah, I know. But I don't want your world, Dee. Your world was smothering me. I look back and it's like I

73

was dreaming all that time. Like I wasn't me yet. And I got a real rough wake-up call but now I can breathe."

Dee's eyes glistened. She leaned down and picked a flower, a yellow tansy flower as round as a button. She gazed at it as though it might reveal the answer, and murmured, "So things can't be the same."

The same? Coral boiled over. "After what happened to me? No way! Oh, Dee, where were you? I thought my mother could do anything!"

Her eyes were stinging, and she saw a tear roll slowly down Dee's cheek too. Suddenly Coral wanted to hug her, to comfort her. No, that'd be some kind of crazy. She swallowed it down and said, "Hey, I'm sorry, that's over. Things are different but we can visit. I'll just do my thing and you do yours."

Dee nodded at the tansy, took a deep breath, and glanced back at the cloud. "Let's get to the shelter, honey. We can talk there."

God, she was right, the sky looked really scary. Coral let her mother take her hand and lead her across the fields. The sickly daylight made Dee's pale hair gleam green.

Most of the other reporters had gone home, but Jake Shaw was on the last paragraph of his water-violations story and wanted to finish. He'd found something at last, a tale not of crime but of incompetence. The water supply was safe but the assholes hadn't complied with state paperwork, so it was still listed as contaminated in the Indianapolis offices. As he typed he wasn't really watching the muted TV screen but something, maybe some shift in the light, made him glance up at it.

Tornado warning, said the marching letters.

Warning!

Jake jumped up. Warning in Monroe, Lawrence, Orange, Dubois, Martin, and Nichols Counties!

He grabbed his camera and his Pacers cap and ran for the Toyota.

The weather advice folks always said a car was a bad place to be in a tornado. But that just proved that weather advice folks weren't reporters.

Jake turned his Toyota's nose toward the southwest.

Marty pushed her barbecued chicken around her plate. Nothing looked very good tonight. Other folks seemed to be enjoying themselves, to judge from the cheerful racket of conversation and laughter. Beside her at the long table, Dawn Arnold and her family were arguing happily about whether the Evanses or the Millers had brought the chocolate cake that the kids had spotted on the dessert table. Chrissie was all the way across the room eating with Janie's family, her yellow T-shirt bright as spring sunshine. Two tables away, his back to her, Romey Dennis and his uncle were talking with the new ear-nose-and-throat doctor and his young family. There was a sag to Romey's shoulders that matched the sag in Marty's spirits.

Boy, Hopkins, you're such a genius, hurting all the people you love best.

And such a genius on the job, too. Why can't you figure out what happened to Stephanie Stollnitz?

Something was niggling at her mind, something far away.

Something about Steffie? Even Doc Altman didn't know what had happened to her. Still, wouldn't hurt to find out if a violent ex-husband from Muncie had come visiting.

She poked half-heartedly at her food.

Across from her, Aunt Vonnie was talking to Shirley Cochran. They were saving the seat between them for Wes Cochran. Where was Coach? He ought to be here by now.

Marty tried a bite of her chicken.

Through the din of conversation, the niggling thing suddenly took form. Shoot, it was the muffled sound of her beeper, buried deep in the shoulder bag tucked under her chair. Marty snatched up the bag and ran for the phone in the corridor outside.

Foley answered. "Tornado warning. You're on duty again. Hang on a second."

Sheriff Cochran's voice replaced Foley's. "Hopkins?"

"Yes sir."

"Shirley there?"

"Yes sir. I'll make sure everyone's in the shelter before I leave."

"Good. The city cops are trying to get the damn siren going. The storm's in the southwest quadrant of the county right now. They've had a confirmed touchdown in Orange County near the county line."

"Yes sir, I'll head out that direction."

"Sims is covering the trailer courts near Dunning, but there's two down there near Steuben, called, um, Crown Courts and that little one, Robin Hill or whatever. I want you to go down there and warn them."

"Yes sir." She ran back to the dining-hall door and blinked the lights. Conversations stumbled to a surprised halt.

How not to panic them? Directions first. "Folks," she called out, "I want everyone to stay in this room, okay? Don't go upstairs, don't go outside. If you've got kids in some other room, round them up right now and keep them here. Everyone got that?"

About half the faces showed instant comprehension. The other half began to babble in confusion. Marty shouted, "Okay, you all understand what to do. Stay right here. This is a public shelter. Now, what's happening is, they just upgraded the tornado watch to a warning. You all know that generally nothing much happens, but it's better to be safe than sorry, so stay right here. You couldn't be in a better place. So just stay calm and follow Pastor Kemble's instructions. Okay?"

She turned and started out of the church basement to the parking lot. Her hand was on the panic bar, pushing the door open, when something hit her from behind.

"Mommy! Mommy, don't go out!"

"Chrissie! Honey, please, go back to the dining room!"

Chrissie's arms were clamped around her waist with all the wiry strength of her eleven years. "Don't go! Don't leave me!"

"Honey, this is a very safe place. You'll be fine!"

"I know! So don't go out! I don't want to lose you too!"

Marty took a deep breath. "Honey, you're not losing anybody. I'll be fine."

"You're not on duty! Don't go!"

"I know I'm not in uniform, Chrissie, but they've called everyone back on duty. I'll be fine. I'll have good information, and backup. And I have to go try to help people now. It's my job."

"Don't go! Please!"

Outside, a great low moan slowly ascended the scale and filled the air with its huge voice. The siren at last. Marty grabbed Chrissie's hand and hurried back to the dining room door. A couple of high-school boys were peering out. She had to shout over the clamor of voices and siren, "Dave! Here, take Chrissie to Aunt Vonnie, okay? Don't let her get away, she's sneaky! Chrissie, honey, I'll be fine. I promise. Don't worry!"

She kissed her daughter's forehead and made sure Dave had a good grip before she let go and ran for her cruiser.

She was grateful for the siren's wail. It kept her from hearing Chrissie's sobs.

Thirteen

They were only steps from the shelter door in the sloping lawn when Coral realized what was happening. "Hey!" she exclaimed, stopping abruptly. "Why aren't we going in the house? It's just a thunderstorm!"

Dee nodded toward the sky behind them. Coral turned. The bulge she'd seen in the base of that vast cloud was longer now, conical, pointed toward the earth. Wisps of cloud boiled around it. "Oh my God!" Coral screamed. "Hoyt!"

"Coral, come on!" Dee urged, pulling her arm.

But Coral jerked free and raced for the BMW. She had to get back to Hoyt, to tell him to get to the shelter. Skell, from Texas, would have known what to do, but he'd left with Duke. Hoyt was from California and had never had to deal with a tornado.

Dee caught her near the parking lot, her hand powerful on Coral's wrist. "Honey, please, it's dangerous!"

"I know! I've got to warn him!"

"I can't lose you again!"

The raw pain in Dee's voice distracted Coral for an instant. She said, "You're not losing me. You get in the shelter, I'll be back. But I've got to go back to him now."

"Coral, don't!"

Shit. Coral ran with Dee to the shelter door, opened it, and bounded into the pit. She waited till her mother was down beside her, then sprang up the steps and closed the door behind her. She sprinted for her car, jumped in, made a sharp U-turn in the empty parking lot, and pressed the accelerator. The BMW surged into the road. In the rear-view mirror Coral glimpsed her mother, struggling with the door, trying to climb back to the surface. "Get down there, Dee, down!" she muttered, but didn't raise her foot from the pedal. The BMW roared through the eerie light.

The highway crossed over the Chapel Road underpass. Two hundred yards south, Marty spotted a peeling wooden sign with a faded-looking robin and once-black letters saying "Robin Hill Court." She turned off and drove into the middle of the dozen trailers, then hit her siren. At the windows a few curtains twitched warily. Looked like law enforcement was usually bad news to these folks. Maybe it was good that she was out of uniform. She saw a pair of pale-haired little girls, maybe six and eight years old, opening a screen door to peer out. Quickly, they were snatched back inside.

Marty got out of the cruiser, ran to the screen door, and pounded on it. At last the little girls and a shirtless young man with a wispy blond beard appeared in the shadows a few feet back from the door. He said, "Yeah?"

"Sir, we've got a tornado warning. You folks have a shelter here?"

"Shelter?" He looked back into the trailer. "Hey, Patty, we got a tornado shelter?"

"Hell no," came a raspy female voice from the far end. "Owner's so cheap, we're lucky to have water."

Like her little sister, the eight-year-old girl was wearing a Disneyland T-shirt and pink shorts. She looked up at the young man. "Granddad said to get in the cave by the creek if there was a tornado."

"Shut up, Ashley," said Patty's raspy voice. "I don't wanna go in no cave."

"Sir, get these children to shelter, please. A trailer's not safe," Marty exclaimed. Chrissie was safe, she told herself as she ran to the next trailer, Aunt Vonnie would keep her safe. Marty yelled, "Hello? Listen, folks, tornado coming! Better get to shelter!"

A heavy man with a massive belly and a stiff gray crewcut had come out of a door across the way. "You kidding us?" he shouted. "Tornado warning?"

"No sir, not kidding."

"Hell, honey, I been in this trailer twenty years and never seen a tornado," the man said, and leered at her. "What I wanna know is how a cute thing like you got ahold of that sheriff car."

Marty looked at him, exasperated, and realized she'd done all she could. No law said you had to get to shelter. Maybe the cruiser's presence was keeping folks inside. If she left, maybe they'd wise up and get to shelter.

She jumped back in and headed for the next trailer park, Crown Court, six miles farther south, just past Steuben. On her way she passed a couple of farm families out studying the sky. They knew already, no need to stop.

78

Crown Court was a cut above Robin Hill, and the owner provided a shelter in the basement of his own brick house next door. Many of the residents were out peering at the sky. As Marty urged them into the shelter, an old gray-haired woman put a frail hand on Marty's arm. "Please," she said. "Could you help with Mama?"

"Mama?"

"She's in her trailer but she won't come out." A tear rolled down the wrinkled cheek.

Marty ran to the door she pointed out. An ancient woman with wispy white hair and pearly clouded eyes sat in a wheelchair.

"Let's go, ma'am. Let's get you to the shelter," Marty said gently.

The old woman gripped the armrests of the wheelchair with knobby hands. "If it's my time to go, I'm ready! I'm ninety-two, young lady, and ready whenever the good Lord snaps his fingers!"

"What about your daughter?"

"Katharine? What about her?"

"She's crying, ma'am. She'll just be sick with worry. She'll feel guilty if anything happens to you, you know she will!"

The old woman's lips worked silently for a moment. Marty could read nothing in the opaque eyes. Finally the old woman sighed wearily. "Watch out for daughters, young lady. They can ruin your life. Help me through that door, all right?"

Marty pushed her out and a friendly neighbor took over. Katharine babbled her gratitude while Marty jumped back into the cruiser and picked up her mike.

"Nichols County Three-twenty-one," she said.

Through static she heard, "Touchdown two miles west of Steuben. Three twenty-one, where you at?"

"Close. State 37, at Crown Court. Near the Lawrence Road."

"Can you see the damn thing?"

"No, but I'll get back on the highway and give a look around."

Jake Shaw was driving west on Chapel Road. It dipped down sharply to pass under State 37, then bent southwest through the wooded hills. He was headed straight toward the vast dark cloud that blocked most of the peach-colored late afternoon sky. Behind him the Dunning city siren faded, but somewhere far off there was a new sound now, a rumbling roar.

He rounded a curve and saw it. Good Lord. A twisting black pillar thick enough to support the heavens was churning up a cloud of dust beyond the trees. He pulled the Toyota to the shoulder, hopped out, and snapped some pictures. Was it headed this way?

79

Hard to tell. Jake got back into the Toyota and drove another half-mile along Chapel to the intersection with State 822. Here a cluster of stores—furniture, hardware, eyeglasses, and so forth—shared a strip parking lot that fronted on the highway. At the Chapel Road end, a neat white diner with blue shutters had attracted a dozen cars. The Country Griddle, said the blue and white sign high on a pole. At the far end of the row of stores, a big-windowed brick building called the Prince of Pizza served the fast-food crowd. Across the highway was Hinshaw Trucks and Campers, basically a big parking lot with the merchandise parked in neat rows.

Jake pulled in near the Country Griddle, but the other cars blocked his view. He climbed up on the Toyota's brown hood.

God, what a monster! Beyond the trees the whirling column was silhouetted against the pastel sunset sky. In the dust billowing up from where it touched the ground Jake could see huge birds circling the funnel. Arching over all, the black cloud filled the sky.

A red pickup screeched into the lot and a man in a John Deere cap jumped out. "Get into the shelter, man!" he yelled at Jake, then jerked open the door of the diner. "Tornado! Get to shelter, folks!"

People ran out of the Country Griddle. Two men got into their cars even though others screamed at them to get to shelter. Three waitresses in ruffled aprons ran toward the Prince of Pizza. One shouted, "Come on, everyone! The pizza place has a basement!"

Jake stayed braced atop his Toyota, shooting pictures, mesmerized by the roaring vastness of the storm.

The man from the red pickup was running along the row of businesses, yelling his message into each door, then he too joined the little crowd and disappeared into the pizza place.

Something heavy slammed across the top of the Toyota and dropped onto the ground. A thick three-foot section of asphalt shingling. My God, thought Jake, somebody's goddamn roof. It wasn't birds circling in the air, it was hunks of houses!

Jake scrambled down from the Toyota and ran like hell for the Prince of Pizza.

Marty turned north from Crown Court and floorboarded it. Highway 37 ran through woods here and she couldn't see much. Black cloud overhead, everywhere except for the northeast, where the sky was still blue. A few drops of rain, a rumbling somewhere. Nothing else. Then the road curved west as it crested a hill, and there it was. Marty inhaled sharply. It was enormous, majestic, unbelievable. *His chariots of wrath the deep thunderclouds form* . . . She keyed on and tried to sound coherent. "Nichols County Three-twenty-one! I see it! It's maybe a mile west of 37!"

"Goddammit, get to shelter, Hopkins!"

"Yes sir, ten-four!"

The road turned northwest again and she had to twist sideways to see it. It was massive, a dark seething cone spiraling up to the dark seething cloud. She could hear its roar. Awesome, Chrissie would say.

She wanted to be with Chrissie.

The cruiser was already going ninety. There was little traffic headed north, though she passed several vehicles in the other lane headed south, away from the storm's path. She could see the storm's movement now as it spun toward State 37. She'd beat it if it didn't change direction, or speed up, or if she didn't have to stop.

She neared the turnoff for Robin Hill. She hoped the people there had got out of their flimsy homes. They'd be real close to the path.

Her foot smacked the brake down and she was skidding to a stop almost before she realized what she'd seen—two little kids in pink shorts, Ashley and her sister, running along the shoulder of the road. Marty backed up, drew even with them. She didn't ask permission, just threw them onto the front seat and started north again.

Ashley shouted over the roar, "We wanted to see it but it was too loud!" Her sister was sobbing, her hands over her ears.

Marty nodded. "You're right about that."

"Mama told us tornadoes always hit someplace else!"

"Not this one, honey."

A bent aluminum chair skidded across the highway and Marty swerved. Once when she'd been tiny her father, drunk and inexplicably furious, had been throwing chairs around the dining room and one had clipped her on the knee. Suddenly her mother was spread-eagled above her, her body braced against the sideboard, shouting, "You hurt this kid and I quit!" with a fury greater than his. He'd crumpled sobbing before her.

Marty breathed a prayer to her mother.

Wes frowned at the map, letting Foley handle all the calls for a moment. The damn thing was headed northeast. Present track threatened the southern business strips and homes, Dunning itself only if it shifted north. His troops were scattered all over the county. Walker and Hopkins, a few miles apart, were closest to the reported track, and he'd ordered both to get to shelter.

The lights went out.

"Shit," said Wes, switching on his flashlight so Foley could see what he was doing. No big surprise to have the power fail. He'd sent Sims down earlier to get things ready, and sure enough, a moment later the rumble of the emergency generator made the floor throb, and the lights blinked on.

"Nichols County Two-twenty," Wes said when there was a lull.

"Two-twenty," came the faint response.

"You in shelter, Walker?"

"Yes sir, the Miller's basement."

"Nichols County Three-twenty-one," Wes said.

No answer.

"Three twenty-one!"

No answer.

Shit. Where the hell was Hopkins?

Jake Shaw, clutching his camera, sprinted past the Prince of Pizza's neat red-upholstered seats and followed the last of the people pushing down the basement stairs. There was a roar like jet engines, and thumps as flying objects smashed into the building. As he started down the steps an enormous crash and a blast of wind made him glance back at the front of the building. The thick plate-glass window had shattered.

Jake helped another man pull the door closed, then continued down the steps. People were crammed in among the boxes of plastic plates and cleaning supplies and trash cans. The roar of the storm was tremendous, although he could hear a couple of women wailing and a toddler shrieking. After a moment a man with a loud voice began reciting the Lord's Prayer. Jake edged his way toward the concrete wall.

The lights went out.

Nothing existed now except the noise. Jake was drowning in a great black pool of thunder and screeching metal and human screams.

For the first time in twenty years, he found himself mouthing the Lord's Prayer too.

It was approaching faster than Marty had thought. There was a cloud of dust seething around the bottom of the tornado, and as she watched, a flock of something as black as crows burst up to circle it too. A roof, probably. Maybe that shopping strip off Chapel Road, the Country Griddle and Prince of Pizza strip.

The roar of the storm filled the cruiser. She saw rather than heard the whimpers of the little girls beside her.

Another branch blew across the highway, and Marty had to brake again. They weren't going to make it to Dunning, she realized. Where the hell could they take shelter? Someplace low, someplace strong—back to the Robin Hill cave? No, she didn't even know exactly where it was. But if that was the Chapel Road shopping strip, they must be nearing the underpass where Chapel dipped under this highway—yes, there it was! Four other vehicles were down there already. Braking, Marty wrenched the steering wheel and careened down the ramp to Chapel, then twisted it again and skidded down to a stop directly under the highway. The roar was incredible.

Dark is His path on the wings of the storm . . .

Marty pulled the two sobbing girls from the cruiser and pointed up at the underside of the bridge. Pushing and tugging, she got Ashley and her sister up the steep incline to where the girders joined the limestone bank. She wedged the girls between a concrete slab and the great steel beams. She waved and beckoned at the other half-dozen frightened motorists and they followed her up.

Both little girls were crying. Marty spread-eagled protectively across them, bracing her body between the slab and the girders, and prayed for Chrissie.

Seconds later it was on them, blasting through their makeshift shelter, whipping weeds to the horizontal, slamming against her taut body. Marty blinked teary eyes at the road beyond the overpass. Objects, fragments of objects, whirled in the churning dust. Black things, white things, and oddly, lots of pink flecks, bubble-gum pink, as though the winds had garlanded themselves with blossoms. Something big, looked like a van, tumbled by. Her ears crackled. She couldn't breathe. There was lightning everywhere, and the gassy stench of ozone, and that ceaseless roar.

It went on for an eternity.

By the clock, it was twenty-two seconds.

Fourteen

In full maturity, the storm was fueling itself. Its funnel pulled in warm, moist winds from all sides, tightening and spiraling faster as it contracted, like an ice skater doing a spin. In its chilly heights, the tropical humidity turned to droplets and to ice crystals, releasing yet more energy. The mighty suction wolfed up the low-level warm air, and with it roofs and branches, trailers and cattle, papers and chimneys, window glass and bicycles, bedsprings and lunch boxes.

But soon the moist tropical air had been consumed and replaced by the cooler downdrafts from around the periphery of the storm. The muscle of the tornado weakened. Its funnel wavered, became thin and ropy, and finally lost its grip on the land. With a mighty sigh, the aging storm flung down its burden of earthly objects and sailed on to the northeast, spending its waning energy in a polite rain.

But a six-mile swath of Nichols County bore witness to the ghastly vigor of its prime.

The crashing and booming stopped. The roar faded. The screams of children and the sobs of women became audible in the blackness, then they diminished too. Jake Shaw took off his cap and passed a hand across his sweaty brow.

"The Lord be praised!" cried the man with the loud voice, somewhere in the darkness.

"Is it over?" asked a woman.

Other voices chimed in. "Is it gone?"

"No, wait, we may be in the center! The center's quiet!"

"No, you can still hear the roar in the center."

"The crashing stopped for a minute back there. Not the roaring, not till just now."

The loud voice returned. "The Lord hath delivered us!"

"Yeah, he's right," said a practical-sounding man. "Let's go look. Just two of us, till we're sure it's clear. Everyone else stand back."

Feet ascended the stairs by Jake's elbow. He heard the clicking

84

of the knob on the door at the top of the steps, and the practical voice again, "Shit, is this thing locked?"

A woman sobbed.

More clicking and grunting. "There! It's opening—no. There's something jammed against it out there."

Jake yelled, "Two more guys up there to help push, okay? We got any linebackers?"

"Naw, but Tank Jones here is built like a bulldozer."

"Send him up!"

In the end it took Tank and five others shoving against the door to open it enough for someone thin—Jake—to squeeze out.

He blinked, stared, blinked again. Where there had been neat tables, red-upholstered benches, and white plastic wall panels, now there was a mass of crumpled metal frames and broken shards of plastic. The roof was gone. Most of the brick walls still stood, but through the gaping holes that had been windows he could see no buildings, no trees, just a moonscape of rubble. Jake raised his camera automatically and snapped a picture.

"Hey, buddy, whatcha doing? Get us outta here!" Tank Jones sounded annoyed.

"Oh. Sorry. This is unbelievable." Jake turned back to the door and managed to wrestle two twisted metal table frames from where they'd jammed against the door. It was sprinkling a little and everything was slick. Jake warned, "Watch your step, now."

Tank muscled his way out and gasped, "Jesus."

Jake climbed over a piece of the serving counter and turned back to photograph the dismay and disbelief as people staggered from the darkness of the basement into this grisly twilight. Then he went out a window-hole and got some shots of the mangled remains of the other buildings of the shopping center.

The ruined Prince of Pizza looked real good in comparison.

Jake knew he was half in shock, that the horror and destruction would hit him hard later. But already within him a little voice was singing, *This is it, this is the story you've been waiting for.*

A woman in a Country Griddle waitress uniform was sobbing, staring down at the wet rubble. He knew her, Karen something. He picked his way toward her, snapping pictures as he went, and asked, "What is it?"

Karen pointed with her toe at a corner of white plastic underfoot. "The sign. See it? The Country Griddle sign." She swiped at her eyes with a tissue and jerked her thumb at a stump of metal. "It used to sit up on that pole there, high and proud."

"Yeah. I remember." Jake photographed the half-buried blue-and-white sign, and also the stump of its pole. "You worked at the Country Griddle?"

"My husband and I owned it." She wiped her eyes again. "I just can't get over seeing that sign down there."

Jake wondered why she wasn't exploring the pile of debris heaped where her restaurant had been. There must be a cash register, salvageable furniture, something. Maybe when the center of your life is demolished you have to absorb it in small steps. Jake's sister had died of cancer a few years before. He remembered when she'd first been told how serious it was, her mind had seized on the side effects of her chemotherapy as though that was the big problem. "My hair!" she'd wailed. "I'll be so embarrassed without my hair!" It was months before she was able to talk about the fact that she was dying. Denial, they called it.

He'd been snapping photos automatically and now found himself out of film. He'd have to go buy some. Might as well call his editor, too, once he got to a phone. He glanced around for his car and realized suddenly that he'd been engaged in some denial himself. His Toyota was nowhere to be seen.

Jake inspected the mutilated landscape more carefully, and finally spotted a familiar brown fender by the massive torn stump of a big maple that had been behind the Country Griddle. Jake worked his way through the slippery debris toward it. Yep, that was it, smashed and twisted with a camper from across the road and dumped by the butchered tree.

Hell.

He turned back and saw a man in a crazily tilted semi cab talking on a CB radio. He hurried toward him through the rubble and said, "I'm press. Let me get a message to my editor, okay?"

"Get in line, buddy," snapped big Tank Jones. Jake realized that half a dozen people were standing anxiously in a ragged line by the tilted truck cab.

He pulled out his notepad, got in line, and started interviewing the people beside him.

"It's gone," said Sims' voice on the radio.

"You sure?" Wes asked into the mike.

"Yes sir. Got real skinny and loopy and finally went back up into the clouds."

"Well, keep your eyes open. They can come in groups."

"Yes sir."

"Cruise by those mobile home lots along the south edge of Dunning and report back."

"Ten-four."

Foley was talking to the Dunning cops. Wes picked up the mike again and said, "Nichols County Three twenty-one."

Still no answer. Wes stared at the map with the sightings marked on it. No way to make it come out different. It had touched down in farmland, moved northeast across State 822 somewhere near Chapel Road, then on across State 37 and more farmland and finally, if Deputy Sims was right, lifted back into the clouds near the southern city limits. Goddammit, Hopkins had been right in the path.

He called again, "Three twenty-one." Nothing.

In the back of his mind her father's image stirred, his buddy Rusty, looking at him as though Wes had betrayed him. Wes slammed a mental door on Rusty and called the next deputy. "Nichols County Two-twenty."

"Yes sir," came Walker's faint voice.

"You back on the road yet?"

"Uh, no, sir, I'm looking out this basement window."

"Tornado's gone, this one anyway. Get rolling, check things out. Start with Chapel Road, you're just west of there."

"Yes sir, ten-four."

"Nichols County Three-seventy."

"Three-seventy." Mason's voice was excited.

"You still at the airport?" Nichols County had a two-bit airport suitable for the Wright Brothers and not much since.

"Yes sir. No damage here, and they're saying it's over. The supercell has dissipated."

"Yeah, Sims saw the funnel lift up. Go take a look west of State 822, Mason. Keep your eyes open for . . ."

"Nichols County Three-twenty-one," gasped a new voice.

"Hallelujah!" cried Wes. "Where ya been, Hopkins?"

"Under the tornado, sir. Underpass where 37 goes over Chapel Road. Eight other people here, all okay."

"Good."

"Uh, sir, are the people in the Cedars of Lebanon church shelter okay?"

"Haven't heard. Probably. What's the damage where you are?"

"I can't see much from under here but you might want to close off Highway 37. Chapel too, there's junk blocking both roads."

"Ten-four. Anything else?"

"Seems worse to the south. I'm real worried about that little trailer park, Robin Hill. And on my way in it looked like that shopping center at Chapel and 822 got hit."

"Yeah, Walker's on his way there. You go check out Robin Hill and report."

"Yes sir, ten-four."

Wes closed his eyes and allowed himself the luxury of a brief prayer of thanks. For all their correct military behavior on the job, Marty was still his best friend's child, still the hotshot kid he'd coached in peewee basketball, still the daughter he and Shirley had never had. So he breathed his thanks to the Lord before jumping back into the job. "Foley!"

"Yes sir."

"I'll check the church shelters and talk to the state cops about the blocked highways. You contact the hospitals and medical centers, make sure they're up to speed. We're going to have some injuries with this one."

But not Hopkins, he thought with relief, not Rusty's kid.

Marty, leaning in the driver's door of the dented cruiser, replaced the mike and straightened. The other motorists looked dazed as they clambered down from the bridge girders. She needed a better look at Highway 37. It was sprinkling a little, and much cooler, so she put Chrissie's slicker on Ashley's little sister and herded both girls partway up the access ramp to look.

The damage to the south was horrendous. The woods that had lined the highway were blasted as though a bomb had exploded, but there was no flame, no smoke, just dead silence and an army of jagged trunks. Stripped branches lay in a jumble with twisted siding, planks, papers, and everywhere tufts of bright pink. Marty touched one that had caught on a guardrail and realized it was fiberglass insulation ripped from somebody's once-snug home.

She'd need help to get to Robin Hill. She grabbed the girls' hands and hurried back down to rejoin the others. "Everybody's car okay?" she called. The vehicles sheltering under the bridge had been shoved around by the winds, but not destroyed.

"Lots of scrapes, but they start okay," called a man. "You with the sheriff, ma'am?"

"Yes sir, I'm Deputy Hopkins. I was out of uniform when they called me back on duty. Now, if we can get that ramp cleared, you folks can probably get out of here to the north if you're real careful."

"I gotta go south," said a young man. Looked about nineteen, with brown hair cut long in the back. He was burly but his voice cracked like a kid's when he added, "My wife and my little baby are down there in Steuben."

"Okay, sir. What's your name?"

"Kurt."

"Okay, Kurt, after we clear the ramp, you come along behind me, help me clear a lane south. I want to get these children back home." She prayed that they still had a home.

They removed rubble from the ramp, then Marty and Kurt set to work clearing a narrow, meandering path through the debris that covered State 37. It took nearly half an hour to travel the two hundred yards to the Robin Hill turnoff. As they approached, the jagged stumps gave way to trees, their branches broken and stripped of leaves, and they in turn gave way to some that had retained much of their foliage. Marty dared to hope a little. The debris on the highway was spottier here, and the light rain had stopped. She waved Kurt on, calling, "I bet your family's fine. They're four miles on." Then she turned the cruiser toward Robin Hill, bumping over branches on the access road until she was stopped by a big piece of siding. "Everybody out, kids," she said, and grabbed her first-aid kit from the trunk.

There was an orange sofa cushion speared high on a broken branch, and a woman's jade green dancing shoe dangling from the bumper of an upended white car.

They were already in the trailer court, Marty realized, although the first three trailers were completely gone. A fourth, roofless, had skidded off its concrete pad and slammed into another. The two leaned drunkenly against each other. The other trailers were damaged too, and some stunned people wandered among them. Marty started toward them. Then a piece of rubble near her stirred and moaned. Good Lord, a man! She dropped to her knees beside him. "Take it easy, sir," she said. Blood all over his green shirt, looked like a chest wound. She glanced at the little girls as she pulled on her latex gloves. "Ashley, honey, can you take your sister down to those people, see if your mama's there? I have to bandage this guy."

Ashley took her sister's hand and tugged her away.

Marty stopped the bleeding, radioed for an ambulance, then hurried toward the little group of people. Halfway there a woman passed her, asking, "You found Larry?"

"If he's wearing a green shirt, yeah. Watch his bleeding, okay? Ambulance is on its way," Marty said.

There were at least half a dozen injured when she reached the people. There were crushed legs, gashes, concussions. A dark-haired woman screamed as a competent fat woman skillfully cut away her bloody T-shirt. The mauled shoulder beneath showed a gleam of white and Marty realized it was bone. A blond woman with an unlit cigarette in her mouth and blood running down her face was hugging the two little girls. Her scalp wound looked superficial, Marty decided, and turned to the others. "Any nurses here?"

"I been a midwife," the skillful fat woman admitted.

"Here, help yourself." Marty put down her first-aid kit. "Has anyone called for an ambulance?"

"Pete went off toward Steuben to find a phone that works."

There was a stink in the air. She said, "Okay, I'll just run back to the cruiser and radio in to be sure. And please don't light any cigarettes. Smells like a gas leak."

The sheriff answered her call. "Yeah, I got one ambulance on the way already."

"We've got anyway eight serious injuries here."

"I'll get more vehicles. Best access is from the south, right?"

"Yes sir. Looks like Robin Hill caught the edge of the storm, and it's better farther south. I'll get the drive cleared for the ambulance. And we've got a gas leak too. I'll look for a turnoff valve, but—"

"Fire department's already on the way. Soon as someone gets there I want you to look over the back roads there between State 37 and the city limits."

"Yes sir."

"And Hopkins, thought you'd like to know, Chrissie and your aunt are both fine."

Tears welled unexpectedly. "Oh, Coach, thanks. Thanks!"

He cleared his throat. "Get to work, Hopkins," he said gruffly.

"Yes sir, ten-four." She brushed her damp cheek and got to work.

Half an hour later, after turning Robin Hill over to the paramedics, she was struggling along the trash-strewn back roads from farm to farm. There'd been injuries here even though most people had basements or even shelters. She'd had to hitch her cruiser to an uprooted tree to pull it off one shelter door, but the family trapped inside was unhurt. As she moved along she became increasingly concerned because it looked like the storm's path might go pretty close to the Dennis place. Romey and his uncle had been at the church supper, so they wouldn't be hurt. But she wanted to be sure.

She hesitated at the Matthews' old place. No problems here. It

90

had been on the fringe of the storm, only a little debris dumped on the road. The house was still standing, she could see a shelter door in the lawn next to the driveway, and in any case there were no cars parked, so probably no one was home.

Still, better give a quick check.

She turned into the asphalt driveway and saw someone lying on the lawn.

Marty jumped from the cruiser, snatching up her depleted first-aid kit, and ran to kneel at his side. Young guy sprawled on his stomach, dressed in black T-shirt and black jeans, long gash across his neck and shoulder from the big piece of aluminum siding that lay beside him. He hadn't bled much, still looked pink and healthy. No pulse, though. She pulled on her gloves, rolled him face up, wiped mud from his lips, and started CPR. One one-thousand, two one-thousand, three one-thousand, four one-thousand, blow one-thousand. Come on, fella, she told him silently as she worked, don't quit on me, help me out here, don't quit! But after fifteen minutes he hadn't responded at all.

Shit, she thought. Shit shit shit.

She broke to radio for an ambulance and got back to work.

Stephanie Stollnitz's image swam into her mind. She wondered if Stephanie would have made it if they'd found her sooner and given her CPR.

Looked like she hadn't found this guy soon enough either.

She went on working another twenty minutes, maybe more. Nothing. And no ambulance.

Marty leaned back on her heels, passed her forearm across her brow, and for the first time looked hard at his face.

She knew the guy from somewhere. Or—no, not him, but his photo. On the mud-streaked T-shirt he was wearing. On a thousand T-shirts, a thousand posters, a thousand album covers.

Jesus. She was looking at the lead singer for Lily Pistols.

Fifteen

"You're kidding!" Wes glared at Deputy Sims.

"No sir, that's what Hopkins said." Sims, as tall as Wes and twice as angular, stood awkwardly at attention.

"Well then, *she's* kidding!" But Wes knew she wasn't. She'd called for an ambulance at the Matthews pig farm and then, astonishingly, for backup. She knew they were stretched too thin to back each other up but she'd repeated her request, without explanation. Wes swore but sent Sims anyway. Had to trust your team. And she was right, she'd needed a messenger, because the phone lines were down and with everybody and his brother tuned to the police frequencies for news, there was no other private way to communicate. Thank God she hadn't broadcast it. This was all they needed in the midst of a disaster, a celebrity death. When this got out they'd be knee-deep in reporters, not just the regional ones hoping to get their fifteen-second shots of the damage into the national coverage, but the big guys too. Might even get a national anchor or two, dolled up in safari gear to prove they were really broadcasting from the untracked wilds of southern Indiana.

Wes sighed. "Shit. Okay, Sims. I'll radio Hopkins to sit tight for now. You track down Doc Altman. He'll probably be helping in the emergency room at Mercy Hospital. Report back when you've talked to him."

"Yes sir." Sims sprang for the door.

The Eagle figured he ought to be jubilant. Triumphant. It had been so easy. The Thunderbolt made it so easy.

And the wrath of God helped, the great wind roaring by like an army. Lying safe in the roadside ditch, a sturdy tangle of hornbeam branches arching over and protecting him from the falling debris, he'd watched the storm pass a quarter mile away.

And the plan had fallen into place. He'd moved to the foot of the driveway after his army passed, waited and watched the shelter door, and everything had fallen into place.

92

The puny gook had cried. The Eagle never cried. Even when they'd flunked him out of flight school, he hadn't cried. They'd told him to stick around, do maintenance. So he had, and he'd heard the stories. "Nothin' to it. Real pretty," said the fighter pilots. "Just push a button and watch those pretty flashes down below."

The guys in the infantry had been quieter about the fighting. They mostly talked about the Vietnamese women, the heat, the leeches. But one grunt told the Eagle that once after a firefight he'd come across the body of a dead enemy soldier. "He was still warm," he'd told the Eagle. "I looked in his pocket, and there was a picture of these little kids and their parents. And he was the father. And he was lying there dead with his guts blown out. And he was a man, like me! A father!" Tears were running down the soldier's face. "He wasn't a gook. He was a man!"

No, thought the Eagle, why think about that wimpy soldier? True, it had been hard, dragging the body to the right place on the lawn, not so much the weight as the warmth, the floppiness. But of course it was important to give the great storm credit for the death. No way to bring him back anyway, he was as dead as the gook, as the drunken soldier's buddy. All the same, the Eagle decided, he wouldn't to it that way again. Made him hear the screaming. Made him think about the wimpy crybaby grunt. Instead he'd think about the fighter pilots, dropping their pretty fire from the sky. Pretty thunderbolts. The Eagle knew he was as safe, as mighty as those pilots, as the storm. King of the air. He too was an instrument of God's wrath.

They'd learn it didn't pay to ignore the Eagle. He was no wimp. He commanded the storms.

The sun was setting at last, but this terrible day was not over. Marty knew she had to rest while she could. She sat sideways in the cruiser, legs out the driver's door, elbows on her knees, chin in her hands. But she was still running on adrenaline, primed to act, not sit around. Her mind jittered from image to image: the limp body on the lawn before her, the van tumbling past in the wind, the woman's shoulder gashed to the bone at Robin Hill, the butchered trees, Chrissie's pleading face, a jade-green dancing shoe, the demolished farmhouses.

This farmhouse wasn't demolished. It was sad to think that the famous Hoyt Heller would have been safer in the house than trying to get to the shelter.

She glanced at his body on the lawn. The last rays of daylight cast a faint shadow from his supine form. There were other shadows, she noticed, looked like faint impressions in the damp lawn. Footprints? They led all the way to the tornado shelter door flat in the lawn near the driveway. And there were streaks, uneven streaks, leading to his body, as though he'd been dragged. But that didn't make sense. He must have been crawling toward the house, the toes of his shoes dragging. She'd found him face down with mud all over his front.

Maybe he'd gone to the shelter and hadn't been able to open the door. She got up and walked across the asphalt to look down at it. Yes—there was a confusion of muddy footprints here near the handle, and at the far end, two parallel tracks about a foot apart and two feet long showed faintly in the lawn, maybe where he'd braced a pry bar. She leaned down and tugged on the handle, and was surprised when the door rose, its hinges creaking but not requiring a lot of strength. There was a sturdy metal brace to hold it open.

She peered inside. The shelter was not much bigger than the door, maybe five feet wide and ten feet long, just a pit lined with cinder block. She went down the steep steps, planks on a frame of steel tubing, that descended at the near end. It seemed pretty dry— only a couple of damp spots despite the rain. At the far end there was a wooden bench. She could see a tuft of black fabric snagged on a splinter. Behind the bench, a shelf held a radio, a kerosene lamp and a box of matches. A flashlight had rolled under the bench. She tried it. The batteries were good. There were no other supplies. This was a tornado shelter, not a bomb shelter meant for long-term survival. For all their faults, tornadoes went by pretty quick.

She released the brace and lowered the door over her head. It was pretty tight for an old door—only a couple of knotholes showed the last gray light outside. It was so close above her head she knew Wes Cochran and Grady Sims would have to stoop. There was a faint smoky smell. Not tobacco, not pot. Maybe he'd lit the kerosene lamp. She pushed the door up again and emerged.

The daylight was fading fast. She walked up the driveway to the big pig barn and looked inside. Nothing, all dark and abandoned. Off to the left in the woods she saw the pink glint of the last rays of sun high on glass. A window? What was it? Then she thought she glimpsed movement along the side of the road. "Hello?" she called, and hurried back to her cruiser.

"Who are you?" The answering voice was female, strong, a little out of breath.

"Sheriff's department. Deputy Hopkins."

"Sheriff? How come? What happened?" There was a thread of fear in the voice now. The lawn was in darkness now and it was hard to see past the cruiser lights. Marty could barely make out the approaching figure, a slim young woman in a light-colored T-shirt, pale hair.

Marty said, "Ma'am, I have to ask you to stay back. We're expecting an ambulance. Who are you?"

"An ambulance! Oh God, no!" She ran up the driveway toward Marty. "Where is he? What happened? The house is okay, what happened?"

"Stop!" Marty barred the way, wishing she had her nightstick. "Please, ma'am, take it easy!"

"Where is he?" In the light from the cruiser the young woman's half-familiar triangular face was remarkably beautiful. Remarkably bedraggled too, smudged with mud, her hair wet and stringy. She struggled in Marty's grip.

"Look, I'm not kidding," Marty said. "If you don't obey orders I'll have to arrest you."

"Arrest me? But—" The young woman stepped back, rubbing her arm, still tense. She had a tattoo that matched the dead man's. "Okay, okay, but you've got to tell me what's wrong! Where's Hoyt? What's going on?"

"What's your name?" Marty repeated.

"Coral Turley."

"Oh yeah, Dee Turley's kid!"

"Yeah."

"You went missing just after school let out last spring. Your mom just about went crazy."

"Look, it's okay, I've seen her! Now where's Hoyt?"

"What do you know about Hoyt? Why is he here?"

"Because we're . . . Haven't you heard, I'm with Lily Pistols now? And we're doing this album and the videos are being filmed around here, and where is he?"

She looked so young to have to bear what Marty had to tell her. She eased the girl toward the cruiser. "Okay, Coral, come over here for a minute while I get this straightened out, okay? Your mother reported you missing in May—"

"Yeah, I know, and then a couple of weeks later they unreported me, right?"

Marty nodded and the girl continued, "The thing is, Dee doesn't understand the music business. Wants me to go to college, maybe marry a farmer. I'm like deeper." Coral frowned at Marty and added, "I know you! You're not wearing your uniform, but you did security at the Harvest Festival the last two or three years. I thought that was cool, you know, a woman officer. Are you plainclothes now?"

"Not really. Just didn't have time to change when they called me in for the tornado."

"Dee said your mother works with Aunt Melva at the bakery."

"Not my mother, my Aunt Vonnie." Marty was glad to make these personal connections. It would make it easier to support Coral if the news devastated her, easier to get an unexaggerated account if the girl knew her story could be checked.

Coral was nodding. "That's right, I remember. And Dee said you used to visit the farm sometimes when you were little, before you moved away."

"Yeah, before you were born. I was about ten or twelve." Marty opened the back door of the cruiser. "You can have a seat right there."

Coral slid in and Marty stood in the open door, still worried that the girl might run off. She went on soothingly, "Your mom was real nice to me, let me help with the farm."

"God, it's so weird around here, like I'm related to everybody! In California everybody's got a clean slate. No roots. It's cool. But here . . . like I thought I didn't have any connections to this place when Duke rented it for Hoyt, but it turns out my mom knows the guy who owns it."

"Your mom knows most of the farmers. Okay, so the situation is, you're traveling with Lily Pistols now?"

"Yeah."

"Do you have a job with them?"

"I sing backup, for chrissake! And I write their songs. Well, some of them. I'm going to have credits on the next album."

"That's great. But you're keeping a low profile here. Nobody knew you were renting this place. How come? So you could visit your parents in privacy?"

Coral shrugged. "Yeah, but the main reason is we try to get away from the fans when we're working. See, the new album has a song called 'Tracks' and we wanted shots of Indy and Churchill Downs. And Hoyt thought it was great to have a tornado warning because another song is called 'Deathwind.' About losing everything." Her eyes, excited and magnetic, met Marty's. "I saw the tornado, you know? It crossed the road ahead of me and I was looking and missed a curve and the BMW went into a ditch. I've got to tell Hoyt, you know? Where is he?"

Marty rubbed her temple. The girl was so young, only four or five years older than Chrissie. "Look, Coral, there's real bad news about Hoyt."

"What? Is he hurt?" She blinked at Marty's silence and added uncertainly, "Is he . . . is he dead?"

Marty nodded. "Yeah. I'm afraid so."

Disbelief and terror warred in Coral's face. "This is some kind of a joke, right?"

"No. I'm sorry."

"Oh God. Oh God!" The girl began to struggle to get out of the car. "Where? I've got to see him! Was it the tornado? Please, let me see!"

"Coral, wait! Can you tell me how to get in touch with his parents?"

"His parents? Yeah." Coral's eyes were glistening with grief, or was it anger? "But I sure as hell won't tell you until you quit jerking me around and let me see him!"

"Look, I'm sorry. But I'm supposed to keep people away from the scene of a suspicious death until the coroner says it's okay. He's on his way, and—"

"Suspicious? You mean he ODed or something? It wasn't the tornado?"

Marty explained, "All deaths are suspicious until the coroner makes a determination. We have to do things the right way, especially . . . well, we have to do things right."

Even in her agitation, Coral was sharp. She said, "Because of the publicity. Because national fucking television will be watching you. If Hoyt was the boy next door you'd let me see! You'd have a heart!"

She was right, it wasn't fair. Marty ran a hand through her hair. "Tell you what. If you don't touch him, and you stay right next to me, I'll walk you over to where you can see him. If you really want to."

"Yeah, I want to!"

Marty retraced her own steps to a point five feet from the body. She held Coral's arm and directed the flashlight toward Hoyt's slack, muddy face. Coral gave a little gasp but didn't try to get closer, just stood staring. Finally she said in a broken voice, "Maybe he didn't OD. See, I told him to get to the shelter if there was a tornado. He was probably looking at the tornado and waited too long to get to the shelter. Got hit by that metal thing." She sobbed. "He was trying to do what I told him."

Marty said gently, "Could be."

Coral rubbed tears from her cheek. "I just can't believe . . . We were doing an album, for chrissakes! He was careful when we were working!"

Marty said, "I'm sorry, honey."

"Are you really sure he's dead? He doesn't look . . . I mean, I thought when you died you got all pale."

"Yeah, sometimes. Not always."

"D'you see a lot of dead people?"

"Too many." Stephanie Stollnitz flashed into Marty's mind. Only six hours ago she'd been working that case. Felt like six years.

Headlights swung into the driveway, illuminating the lawn and everything on it. Marty tugged on Coral's arm. "Come on. It's the coroner."

Still staring at Hoyt's body, Coral muttered something that sounded like, "You bastard!"

"What?"

"Nothing." Coral turned, eyes too bright, and allowed Marty to lead her away. "Or maybe everything. It's not just him, it's the whole band. It's my future. We can't stop now! Shit!"

Doc Altman was walking toward them across the lawn. He looked weary and shaken, his curly hair frizzing out like steel wool, his wire-rimmed spectacles slightly askew. "What've we got here? Sims told me—" He paused, glancing at Coral.

"This is Coral. She's with the band. Um, Dr. Altman, could you approach from this side? In case you want photos."

His eyebrows rose. "Like that, is it? Well, I already asked Deputy Sims to track down Kev."

Kev was the police photographer. Marty said, "Good. I'll keep the rest away."

She took Coral back to the cruiser. Coral sat but said, "I've got to tell the others!"

"What others?"

"Skell and Brian. The guys in the band, and the guys that help us. And Duke."

"Where are they now?"

"They're staying with Brian's friend in Bloomington. Actually Skell stayed here with us for a couple of days because he and Hoyt are working on some songs I wrote."

Sounded like Coral had something going with Hoyt, if the two

98

of them were staying here and the rest in Bloomington. Had she really said "Bastard?" Marty asked, "Coral, were you, um, Hoyt's lover?"

The girl's eyes, young and ancient all at once, met Marty's. "Hoyt was my lover, yeah, you can say that."

"God, Coral, I'm sorry." The girl looked away and Marty pulled out her notebook. "What's the band's Bloomington address?"

Coral gave it, and added a phone number. Marty said, "It's going to be hard to contact them right now. See, the phone lines are down, and we don't want to broadcast because the media folks are tuned in to the police frequencies."

"Oh, God, the media." Coral closed her eyes and shook her head. "What the hell can we do about the fucking media? Did they hear you call for the coroner?"

"No, we sent a guy in person. We haven't broadcast anything."

"Good. Oh, God, it's so awful! How the hell are we going to play this?" Coral threw herself back in the cruiser seat and propped her right foot on her left knee, frowning.

The girl was upset, Marty thought, but she sure wasn't reacting like a kid whose boyfriend had just died. What had gone on between those two?

When Kev the photographer arrived Marty led him to the shelter door. Doc Altman bustled over to them, looking more like his old eager self. "God, the dead ones are so much more interesting!"

"What do you mean, sir?" Marty asked.

Doc turned cagy. "Can't say yet. Gotta check something in the lab."

"Should we photograph those footprints or whatever they are?" She played her flashlight on the lawn.

Doc squinted at it. "Aha! So he was in the shelter!"

Altman must think there was more to it than the tornado. She said, "Yeah, my reading is he got to the shelter and crawled out later."

Doc nodded happily. "Good, good." But he held up a warning hand as he saw Marty writing in her notebook. "This is not, repeat not, official."

"Yes sir. But we'll need all the help we can get. This'll be a real high-profile case."

Doc looked startled, and Marty realized he'd been so involved with the scientific puzzle that he'd forgotten who the dead man was. "All the more reason to keep it to yourself," he said, then turned to the photographer. "Okay, Kev, let's hurry it up so I can get this guy on the table."

Sixteen

Wes arrived at the old Matthews place just as Doc Altman's assistants from Pinch's Funeral Home were loading the celebrity body into the coroner's van. Art Pfann, the county prosecuting attorney, was talking to Doc. Behind them, leaning on her cruiser, Hopkins talked quietly to a slender young blond woman with an intriguing big-eyed, triangular face, vaguely familiar. Kittenish—no, she looked stronger than a kitten, Wes decided. More like a young lioness.

He headed for the two men. "Howdy, Art. Doc. What've we got?"

Art Pfann wasn't tall, but had a booming voice, very effective in a courtroom. "Victim's name is Hoyt Heller—lead singer for this rock band, um, Lily Pistols. Looks to me like he didn't make it to the tornado shelter and was struck by flying debris. See that sharp piece of aluminum siding there?"

Doc said sharply, "Gotta get the lab results."

"But you just said the aluminum siding could have killed him."

"It's one possibility, but there are others!"

Wes studied Doc's perturbed face. He'd worked with the man often enough to know there was a problem. He asked, "You want us to hold off comments about cause of death?"

"But I've got to say something to the press!" Art turned angrily to Wes. "Soon as word gets out we're going to have reporters crawling all over us, national reporters too, and if they think we don't know what happened they make us look like hicks!"

Wes rubbed the back of his neck. He knew this argument, P.R. versus caution, politics versus science. "Okay, Art, you're right," he said, and held up his palm to stop Doc's indignant sputtering. "We don't want to look like hicks. How about—okay, Doc, Hopkins found him lying on the lawn with a gash on his neck from the siding, right?"

100

"I'm not saying she didn't, but—"

"But you aren't willing to say that it killed him?"

Doc glared at Wes. "Am I really hearing you say that you want to jump to conclusions? In front of national reporters?"

"Hey, take it easy," Wes said. "I'm saying maybe we can agree on a few facts. Suppose Art tells the press three things. One, that's how he was found. Two, top-notch scientists will soon issue an official autopsy report. Three, tornadoes kill about fifty or sixty Americans a year, we need to improve our warning systems, bla bla bla."

Doc shrugged. "Fine by me. Especially the part about top-notch scientists."

Art nodded slowly. "Okay, but it'll only hold them a couple of days."

"There'll be plenty of tornado stories to keep them busy," Wes said. "And Doc is right, we need to be real careful and back up every fact, because the wildest imaginations in the country will be working on this. First thing you know we'll have aliens involved, and conspiracy theories up the kazoo."

"And fans making pilgrimages. And after-death sightings. Wait and see," said the blond girl behind them. Her voice was strong with a husky edge, just right for a young lioness.

Wes turned to her. "Yeah, that too."

"Sheriff Cochran, do you remember Coral Turley?" Hopkins asked. "She's in the Lily Pistols band now."

"Oh, yeah, I knew you looked familiar," Wes said. She'd matured a lot from the pretty little kid he'd known. He added, "I'm real sorry about what happened here."

"Yeah." Her mouth trembled.

"Have you told Deputy Hopkins about it, Coral?"

"I don't know much," the girl said.

Hopkins said, "She went to visit her mother and left Mr. Heller here working by himself. When she saw the tornado coming, she tried to get back here to warn him but her car went off the road in the storm and she didn't get here until half an hour after I did."

A van carrying the state evidence technicians pulled into the driveway. Wes saw Altman and Pfann greeting them, Altman pointing at the tornado shelter door.

Wes glanced back at the girl. "We'll be busy here for a while. Why don't you go wait at your parents' place?"

"But—" She seemed uncomfortable at the idea, and wiped a hand across her forehead to push aside the damp blond strands. She

101

suddenly looked very young and sad to him. "I gotta talk to the other guys in the band."

Hopkins said, "I could take her to White Oak Farm, see if her mother's up to it. When the other band members show up, we can send them there."

"Okay." Wes wanted to get the poor kid away from the bustle and black jokes of the evidence crew. "And after you drop her off, finish checking this section of the tornado path, up to Vine Road."

Len Abbott thumped the heel of his hand against the T-bird's steering wheel. He'd been sitting in this traffic for weeks, it seemed. He should have been in Nichols County by nine P.M., but the last thirty miles had been a horror, only inches at a time. Around ten P.M. he'd pulled off for gas and a snack, hoping that maybe the traffic would ease while he was away, but when he came out it was as bad as ever, and it had taken ten or fifteen minutes of waiting before a van driver took pity on him and let him rejoin the creeping line of cars.

This kind of stop-and-go traffic was hard on engines. When he got out of the service, he'd gone into heating and air conditioning in part because he respected the mechanisms that clever men had developed to keep people warm or cool when cruel nature made them suffer. The other part was that it offered a solid career, if a man was willing to keep himself up-to-date, take courses from time to time, put in the hours. He'd done all that. He'd been a good provider for his wife and daughters, working his way up at the firm until he was foreman. And for what? His wife had taken the girls when she ran off, all the way to the West Coast. There had been two terrible years of lawyers and accusations, and it had settled down to strained visits. Sweet Steffie had come back to finish high school in Muncie, but Joss had taken her mother's part and when she was old enough she quit visiting.

He should never have let Steffie marry that drunken bastard Stollnitz. He'd given in at last because he feared if he held out she'd run away, and because her first boyfriend had wanted to join the Air Force and live God knows where, and Clay Stollnitz at least planned to stay in Muncie. But that had sure backfired. The year wasn't up when she'd come knocking on his door with bruises all over, and a couple months later he'd had to drive her to the hospital with a broken collarbone. And when even the order of protection wouldn't keep Stollnitz away, she'd decide to move. She'd kept in touch with her father, but it wasn't the same.

Now that bastard had taken Steffie away again. For ever this time.

102

Len glanced across the median, where the outward-bound traffic was heavy but moving. He could probably be home in Muncie again before he got to the Nichols County Sheriff's Department.

But he was not about to let them forget about Steffie.

He was not about to let Stollnitz get away this time.

The brake lights of the car ahead went off, and the line of cars rolled forward another thirty inches before it stopped again. I'm trying, Steffie, I'm trying, he whispered to his daughter.

Lights welcomed them to White Oak Farm, shining from the house and the parking lot, glinting on the damp leaves of the surrounding oaks and forsythia and yew. Marty cut the engine, hoping Tom was around, fearing that Dee would be too ill to take responsibility for the girl. In fact she and Coral were barely out of the cruiser when the door of the big white house burst open and Dee came running out. "Coral! Oh, thank the lord, you're okay!"

Marty was surprised at Dee's radiance. Her hair was braided into a bright coronet, her workshirt in harvest colors was neat and cheerful. Only yesterday she'd looked ancient, wasted. But as she embraced her daughter, Marty thought her eyes looked puffy from weeping.

The girl seemed reluctant, edgy even, but let herself be hugged. Dee stepped back and said, "Honey, don't worry, I had time to think things over while I was waiting for the storm to pass. And you're right. I don't want to smother you, I promise. I know what that's like."

"What do you know about it?" Coral asked, and Marty remembered that she'd been suspicious of her own mother, especially when she started doling out advice about things she knew nothing about.

But instead Dee said, "My family wanted me to work in the bakery like your Aunt Melva. But I wanted to farm. And that's why I married George Meade, because he was a farmer, and because if I'd stayed at the bakery I would have felt smothered."

Coral stared at her a moment and then reached out to her suddenly. "Oh, Ma, things are so awful! Hoyt's dead!"

"Oh, honey, that can't be!" Dee hugged her again.

"But it's true. It was the tornado."

"Oh, honey, this is terrible for you!"

"Are you glad, Ma? Or sad?"

Dee said honestly, "Some days I prayed for it, honey, but not really. Do you understand? Never really."

"I know. Me too." The two were so absorbed in each other that Marty felt invisible.

103

Finally Coral stepped back. "Dee, what I said before still goes, okay?" She was still snuffling, but her voice was firm. "I belong with the band. Hoyt's gone but that doesn't change things. I belong with them now."

Dee said, "Okay, I understand. But there's one other thing. You're also connected to me."

"Yeah, I guess." The girl shrugged and suddenly blurted, "That first time I called—Tom said you'd call back. You didn't."

"I tried, honey. But Tom was so rattled he wrote down the number wrong and you never gave us another one."

"You tried? Oh God." Coral shook her head. "I had this feeling— you know, my mother can do anything—so I thought you were mad, you'd rejected me . . . oh God."

A wave of sorrow at the missed connection rolled through Marty, and she realized she was mourning her own mother too, the conversations that would never be. Dee touched her daughter's cheek gently. "Honey, you know you've always been my other half. I thought you'd rejected me. But that's over. Can I help now?"

"I don't know. I have to talk to the guys in the band."

They were going to be all right. Marty cleared her throat to announce that she had to go, but Dee was still focused on Coral. "Hoyt was real important to you, wasn't he?"

"The music is important. Always was. And Hoyt gives—gave me a chance to do it."

"I wish I could help, honey." Dee studied Coral for a moment. Marty thought she was puzzled too.

Coral said again, "I've got to get in touch with the band somehow. That's where I belong now."

Dee looked at Marty. "Is there any way to call? My phone is out."

Marty said, "They're out all over the county."

"Is there an emergency center? Red Cross, fire department?"

"They're talking about setting up near Rockland Mall."

"Talking! We need phones and things now, not next week!" Dee snorted, then sudden enthusiasm lit her face. "Marty, there'll be lots of people wanting to help right now. The radio said the tornado hit a trailer park and the Chapel Road shopping center."

"That's right. There are lots of injuries, lots of property damage."

"Was Holy Spirit Church damaged?"

"No, the storm track was mostly south of Chapel Road."

"Then we'll set up there. And I'll get the phone company to run in a line. Tom? Tom!" She shouted toward the house, then strode

104

across the asphalt to the white van that was parked opposite the store, opened the rear doors, and climbed in to clear it out. She pushed a greenhouse heater to the door and called, "Coral, honey, you want to give me a hand? Just push these things out of the way. We'll back the van over to the door there and load some vegetables. People need to eat."

Coral lifted the heater down to the asphalt and slid it out of the way, then helped Dee muscle a power mower down from the van. Marty, wondering at Dee's sudden vigor, jumped into the van to give them a hand. "Dee, you've been sick. Are you up to this?"

Dee smiled. "What I'm not up to is sitting around when people need me. I'm just like you, Marty honey. Besides, I've got to get a phone for my daughter."

"You're sure you're okay?"

Suddenly serious, Dee nodded. "Yeah, I'm okay. I'm finally learning to deal with how much of motherhood is loss."

Tom Turley came hurrying from the house, and Dee called, "Tom, honey, we're setting up a kitchen and volunteer center at Holy Spirit. We're going to need all our potatoes and beans. Salad things too. It's so sad that the harvest was bad this year. But people will bring things in from other counties tomorrow, so let's take all ours now."

Tom looked worried. "But it's been such a hard year!"

Dee waved a dismissive hand. "So much the worse! Right now we've got people to feed!" She handed down a shovel and rake to Coral and glanced at Marty, who had jumped down to the asphalt and was walking toward her cruiser. "Honey, when you see your Aunt Vonnie, ask her to come help, okay? Holy Spirit Church hall."

Marty said, "Sure, I'll tell her. Coral, we'll have your statement ready to sign in a day or two, after the other emergencies are taken care of. Keep us posted where you are, okay?"

"Okay." Coral leaned the shovel and rake against the lamppost.

Marty drove away from the brightness of White Oak Farm and into the dark. Midnight already. Except for the two hours between the end of her shift and the church supper, she'd been working since seven A.M. yesterday. Marty flexed her tired shoulders. Poor Dee! She was trying to bounce back, but it was as though she didn't feel complete without her daughter. Well, Marty could sure sympathize with that. If Brad—

Quit worrying, Hopkins, she scolded herself. Don't waste energy when you've got real work to do. Chrissie's alive, and you're alive, and you've got more farms to check.

And a celebrity death to worry about. And Stephanie Stollnitz needed attention too. Her ex-husband, her lawyer—there were people to talk to. The urgency of the tornado work and the fame of Hoyt Heller didn't mean that Steffie wasn't important.

Marty finished her assigned area of the storm track, three more farms. Like the Matthews place, they had only minor damage. At the middle one, Sam Meisner was contemplating a four-inch-thick branch that had fallen across his pickup's hood. Marty was sorry to see a beer can in his hand and several empties strewn around him. As Marty walked up the drive he managed a bleary grin. "Well, look what the storm blew in! Hi, baby."

"Do you need any help here, Mr. Meisner? Is your wife okay?"

"She's with her sister. What's this Mr. Meisner? Do I know you, baby? Hey—you're not that Deputy Hopkins, are you? She wears a uniform."

She'd had to arrest Sam once. He'd been with three other drunks, banging on the window of somebody's terrified ex-girlfriend. She said evenly, "Just let us know if you need any help."

He focused unhappily on the cruiser at the foot of the drive. "You are Hopkins, aren't you? Shit! I didn't do anything!"

"Nobody said you did." Marty got back in the cruiser, muttered, "Bonehead!" under her breath, and called dispatch.

The radio was jammed with messages and it took a long time for Foley to answer her. He said, "Sheriff wants you to report back here for vital paperwork."

Yeah, it was true, with a case like Heller's they had to do it by the book, no matter how many catastrophes Nature was hurling at them. She said, "Okay, tell him I'm going to take five minutes to get into uniform, so I should be there in twenty minutes."

"You're going to change clothes? Sheesh!"

Foley could be a jerk too. She thought about pointing out that it wasted time when she had to keep explaining that she really was a deputy, but instead she sighed and keyed off. She and the jerk both had more important things to do.

When she got home, Coleman lanterns glowed in the kitchen and living room and a kettle steamed on the gas stove. "What happened to your hair?" Aunt Vonnie demanded. "It's pink!"

Marty ran her fingers through her curls and discovered tufts of insulation. She grabbed her comb. "Aunt Vonnie, I have a message from Dee Turley. She's setting up a kitchen and volunteer center in Holy Spirit Church hall to feed the victims. Wants to know if you can help."

106

Aunt Vonnie actually looked relieved. "Of course! I've been pacing around wanting to do something. So Dee is feeling better?"

"Must be. A total change from yesterday."

"A volunteer center is a great idea. Sounds like the old Dee."

"Where's Chrissie?"

"Fell asleep listening to the radio. There's no real information yet, just Fiscarelli on some kind of radio link. You know, the editor of the *News*."

They tiptoed in to look at the girl, sprawled fully clothed on the sofa in the total relaxation of the young. She was gawky, coltish, and absolutely beautiful. The portable radio on the coffee table still chattered. Marty murmured, "Let her nap until you leave. But take her along, she'll want to help too. Aunt Vonnie, do you think Dee is up to this?"

"I hope so. Used to be the best organizer in the county. I suppose you're still on duty?"

"God, yes. I'm just taking five minutes to get into uniform."

Marty kissed her sleeping daughter on the forehead, changed, accepted the thermos of coffee Aunt Vonnie handed her, and headed out again into the devastation.

Seventeen

Wes, still pondering the best way to handle Heller's death, got back to the station shortly before midnight. Cars choked the darkened courthouse square and chaos reigned inside. Foley, alone at the dispatcher's desk, was besieged by blinking lights and by forty or fifty people hollering at him. Is Johnny Jordan okay? Have you seen Kerry Hays? Wes was suddenly angry at Heller, angry at the fame that would make it so much harder to help the ordinary folks here, who so desperately needed and deserved his help.

Don't get angry, get busy. For starts, a little order would help. Sometimes it was good to be six-four and in uniform. Wes waded into the crowd and bellowed, "Okay, folks, over here with your questions! Let the dispatcher do his job!"

They pressed around him. Wes scanned the crowd quickly.

Whitcomb from the Red Cross he'd better talk to, and— My, my, there was Hollenbeck himself, the Dunning city police chief. Wes held up a hand for quiet and said, "What can I do for you, Chief?"

"You've got to get better communication with the emergency workers," Hollenbeck said. "A couple of my men just got back from South Dunning hospital, and they've got about a hundred patients."

"Foley's been telling the ambulances to take them to all three hospitals."

"Maybe so. But a lot of people are driving relatives in themselves, and South Dunning's the nearest hospital to the tornado damage."

"Okay, Chief. Can you spare a man to work with the South Dunning staff? We need to set up some kind of triage, you know, send the victims who aren't emergencies to the hospitals on the other side of town. The medics can decide on the plan, but people will listen to a uniform quicker than to a scrub jacket." When Hollenbeck nodded, Wes yelled, "Foley!"

"Yes sir?" The dispatcher turned harried, sunken eyes to him. Foley was a couple of years from retirement and not in good health, but you had to use what you had.

Wes said, "Tell the troops that the Dunning police are in charge at South Dunning hospital. Whitcomb, what's up?" He turned to the grizzled Red Cross director.

Whitcomb gestured at the crowd. "Well, Sheriff, a lot of these folks are here because they want information about their relatives. We've been trying to start a casualty list but South Dunning won't give us information. Patient confidentiality, they say."

"Sheesh. Chief Hollenbeck!"

"Yeah?" Hollenbeck paused at the door.

"Tell South Dunning that the Red Cross is authorized to collect casualty information, and nobody's gonna sue them, okay? Whitcomb will be along in a minute to get the list. Whit, are you set up somewhere to give out the information?"

"Yes sir, we're next to the Rockland Mall. We have a big sign so people on the highway can see it."

"It says 'Tornado Disaster Information,' but they've got no information!" complained a woman with curly red hair.

"Yes ma'am, we're working on it. How many of you other folks are trying to find relatives?"

About two-thirds of the crowd waved their hands. "Okay. You all go to the Rockland Mall. Mr. Whitcomb here will be there soon with the current information." As the crowd started for the door,

108

Wes beckoned Whit closer and murmured, "One little complication, Whit. Guy named Hoyt Heller got killed. Turns out he's famous."

"Never heard of him."

"Well, they tell me he's got a million teenage fans. When word gets out we'll have crowds like Graceland."

Whit grimaced. "Just what we need."

"So keep it quiet. If you get questions about him, refer them to the prosecuting attorney. Art'll be in his office."

Whitcomb nodded and left. Wes saw Hopkins hurry in, back from delivering the Turley girl to her parents' place. Wes turned to Stewart from the State Police. "What's up?"

"People are jamming the highways. They can't get through on the phone, and everybody's relatives for miles around are trying to get in here. We've set up roadblocks but they get in the back ways. Ambulances are having a hell of a time."

"Highways are clear around the Rockland Mall, right?"

Stewart shrugged. "Same thing. We clear a lane and it jams up. Some people park their cars in the clear lane and try to get to their relatives on foot."

"Yeah, one of my deputies had to haul a couple of folks from Martinsville out of a sinkhole next to the highway. Foley!"

"Yes sir?"

"Ask the radio stations to tell people to stay away, not to clog the highways."

Foley began to speak into the mike. Watching his slumped, weary dispatcher, and Hopkins, who hadn't even sat down, Wes wrote himself a mental note to order the troops to take turns resting up. Otherwise his people would work till they dropped.

A rumpled curly-haired man pushed his way through the remaining crowd. "Sheriff?"

He was about five-ten, in his fifties, a face that might have been pleasant if it weren't so tense. Business jacket, maybe a salesman. Wes said, "If you're asking about a relative, sir, please go to the Red Cross information center."

"I'm Len Abbott, Sheriff. Stephanie Stollnitz's father."

Shit. Wes said, "Hopkins, c'mere a minute!" and added, "I'll be right back, folks," to the people waiting. He showed Abbott into his office. "Mr. Abbott? Come on in. Have a seat. I'm Sheriff Cochran."

Abbott sat, his eyes circling the office. Wes had a sudden image of the man as a little boy after his first run-in with the playground

109

bully, the world seeming suddenly unreal because he couldn't believe in it, couldn't understand it, couldn't figure out what rule he'd broken to cause this pain. Wes had walked around like that after his Billy died.

He sat sidesaddle on the edge of his desk, facing Abbott. "I'm real sorry about Stephanie, sir."

"Thank you." Abbott's hands clenched as he asked, "What did he do to her?"

Wes asked, "Who?" though he suspected the answer.

"Clay Stollnitz! He used to be her husband! I told you!"

"Yes sir. See, the thing is, we don't know yet what happened. They're still doing some tests. Right now it looks like it was a real peaceful death."

He looked confused. "Peaceful? I don't understand. How did she die?"

"We don't know yet," he repeated patiently. "The coroner's working on it."

"Is there anything I can do to help? To speed things up? I know it's crazy with all the tornado stuff."

"Well, yes sir, if you could answer a few questions about Stephanie it would help a lot. Let me introduce Deputy Hopkins. She's working on this too."

"Hi," Abbott said without much interest.

"Hopkins, take notes, okay? Now, Mr. Abbott, it could help us figure this out if we had more of Stephanie's medical history. Did she have a heart problem, for example?"

"No! Not Steffie." He took a deep breath. Wes could see him struggling to control his anger and grief and frustration. He said evenly enough, "I'm not just saying that. I'm sure because we checked on it. Joss, her sister, had rheumatic fever, just a mild case and we treated it soon, but of course we checked her heart every year, and Steffie's too, just to be sure. Steffie was always the healthy one. She played tennis and loved to dance, and in high school she was a cheerleader. Always healthy."

Wes cleared his throat. He had a soft spot for cheerleaders. He'd married one. He asked, "Was she taking any medications?"

"Medications. Is that what happened? He poisoned her?" Abbott asked eagerly.

"We're just trying to find all the possibilities. To help the coroner."

"She had some anti-depressants, because of the divorce, but—" Abbott hesitated and added in dismay, "You're thinking it was suicide, aren't you? But she wouldn't do that! She knew she could

110

come back to me if she got to feeling blue! You're wrong, it absolutely wasn't that!"

"Yes sir." Wes decided not to argue the point with a family member, certainly not with a father. He asked, "Did Stephanie tell you about her friends after she moved here? Her activities?"

"Well, there's Mary Jo Osborne, who helped her get the job, I remember. And she's rooming with Gus and Clara something— Jackson, maybe. And she said she liked to go—"

The buzz of the intercom interrupted. Wes said, "Sorry, Mr. Abbott, just a sec," and barked, "Yeah?" at it.

"Guy out here named Stollnitz," Foley announced.

"Tell him to wait a minute," Wes said.

Abbott was on his feet, staring at the intercom. "Stollnitz? Is it that son of a bitch Stollnitz?" He shoved his chair out of the way.

Hopkins, who'd been leaning on the doorjamb, straightened. "Take it easy, sir, okay?" she said gently.

"Where is the bastard?" Abbott's voice rose.

"Who's a bastard?" The door opened and a man in a Colts sweatshirt, six-three and beefy, his skin beaded with raindrops, loomed suddenly over Hopkins, who had turned to face him. She was no longer taking notes, Wes saw, and her hand was on her nightstick. Wes moved around his desk to control Abbott, deciding that Hopkins's sisterly approach might work with the big guy at the door.

"Sir, please wait a minute out there," Hopkins said to the newcomer over the background clamor of the crowd outside.

At first he didn't seem to see her, looking over her head and waggling his fingers at Mr. Abbott. "Hi, dad-in-law."

Wes felt Abbott's muscles tensing under his hand.

"Sir." Hopkins stepped forward firmly and took Stollnitz by the elbow. Wes decided the guy had probably been a football hero and high-school heartthrob in his day, now thickening and going jowly from too many hours in bars but still curvy lipped and twinkly eyed. He had eight inches on Hopkins and was probably double her weight, and shook his arm free easily, but she'd caught his attention now and Wes could see his puzzlement as he stared down at her.

"Come on, sir, you don't want to cause a scene here," Hopkins said, half soothing and half commanding. "Just let us finish up with him so we can listen to you."

The newcomer gave her a crooked grin that reminded Wes of those Elvis Presley stamps. "Damn right! I'm not here to cause a scene.

111

But I figured if old man Abbott was coming down to give you an earful, I'd better come too and make sure you heard the truth."

Hopkins nodded. "Yes sir, that's what we want too. Now just wait out here—" She started to lead him through the crowd.

He was turning away, going along with Hopkins, when Abbott yelled, "Goddammit, he killed her! Can't you see? He murdered her!" He lunged after him. Wes caught him in a lock and Hopkins closed the door.

"Mr. Abbott, take it easy," Wes said.

Two heavy blows thudded against the other side of the door, then Wes heard Hopkins's soothing murmur: "Come on, Mr. Stollnitz, breaking the door down won't help things. Let's go over there until they're finished."

"But he did it! Somehow, he did it!" Abbott insisted.

There was no more pounding. Wes said, "Sir, take it easy. We'll find out what happened to your daughter. We have to do it all legal or the judge will throw it out."

Abbott stopped struggling but yelled, "That bastard! You know he broke her collarbone!"

"Yes, I know."

"You do?" Startled, he focused on Wes for the first time since Clay Stollnitz had appeared.

"We've got the whole divorce record. I reckon that's why Mr. Stollnitz came, because we asked the Muncie police to talk to him too."

"But this proves he knows where she lived!"

"He wasn't supposed to know that?"

"She had an order of protection in Muncie, but he ignored it. She got him arrested twice but of course they just let him out again. So she moved away."

Wes asked, "How did Mr. Stollnitz react to that?"

"For a few months he came pounding on my door every time he got drunk, demanding to know where she'd gone. Then I told him I had a shotgun. That made him quit. I hoped he'd given up."

"Did you hear from him yesterday or the day before?"

"No. Not for six months or so."

"Okay," Wes said. "We better talk to him, since he's here."

"He'll lie to you," he warned.

"We're aware of that possibility. Sir, we'll tell you as soon as we know anything. Make sure we know how to reach you."

"Don't worry. I'll catch a nap somewhere and check back tomorrow."

We're already working as fast as we can, Wes thought, but he said nothing. He knew the man needed some function, something to do, in this dreadful time when there was nothing that could be done. He accompanied Abbott through the yelling crowd to the door, telling people he'd be with them in a minute. On the far side of the room Clay Stollnitz was sitting talking to Hopkins, and this time ignored his ex-father-in-law except for one mild glance, thank the Lord.

Eighteen

When Abbott was safely out Wes turned to Hopkins and jerked his head toward his office. She brought Stollnitz in and they closed the door again. Stollnitz was already talking. "You know, Sheriff, like I was saying to Deputy Hopkins here, I hope you don't get the wrong idea from the old man. I won't kid you, he's got one hell of a temper!"

Wes nodded at Hopkins to take notes again and perched on the edge of his desk. "Have a seat, sir."

Stollnitz glanced around, beefy and friendly, just the normal amount of edginess that folks usually got in the sheriff's office. He took the chair where Abbott had been sitting, rocked it back on its hind legs, and rubbed a hand through his rain-moistened brown hair.

Wes asked, "Did you give Deputy Hopkins your address and phone already? We want to be able to reach you."

"Yes sir. Uh—can you tell me what happened to Steffie?"

"We don't have the coroner's report yet. Mr. Stollnitz, where do you work?"

"Seale Distributors in Muncie."

"What kind of outfit is that?"

"We deliver beverages to restaurants and so forth. My boss says we're a vital link in the food chain." Stollnitz had a direct, good-humored gaze.

"Worked there long?"

"Three years. Before that I was in auto repairs. But I figured there was no future in that."

Wes decided not to get into Stollnitz's future, though privately he thought that auto repair sounded like a more promising field than lugging cases of beer. "You ever work for a pharmacy? Medical supplies? Hospital?"

Clay Stollnitz looked puzzled. "No sir. Nothing like that."

"Okay, Mr. Stollnitz, what do you want to tell us? Why'd you come?"

"Well, I came to ask you what happened to Steffie. The cops in Muncie told me she'd died here but they wouldn't tell me any more." Stollnitz leaned forward. "And, dammit, I was married to her! I loved that woman!"

"Yeah," Wes said. Stollnitz looked intense now, the twinkly eyes blazing earnestly, the Elvis mouth curved sadly down. Guy might be telling the truth about that, or part of it. Didn't mean he was innocent, though. Wes asked, "Why does Mr. Abbott think you had something to do with Steffie's death?"

"Because he's crazy, that's why. Can't let go of his little girl. Says everything that goes wrong is ol' Clay's fault. See, sir, I loved Steffie. I'd never hurt her!"

"She got an order of protection against you."

Stollnitz waved emphatically toward the door. "That's his doing! Steffie and I were fine, only trouble was her father!"

"Stephanie divorced you, Mr. Stollnitz."

"Look, sir, that was a misunderstanding. We both made some mistakes. It would've worked out, I swear."

He was so earnest that Wes figured he actually believed his own bullshit. Time to move on. "Mr. Stollnitz, can you tell us what you did the last couple of days?"

"Me?" Clay Stollnitz straightened, surprise on his face.

"Don't give me that, Mr. Stollnitz. Here's a woman ends up dead at a young age, and she's had an order of protection against you. You really expect us to ignore that?"

"Yeah, okay." Stollnitz ducked his head a moment, pushed his damp hair back from his forehead, and faced Wes again. "You see, sir, I was in Muncie, and I answered these questions for the Muncie police. I thought they'd told you already, that's all."

"We got a lot to do, don't waste our time. Talk. Start with Tuesday."

"Yes sir. I worked, regular deliveries."

"And after work?"

"I usually stop off at the Blarney Stone for a drink and dinner. Friendly place."

"When did you get there?"

"I get off work at six, and went straight over there. Six fifteen, maybe."

"When did you leave?"

"Just before eight. A bunch of us decided to go bowling. Morgan's Lanes. Finished up at ten thirty. See, I like to stay in shape. I'm not a bad athlete. State championship football team a few years back." He flexed his right leg. "Man, if I hadn't torn a tendon senior year, I could've— Well, no sense whining. What happened, happened."

"Yeah, you gotta get on with your life." Wes too had been on a state championship team—basketball—and Clay Stollnitz reminded him of some of his teammates, frozen in those times, as though those glory days were the only time they'd been alive, and they'd been sleepwalking ever since. Hell, not just his teammates. Wes had been in combat, had won political races, had faced some hairy moments as sheriff, but nothing tasted the same as his long-ago hoop dreams. With more sympathy, he asked, "And after bowling?"

"After bowling, we went back to the Blarney Stone for a nightcap."

"When did you leave?"

The direct blue eyes shifted. "Uh, about closing time. Midnight or whatever." He glanced back at Wes, pain in his face. "Hey, I won't kid you, I've been real lonely since Steffie ran off. I probably hang around bars more than I should. But that apartment's real empty when I go home."

Wes believed him. But hurting made the guy more likely to lash out at the source of his pain, not less. Wes asked, "So you went home sometime around midnight Tuesday?"

"Yes sir."

"Spent the night at home?"

"Yes sir, of course," Stollnitz said, too quickly.

Wes was aware of Hopkins near the door, shifting her weight as she noted down his answer. She'd picked up the same vibes. Wes followed up, "You didn't go out at all?"

"No sir. Gotta admit, I'd had maybe a couple too many. I was dead to the world."

Yup, and so was Steffie. Wes asked brusquely, "Did you go to work on Wednesday?"

"Yes sir. Nine thirty to six, same as always."

"Okay. Anything else, Hopkins?"

Hopkins asked, "Mr. Stollnitz, how come you arrived exactly the same time as Mr. Abbott?"

"Well . . ." He pushed the hair out of his eyes again.

Wes picked up the line of inquiry. "Were you watching Mr. Abbott?"

"Well . . . look, what happened was the Muncie cops came and questioned me, and I was all shook up, okay? And I just happened to drive by the Abbott house and saw the police cars still there in the driveway, so I parked a couple blocks away. And then the police cars left and a minute later old man Abbott came out of his house and jumped in his car."

"So you followed him here."

"See, I got curious when I saw him head out of town. And when I saw him come in here, I knew he was going to fill all your heads with lies about me, same as he always does. And it looks like I was right."

Wes said, "So you want us to believe that you only now found out that Stephanie lived here."

"It's true!"

"And you want us to believe that the night she died, you got yourself drunk, and you didn't drive down here to see her, you went home sweet as pie and slept it off?"

Stollnitz licked his lips but kept his earnest gaze on Wes. "That's exactly what happened, sir."

Wes looked at him, flat-eyed. Stollnitz said, "Look, you can ask the guys at the Blarney Stone!"

"We'll get a statement for you to sign. On your way back to Muncie, you think if there's anything more you want to tell us."

"Yes sir." He seemed eager enough to leave now, no longer the noble, unjustly accused football hero, now just a schmuck who beat up women because he was no longer a contender. Hopkins showed him out and returned immediately.

"We gotta get back to work," Wes said. "But what do you think?"

"High-school dreamboat turned into a Jekyll–Hyde drunk," Hopkins said.

"Yeah. And if he left the bar in Muncie at midnight he coulda been here by three A.M. But right now let's get out and help those people."

For hours, Marty had been escorting emergency-repair crews from the electric company from one damage site to another, getting people to move their cars out of the way or moving them herself.

116

At five A.M. Deputy Walker hailed her at the substation near Chapel Road and State 822. "Hey, Hopkins, the boss says you should take an hour off and take a nap."

"I don't need—"

"And eat some breakfast. He says that's an order."

"Have you had breakfast?"

"Yeah, that's why he sent me to relieve you."

Coach was right, she realized, she was starving. She headed for the Red Cross center at the Rockland Mall. A crowd stood around the information desk, and some workers were laying out forms on a table, but nothing else had yet been organized. Remembering Dee Turley's plan to set up a kitchen, she made her way through crowded highways to Holy Spirit Church.

The fellowship hall was teeming with victims and volunteer helpers alike. Along one side, people were stacking bundles of clothing. In the center they'd set up a table to fill out insurance forms and government disaster-relief applications. Behind, the phone company had set up an emergency line, and people waited their turn to call out. Someone was painting a sign, "Volunteer Center." Across the room, long tables had been set up in front of the church kitchen, and Marty saw Dee Turley, looking radiant as befitted a miracle worker, directing a small mob of volunteers in a breakfast set-up. What a change from the bedraggled, depressed woman she'd seen only yesterday. And there was what seemed to be the reason for the transformation, young Coral Turley, her pretty eyes red-rimmed, helping Dee's sister Melva put out little bottles of fruit juice. Clara Johnson was stacking mini-boxes of cereal. Three big coffee urns smelled real good. As Marty crossed the room she spotted bottles of maple-flavored syrup. Pancakes? Could there actually he pancakes today? She picked up an orange juice and looked around.

Her own Chrissie came out of the kitchen carrying stacks of paper plates and a box of drinking straws.

Marty ran around the table and gave her a big hug. "Hey, kid, how're you doing?"

Chrissie pulled away. "Where've you been?"

"Helping people. Same as you. When I checked at the house you were asleep." Marty took one of Chrissie's straws for her juice and added, "C'mon, I need a hug."

Chrissie said icily, "You always run off when I need you!"

Guilt bubbled up in Marty, and childish anger. Damn kid was such a—such a kid! Couldn't think of anything except herself, how scared she'd been. Marty couldn't decide whether to comfort her

117

or whack her a good one, so she did the only sensible thing. She said, "I do not!" and blew the wrapper of the straw at Chrissie. Bull's eye on the heart.

Chrissie, startled, pulled out a straw of her own and blew it at Marty. "Do too!"

"Do not!" Marty grabbed a handful and jumped into combat stance.

A grudging giggle escaped Chrissie and she hugged Marty at last, mumbling, "Okay, idiot Mom. But all the other kids' families were there."

"And you know why? Because I was on the job and told them what to do! Listen, Chrissie, it's great that you're helping. We're all doing our jobs. Are you really going to have pancakes?"

"Yeah, Aunt Vonnie and Mrs. Yeager are fixing them now."

Dee Turley sailed through the kitchen door, blond and beaming. "Hi, Marty, honey. We've got plain and buckwheat both. Grab a plate and take it back there. Tell them to sneak you a couple. Now, where has Tom got to? Never mind, I'll send Coral." The girl turned at the sound of her name. Marty could see she'd been crying. Dee put an affectionate arm around her daughter's shoulders. "Honey, here come the men from the Save-More with some bread. Go ask them to bring it back here, okay? Shelves next to the dishwasher."

Marty took a paper plate and went back into the big kitchen. Aunt Vonnie, pancake-turner poised for action, her face pink from the heat, looked Marty over and frowned. "Hey, now I see you in the light, you got yourself scuffed up pretty good."

"It was pretty windy out there for a while," Marty said. This was not the moment to discuss narrow escapes. The pancakes were beginning to sizzle around the edges. "Chrissie's mad at me, isn't she? Thinks I ordered up a tornado just to embarrass her."

"Gets that from you." Aunt Vonnie flipped the pancakes. "When you were Chrissie's age, you used to blame your mother for everything, including acts of God. Your dad would drink up his paycheck, but when there wasn't enough money for your new basketball sneakers, you'd blame her."

This was an old, tired fight. Marty raised a palm for peace. "I know, Aunt Vonnie, we've been through all this. I know it was hard for Mom. But he seemed like a wonderful dad to me. We both loved basketball and we had fun together. I was just a kid."

Aunt Vonnie nodded wisely. "And so is Chrissie. Don't forget it!" She slid the turner under a pancake and Marty held out her plate. Laurie Yeager came over with a bowl of batter and began spooning it onto the griddle as Aunt Vonnie removed the cooked ones. Aunt Vonnie changed the subject. "Grady said that Al Evans got killed."

They knew Al Evans slightly, a crusty old gent who sometimes came to their church. Marty said, "Yeah, I'm afraid so. He was in his car and it got tossed off the road."

Laurie said anxiously, "I didn't know Mr. Evans, but I heard there were lots of people injured."

"I don't know the count for sure. Someone said close to a hundred."

Laurie shook her head sadly. "Where exactly did it hit?"

"Well, it started on the Buehl's farm, took out some sheds. Then it wiped out that shopping center at 822 and Chapel Road. And the RV lot across from it, and half of that little trailer park on 37 south of Chapel. And it took off a lot of roofs from farmhouses, and a few businesses south of Dunning. The car wash, half of K-mart and Walgreen's, the bridal shop." Laurie's shocked face reminded her of another question. "Laurie, you said you saw a tornado movie on TV late Monday. What time was that?"

Laurie said, "Started at midnight. But you know, it sure didn't show all this. It just showed one family being rescued. When Gordon came in I asked him if we were safe and he said the emergency teams were very good now. They are, aren't they?"

She looked at Marty beseechingly, wanting confirmation, but Marty could remember only that terrible forty-five minutes trying to resuscitate Hoyt Heller, waiting for an ambulance that she knew wouldn't come, what with the clogged roads and hundreds of other injuries. Marty said lamely, "Well, we do our best, but we can't be everywhere at once. Listen, I better get me some syrup before my pancakes get cold."

And, she thought, she'd better ask Gordon what he'd been doing out so late the night one of his clients died. But first there was a lot more search and rescue and clean-up to do.

Coral Turley, a sad, distracted frown on her face, was standing in line for the phone. So was Chrissie. Calling her dad, probably.

Feeling suddenly alone, Marty ate quickly and hit the road again.

Nineteen

Jake Shaw's Toyota was still wrapped around the tree. He'd hitched a ride to the *News* office with relatives of the Country Griddle's owner. He'd spent the rest of the night working side by side with his editor, Fiscarelli, and a ham operator named Rudy who was their only way of transmitting information out. It was a night of frantic activity as Jake readied his eyewitness accounts for the wire, ran out to interview the sheriff or the police chief, and wrote up stories from the scribbled notes he got from Betty and the other reporters who still had cars. They'd reported one death, Al Evans, an old redneck who'd foolishly got into his car to go check on a neighbor and died when his car was blown from the road and dropped in the nearby woods.

Towards dawn Fiscarelli pushed back his aviator glasses, rubbed his eyes, and tossed the keys of his Maxima to Jake. "Check the hospitals," he said. "See if the Red Cross casualty lists are up to date."

At South Dunning Hospital they were triaging the patients, keeping only those who needed instant emergency attention, sending the others to the two city hospitals. The numbers checked out close enough with the Red Cross list, and Jake debated for a moment if he should even bother with the other hospitals. Hell, why not, it was good to be behind a wheel again, even his editor's wheel. Maybe he'd get a Maxima like this when his insurance came through. Although his totaled Toyota wouldn't bring in a whole lot. Maybe nothing, he thought glumly. The insurance people would get off the hook because a tornado was an act of God.

City Hospital had no additional information, and Mercy also claimed to have none. But when Jake persisted in his questioning, wondering if someone might have died of injuries after being brought there, one harrassed nurse became edgy and said, "Go ask Art Pfann."

Art Pfann? Jake's antennae went up. He asked, "The prosecuting attorney?"

Suddenly tight-lipped, she turned away to her next patient.

Jake beelined for the county building on the courthouse square, driving on sidewalks when he had to get past jams, and parking the Maxima on the rain-soaked courthouse lawn. He could see lights in the prosecuting attorney's office.

Art Pfann looked exhausted, with bruised-looking dark circles under his eyes, but he came across with a zinger. "Yeah, we had a second death," he told Jake. "We haven't announced it because I had to drive twenty miles to a working phone to get through to the next of kin in California. Guy's name was Hoyt Heller."

"Heller? Wait a minute—isn't that the same name as that guy in show business? What is he, an actor or singer or something?"

Art just looked at him. Headlines about huge concerts in Bloomington and Evansville stirred in Jake's memory and he said, "That band. Lily Pistols."

"That's the one," Art admitted.

"You're kidding!"

"Wish I were, Jake."

Jake whistled. This story wasn't big. It was gigantic. "What was he doing here? I didn't know he was even in the state!"

"No one knew." Art's voice boomed even when tired. "I understand he was making a music video in Indianapolis and Louisville."

"So what happened to him?"

"Well, Doc's working on the report right now."

"C'mon, give me a hint! Where was he found?"

"Lying in the yard of the place he was renting, between the house and the tornado shelter." Art gave the address.

"What happened? Did you see the body?"

"There was a piece of siding next to him, and a gash on his neck."

Jake winced. "Ouch. So the wind slammed him with the siding, I guess. Is that safe to say?"

Art said stiffly, "The coroner wants us to wait for his report."

"You mean there's a question?" Jake asked suspiciously.

"Not that I know of. But I'm not the coroner, Jake, and the coroner's in charge. You know that."

Jake grinned. "Altman's flexing his muscles, huh? I'll get it from him, then. Now, what about the rest of the band? Are they hurt?"

"No, they were all in Bloomington, except . . . I understand they're staying with a friend there." Art massaged the bridge of his nose.

What had that "except" meant? Jake asked, "You mean he was all alone? There was no one with him?" When Art continued to rub his nose, Jake added, "A girlfriend, I bet. Who? Is she hurt?"

Art gave a little nod, acknowledging Jake's good guess. "No, she was in another part of the county at the time."

"What part? Is she still around?"

Art studied him a moment, then said, "Hell, it'll come out soon enough, you might as well have it. It's a local girl, the Turley kid. She's got some sort of job with the band, and they were staying together in that rented farmhouse."

"The White Oak Farm Turleys? That kid who ran away?"

"Yep."

"I was there last week, and Tom didn't say a word about her coming back!"

"So? Maybe they didn't want any attention." Art sighed. "They've got no choice now."

"Okay. Is there anything else you can tell me about the death?"

"Just that tornadoes kill a lot of people every year, and it's important to know what to do when they strike."

"Yeah, yeah, see you." Jake bounced out of the county building and headed for the *News*, a fizz of excitement in his veins.

Marty wiped her syrup-sticky lips and glanced at her watch before turning the ignition. Five twenty-five A.M. The sheriff had given her an hour for breakfast and a nap, but there were just thirty-five minutes left. She decided to skip the nap and reassure herself about a different worry. Romey Dennis would be okay, she told herself, he'd been safe at the church supper like Chrissie. Plus Grady Sims had checked those farms and found no injured people. But she had to see for herself. She turned on to Vine, driving slowly, trying to judge the path of the storm from what she could make out in her headlights.

It had passed just north of the Dennis place. But, as at the Matthews farm, the storm had dumped debris as it passed. Marty drove up the driveway. Her headlights showed branches down in the yard. Romey's uncle's house was okay in front and on the side, but when she reached the rear she saw a huge downed tree. It had broken some windows and damaged the roof of the kitchen addition. And a big branch had hit the trailer. Shoot. The door hung askew, and what she could make out of the roofline didn't look square.

The Taurus was parked by the addition. She pulled in beside it and grabbed her flashlight.

When she stepped through the trailer door, she almost stumbled. Chairs were tipped over and cabinet doors gaped, the contents

122

tumbled on the floor. The framed photo of their long-ago basket-ball team, the Stonies, on their way to play their archrival Little Pistons, lay shattered and torn on the carpet. Half of her own ten-year-old face and Romey's grinned up in the flashlight beam.

She became aware of a glow from the back room. A candle, she saw, stepping closer. She switched off her flashlight and said softly, "Romey?"

"Hey, Marty," he said dully. He was sitting on the floor next to the bed looking at a heap of broken ceramic. The beautiful Greek plates he loved so much. Even the Stonies' trophy, the loving cup, was dented. And in his hands— Oh, shit, it was his mother's photograph, crumpled and torn, frame broken. He could get another copy of their team photo, but that was the only one he had of his mom.

Marty had been keeping her feelings at bay, but somehow this tiny tragedy cracked the barricades and the sorrows flooded in: Hoyt's death, and old Al Evans's, and Stephanie's. Wrecked homes at Robin Hill. The grieving eyes of Stephanie's father. Dazed and bleeding people, and the hard-earned daily comforts of hundreds of lives hurled carelessly across the ruined landscape. She blurted, "Damn, damn, damn!"

Romey looked up at her. The candlelight made his bearded face softer and more mysterious. He took a deep breath and said, "Hey. Why did the Little Pistons grab a rifle when they heard the tornado warning?"

She knelt beside him. "Why?"

"Because they wanted to shoot the breeze."

"God, if only we could!" She tried to smile, her throat tight, and touched his face. The skin was damp. She felt tears welling in her eyes too and said, "Romey, I'm so sorry," and pulled his head to her breast. For a moment they clung to each other, mourning for the newly dead and the long dead, for smashed homes and hurt people and ruined beloved photos. He smelled of sweat and his spicy soap. She stroked his hair and he nuzzled the hollow of her throat. In a moment they found themselves stretched on the carpet in the midst of the wreckage, unbuttoning each other's shirts.

Romey paused, pushed himself to a sitting position, and pressed his palms to his eyes. "Oh boy. Sorry, sexy lady. You know you taste like maple syrup? I got carried away. I know you don't want . . ."

"The hell I don't!" said Marty fiercely, and handed him the dented loving cup. She wanted to rip this horrible night apart, to find the joy the storm had tried to smother.

He said hesitantly, "But your lawyer . . . you're sure?"

"Romey, you're alive! And I'm alive! That's so great!"

Romey grinned suddenly and went for her last buttons. "Yeah, you're right, let's keep our priorities straight." And in the candle-glow, surrounded by the shards of the past and the shadows of the dead, they celebrated being alive.

Twenty

On her fourth try, waiting through the long line for the emer-gency phone, Coral got through to Skell in Bloomington. He grunted, "Coral, you bitch, you know what time it is?"

Coral said, "Six A.M. Skell, there was a tornado here. You heard?"

"You're kidding! And we missed it! Fuck!"

"Skell, listen!" She glanced over her shoulder at the impatient people waiting for the phone and lowered her voice. "There's a crowd here. I can't say what happened. But it's real bad."

Skell groaned. "Look, I been asleep maybe fifteen minutes, you wake me up to play guessing games?"

"Good idea," Coral said briskly. "I'll tell you when you get warm. Here's a clue: it's real bad."

"You're pregnant."

"Nothing to do with me."

"Hoyt's pregnant."

"No, but it's about him."

"What's wrong with you, babe? Lost your sense of humor? What happened? It's not AIDS, is it? Say it's not AIDS!"

"Worse than that, Skell."

"Worse? C'mon, he can't be dead!"

"You got it." A memory of Hoyt's magnetic grin swam into her mind and she choked back a little sob. Hell, what was wrong with her? It was as though she really did love him, in spite of what he'd done to her. Could you love and hate at the same time?

Skell was sputtering, "Fuck, woman, you're putting me on!"

She managed to say, "No. I saw."

Skell's conversation disintegrated into curses about her dumb

124

taste in practical jokes. Coral took a deep breath and broke in, "Hey, we're still a band, right? Brian and I can do vocals. So what do I tell the press?"

"Fuck the press!"

Chill, Coral told herself, don't yell at the asshole. "Look, if we don't say anything they'll make something up. I mean, you want them to define us?"

"Coral, baby, number one is, I don't believe you. Number two, if anything did happen to Hoyt, we'd have to think about it real careful. After that we'll talk to Ned. I can manage Ned."

Hell, thought Coral, anyone could manage Ned. Their PR man had been hired because he followed Hoyt's orders without ever inserting a thought of his own. She said patiently, "Ned's in Bermuda, Skell. The press'll be here any minute!"

"We have to think about it longer!" he shouted. "Number three, when we do make any announcements, I'll make them, not you."

"They'll be here, Skell, not there! Now, not later! Anyway, what do you plan to say?"

There was a pause before he muttered, "Shit. Are you at the farm now?"

"Farm's got police tape all over. I'm at the volunteer center, the Holy Spirit Church of Christ."

"Shit. What's the phone number?"

"You won't be able to get through. I'll call you back, maybe half an hour."

Brow furrowed, Coral marched back to the kitchen. So Skell wanted to speak for the band! Idiot. Hoyt had never been able to get through to Skell even the most elementary ideas of what the media wanted. She could see Skell in her mind's eye, spaced out and babbling nonsense, everyone's future down the tubes.

He didn't believe her, didn't understand that the reporters would be here, filming the destruction, recording breathless commentaries on Hoyt's final moments at the farmhouse—no, she could almost hear Hoyt saying, not the farmhouse, not enough damage there. In front of one of the really flattened houses. They wouldn't give a shit where he'd really died, they'd want good visuals. She imagined what they'd air: a broken chimney surrounded by a pile of boards, the earnest anchorperson in the foreground, clips of Hoyt performing old songs.

Nothing about the rest of the band. Nothing about Coral. Nothing even about "Deathwind," which hadn't been released yet. Because Skell was a PR idiot. Musical genius, yes, and she'd always be grateful because he'd been the one who noticed her songs, made Hoyt try them, elevated her from plaything to band member. But all the same, a PR idiot. And Ned would follow his orders.

They had to deal with the media now. They had to give them a story. Bastard though he was, Hoyt had understood that. Hoyt had always given them good stories.

Coral took a deep breath. Dee would hate this, but it had to be done.

She found her mother collecting cartons of carrots and cabbage and carrying them to Clara Johnson, who was scrubbing and shredding them for coleslaw. Dee looked up at her as she approached, her happy welcoming smile fading at something in Coral's appearance. "Problems?" Dee asked.

"I need to borrow the van, Ma. It's about Hoyt."

Consternation tightened Dee's face. "Honey, is it really necessary? All these people have to be fed. We may need the van."

"Yeah, it's necessary. It's like my whole future. And look, you've got about two zillion volunteers already wanting to help out. Use their trucks." Coral waved at the church hall, where more volunteers were appearing every moment. The Scouts were bringing in camping supplies and old-fashioned litters, someone had lettered "Search and rescue crews: Sign up here," onto a big cardboard carton and was doing a brisk business, a bearded guy she'd never met with a Dennis Rent-All shirt was whistling as he piled chain saws, ropes, wrecking bars, and other equipment along the wall for the crews. The little radio behind Dee announced the location of this volunteer center periodically.

Dee looked where Coral indicated and said fondly, "They're wonderful, aren't they? But honey, what do you mean, your future?"

"Just something I have to do for the band. I'll be back in twenty minutes."

"Mrs. Turley? Excuse me." The speaker was a thin man in his fifties, wearing a Pacers cap and carrying a notebook. Oh God, thought Coral, he has to be press. She wasn't ready yet. But he was eying Coral curiously even while he spoke to Dee. Coral stepped back.

Dee saw him looking, reached into her jeans pocket and, without glancing at Coral, tossed her the keys.

Coral snatched them and ran for the van. Behind her she heard her mother say, "Hi, Jake, honey. What can we do for the *Nichols County News*?"

Smooth. Sometimes her mother amazed her. Coral climbed into

126

the van, her mind shifting to the band's problems again. Good to know that what's-his-name in the Pacers cap worked for the *News*. Coral was after bigger game, but he'd be a start.

She turned toward the Matthews farm, toward the place Hoyt had died, easing the van through the crowds of people heading for the volunteer center. Their faces seemed to glow pink, as though they'd been resurrected from the dead, she thought. Worthy subjects for the Queen of the Bones.

Or maybe it was just the sun rising.

Two hours later, Jake Shaw sat in Denny's, the nearest restaurant that still had electricity and running water. No phone, though. He sipped his coffee and put the last touches on his article. Fiscarelli had spoken to his counterpart at the *Herald Times* in the next-door county, and the H-T would run the *News* on their presses. Jake's story would likely hit the street in three hours. Jake was still kicking himself for letting the Turley girl slip away from him at the volunteer center. But he'd reach her before anyone else did. He was way ahead.

Still, he'd better move on it as soon as he ran this up to the H-T office. He was meeting his editor outside in ten minutes for the ride to Bloomington. There, he hoped to rent a car. Here in Dunning nothing was available. Even the trucks at Dennis Rent-All were already rented.

Trying to think of a fresher way to say "rock star," Jake was gazing out the window when he noticed a man in the parking lot opening the door of his gray Lincoln. It was the Ohio man with the mustache who was staying at Asphodel Springs. Who the hell was he? The man glanced in his direction before he climbed into the car, and because Jake was just finishing up a roll of film he snapped a picture through the glass.

Someone cuffed him on the shoulder and cried, "Hey, Jake, ol' man! How's it going?"

Jake looked up. Wavy dark hair, coffee-colored skin, square-jawed. "Well, look at what just blew in! How you doing, Stu?"

"Not bad at all. I'm with ABC in Chicago, six o'clock local news."

"Yeah, I heard you were doing okay. Long way from the Indiana backwoods." Nine years ago, while still an undergraduate at J-school in Bloomington, Stu had talked the then-editor of the *News* into letting him write features on young people. Jake had enjoyed showing the ropes to the eager youngster, and had been interested to hear later that Stu had used his news background and his genial, square-jawed good looks to move into television news and eventually big bucks in Chicago. Jake hadn't been surprised. Envious, yes. But he'd always known that scrawny guys whose Adam's apple stuck out like his were just not made for the age of television.

Stu pulled out a chair, signalled the waitress for coffee, and said, "Tell me about this tornado!"

Jake hesitated. He had a strong urge to keep it to himself, but an even stronger one to see his story on the national news. He said, "You'll have to say I broke this story. My name and the *Nichols County News* up front."

Stu wasn't interested. "Hey, I'm only in the area to cover the auto show in Indianapolis. Tornadoes are a dime a dozen, unless they do a lot of damage, or hit close to Chicago. This one's pretty marginal, Jake. They'll only run something if I get exciting footage. So tell me what's exciting. Thirty seconds at most, if it airs at all."

Jake was grinning smugly. "It'll air, I guarantee it, if I tell you what I just found out."

Interest quickened in Stu's intelligent eyes. He waited while the waitress delivered his coffee, then said, "That good? If it is, of course I'll say you broke the story. Hell, I may even put you on camera. You've got a real banks-of-the-Wabash look to you, Jake. Promise to wear your Pacers cap."

"Tell me exactly what you'll say for a big story."

Stu leaned back and intoned in his best on-camera style, "Jake Shaw, writing in today's *Nichols County News*, reports that Elvis was sighted today in southern Indiana."

"That'll do for now. There's a local angle I'm checking too." He flipped his hand-scribbled story toward Stu. "Here you are. Hotter than hot off the press."

"Christ, man, you write longhand still?"

"Sure, every time a tornado knocks out the power. What do you do when there's no electricity, Stu?"

Stu laughed. "Hey, man, when there's no electricity I don't even exist. That's why we carry our own in the truck. Let's have a look, here."

He picked up the pages, squinted at Jake's opener, then let out a delighted bellow that turned heads. "Hoo-ee! Jake, my man, I think I just made co-anchor!"

"So when do I get interviewed?"

"Let's set up in front of some tornado damage. Where's the best place?"

"Mm. The place I hunkered down is as good as any. Shopping center a couple miles from here, State 822 and Chapel Road."

Stu was still puzzling over the handwriting. "My God, you were right under the damn thing!"

"Yep," Jake said modestly. "Right here in one guy you've got the big scoop, the follow-up, and the eyewitness account of the tornado."

"Okay, tell you what, I'll meet you there in forty minutes, okay?"

"Sixty minutes. I have to file this story from the next county."

"Okay. See you in an hour!" Stu gave him high five and bounded out the door, leaving Jake to pay for both coffees.

No telling when the *News* darkroom would be functioning again. He dropped his finished rolls of film at the photo place next door, reloaded, and was ready when his editor's Maxima rolled up a minute later.

Len Abbott had spent the night in his car, because every goddamn motel room in the area was taken up. He woke up creaky from the too-short, uncomfortable backseat. It was later than he usually got up. He drove to a crowded McDonald's. The lines were long for coffee and even in the men's room. He wasn't the only guy around here who was homeless at the moment. He waited his turn to shave and finally, feeling grungy, went back out to stand in line for breakfast.

A tall blond man was already in line, looking up at the posted menu. Goddammit, Clay Stollnitz! Was the guy following him or what? Len crushed his impulse to take a swing and instead slipped out the glass door behind him and got back in his car. He'd go to another diner. And if Stollnitz showed up there too he'd have proof that the guy was tailing him.

What did the bastard want? And what had happy, sweet Stephanie ever seen in him? Okay, okay, football hero, handsome face, bla bla bla—those were surface attractions, he'd tried to tell her. He'd argued with her for months about Stollnitz but she'd believed the guy's lies. And okay, back then he'd thought there was a chance she was right, that he was being a possessive, unreasonable father, and at least Stollnitz wouldn't move away from Muncie. And so he'd given in.

And now Stollnitz had killed her.

But how? The sheriff had said it wasn't violent.

Len decided to stop by Stephanie's apartment to see what the landlords had to say, and to warn them that Stollnitz was in town.

And he'd better warn the funeral home too, no telling what the guy might ask for. Then he'd go corner the sheriff again. With all the tornado damage, it would take some work to keep the law focused on justice for Stephanie.

But it was so simple. All they had to do was arrest Stollnitz. Convict him. Fry him.

Len saw his fist pounding on the dashboard. Slow down, he told himself, get your facts together. Don't let the goddamn sheriff mess up.

Twenty-One

Balanced among the branches, Marty checked to be sure the rope around the huge fallen maple was snug, ran down its slanting trunk, waved her hand at Bert Mackay behind the wheel of his tow truck, and watched nervously as the truck hauled the massive tree off Carson and Alice Rowe's house. When it was clear, Marty stepped carefully into the roofless ruin, heaped with two-by-fours, wallboard, and shingles, that had once been a home. "Mrs. Rowe?" she called. "Are you here?"

"She doesn't answer. I been calling for hours, but I couldn't get in," said Carson Rowe. He was cast in the old-fashioned John Wayne mold, a tall, rugged sixty-year-old with a cleft chin, grizzled hair, and a limp from a tractor accident.

"Well, we better have a look, sir." Marty worked her way on through the rubble. She was exhausted but still too keyed up, too angry at the brutal storm, to rest. This was the fourth house they'd worked on, this casually assembled rescue party that was searching carefully, in daylight, the same ground that Marty and the other deputies had covered so hastily last night. The groups were mostly volunteers, but where possible included a professional emergency worker like herself. Her group had also snagged Mackay and his tow truck, and was checking houses the deputies hadn't been able to search because trees or other damage blocked access.

They weren't the most efficient work crew in the world, but they laid into the smashed trees and fallen buildings with a fury that got the job done. The work was helping burn off Marty's rage at the cruel storm, and she suspected the others were energized by the same anger, the same desire to destroy the destruction.

Their highest priorities were homes of people who, like Alice Rowe, were reported missing by distraught friends or relatives like her husband Carson.

"Mrs. Rowe?" she called again. She'd seen Alice Rowe on the church supper clean-up crew just last week, tense and birdlike as she scraped the plates so energetically that Marty was surprised none of them cracked.

She strained her ears for a moan, a whimper, a knock on a wall. But there was no answer.

The house was a roofless shell, many of the walls fallen and the rest sagging. Others in the group were checking what Marty took to be the living-room area and the garage. Marty saw a crumpled refrigerator near her. On the almost-intact facing wall, the capricious winds had left a yellow stove, cheery and unhurt, with a flower-painted teakettle still sitting on one of the burners.

Near her right foot was a depression in the pile of debris. She grabbed a board, pulled it aside, and saw the corner of some steps. It was the basement stairwell, filled with rubble from the smashed house. If Alice Rowe had had any warning, that's where she'd be. Marty called down, "Mrs. Rowe?"

Still no answer. "Hey, guys!" she yelled, and Carson Rowe and two others who'd been searching the living room waded through the rubble toward her and helped her remove a big beam that blocked the stairwell. She skidded her way down to the dark basement floor and flipped on her flashlight. "Mrs. Rowe?"

Nothing.

Most of the basement ceiling was intact, but part had collapsed against the northwest wall, and there was a foul smell. Oh God. Her tired mind registered the problem at last. Marty turned and scrambled up as fast as she could, stopping Carson Rowe on his way down. "Get out of here, Mr. Rowe!" she gasped. "Gas leak!"

Hands pulled them up the last treacherous steps. Marty added, "Where's your damn propane tank?"

Carson pointed toward the debris-filled yard behind the stove wall. Grimly, the crew set out to find the shut-off valve while Marty radioed for the fire department to send someone with a gas mask to check the basement. Damn.

A television truck from Indianapolis rolled by slowly. Marty looked at it, depressed. Outsiders couldn't help Alice Rowe. They

131

couldn't even understand. Dorrie Yeager had been right—television, at best, could picture the rubble and tell one person's story. It couldn't record the vastness of the horror, nor the emotion of a whole community when so many friends and neighbors faced terrible losses.

Besides, Marty knew that as soon as the news about Hoyt Heller got out, the fickle media would forget everyone else's tragedies.

"Got it!" yelled Bob Turner from the backyard. He'd found the propane tank in the rubble and was turning the valve.

"Mr. Rowe, why don't you stay here to show the firemen where the basement is?" Marty suggested. "We'll come back after the gas is cleared."

He nodded mutely, no tears escaping his John Wayne eyes but his fists clenched.

Back in the cruiser, Marty glanced at the clock. Twenty-four hours ago she'd been haunted only by the image of Stephanie Stollnitz, her skin pink against her turquoise clothes, so peaceful that her death jarred. Now Stephanie had been joined by crueller images: Carson Rowe, struggling to contain his grief; Hoyt's limp form, still seeming to bloom with youth in his death's-face T-shirt; the injured woman at Robin Hill with white bone jutting from her shoulder; the whirling, pink-streaked, stinking winds.

Ahead of her, the tow truck turned up another farmhouse driveway. Marty followed it, called in her location, and set to work with the others pulling debris from the house. A few minutes into the job, Wes Cochran's cruiser pulled up. He looked worn, Marty thought, saggy-faced and unshaven. He probably had bags under his eyes behind those sunglasses. He got out and watched the men hitching the tow truck to the beams while she walked toward him. As soon as she was in earshot the sheriff said, "You're outta here, Hopkins."

"What?"

"The way I figure it, you morning-shift officers have been about thirty hours without sleep, unless you got a nap last night when I told you to get breakfast. Take a couple hours now, report back about one o'clock."

"Don't know if I can sleep, sir."

"Don't tell me your problems, Hopkins, just catch some z's. That's an order. Go."

"Yes sir." She went.

She stopped at the volunteer center first to see how Chrissie was doing. Dee had put the girl in charge of clearing coffee cups and

132

bringing clean ones out to the big urns, where a steady line of weary emergency workers, shaken victims, and excited volunteers were gulping it down. Chrissie too had enlisted a helper, her friend Janie Tippett. When Marty came in she was saying importantly to Janie, "Be sure to check all the tables in this hall. People take cups over to talk on the phone, or sign up for a clean-up team and then don't bring them back." Her dark eyes flicked up to meet Marty's. "Hi, Mom."

"Hi. How're you guys doing?"

"Okay."

"Ready for a break?"

"Are you on a break?"

"Sheriff's orders."

Chrissie looked around. "Well, I can't leave for long, but—see, Janie got to see where the tornado hit the roof off of K-Mart and everything."

Janie was a freckled honey-blond eleven-year-old, shorter than Chrissie because she hadn't yet started her growth spurt, but still one of the few who could keep up with Marty's active daughter. Both girls wore identical jonquil design earrings. Janie said, "I can do this for you for a few minutes. You really oughta see it. It's awesome."

"Let's go, Chrissie," Marty said. "Janie, we'll be back in fifteen minutes. Maybe twenty, the traffic's bad."

Chrissie climbed into the cruiser and buckled her seat belt. She looked like spring, Marty thought, with her leaf-green jeans, white top, and flower earrings peeking from her dark curls. Her legs were finally long enough to fit comfortably in an adult seat. Another year and a half and she'd be a teenager, Marty realized with dismay. She had no idea how to deal with a teenager.

Marty spoke over the background crackle of the radio. "So do you want to see what Janie saw near town, or do you want to see the Country Griddle? Remember, where we had breakfast a couple of times? It's in the shopping center that really got smashed."

"Yeah, the Country Griddle!" Chrissie agreed. "Janie said nobody was allowed to go there."

Marty smiled to herself. So there were advantages every now and then to having a mother with an official job, a job that Chrissie complained about as intrusive and obnoxious. Well, it was that too, Marty had to admit.

The troopers on State 37 waved her on. The road was mostly clear now and she made her way cautiously to Chapel Road. "Oh my God," said Chrissie, bolt upright in the passenger seat and squirming around to see everything. "Oh my God. Where are the trees?"

Suddenly uneasy about the effect of all this destruction on her daughter, Marty tried to lighten the mood. "Looks like a giant Weed-Eater went by, doesn't it?" She eased down the ramp on to Chapel. "Want to see where I was when it hit?"

"Yeah."

She left the cruiser at the side of the road and walked Chrissie back to the underpass. The sloping sides looked steeper now, but when she pointed up to the niche between the support girders where she and the little girls had sheltered, Chrissie scrambled up the incline to look. "Was it here?"

"Yeah." Marty climbed up to join her, glanced out under the bridge as she had before, and suddenly in her mind she saw that whirling pink-spangled dust cloud and she smelled that stink and she heard that incredible roar. She closed her eyes and braced herself against the wind.

"Mom, you okay? Hey, you okay?" Chrissie's hand was shaking her shoulder, Chrissie's anxious voice was breaking through the roar in her ears.

"Sorry. I'm real tired." Marty took a deep breath and opened her eyes. The terror on Chrissie's face snapped her back to the present. Here was her daughter, already mourning her father's absence, terrified that she'd lose her mother too. Marty hugged her. "Hey, everything's fine," she said.

"You could be dead!" Chrissie said into her shoulder.

"No way! Gotta stick around to hassle my daughter." She forced her shaky knees to stride confidently down the incline, but when she got to the cruiser her hand still trembled as she put the key in the ignition.

She drove cautiously down Chapel toward 822 and began to feel stronger. Chrissie was exclaiming every few feet about the ravaged trees and houses. When they reached the corner she fell silent. Finally she whispered, "Where's the Country Griddle?"

"Let's see. I think it was the closest to this corner. Yeah, see that stump of a pole? Its sign was up on a pole."

"Oh, yeah. Oh my God." Chrissie stared at it as though transfixed. Marty saw a slow tear roll down her cheek.

"Chrissie? Honey, what's wrong?" Marty turned off the radio.

"Nothing."

"C'mon, honey, what is it?"

134

Chrissie gestured at the bleak wreckage around them. "It's like my life. It's all just smashed."

"Your life isn't smashed, honey!" Marty protested. "You'll have a wonderful life! You're smart and tough, and all of us love you so much!"

"You and Daddy don't love me enough to get back together."

Please God, not that again, not now when she could barely hold herself together! But there sat Chrissie in the midst of the debris of her world, lip trembling, needing to talk now. Marty took a deep breath. "We both love you, Chrissie! Our problems have nothing to do with you. It's just we can't seem to live with each other."

"Yeah, I guess I know that. I've known that a long time. But you were never so mean to each other before. And I tried so hard!" The girl was sobbing openly now. "I was really really good the last six months, did you notice?"

Marty wanted to cry for her too. "You've been great, yeah. But you were never the problem, Chrissie. Daddy and I have other problems."

"And I didn't tell you the things Daddy said about you after you started the divorce. I just pretended not to hear and tried to be good. But it didn't make any difference! And today I waited for the phone at the volunteer center to call him and say everything was okay, and he just complained about you."

Damn Brad! How could he do that to his daughter? Marty said, "Chrissie, look, what you do doesn't make any difference because it's not about you. I know it's hard."

"Yeah, that's what I mean. It's like a tornado. I can't do anything about it except hide."

Marty ached for her daughter. "Maybe. But remember that I'll love you if you're good or if you're bad, and so will Daddy. You can't do anything about that either. Of course we'll be happier if you're good but we love you no matter what."

Anger flared in Chrissie's eyes. "Yeah, you said that about each other when you got married, right?"

Chrissie knew where the guilt lived. Marty closed her eyes, thinking, yes, she'd believed her marriage vows back then, dammit! Maybe Brad had too. And she'd tried, for twelve years she'd tried, raising Chrissie, staying behind when Brad said he had to go to other places to achieve his dream, encouraging him after each failure, taking this job because it paid enough to hold the family together. And after all that, they'd found that they had nothing in common any more. After all that, she could not go back to being his cheerleader. And he sure wasn't about to come back to be a cheerleader for her.

Should she have tried harder, for Chrissie's sake?

No, dammit, when she was with Brad she didn't feel whole. Chrissie deserved a whole mother. Marty said to her gently, "It's not the same with you and me. We're mother and daughter for ever, honey."

Chrissie wouldn't leave it. She pounded the seat beside her. "Till death do us part?"

It was impossible to hug her across the radio equipment between them, but Marty reached for her daughter's clenched hand. "More than that, honey. It's . . . look, maybe you won't understand, but when I was up in the girders of the underpass back there and the tornado came, I was really scared."

"Yeah." Chrissie looked at her, still angry but interested in spite of herself, and wiped her damp cheek with her free hand.

"And I had plenty of arguments with my mom, but at that moment I remembered how she protected me when my dad was drunk and throwing things around. I was trying to protect those kids, and it was like she was there protecting me again. It was like she *was* me."

"Well, I don't want to be you!"

"Good, because you're yourself. I'm myself too, I didn't mean I wasn't. I'm just saying, that, like it or not, we have a connection we can't get away from."

Chrissie digested that for a minute, then said, "Daddy never throws things."

"Your dad is a good man in lots of ways, Chrissie. But it turns out there's no way for both of us to be the people we're supposed to be and still be married to each other."

"Well, if he's so good, why do you say all those bad things about him?"

"What bad things?"

"In the divorce papers. About not supporting us, and abandoning us, and being an unfit father. I'm not stupid, Mom, I can read!" She was crying again. "You keep saying the divorce doesn't change anything because he's lived away from us for so long. But you never said those things about each other before! You were never so mean to each other!"

The truth of the child's words rang deep in Marty's bones. "Yeah, you're right. It's like writing it down makes it a lie, even when we're trying to just tell the facts."

136

"So why are you doing it?"

"Because those are the rules. The law. That's what people have to do to get divorced. Look, honey, I'll talk to Daddy about trying to be nicer, but he generally does what he wants to do, and he's pretty mad these days."

"Well, I'm mad too. Maybe I'll just go live with him."

Marty felt as though the bottom had dropped out of her universe. She forced herself to say calmly, "I'll try to talk to him, honey. Because you're right, people shouldn't be so mean."

"Yeah." Chrissie rubbed her cheek and took a shaky breath. "I better go back now. Janie can't handle the job alone."

Mother and daughter drove back cautiously through the rubble of many lives.

Twenty-Two

Jake Shaw parked his newly rented blue Geo Prizm in the crowded Holy Spirit parking lot, slung his Nikon around his neck, and hurried toward the church hall. He saw a gray Lincoln that slid into a space near the back of the lot, but didn't think about it because he was focused on finding Coral Turley. If she was at the church, he'd arrange to talk to her after his TV taping with Stu.

The church's parking-lot door was topped by a hastily lettered "Volunteer Center" sign. As he approached, a young woman dressed in black headed him off. Short black vest, skinny black leather pants on a nice pair of legs. Black boots, black gauzy scarf tight around her neck. Big beautiful eyes in a pale face, but the nose ring and a wild explosion of corkscrew curls spooked him a little. She said, "You're the reporter for the *News*, right?"

"Sure am."

"D'you know any TV people?"

"I might. Listen, you're not—you *are* Dee Turley's daughter, aren't you?"

She put her fists on her hips, on the edge of belligerence now. She wore metal cuff bracelets, he saw, and the black studded leather vest had chains and metal zippers with huge teeth. She managed to look simultaneously like a sex kitten and a soul-snatching harpy. Whatever had happened to the pretty girls in flowered dresses that Jake remembered from his youth? For that matter, what had happened to the sweet, unpainted Coral Turley he'd seen with Dee just an hour ago?

She said, "Yeah, I'm Coral Turley. I'm a singer and songwriter with Lily Pistols. I'm Hoyt Heller's lover and I can tell you about his last hours. Are you ready to deal?"

So that was it. Jake's heart sank as he saw the story of the century slipping away from him. "The *News* doesn't have money for—"

She shook her firecracker curls impatiently. "Not money. I want television coverage. Right away."

Jake felt a grin spreading across his face. "That I can do. You give me the story and I'll lead you straight to where they're shooting."

She smiled, a smile that might light up the world, then added uncertainly, "Uh—you got a car? I have to leave my mom's van here."

Now Jake could see the timid girl behind the brazen leather and metal. He said, "Yeah, a little rental car. The tornado smashed my car."

"Wow! Mine too! Sort of. It's still in a ditch. Won't be able to get a tow truck for days."

"Yeah. Let's go find a place to talk, okay?" He glanced at his watch. Stu would just have to wait a couple more minutes. He asked Coral, "May I take a couple of pictures of you?"

Her hand was instantly on his Nikon, blocking the lens. "Not here. Not at the church. Let's take pictures with tornado damage behind."

"Okay, that'll be better." He hid his amusement at her precocious media savvy and gestured toward the Geo Prizm. They started toward it. "Tell me, Coral, how did you get into Lily Pistols?"

"I had a summer job at Asphodel Springs resort," she explained. "Lily Pistols did a gig in Bloomington and they were on their way to Evansville, and they stopped for lunch. They told us it was Skell's birthday—he's the lead guitar—and they, you know, flirted with us. Well, I hammed it up a little. See, I'm a songwriter and I had this gloomy version of 'Happy Birthday.' How you're a year closer to the grave, you know, that kind of thing. Well, they loved it but they drove off like any other customer and I didn't think anything of it. Then two days later they—sent for me." A shadow darkened her splendid eyes. "Anyway, pretty soon I was singing backup and writing songs for them and so forth."

138

"You say they sent for you. Your mother took it pretty hard, as I remember. Reported you kidnapped."

Her eyes were opaque now, her mouth resentful. "I'm not going to talk about that, okay? She didn't understand. Anyway, I thought you wanted to talk about Hoyt."

"Okay, sure," said Jake agreeably. That was in fact the main thing he wanted to talk about. But there were interesting undercurrents here, and he promised himself he'd come back to it later. For now, he asked, "Hoyt Heller was found near a tornado shelter, right? Was he trying to get in?"

"Hoyt lived on the edge," Coral said, pausing on the passenger side and looking at Jake across the top of the car. "He danced with death. He wouldn't take shelter, not Hoyt. Did you know he has a new song called 'Deathwind!'?"

"'Deathwind.'"

"Yeah. I'll sing it for you sometime." A breeze picked up the gauzy black scarf and it waved beside her like a dark banner as she opened the door of his car.

The stream of people moving past Wes's desk seemed endless. The station's communication capabilities were not as up-to-date as they'd be if the County Council would pass his budget requests. But they were still the best in the county, and until the Red Cross got its act together, coordinating this emergency was in his lap. Poor old sunken-eyed Foley, the dispatcher, was dealing with all the emergency workers, local and from nearby counties. Wes was directing people who showed up in person—some to the Red Cross information center, some to the ham radio set-up, some to Dee Turley's volunteer center—always trying to protect Foley from their questions. The station was especially short-handed now, because he'd sent the first shift workers home for some rest. As soon as they reported back, he and Foley could catch some z's too.

He needed rest. Half an hour ago he'd had to take a nitroglycerin tablet, the first one in months. And he was about to nod off right now while some retired cop from Kentucky tried to pull rank and get a personal tour to check on his brother.

Wes roused himself and said, "We'll get to it soon as we can, sir. You've worked emergencies, you know we have to take care of the injured first. Okay?"

The man moved on, grumbling, and Wes glanced at the next person in line. Oh shit. He was rumpled this morning, as baggy-eyed as Foley, but unlike most of the people here he'd managed to shave. Same bruised and angry eyes as yesterday. He said, "Sheriff Cochran, you haven't arrested him!"

Wes took off his Stetson, smoothed back his hair, replaced the hat. "Mr. Abbott, we haven't forgotten your daughter, believe me. But you can see we've got a major emergency on our hands right now."

He thumped his hand on Wes's desk. "The radio said there were only two deaths from the tornado. Well, my daughter is dead too!"

"Yes sir, and we're working on it. The Muncie police are working with us—"

He snorted. "I talked to them. They say they can't prove he was out of town. Or in town, either. They say it's up to you. And I talked to her landlord this morning, and he said you hadn't been by, only your deputy!"

"Look, Mr. Abbott, our department has a real good record of nailing murderers. If the coroner tells us it was murder we'll get him. But right now things aren't normal."

"Normal! Stephanie is dead, Sheriff Cochran. Dead! That will never, ever be normal!"

Wes closed his eyes, rubbed his face. He was right, of course. Wes lived with the daily knowledge that his son Billy was dead. But it never seemed normal. Familiar, yes, but never normal, never okay.

Abbott said, "Dammit, do I have to get a gun, waste him myself?"

"Mr. Abbott, were you ever in the service?"

"I had a tour in Nam, yeah," he said suspiciously.

"Well, then, I don't have to tell you how things are in a mass casualty situation. All of us right now have to try to prevent those two tornado deaths from turning into three, or four, or five. We'll get back to the other investigation as fast as we can."

He looked at Wes with tired, angry eyes. "That's what I figured. You've triaged her out of your life."

"You know that's not true, sir."

His lips tightened. "Well, I'll be back."

Wes knew there would be no peace until he could tell Abbott what had happened to his daughter. And dammit, the man was right, that was what Wes's job was supposed to be about. With renewed determination to get this crisis behind him, he turned again to the line of victims.

Marty sat up foggily, stumbled across her bedroom to the old wind-up alarm clock on the dresser, and punched the button to stop the ringing. So she'd fallen asleep after all. Amazing. She remembered lying for what seemed like hours, images sputtering through her mind: Hoyt Heller and Stephanie Stollnitz, Alice Rowe's crushed house and Chrissie's tears, bleeding people and broken trees. Though she remembered, almost, a couple of coherent thoughts just before dropping off. What? She struggled to resurrect them, but discovered only that she had a dull headache and aching shoulders and three broken fingernails, and a brief fifteen minutes to get back to work.

No electricity for the coffeemaker. She put water on the gas stove, took a one-minute hot shower and an aspirin, got into her uniform again, and remembered one of her pre-nap thoughts, a way to approach Brad. Not enough time now, but— She picked up the phone. Still dead. She shrugged, splashed hot water into a mug, stirred in the instant coffee, and carried it out to the cruiser.

At the station a set of first-shifters, all looking as weary as Marty felt, prepared to relieve the even wearier second-shifters. Poor old Foley, she thought, watching the dispatcher limp toward his locker. There was no love lost between her and the dispatcher, who seemed to think the presence of a woman in the department was a personal insult to all red-blooded American males. Still, she felt sorry for the old guy today.

She saw rangy Grady Sims and asked, "Did they find Alice Rowe in that basement?"

"No, she's still missing."

"Really?"

"Yeah. Fire department looked around pretty good but only found a couple of dead mice in all that gas. So old Carson Rowe got a bunch of buddies and they're stomping through the woods now, there where it's all tore up."

Marty shook her head sadly. "God, I hope she turns up soon. I feel for the guy."

The sheriff levered himself up from his desk. He looked older to Marty, weary lines in his face, a slump to his shoulders. He glanced at the long line of people waiting to see him and beckoned the deputies over to give them their assignments. Marty's job was to relieve him at the desk so he could get into the field. After the others trooped out Marty asked, "You tired, sir?"

"You're no vision of freshness yourself, Hopkins!" he snapped. Then, relenting, "I'm okay. Worst thing is realizing how much has to be done. Hard to get a handle on it."

"Yeah, everybody's pitching in real good, but there's sure a lot to do."

"Tell me about it," the sheriff grunted, and waved her into his chair to face the long line of questioners.

Twenty-Three

Coral had wowed the news guys, she could feel it. Old Jake Whatsis was in the palm of her hand. Maybe too much, now he was trying to act like her father or something, real possessive. The black smoothie, Stu from Chicago, was coming on to her, nothing blatant but lots of extra winks and twinkles when he spoke to her. Fine with her. He'd do a better job on her story.

She stood with Stu in front of the blasted remains of the Country Griddle restaurant. Stu's assistant had shooed away the people who were looking through the rubble, promising to interview them in a moment. Stu directed the camera to a position where the maximum damage would show behind them.

Jake said, "Don't tire her out, Stu. She's been through a lot."

Stu nodded impatiently, put on a serious face and said, "Coral, the entire nation is shocked to learn of the death of a young, vital, well-loved star like Hoyt Heller. Tell us, as someone who was close to him, what was he— Oh shit." Stu pointed the mike down and coughed. "Hey, anybody got a soda? My throat's getting dusty. Want a soda, Coral?"

"Sure. Sounds good."

But the only thing Stu's assistant could find in the van was someone's apple juice. "Worse than dust," Stu grumbled.

"Well, none of these places are open." The cameraman pointed at the wrecked shopping center.

"I'll go pick something up at the Save-More. If I take the back roads I should be back in fifteen minutes," Jake said, then paused. "Save-More's probably lost its electricity like everybody else. So they won't be refrigerated."

"Right now I want wet. Cold's not important," Stu said. "Thanks, Jake. Coral and I will talk through a couple topics, then when you get back we'll wet our whistles and do the real interview."

Jake nodded. Coral watched him drive off in the little rental car.

Shit, she was tired of waiting, why couldn't they get on with it? She kicked at a cracked plastic bucket that lay in the rubble.

One of the onlookers approached Stu, a woman with tired hazel eyes. "I brought a six-pack of Coke," she said. "You want some?"

"Bless you, kind lady!" Stu exclaimed. "Who are you, and why are you here, doing good deeds?"

She laughed. "I'm Karen Fairleigh. I own the Country Griddle. That pile of sticks over there."

"Oh God, sorry about that. Karen, I'll want to talk to you in a few minutes too, if you're willing."

"Sure. People ought to know what happened to the people who live here." She glanced resentfully at Coral.

Like nothing had happened to Hoyt? Coral pointed at the rubble and shouted, "Listen, lady, you may have lost your little diner. But the whole world lost Hoyt Heller! He's one of the greats! He turned music in a whole new direction!"

"Well, my diner was important to me," said Karen Fairleigh, tears welling, and walked off.

Coral felt a pang of guilt. But as she was turning away, she noticed that the camera was still on her, and changed the movement to a slow spiral collapse into a crumpled lotus position, her face bowing down into her hands.

"Did you get that? Did you get that?" she heard Stu whisper excitedly to his cameraman.

It was time. She reached for the cracked bucket that lay in the wreckage before her and began to slap it in the complex drum-rhythms of the song. In a moment, she threw back her head and looked at the camera, eyelids half-lowered. "Make love to the mike and the camera," Hoyt always said. He'd sure as shit been better at that than at making love to a woman. As she stood up again Coral felt the old rage surge through her body, through her braced legs, through her drumming fingers.

And through her voice as she sang, "The sunlight gleamed on the blackbird's flight when I searched for you, but the deathwind blew. Baby, love is the light but its sun sets too. Now all I can see is the wind of death, the wind with dark on its breath."

She missed Skell's arrangement, the smoky chords spiraling around "death" and "breath," but the song still felt true, achingly true. Pain made her voice huskier, the beat more urgent. "The meadow was warm, the blossoms alight when I reached for you, but the deathwind blew. Baby, love is so warm but it freezes too, and all I can feel is the wind of death, the wind with ice on its breath."

Tears stung Coral's eyes, angry tears or sad tears, she didn't know which. She cried, "The air was fragrant, the poppies bright when my lips touched you, but the deathwind blew. Baby, love is the answer but love dies too, and all I can smell is the wind of death, the wind with blood on its breath."

She bowed her head slowly, letting the corkscrew curls fall over her face, letting the drum-patter fade.

There was a little pause. "Christ," said Stu. "Coral, baby, you're a natural. Did you get all that, Biff?"

"Yup." The cameraman nodded.

Stu cleared his throat. "That's the tornado song you were telling us about?"

"Tornado, whatever. It's called 'Deathwind' and it'll be on the new album. In memory of Hoyt."

"Look, it's okay for us to use the footage, right? No copyright problems?"

Coral shrugged. "The label usually okays promo stuff."

"Terrific!" Stu, enchanted, messed around for another hour, shots of her doing this and that, questions about Hoyt, about the band, about love and death. Finally he looked at his watch, spent a couple of minutes with Karen on losing her restaurant, and said, "Guess old Jake decided not to come back. Need a ride, Coral? Maybe lunch?"

"A ride to Bloomington, yeah. And if you can get me to a working phone, I'll make that call to the label for you."

He pulled out a cell phone and Coral grinned as she took it. She didn't need Jake any more. She'd be singing on Chicago TV tonight. From here it was straight to the top.

Queen of the Bones. Yes!

It took Wes an hour and a half to tour the damaged areas one more time. Professional crews with much better equipment than the volunteer clean-up crews were appearing from a dozen counties to work on pipes, roads, and trees. Dee's volunteer center at the Holy Spirit Church was rolling along like clockwork, and the Red Cross had finally gotten geared up to work on the damage-assessment forms necessary for help over a longer haul. Wes decided things were enough under control for a nap. He went back to the station to tell them he'd be off for a couple hours.

But Hopkins said, "Doc Altman's waiting in your office, sir."

A couple of people in the line shouted, "Sheriff!" as he walked by.

He didn't pause, just waved and said, "Hey Vernon. Hey Pete. Help you in a minute," and went into the private office. "Howdy, Doc. What's happening?"

Doc rocked back in the scuffed visitor's chair. He was at his weediest, clothes rumpled and hair frizzy, but behind the round spectacles his eyes shone like spotlights. "Up all night on this," he began.

"Yeah, tell me about it," Wes grunted as he sat down.

"Yeah. Well, it's what I suspected." There was triumph in his voice. He pulled a folded paper from his pocket and tossed it on the desk in front of Wes. "Here you are. We'll print it out all pretty for the official release, but I thought it'd help you to have a copy of the rough draft now."

Wes unfolded the paper. "It'd help more if I could read your chicken-scratches," he said. "This is on Hoyt Heller, right? Cause of death—" He frowned.

"Carbon monoxide poisoning," said Doc.

"Are you kidding me? The guy had a hunk of sheet-metal in his neck!"

"Not for me to say," Doc said piously, "but Deputy Hopkins pointed out the footprints around the tornado shelter. We got photos of them before the rain washed them away. The shelter was a snug little hole. And there was a kerosene lamp in there."

"So you say he— Wait a minute." Wes got up, stuck his head out the door, and yelled, "Hopkins! In here a moment." He held the door for her, then sank back into his chair. She stood against the wall. Wes repeated, "Hopkins found the guy in the open air. Not in the shelter. Right, Hopkins?"

"Yes sir." She shot a curious glance at Doc.

Doc said, "What happens sometimes is, instead of passing out as usual, they realize something's wrong. Try to crawl into the clear. But it takes a while for the carboxyhemoglobin to leave the blood-stream—"

"The what?" Wes asked.

"Carbon monoxide poisons us because it combines with our red blood cells better than oxygen does, over two hundred times better. So when sixty percent of your red cells are clogged up with carbon monoxide, only forty percent are carrying the oxygen your other cells need. If you get back into the open air, the percentage of red cells carrying carbon monoxide decreases, but slowly. If you're at sixty percent like Mr. Heller, it'll take hours of breathing to reduce your level to thirty percent, hours more to get to fifteen percent,

145

and meanwhile more and more of your body's cells are starved for oxygen. So even if we get victims to hospitals, they often keep on getting worse and die."

Wes rubbed his tired face. "Okay. You're suggesting he went into the shelter, lit the kerosene lamp—isn't a lamp pretty small?"

Doc shrugged. "Shelter's small too. Spend enough time in there with the lamp burning and it'll do the job."

"So Heller figures out that something's wrong, crawls out a few feet, passes out, and dies." Wes placed both hands on the front edge of the desk, pushed himself back, and glared at Doc. "Hell, Doc, this story won't help. We'll still have the conspiracy theories and the murder-by-alien theories and the axe murderer theories and the mysterious woman in black theories."

"Sure," said Doc cheerfully. "And I bet some people will even say it was the tornado. But that's your problem and Art Pfann's, not mine."

"Yeah. Shit. Hopkins, got any questions?"

"The siding cut his neck after he died, then?"

"Right. You were there. Not much bleeding for a cut carotid."

Hopkins said thoughtfully, "So you say he was in that little shelter—"

"That's for others to decide," Doc protested. "All I can say is, he died of carbon monoxide poisoning, with post-mortem injury consistent with being hit by that piece of metal siding."

"Yes sir." Hopkins was in a bulldog mood, Wes saw. She pressed ahead. "He's in that little shelter, realizes he's about to pass out, gets the door up, crawls out, closes the door—"

"Closes it?" Wes asked.

"It was closed when I got there, sir."

"Could it fall shut behind him?"

"Or get blown shut," she said, her gray eyes serious. "Maybe. Dr. Altman, is it unusual for someone with carbon monoxide poisoning to be able to crawl that far?"

"It's not common, but it happens. Not in suicides, of course, they're not trying to get away. In the accidental deaths, the common thing is they'll go into a coma, linger from a few minutes to a few days, and then die. They die even though the actual blood level of carboxyhemoglobin has dropped to near-normal. But a few manage to get out before the coma hits."

"I found him two or three hours after the tornado. If he could crawl out, why wasn't he just unconscious when I found him?" Hopkins asked. Wes could see the effort it took to keep her voice steady. He knew the real question was, could I have saved him somehow? He sympathized. It was real hard to lose one.

Doc said, "There's a lot of variation. Could be that his struggle to get out speeded up the process, used up his few reserves of oxygen." He squinted at Hopkins and his voice softened. "Almost a blessing, really. If he'd lived, he would've been a vegetable."

"Yes sir. Thank you, sir." But there was still a line between her brows.

Wes said, "You're not happy with this story, Hopkins?"

"Okay, sir, it's possible he crawled out. But it's also possible that somebody pulled him out of the shelter. Pulled him out, closed the door, and ran off to get help. Or something."

"But why didn't they come back?" Wes demanded.

"Lots of possibilities. Sir, let's talk to Coral Turley again."

Wes nodded. The Turley girl had come back to the scene. But she hadn't said anything about being there before. He said, "Okay, Hopkins, no big rush, but soon as we can take a breather from the tornado work, talk to the Turley girl, and cruise by the Matthews pig farm again and take a look at that lamp and anything else that produces carbon monoxide."

They spent another couple minutes chewing it over, but no one came up with anything more. Wes sent Hopkins back to her post, said good-bye to Doc, checked with Adams for messages—no new emergencies—and headed out once again. Not for his nap, not yet, but to tell Art Pfann what Doc had said.

As the door closed behind him, he heard a phone ring.

Communication at last! He joined in the general hurrah for the phone company.

Twenty-Four

By four P.M. Thursday Marty felt as though she'd been working on tornado problems for weeks. It hadn't even been twenty-four hours. The sheriff returned from his break to relieve her at the desk. He looked weary still, but was shaved and wearing a fresh uniform. "Okay, Hopkins, I want my sit-down job back. Anything I should know?"

"I heard Adams briefing you as you drove in, sir. Nothing to add, except for that accident victim in the rented car."

"Oh, yeah. The one the Boy Scouts took to Mercy Hospital? The doctors said he was pretty banged up, I recall."

"Yeah. The Bloomington Avis office just called with info on the car. It was rented to the reporter. Jake Shaw."

"Jake! Shit!"

"Yes sir. They got him stabilized, I guess you heard that from Adams. I don't know any more. Mason might, he took the call, but by the time he got there the scoutmaster had driven Jake to the hospital. Do you want me to stop by?"

"I'll be going by anyway a little later. Right now, you and Adams take twenty minutes, grab a bite to eat. Then I want Adams back here and you out at that Robin Hill trailer court for a couple hours till Sims gets back. After that find out where the Turley girl is and check the Matthews farm again. We need to know how her boyfriend gassed himself."

Marty nodded and went out to the square.

She was starving but Chrissie's tears that morning still haunted her. The kid was right, the lawyers were encouraging her and Brad to cut each other up. There had to be a better way. She'd use her twenty minutes to call Brad.

Phone service still hadn't been restored in some areas and there were long lines at the drugstore and at the diner, so she crossed the square to Reiner's Bakery. Melva was baking muffins—her sister Dee needed more at the volunteer center, she said, so in addition to doing both her and Aunt Vonnie's jobs, she was fixing extras. She told Marty to use the phone by the back door.

He should be home, Marty thought as she listened to it ring. With a night show, he didn't have to be at the radio station until seven thirty. He got off maybe two thirty A.M.—that's when he called to hassle Marty—and slept late every day. And he expected to get Chrissie off to school on time?

C'mon, be fair, Hopkins, she scolded herself. You have your share of late nights too. It was Aunt Vonnie who kept Chrissie's life orderly. Aunt Vonnie was the one who should get custody. What a depressing thought.

When he picked up she said, "Brad, it's Marty."

"Is Chrissie okay?" His voice was anxious. Shoot, he did love the kid.

"Yeah. Yeah, she's fine. She said she called you."

148

"Yeah, but she sounded so scared. About you. Said she hadn't seen you."

"Well, when I stopped by the house last night she was asleep, and I had to go right out again."

"So you went right out and left your daughter all alone to face a tornado? Hey, we've got you now, Deputy. What kind of mother leaves her kid alone in the middle of a major disaster?"

"Brad, you know it wasn't that way!"

"Tell it to the judge, Marty! We've got you now!"

It's a game, she reminded herself, a game. Even when your secret goal is to get out of the game. So if that's the way he was going to be, that's the way she'd play it. She took a deep breath and said, "I don't think so, Brad. I can spend as much money as you to prove she got excellent care."

"Spend, spend, spend! God, Marty, don't you even care about the kid's future? You're driving us both to the poorhouse."

"If you spend money to bring up new issues, I have to spend money to refute them."

"You know, Marty, your problem is you're so short-sighted. Swear to God, you can't see a day beyond tomorrow."

This from the guy who'd ignored years of her attempts to get him to notice the problems in their marriage. Marty damped down her anger and focused on the goal. She said, "I guess we'll both spend what we have to. Anyway, there's no cheaper way."

"Sure there is! Remember, we suggested mediation? That's cheaper!"

"Oh, that." Marty let herself sound scornful. "My lawyer says to steer clear of that, because you'd just sweet-talk something through."

"No, he says that because he sees his cash cow drying up. That's why he doesn't want you to do it."

"Really? But—"

"Yes, of course really!" He was getting wound up now. "Your problem is you've never understood finances. But just look at how much they charge per hour! Anyone but you can see the mediator's a better deal. And just as good as lawyers, because the lawyers check out the agreement afterward, make sure nobody gets screwed."

"I don't know, Brad. The mediator guy's way down in Evansville, right?"

"Yeah, that's just like you, Marty! You never think of how long it takes me to get from Memphis to Dunning. You only care about your own convenience."

"I don't want to go to Evansville to save fifty bucks."

"Jesus, Marty! It would save thousands!"

Marty let a beat pass, then said slowly, "Well—look, I want to save money too, you know that. But I don't want to be railroaded into anything. You've always been the talker, Brad. I mean, God, that's how you earn your living! I feel more confident with Chip presenting my side."

"Yeah, I know. You're willing to spend your daughter's education money on your mouthpiece!"

"That's not true, Brad!"

"It is true, if you'd bother to think about it."

"Look, if it's really that much cheaper, I'll try the damn mediation!"

"Well, that shows some sense, finally!"

"Wait! I mean, if it's not cheaper, or if it's not fair, I won't want to—"

"Hey, don't back out now!"

"Well, it better save money, is all I can say."

"It will, it will! I'll call up and get the process started. Bye, kitten."

Marty hung up too, drained and apprehensive. He'd bought it. She'd done what she set out to do. She'd gotten Brad committed to mediation, gotten him away from the damn finger-pointing lawyers. Not that she felt victorious—it was scary to think of going up against Brad without Chip. But it was the only way they'd have a chance of working together to get out of this mess.

And dammit, they owed it to Chrissie to try to work together.

Don't fret about it now, she told herself. You have to go help out at Robin Hill Trailer Court, and then find Coral Turley to figure out what happened to Hoyt Heller, and then if you still don't know, go look at the tornado shelter on the Matthews farm. Puzzling over Heller's death, she accepted the muffin Melva offered and headed for Robin Hill.

Jake Shaw woke up to a glare of pain. Through it he could make out blinding fluorescent lights, brilliant white ceiling, dazzling white walls. Something else white was pressing him down. Was it the man with the mustache? Panicked, he tried to move his arms. More pain, but no movement. He tried to yell and couldn't open his mouth any further. But he did manage to say "Unh!"

"Hello, honey, take it easy now." A pleasant-faced black woman in nurse's whites moved into view and adjusted a drip bag. "It's good to see you waking up."

"Unh?" asked Jake.

"Just relax, don't try to talk. You're in Mercy Hospital. You had a little car accident but Dr. Collins fixed you up again. I guess you don't know what we did, do you? Your jaw is wired shut for a little while, and you've got—"

The woman's smile receded into the glare. Jake didn't fight it. He slept again.

"So what are we doing here, Grady?" Marty asked Deputy Sims when she pulled into Robin Hill.

"Just helping. Guarding against looters, too, but I haven't seen one. So I just keep things cool. We've got some short fuses here."

"Okay. See you in a couple hours." And don't be late, she added silently, itching to ask Coral Turley more questions.

She left her cruiser and hiked into the trailer court. Still looked like a bomb site. Then her heart gave a happy lurch. Romey was helping a group of volunteers stack twisted pieces of trailers into a Dennis Rent-All pickup. His eyes smiled a hello but he kept on working. The residents were sifting through the rubble, or staring at it. Marty recognized the plump midwife, who had found some laundry baskets and was picking up muddy bits of clothing. The brunette woman who'd had the ghastly shoulder injury wore a splint and bandages now as she hunted for her pocketbook. "It's got to be here," she muttered. "The blender was here."

People moved stiffly, and some cried, but most seemed to be finding items to save. Only one old woman, dazed, sat unmoving in a bent lawn chair, her liver-spotted face turned toward the southwest.

Little Ashley spotted Marty and edged away nervously. Marty took off her Stetson and asked, "Hi, honey, what's wrong?"

Ashley scurried back toward her mother, who was picking up some battered saucepans. The woman glanced back, her bandaged forehead gleaming white, and said, "Yeah, I told you she was the fuckin' law, Ashley." She took the cigarette from her mouth and added grudgingly, "Thanks, ma'am. Ashley tells me you took care of her and Jessie in the tornado. I had a real bad half-hour there before you brought them back." The blue eyes blinked and for an instant Marty glimpsed the terror and bleakness the woman had suffered in those moments.

She said, "I was glad to help, ma'am. I have a little girl of my own."

"Yeah." Ashley's mother had her defenses up again. "C'mon, girls, go get the raincoat she loaned you. Lady wants it back."

"No, that's not why I came," Marty protested. "I'm supposed to be here helping you!"

"Yeah, everybody's helping now, thanks a load." She waved her cigarette at the volunteers. "Where's everybody gonna be when Ashley and Jessie need new shoes for school? Who's gonna help then? Not you. Not all those folks driving by, gawking at us, like we're zoo animals or something."

"Yeah, it's tough." The woman was probably on welfare, and Marty could remember how hard it was to make ends meet on welfare. "Have you been to the volunteer center at Holy Spirit Church? They've got a lot of disaster-relief stuff."

"Disaster relief! Man, my whole life is a fuckin' disaster!" She puffed fiercely on her cigarette.

"Can I maybe drive you to the center later? I'd like to help," Marty said.

The weary blue eyes met Marty's with the first glimmer of humor she'd shown. "Help? You can't. Not unless you're giving out magic wands. I thought there was supposed to be a wizard. What the hell happened to Oz?"

Marty laughed. "Maybe we're all wearing the wrong color shoes."

She turned away, replacing her Stetson, because she'd heard angry voices across the way, two middle-aged guys in grimy T-shirts. "That's my toaster!" said the wiry one with the curly hair.

"No, it's mine! Black and Decker, see?" the balding one yelled.

Marty grabbed the curly-haired man's cocked arm before his fist could connect with Baldy. "Hey, guys, take it easy!"

"This asshole's trying to steal my toaster!" Curly said.

If she had to call for backup it'd take hours for them to get here. She said, "Look, just take it easy. Maybe there's two toasters here somewhere."

Baldy wasn't having any. "This guy's been in jail for burglary, and he says *I'm* stealing?"

"Take it easy," Marty repeated.

"Hey everybody!" Romey yelled. "We found a six-pack! Let's party!"

"I got popcorn!" sang out the midwife. "And pretzels!"

Ashley's mother set a big bottle of Coke on the tailgate of Romey's half-loaded pickup. "Here's something for the kids."

Someone produced foam cups, someone else a bottle of Four Roses. The Robin Hill residents grouped themselves around the

152

tailgate. The two would-be fighters, macho honor saved by the diversion, left Marty and ambled over to join them. Behind their backs she thanked Romey with a thumbs-up.

A couple of the volunteers with IU T-shirts looked up from their stacked branches, frowning.

"Whatsa matter?" Ashley's mom yelled at them. "We're having open house! You ever seen a house this open?"

The Robin Hill group guffawed. The volunteers grinned uneasily and went back to work.

Marty eased over to stand between Curly and Baldy just in case.

"Hey, you guys know that old song, 'Alive Alive-Oh'?" Romey asked the party group, waving a pretzel for emphasis.

Ashley's mother nodded. "Yeah, the girls learned it in school. About fuckin' cockles and mussels. Sounds dirty to me."

Romey laughed. "Well, I've got a new way to sing it." Muscular and nimble, he jumped up onto the tailgate and sang, "'Alive alive oh, alive alive oh, singin', "Fuck you, tornado! I'm alive alive oh!"'"

Laughter and cheers. Romey said, "All together now! 'Alive alive oh . . .'"

Standing as a buffer between Baldy and Curly, Marty saw that Ashley's mother was singing along lustily. So was Ashley.

So was Marty. Watching Romey sing, she could think of nothing in the world she'd enjoy more than an hour in his bed, forgetting the world's problems and her own.

Too bad that as soon as Sims returned from his break, she had to find Coral Turley and try to figure out how Hoyt Heller had died.

Twenty-Five

The Eagle loaded in the Thunderbolt, just in case. It was always best to be prepared. No more mistakes, no dragging bodies around and letting them get on your nerves, so young and dead. He'd be like the fighter pilots, or the reconnaissance pilots who flew into storms and out again. Had to be ready to grab opportunity when it knocked. Like yesterday. He'd waited at the driveway until the storm had passed, and when the tornado shelter door began to open, he'd gunned the motor and driven right into it, knocking down the young figure within. And then he'd parked right on top of the shelter door, so the gook couldn't get out again. He'd grabbed his opportunity, found the perfect plan.

Two to go, two who'd insulted him, two who didn't know the Eagle's value.

She'd known his value once. She'd smiled at him and made his joints melt with joy. Now she looked through him, didn't see him at all. But he'd make her smile at him again. He was already halfway there.

Two to go.

Wes Cochran stood awkwardly by the hospital bed, Stetson in hand, sorry to see how banged-up Jake Shaw was. Dr. Collins had told Wes that Jake was doing well, considering, and that he'd been lucky that the scoutmaster who'd found him hadn't waited around for one of the overworked ambulances to get there. True, bouncing along in the scoutmaster's backseat had taken its toll on Jake's broken and inadequately splinted arms, but the scoutmaster had managed to stop much of the bleeding and the hospital had cleaned out the bloody airways. "He's doing good now," his nurse agreed. "He can wiggle his toes and he's breathing okay. Liquid diet, of course."

"Can he hear me?" Wes asked her.

"I think so. His left eye is bandaged but his right eye looks around and he can sort of grunt when you talk to him. He's on a lot of painkiller, of course. May not stay awake long." She headed for the door, adding, "Gotta go. It's busy days here."

Wes nodded and looked again at the bandaged bundle in the hospital bed. The mouth was slightly open, held rigid with wires, and the eye he could see was closed and bruised. Well, give it a try. He stepped closer to the bed and said loudly, "Hey, Jake, that was some door you banged into."

The unbandaged eyelid flickered, and Jake's blue eye gazed up at him dully.

"Can you hear me, Jake?"

There was a beat before Wes heard a faint, "Uh-huh."

"I don't know if you can see me very well. It's Sheriff Cochran."

"Uh-huh."

"First of all, they tell me you're coming through this real well. You're a tough old buzzard, Jake. Another guy woulda been taken out by what you've been through."

154

"Uh."

"Second reason I'm here, we've got some questions. You remember you were driving a little Geo Prizm you rented from Avis?"

"Uh-huh."

"Good. Well, at first glance it looks like your car didn't make the turn and you went into the sinkhole there at a high rate of speed."

"Unh-unh!" Jake protested.

"Yeah, we're thinking there's more to the story. I just talked to Deputy Mason, and he says he spotted a dent on the front fender. Looking at how the car landed, he couldn't figure how the sinkhole could have done it."

"Uh-huh! Uh-huh!" Jake's eye seemed brighter to Wes.

"We thought there might've been another car involved."

"Uh-huh! Uh-huh!"

"Getting warm, am I? What'd he do, crowd you off the road?"

"Uh-huh."

"And then left you in that damn sinkhole? Didn't he stop to see how you were?"

"Uh-huh."

"He did? Well, if he stopped, why the hell did he leave you there? Wait a minute—did he steal anything?"

"Uh-huh! Uh-huh!"

"Goddamn! We'll catch the skunk who did this, Jake. He took your wallet?"

"Unh-unh."

"He didn't? What else—your camera!"

"Uh-huh! Uh-huh!" The feeble grunts sounded excited now.

Wes laid his hat on the bed and took out his notebook. Old Jake was coming through for him. He asked, "Okay. Next question is, who did it? Did you get a look at the driver?"

"Uh-huh."

"Do you know his name?"

"Unh-unh."

"Didn't figure it was one of your buddies. Okay, Jake, let's work on a description. Is he a white guy?"

"Uh-huh."

"Is he taller than six feet?"

"Unh-unh."

"Taller than five-ten?"

"Uh-huh. Unh-unh."

"No and yes? Oh, I see, he's pretty close to five-ten?"

"Uh-huh."

Who said kiddie games like twenty questions were foolish? Wes learned that the guy weighed about one-sixty and was maybe forty years old. But Jake was tiring. Wes said, "Hang in there a minute for me, Jake. Hair color, now. Brown?"

"Uh-huh."

"Brown hair. Any facial hair?"

"Uh-huh."

"Beard?"

"Unh-unh." Jake's eyelid was drooping.

"Mustache?"

"Uh-huh."

"Did you notice his eye color?"

"Unh-unh."

"Jake, you're doing great. Just stick with me a few more minutes here. Shirt color, now. Was it—"

"Unh-unh. Uh-huh."

"You don't know his shirt color. Was he wearing a hat of any kind?"

"Unh-unh." Suddenly the eye opened wide. "Uh-huh! Uh-huh!"

"Good, let's work on the hat. Cowboy style?"

"Unh-unh."

"Baseball cap? Like your Pacers cap?"

"Uh-huh! Uh-huh!" It was real hard to tell but Wes thought he was excited.

"Was it a Pacers cap?"

"Uh-huh! Uh-huh!"

"Okay, we're doing great. Guy's Caucasian, brown hair and mustache, forty years old, five-ten, about one-sixty, wearing a Pacers cap. Is that right?"

"Unh-unh." Jake's eye closed wearily.

"No?" There was no response. Wes sighed. "Tell you what, Jake, I'll get the state evidence technicians to check out the car real careful before we return it to Avis, and you and I will work on the description some more tomorrow."

There was still no answer, only the hoarse breathing. Damn, he still hadn't learned anything about the other guy's car. But considering Jake's condition, the interview had been surprisingly successful. And catching a reckless driver and thief who hadn't actually killed his victim had to be lower priority than the tornado relief effort or the Hoyt Heller case or even Stephanie Stollnitz's mystifying death. Wes said, "See you soon, pardner," and walked out quietly.

*   *   *

156

The cold northern air mass still pressed south, and the moist gulf air, halfhearted now but still powerful, continued to resist. And so, again, a churning, crackling thunderhead built up over southern Indiana.

Far below, worried eyes turned skyward. Volunteers at Dee Turley's center crowded around the window of the church hall, ignoring the aromas of fried chicken and peach cobbler while they gazed at the approaching cloud. Tom Turley gave it a nervous glance through the windshield of the cleaning service van as he started on his rounds. Wes Cochran, saying good-bye to the deputies who guarded Mercy Hospital from crazed fans who might want to photograph or body-snatch Hoyt Heller's corpse, frowned at the cloud and muttered, "Shit." Len Abbott, who was furtively following his hated ex-son-in-law Stollnitz to see what he was up to, squinted anxiously through his windshield as the daylight dimmed, but managed to track the younger man's blue Ford Tempo to a gas station. Gordon Yeager, Esq., working late at the Hansen and Yeager office, looked out at the darkening sky and switched on his desk lamp. At Robin Hill Trailer Court, the old woman named Bella, who despite Deputy Marty Hopkins' best efforts had not budged from her bent lawn chair for hours, suddenly pushed herself to her feet, pointed with a trembling hand, and cried, "The end is coming! The Lord's chariots of wrath will come upon us!"

A chill ran down Deputy Hopkins' spine and the words to the hymn chimed within her: *Dark is His path on the wings of the storm.* All the same she attempted to soothe the terrified residents and crying children, saying, "C'mon, folks, it's just a plain old thunderstorm."

Deputy Hopkins spoke truly. Today there was less energy, less wind aloft to set the air rolling horizontally like a log, and less updraft to tip a whirling cylinder to the deadly vertical. The cloud spewed out rain, thunder, lightning, and gusts of wind; and that was all.

The storm rumbled away to the northeast, and Nichols County residents breathed a sigh of relief.

When Grady Sims came to relieve Marty at the trailer court, he brought word that Sheriff Cochran wanted to see her at the station in forty-five minutes. Didn't leave much time to locate Coral, but she'd try.

Still a little giddy from the fact that this time the storm had involved only rain, on her way out she slowed her cruiser as she

157

rolled past Romey Dennis. Boots, jeans, and arms streaked with mud, he was throwing more trash into his pickup. "Hey, thanks for the little singalong. Helped calm things down," she said.

Romey wiped his forehead and got mud on it too. He said, "Yeah, there's magic in wine, women and song. Glad to be on your team, Deputy Hopkins."

"Yeah."

His voice dropped to a murmur so no one would overhear. "And when all this is over, how about this team taking a couple days off? Meet me in Louisville and we'll play an away game."

"But—" No, he's right, he's right, clamored the secret rowdy Marty inside. She felt her mouth curving into a wicked smile. "Yeah, I was just thinking the same thing. When all this is over."

He gave her a grin and a thumbs-up and whispered, "Whoopee!" Then, all business, he picked up a bent gutter and threw it into the truck.

Marty made good time to Dee's bustling volunteer center but Coral wasn't there. Shoot. She saw Aunt Vonnie and Chrissie at one of the long tables, finishing a chicken dinner. Her daughter looked very serious and competent. Marty ran over to give her a hug. "Go get something to eat and join us," Aunt Vonnie commanded.

She was right. Things smelled real good. Marty saluted and obeyed. At the serving table Dee was replacing the depleted coleslaw container with a new one, heaped high. Dee looked wonderful, skin flushed a little from the steam, hair braided like a golden crown around her head, eyes smiling at the bustling church hall with compassion and serenity. Marty flashed on the sickly, shuffling Dee she'd seen two days before and wondered again at the transformation. She said, "Hi, Dee. Is Coral around?"

"She called and said she was in Bloomington dealing with the press and the rest of the band." She gestured at the television someone had set up in a corner of the hall. "Coral's going to be on the ten o'clock network news tonight. I just saw her on the six o'clock news from Chicago. Did you?"

Marty shook her head. "Missed her."

Dee laughed. "You might not have recognized her. All in black, skulls and things." Her eyes became thoughtful, as though looking far away. "She sang a strange song, quite beautiful. I didn't know she understood—"

"Understood what?"

"Loss. Striving and sorrow. It's like I didn't know my own child."

158

"Yeah. Chrissie fools me all the time. So will Coral be in Bloomington long?"

"She said she hoped to get back late tonight."

Shoot, that meant she might not see Coral till tomorrow. Marty said, "Tell her we need a statement soon, okay?" She spooned some coleslaw on to her plate, took a preliminary bite of Melva's sweet buttery corn muffin, and went to join Chrissie and Aunt Vonnie, who were in the middle of an argument.

"Look, Chrissie, things are slowing down now that most folks have had dinner," Aunt Vonnie was saying. "And there's school tomorrow, so you've got to go home to do your homework. We've got math problems to do."

Chrissie protested, "But who'll clean up if we're not here?"

"Well, I can do it." Laurie Yeager had come in behind them. She put her thin hand on Chrissie's shoulder.

"What're you doing here, Laurie?" Aunt Vonnie demanded. "I thought you had to go home to fix dinner for Gordon!"

"Yeah, that's what he said this morning, that he'd be home at six." Hurt lurked under Laurie's controlled voice. "So I leave here when everything's at its busiest, and I go home and fix him a nice meal, and it starts getting cold so I eat mine, and then he calls and says he'll be another couple hours. So I told him it would be in the refrigerator and came back here."

"Everybody's schedule is messed up right now," Marty said around a mouthful of fried chicken. She glanced uneasily at Aunt Vonnie, who constantly and justifiably complained about Marty's unpredictable hours.

"No, it's not just now." Laurie's hurt was turning to anger. "He's late a lot, that's the kind of job he has, but he ought to call sooner! Dammit!"

Marty said, "Have you asked him to call you sooner?"

"Yeah, but he says he's working late because of me. He gets mad." Laurie jerked a tissue from her bag. "Oh, damn, let's not talk about this any more!"

"I gotta go now anyway," Marty said. But she found herself wondering about the Yeagers. All was not sweetness and light there. And was Gordon really working late? Specifically, had he been working late on Monday night?

Marty kissed Chrissie and Aunt Vonnie good-bye, buttered another corn muffin to eat in the cruiser, and headed for the station to meet the sheriff.

Twenty-Six

Wes stretched back in his rolling desk chair, clumped both shoes onto the edge of his desk, and closed his eyes. He was bone-tired. But you didn't take this job for the easy hours. He took a swallow of departmental coffee, made a face, and grunted, "So little Miss Coral is out of town."

"Yessir," Hopkins said. "In Bloomington with the rest of the Lily Pistols. And her mother says she's on TV."

"Yeah, Art Pfann told me." The prosecutor always took a personal interest in how the media treated the county crises. Wes couldn't help smirking. "And boy, was Art disappointed. Man loves the sight of his own mug on TV. And on two channels they show him for maybe a second and a half before they cut to clips of Hoyt Heller, and on the third they don't even bother to show him, just Coral singing plus the Heller clips."

Hopkins was grinning too. "Poor Art. I bet this time he thought Hollywood would come knocking for sure."

"Yeah. The ten o'clock news will probably be even worse. But—" He looked at Hopkins directly, "—we've still got to get her statement. Now that we know it wasn't the tornado we've got to push a little more about where she was when he died, and what Heller was doing right before the tornado."

"Okay, soon as I can track her down. How's Jake Shaw doing?"

"Jake's in really bad shape. All he can do is grunt yes or no because he's got both arms and his jaw broken."

"God, I didn't realize!" Her gray eyes were warm with sympathy.

"Besides forcing him off the road, this scumbag stole Jake's camera. I got kind of a description from Jake. Caucasian male in his forties, five-ten, one-sixty, brown hair and mustache, with a Pacers cap like Jake's, maybe. Jake confirmed each of those things, but when I read the whole thing back he said no and drifted off to sleep."

"So somebody has to check again?"

"When somebody has a minute." Wes sighed. "Interviewing Jake

160

is like playing twenty questions. Takes for ever. Plus he drifts in and out, he's on so much painkiller. But yeah, I want to go back and ask about the car that forced him off."

"He said the guy wore a Pacers cap?"

"Yeah." Wes frowned. "First he said there was no hat. Then he said, yes, yes! And I established it was a Pacers cap. But then he denied it and drifted off."

"If the guy stole a camera, maybe he stole Jake's cap."

"You mean he stole the cap and not the wallet? Must be some Pacers fan."

"Sorry. Dumb idea."

"We're all tired. But hell, I'll check on it next time I go by the hospital." Wes pulled his feet from the desk, straightened, and put the coffee mug down. "Well, that's it, unless you've got something else."

"One small thing, sir. About Stephanie Stollnitz."

"Yeah?"

"Gordon Yeager told us he left his office about six thirty to do errands, and the janitor confirmed that. But his wife says he got in real late Monday night. Like one or two A.M. Everyone agrees he often works late, so I'm wondering if he came back to the building later. And if not, where was he?"

"Interesting. Yeah, we better talk to the guy again. I'll swing by his house on the way to see Jake tonight. Meanwhile, you track down our famous Miss Coral."

"You mean now? Go to Bloomington?"

"We need to know. I'll talk to the department there." He reached for the phone.

Len Abbott sank back in the driver's seat, his lower back complaining that he'd spent too many hours in this position, and bit into his cheeseburger. The sun was low in the western sky, and the clouds that had brought the dinnertime cloudburst were blowing eastward. On the other side of this crowded parking lot sat his ex-son-in-law's old blue Ford Tempo. Guy couldn't even afford a decent car.

Len had been tracking Stollnitz for hours. He'd picked up the trail in the early afternoon, shortly after he'd spoken to the sheriff and learned that they were doing nothing. It was clear that Len would have to get the evidence himself.

He'd soon spotted Stollnitz's Tempo in the parking lot of the funeral home. Len had been there first thing this morning to make arrangements for them to work with the Muncie funeral home, and had thought to warn the director that the ex-husband might try to claim the body. So he was fiercely pleased when Stollnitz came out with his handsome pouty face drooping.

Why hadn't Steffie been able to see past that handsome face? Why had she discounted her father's warnings?

Stollnitz had headed straight for Steffie's apartment—proof that he'd known where she lived! Damn bastard! The guy didn't notice Len a block behind him. Len parked around the corner by a shrubby yard, where he could see the front door of the Johnson place through the branches. No one was home. Stollnitz waited, knocked again, and when there was still no answer, walked to the sidewalk before turning to inspect the house carefully.

Stollnitz was still wearing the Colts sweatshirt he'd had on yesterday. Looked grubby today. Len didn't feel much neater after a night in the car and a quick wash in the McDonald's restroom, but at least he'd brought along a fresh shirt. Finally Stollnitz gave up and climbed back into the blue Tempo. Len revved up his T-bird and followed.

Stollnitz drove to the bank where Steffie had worked and went in briefly. Then he came out again, rested his head a moment against the steering wheel, and then started to drive around aimlessly. Len had followed him on a tour of the tornado damage, then to a grocery, then to gas up, then back to Steffie's house—still nobody home—and finally to this Burger King. Stollnitz had gone inside, and Len, by now as hungry as his quarry, went to the drive-through window to order his cheeseburger and coffee.

Now he sat chewing and watching the Tempo, wondering what Stollnitz was up to. So far, after hours of trailing the younger man, he'd come up only with the information that Stollnitz knew where she'd lived—and the bastard would probably tell the sheriff that he'd only just found out. Len wanted to do better than that for Steffie.

The Burger King lot was still fairly crowded, although people were starting to leave. The bank lot next door was mostly empty. A cleaning van and a Pontiac were near the back door, a couple of smaller cars and a pickup toward the front, but they might be overflow from the Burger King rush hour. A dark Chevy Caprice rolled up to the back door and a uniformed security guard got out and entered the bank.

Len's fist crushed the foam cup that had held his coffee. Where the hell had the security guard been when Steffie was killed?

Ten minutes later he had his answer. The guard came out again and drove off. Probably had other buildings to guard, if guard was the right word for this slapdash drop-by approach.

Then Len sat up straighter. Stollnitz was walking toward the back door of the bank! Shit, Len had been so busy watching the guard he hadn't even seen the guy leave the Burger King. Stollnitz was already halfway across the lot. When the door opened and the green-uniformed janitor came out, Stollnitz stuck his hands in his pocket and shifted direction so it wouldn't look like he was heading for the bank. The janitor glanced at Stollnitz, then stowed a vacuum cleaner into the back of his van. He left the van doors open and disappeared back into the bank.

Stollnitz ran to the door and hid in the shadows on the far side. Sure enough, when the cleaning man came out with a second machine a moment later, Len saw Stollnitz stick something in the hinge side of the door. The door didn't close completely behind the janitor.

The janitor closed up his van and drove away. A moment passed. Another. Then Stollnitz went in.

Len was in turmoil. Should he follow the bastard in to see what he was doing? He started to open his car door and paused. Should he call the cops now? Would this bank break-in be enough for that sheriff?

No, it wouldn't. Len had seen the chaos at the sheriff's office, had seen lots of deputies working in the tornado-damaged areas. It'd take more than this sneak visit to catch the sheriff's attention. Better go see what Stollnitz was doing.

Or should he do both? Call the sheriff, then follow up?

But as Len hesitated, the door opened and Stollnitz rushed out. He took a few steps, pulled out a handkerchief, blew his nose, and then hurried to his Tempo, almost at a run.

Len followed Stollnitz back onto the highway. Couldn't quit now! Things were starting to happen. He'd follow up, and call the sheriff first chance he got.

Don't worry, Steffie, I'll get him, he promised as he followed Stollnitz into the dusk.

Gordon Yeager lived in Evergreen Hills, an upscale development on the Bloomington side of town. Gordon's neighbors were other lawyers, doctors, and a stray professor or two from Indiana University. The houses were modern versions of colonials, lots of brick, columned porches, small windowpanes instead of the fifties picture windows favored in Wes's neighborhood. He drove up the asphalt driveway. The porch light was on, but no other lights, and it was going on nine and plenty dark. No one answered the door. Wes shone his flashlight in the garage window. No cars.

Suddenly his radio crackled. Man with a gun at the White River Bar. Deputy Culp, an eager rookie, had called for backup. Wes jumped into the cruiser and hit the siren. Damn. The tornado had distracted the local scum for a few hours, but here they were starting up again, causing the ordinary disturbances that normally took one hundred percent of his department's time.

He was the third unit on the scene. Culp and Mason had wrestled a guy onto the blue-and-black checked carpet and were handcuffing him while an excited, relieved crowd looked on from the back of the bar. A Ruger revolver lay under a booth table nearby, a nasty-looking .44 that could've drilled four or five patrons with one shot, if they were lined up right.

Nobody looked drilled, thank the Lord.

Culp and Mason jerked the guy to his feet while Wes radioed that the suspect was in custody. "So what's the story?" he asked.

Culp, still pumped, spurted out words. "I take the call and when I get here, this guy's drunk as a sailor. Waves the .44 around and yells that he's going to kill the bitch. I tell him to take it easy and try to talk him outside, but he keeps yelling. So I ease around beside him and when Mason comes through the door the guy looks around. That's when I knock the gun from his hand." Culp was flushed and glistening with sweat. He'd relive that moment for years.

Wes caught Mason's eye and jerked his thumb at the Ruger. Mason unloaded it. Wes asked, "What's your name, buddy?"

The man was staring at the checkered floor and didn't look up. Someone at the bar said, "He's Carson Rowe."

Shit. This was the poor guy whose wife was in that basement with a gas leak. Wes said, "Take it easy, Mr. Rowe. We haven't even found Alice yet. We don't know for sure that she's hurt."

Carson Rowe looked up at last, tears running down his cheeks, alcohol strong on his breath. "She's not hurt! Bitch! And I thought she was dead!"

"What, you heard from her?"

"She called. Bitch! She went to her cousin's in Mitchell! I thought she was dead!" Rowe, cuffed and unable to hit now, kicked a chair.

"Take it easy, Carson. You oughta be happy she's alive."

"She just ran off! Says she's never coming back! And I thought—" He ducked his head again.

"Well, tell you what, buddy. You stay with us for a few hours. Tomorrow we'll figure what to do." Wes nodded at Culp, who led

Rowe stumbling out to the cruiser to transport him to the jail. "Take statements from these folks," Wes told Mason, and got back in his cruiser. He felt for Rowe. Terrible to lose your wife to an act of God, worse somehow if she left you. But if the guy was going to drown his sorrows, he'd better keep his hands off firearms.

The Monroe County sheriff's department directed Marty to the back room of a Bloomington bar, where Coral was standing on the little makeshift stage behind a bank of microphones. A crowd of reporters and photographers jammed the room. A middle-aged man with a mustache supervised the band's private security force, four muscular young men in black death's-head T-shirts. Coral herself was in black leather, nose ring, and a breezy explosion of blond curls. The sensuous flower tattooed on her arm looked right at home now.

"We're really, really tired. One last question," Coral said. There were shouts and hands all over the room. Coral picked someone who wanted to know if the band would continue. "You bet!" Coral exclaimed. "Hoyt would want that. We all contribute to the band, that's why we're together. And the important thing is, Hoyt wrote some songs that haven't been recorded yet, and he'd want them to see the light of day. They're like love letters to his fans, you know? Okay, thanks, folks, see you later!" She waved her hand, ignoring the shouted questions, and turned to the others on stage, her back now to the audience. The reporters began to pack up. Marty made her way past the security men to the edge of the stage.

"What the fuck songs are you talking about, woman?" she heard the bearded member of the band ask Coral. "Hoyt hasn't written anything for months!"

"Don't sweat it, Skell, we'll sign his name to a couple of mine."

He started swearing, and Coral looked around almost gratefully when Marty said her name. "Hey, Deputy Hopkins, good to see you."

The other band members backed off hastily. Probably all carrying drugs, Marty figured. She ignored them and said, "We need your signature on the statement, Coral, and we've got a couple more questions."

"Sure. I'm going back to my mom's now."

The middle-aged man asked, "Want me to drive you?"

Coral said, "Thanks, Duke, but I bet Deputy Hopkins wants to take me home."

"Sure thing," said Marty. "We'll talk on the way."

Once in the cruiser, Coral settled back with a sigh, more inclined to sleep than talk, but Marty said firmly, "Let's get this over with, okay? We found Hoyt lying in the yard. A few minutes later you came up the road."

"God, that was so awful!" Coral covered her face with both hands.

"Yeah. That was about nine P.M. yesterday."

"Twenty-four hours. God, it seems like a couple years!"

"Sure does. What was Hoyt doing when you left?"

"He was working on a song. We needed some more lyrics to go with a musical idea Skell had. Hoyt's like me, when the ideas are coming he hates . . . hated to stop working on them."

"Did he say anything about meeting someone?"

"No."

"Okay. So you were at your mom's, and you started back a few minutes before the tornado hit, maybe six ten. Right?"

"Yes. But to get back to the pig farm I had to cross the tornado path." The girl shuddered. "It was awesome. I could still see it going away. That's why I wasn't watching and ran into the ditch."

"Where exactly?"

"Thompson Road was the nearest intersection. I bet I broke an axle or something."

"So this is maybe six thirty?"

"Yeah. Oh, God, was he already lying there?" The girl turned stricken eyes on Marty. "If I'd got there sooner, could I have helped?"

She seemed sincere. Marty said, "We don't know for sure. But I'd like to know what you did next."

"I was trying to get there, honest!" She looked suddenly very young to Marty. "See, first I tried to back out of the ditch. But I couldn't get it to move. I tried and tried."

"How long?"

"I don't know. Half an hour, I guess. Maybe even more. It was raining a little and the ditch was slick, so I got branches to put under the tires but it still wouldn't move."

"Okay. And then you decided to walk?"

"I decided to hitch. I went back to the highway."

"So you were there by around seven?"

"Maybe. I don't know for sure. But there weren't any cars. So after another half-hour I started walking."

"It's two or three miles from there, right?"

"I don't know. All I know is, it took a long time."

"So the first time you got there, where was he?"

"Right there in the yard. You showed me." She looked confused.

"Where else would he be? What do you mean, the first time? You were there!"

"You didn't see him when he was in the tornado shelter?"

"In the shelter? What do you mean? He was on his way to it!" Coral stared at her. "What are you saying? That I got there earlier and then went away and left him? God, how could anyone—"

"Take it easy, Coral! We thought maybe you went for help."

"No! Help was there already! You were help!" The girl's beautiful eyes glittered with anger. "Are you trying to cover your ass or something? You mean you could have saved him and you're trying to get me to say something to bail you out?"

Marty bit back an angry retort. Cool it, Hopkins, you feel rotten because you failed to revive him. You'll only make it worse if you botch this interview. Marty said coolly, "I gave him CPR for forty-some minutes. Nobody could have saved him unless they got there much earlier."

"I was trying to get there! But the car went in the ditch!"

Marty sighed. It sounded like truth. But could she believe Coral? She'd just heard this kid lie to a roomful of reporters, smooth as silk. A born performer. Marty shifted to another topic. "Were you ever in the tornado shelter?"

"Why are you asking me all these questions? Do you think somebody was there earlier?"

"That's what we're trying to find out. Coral, were you ever in that shelter?"

"Yeah. Couple times. With Hoyt."

"How come?"

Coral pulled up one long leg, placing her Doc Marten boot on the taxpayer's upholstery and hugging her knee. "Why do you think? Sex. He liked weird places."

Oh boy, Hopkins, don't lose her now. Marty said, "Doesn't sound real comfortable."

"At least there was a bench. It was a hell of a lot better than that dried-up lawn, all full of stones. Talk about scratchy."

"Yeah, I guess so."

"Plus he liked the shelter because of my song. 'Deathwind.'"

"You keep talking about what he liked. Did you like it?"

"I wanted to be with him, sure. We made a real good team."

Was that true, or was that the public Coral who had lied to the reporters? No way to tell till she had more information. Marty shifted direction. "Tell me, when you were in the shelter, did the door work okay?"

167

"Sure. That metal thing that holds it open was a little stiff, but it worked." She frowned across her knee at Marty. "He was in there, you think? With somebody?"

"We're trying to find out. Can you think of anyone?"

"Besides me, you mean? Not off-hand," Coral said bitterly, letting her leg down and staring out at the passing lights.

"Well, think about it and let me know. When we get to the station we'll get it all in writing." Marty gave her a few minutes to reflect, but when she looked across, she saw the girl was sound asleep. Looked like at least one of her statements was true: she was really, really tired.

Wearily, Wes turned back on to the highway. It was definitely time for bed. Ordinarily a drunk with a gun like Carson Rowe would keep him revved up for hours. Tonight his pillow seemed the most attractive thing on earth.

But as he drove by the Montgomery State Bank he saw light seeping around the blinds of a window on the third floor.

There was a Pontiac in the lot. Nothing else.

Wes pulled in next to the front door, got out of the cruiser, and banged on the glass. No one was around.

He ran the license plate of the Pontiac. Gordon Yeager's. He telephoned the Hansen and Yeager office number, but got only a machine, and no one picked up when he spoke to leave a message. He was ready to call it quits and get to his scrumptious pillow when the paunchy security man arrived to make his rounds. Wes yelled out the cruiser window at the ex-cop, "Hey, Glenn, can you let me in here?"

"Sure. Come on around back."

They met at the back door. "Hi, Sheriff. Do we have a problem here?" Glenn asked nervously. He wore a blue uniform with the security company's square gold badge.

"Just want to talk to the guy on the third floor," Wes said. "He won't pick up his phone."

"Sure. Come on in." Glenn sounded relieved. He was supposed to tour the bank building once every hour, Ed had said. He was probably late tonight and uneasy about being checked on.

Glenn had keys to the upstairs offices. "Only for emergencies," he explained to Wes. "I don't actually check the offices, just walk the halls and test the doors."

"Light's on in there."

"Yeah, Mr. Yeager works late a lot. Uh . . . he doesn't like

168

interruptions." He opened the door marked "Hansen and Yeager" and stepped back to let Wes take the brunt of Yeager's displeasure.

The outer office was dark, except for tiny signal lights on the telephone and the glow through the window from the parking lot below. "Which one is Yeager's office?" Wes asked.

Glenn indicated the door to the right of the coat closet. Wes knocked and yelled, "Gordon? Sheriff here! Open up!"

There was no answer. He tried the knob.

It opened easily.

There was a small lamp on the desk. It lit Gordon Yeager's body, slumped across his desk, and his very red, very dead face.

Twenty-Seven

After Coral signed her statement, Marty drove her to the volunteer center. As the girl walked in, all metal and black leather, Laurie Yeager waved at her. "Hey! Here's our TV star!"

Shouts and applause, a big smile from Dee. Marty, walking behind Coral, saw the girl straighten her tired shoulders and lengthen her stride, suddenly regal, and Marty wondered again if she'd told the truth. Coral gave Dee a hug. They were so like each other and yet so different, even the two blond heads, one a wheat-gold coronet, the other brighter, almost sulphur-yellow in the artificial light. Dee was mature, robust, ripe; Coral was harder to pin down—delicately tender, yet full of darkness; spring, yet winter. It seemed to Marty that Coral was Dee's youth and death all at once.

"Hey, honey, got to get to work," Dee said, and released the girl, and maybe only someone like Marty, who might lose a daughter too, understood the fleeting sadness in Dee's eyes. We all want to keep them for ever, Marty thought. My mother clung to me, I cling to Chrissie, Dee clings to Coral. She remembered Dee's words: I'm finally learning to deal with how much of motherhood is loss. Yes. And letting go was necessary to keep them. The lesson of Solomon.

But the legal system didn't work that way. It didn't award custody to people who let go. No Solomons today, only Judge Fischer and Judge Schmidt.

Marty's portable radio sputtered to life, told her to phone in. She commandeered a phone in the church office. Adams was on dispatch. "Hopkins? Gordon Yeager's dead."

"Gordon?"

"In his office, Montgomery State Bank. Sheriff's with the body. Wants you over there."

"Okay. Uh . . . Laurie Yeager's here at the volunteer center."

"Better not tell her. It's not official yet."

"I'll get someone to wait with her." Marty hung up and glanced around the church hall. Melva Dodd was wiping off a table. Marty murmured, "Melva, something's happened to Gordon Yeager. Can you stay with Laurie until we've got some news?"

"Sure thing."

Marty sent Laurie home, apprehensive and full of questions but soothed by Melva's motherly presence. She promised to get word to them as soon as she knew something, then headed for her cruiser and hit the siren. She blasted a wriggly path through heavy traffic to the bank. A nervous-looking, paunchy security man greeted her. "Sheriff Cochran's upstairs with the body," he said.

When she entered Gordon's office the sheriff looked exhausted, leaning back in the black sofa. Kev was there already, photographing the office. Doc Altman was peering at the body slumped over the desk. The sheriff raised a tired hand in greeting.

"What is it? Stroke? Strangled?" Marty asked, peering around the photographer. "What is it, Dr. Altman?"

The sheriff turned his head slowly to look at the coroner.

"Classic," Doc announced. "Cherry-red coloring. Only about twenty percent of them look like this, but when they do, it's clear. Carbon monoxide."

"Not a stroke, then." Sheriff Cochran heaved himself up from the sofa and shuffled toward Marty.

Doc said, "Kev, get some shots of the body in place. Make sure you get the color."

The sheriff, moving to give the photographer room, stumbled.

"Sir, you okay?" Marty asked.

"Yeah. Just tired," he grunted. "Too many hours on the job. Headache."

"Jesus!" Doc exploded. He grabbed the sheriff by the elbows and pushed him out the door. "Get out of this room, Cochran! Everybody *out!*"

Marty, struggling to help Doc with the collapsing sheriff, saw

Kev look around in bewilderment. "Come quick, Kev!" she yelled. "This air is poison!"

Kev came quick.

They closed the door behind them and steered the sheriff to the elevators and the parking lot. He protested but Doc made him lie down on the asphalt. "How long was he waiting for us up there?" he demanded of the security guard.

"Twenty minutes, maybe."

Marty started to call the fire department, but saw their emergency medical truck turning into the lot just ahead of the state crime scene van. "I'm okay," the sheriff said thickly.

"You're not okay until I say so," Doc informed him brusquely. He was kneeling by the sheriff, beaming a flashlight at his eyes.

The sheriff mumbled, "Hopkins? Check things out."

The firemen put an oxygen mask on Sheriff Cochran and loaded him into their truck. They left a couple of guys behind with gas masks and air tanks. Marty appropriated a spare mask and tank and showed them up to Gordon's office. "Don't disturb anything. The crime scene unit's here," she said.

"Sure thing," said Ray Bramer, who'd gone to grade school with her. She watched helplessly as the firemen clumped into the office to set up their equipment.

In the outer office, nothing seemed out of place. Bookcase, computer and printer, rubber plant, all neat. Even the telephone was lined up straight on the uncluttered desk. No sources of carbon monoxide that she could see—no faulty heaters, no gasoline engines, no autos with hoses attached to their tailpipes. There was a grille under the window for the central heating and air-conditioning. That's what they'd better check. She adjusted her mask, which was rubbing her ear, and glanced into the coat closet. Chipped paneled walls, carpeting, its nap mashed and grooved, some reams of letterhead paper on the floor at the left, envelopes and paper clips on the shelf over the rod, and Debra's rose-pink cardigan on a hanger. The small bathroom contained only standard fixtures, liquid soap, paper towels and tissue, and a green plastic air-freshener. Marty closed the door and went back down to the security man.

"I want to see the heating system," she said, relieved to have the mask off for a moment.

He looked startled. "God, that's probably it! But I can't leave here."

"Right. So give me the keys and the directions."

He eyed her suspiciously, an old guy who'd done his police

171

service before women were on the job. Marty said wearily, "Sheriff Cochran told me to check," and held out her hand.

He gave in, dropping the keys into her hand. "Sub-basement, metal door, says 'Authorized Personnel Only.'"

The basement room was a tangle of ducts and pipes. If there was a malfunction, or if someone had tampered with the furnace or air system, a layman like herself couldn't tell. As she left the room, Bramer and his fellow fireman approached her from the elevator. "Got it solved, Marty?" he said edgily.

"No more bodies in there, anyway. Let us know where the gas is coming from," she said, holding the door for him.

She left the mask by the back door, returned the security man's keys and walked across the parking lot to where Doc Altman stood talking to Kev. She tapped his arm. "Dr. Altman? Will Sheriff Cochran be all right?"

"Didn't look bad. But you gotta be cautious." She remembered what he'd told them earlier about patients continuing to worsen in the hospital. He adjusted his wire-rims. "I sent him to Mercy for observation and extra oxygen. He's got that heart condition."

"Yeah. When'll we know?"

"A few hours. Guy needs some rest anyway. We all do."

"Look, I have to go notify Laurie Yeager officially that her husband is dead. But I've got a question. Gordon Yeager died of carbon monoxide poisoning."

"I'll be real surprised if it turns out to be something else, but that's not official. You know I have to do tests."

"I know, sir. And Hoyt Heller also died of carbon monoxide poisoning. That is official."

"Yeah."

"So my question is, did Stephanie Stollnitz die of carbon monoxide poisoning?"

Doc shook his head. "Nah. Wish it was that easy. We checked, of course, but her carboxyhemoglobin level was in the normal range. Besides, where'd she get it? She was in that huge lobby. Gordon just had a few cubic feet of air in that little office of his."

"Heller was outdoors."

"But he'd been in the tornado shelter, looks like."

"Well, suppose Stephanie was in a smaller room. Maybe in Gordon's office for some reason. And whatever malfunctioned tonight did it that night too. And suppose Gordon found her in there, dead or almost dead. And—" Suddenly she could picture it, Stephanie's limp form, not on the gold carpet of the lobby, but on

172

the sofa in Yeager's office. Gordon bending over her, trying to revive her. "Maybe she passed out there. He could've moved her downstairs. And her face was wet, remember? Well, one end of Yeager's sofa was wet the next day. I bet he splashed water onto her face!" And I bet he knocked over that soda can on purpose, to make Marty think the wet spot had only just occurred. Neatly done, Gordon, she thought, but why didn't you tell the truth?

Doc wasn't yet convinced. "Okay, I'll check again, because of this second carbon monoxide case. God knows I'd be glad to get a cause of death on the Stollnitz woman. But her blood level really wasn't high enough."

"I thought you said the levels went down over time, if you were still breathing, even when you die eventually."

"That's right. But in a fatal case the level would start out so high to begin with, it would take hours of breathing to come down to normal. So it's much more likely it was never high."

Marty was trying to remember what he'd said before. "Didn't you say her level was a little elevated?"

"Sure, but still normal for smokers. Millions of people walk around every day with levels the same as Stephanie Stollnitz's."

Marty stared at him, remembering the moving cartons still in Stephanie's apartment, the never-unpacked ceramics. "Doc, the thing is, Stephanie owned ashtrays but hadn't ever unpacked them! Not in a year and a half! She didn't smoke!"

"Stephanie Stollnitz didn't smoke? I just assumed—" Doc scowled at Marty, probably embarrassed that in the confused aftermath of the tornado he hadn't bothered to confirm his assumption, but excited too as he now glimpsed the solution of his scientific puzzle. "Okay. I'll check again, let you know. But if you're right, if Gordon Yeager is the third—" He shook his head. "I'm glad I'm not the one who has to make sense out of all this!"

Twenty-Eight

Holding Laurie's hand, Marty sat on the white leather sofa that faced the massive stone fireplace in the Yeager living room. Gordon's new widow was a little more composed now after her first rush of tears, but still pulled tissues from the box that sat next to Marty's Stetson on the brass-and-glass coffee table before them. Through the arch to the dining room, Marty could hear Melva Dodd bustling in the kitchen, making coffee.

"Thanks, Marty." Laurie blew her nose. "You know, it's terrible. I shouldn't say this. But I got so mad at him! Even with the tornado he went to the office instead of staying with me!"

Hating to ask, Marty said gently, "You think he was meeting someone? A client or . . . someone?" The scene she'd imagined fit all the facts—almost. Gordon could have met Steffie, tried to revive her as she lay comatose on his office sofa. But now she was gone. Who would he be meeting tonight?

Laurie shook her head. "No, he told me it was paperwork. Didn't say much—he never does—but he seemed really down about having to go in. But now . . . I mean, he should've known it was dangerous to be there, right? Because you say that bank teller died of the same thing."

"We haven't confirmed that yet, Laurie." She remembered Gordon's question the next day, deep concern in his dark eyes— *How did she die*? "He probably didn't know why she died any more than we did."

"Well, he knew she died in the bank! And I kept telling him he shouldn't work so hard. We hardly ever saw each other these last few months. There must have been some other way! I told him to let Chip do some of it but he said we needed the money because . . . anyway, we needed it."

Marty's tired senses jumped to attention. She probed gently, "You've got a real nice house here. A lot of men like to show they can earn enough for a place like this."

"Yeah. He loved this place," Laurie snuffled.

"Chip's house is nice too," Marty observed, thinking of the bills she'd paid already for her divorce. She probably owned Chip's dining room by now. "But maybe you all had other expenses too, besides the house."

Laurie burst into tears again. "Oh, God, I didn't mean to!"

Was this guilt? Why? Marty put an arm around her shoulder. "Hey, take it easy, Laurie. I know you wouldn't mean to do anything wrong."

"I was just getting so bored here!" Laurie sobbed. "And my girlfriend in California invited us to LA for a holiday. And at the last minute Gordon wouldn't come because he had a case, and he said I should go without him. So I did. But I was still mad at him." She blew her nose again.

"So it was your girlfriend that caused the problem?"

"Yeah. Good old Dorrie. Dorrie and Laurie. They called us Bobbsey twins just because our names rhyme. We don't look alike. Anyway, we worked together in the law school offices at IU, that's how I met Gordon. And in those days we used to have fun, you know, the office pools, even Churchill Downs a couple times."

Marty remembered Laurie pulling out her money in the bakery, the bettor's ticket that fell out of her purse. She said neutrally, "A lot of people enjoy that."

"Yeah. It can be fun. Real exciting," Laurie said. "But see, I didn't know this fancy LA casino she took me to had these illegal games in the back. Dorrie quit pretty soon but I'd had a few drinks and I went on playing, because I was winning a lot. Nine thousand four hundred dollars. I told her I'd stop when I reached ten thousand."

Marty had heard this one before, though seldom in such rich surroundings. She nodded sadly. "Yeah."

"And then my luck turned. Gordon said later it was probably rigged. Anyway, the first thing I knew I owed them fifty thousand. They made me max out three credit cards but even so I couldn't pay it all, and I had to sign a paper promising to pay all kinds of interest. Gordon said it was all illegal. But if I brought charges I'd go to jail too, and Dorrie. Couldn't do that. So I tried to pay but I got behind, and they said they'd—well, you know, break my bones and so forth."

"Yeah."

"So finally I told Gordon. I thought he could fix it somehow. He always knew what to do. But he got really mad, and said we didn't have a handle on them, so we had to keep paying until he could figure something out."

175

"What kind of a handle?"

"I don't know. Gordon didn't talk about it much after that. He didn't talk to me about anything, really. And the last couple days he just sort of stared into space, like he wasn't here."

Interesting. Marty moved on. "Who were the people who talked about breaking bones, Laurie?"

"I'm not supposed to say anything." She looked suddenly frightened and poked a finger at the Stetson on the coffee table. "God, Marty, you're police, aren't you? I kind of forget. You don't seem like police. Please, don't do anything, or say anything! Gordon said I'm especially not supposed to tell the police!"

"Laurie—" Marty paused to think a moment. Difficult as Laurie's problem was, racketeers generally preferred live, paying customers. Besides, if it was a hit man who uncharacteristically preferred carbon monoxide to firearms, it only accounted for Gordon's death. Why Steffie?

Laurie was still pleading, "Don't do anything! They're dangerous! They're—"

Melva Dodd came in with a tray of coffee and cookies. "Here you are, Laurie honey. Let's have some coffee."

Marty said, "Thanks, Melva, this is wonderful. Could you give us another couple minutes alone?"

Melva looked hurt. "It'll get cold!"

"Why don't you pour us both a cup?"

Melva did so and retreated reluctantly across the dining room to the kitchen. Marty said in a low voice, "Okay. Now listen, Laurie, this is important. If you hear from these people, let us know right away."

"I'm not supposed to—"

"Look, they probably had nothing to do with it. But just to play it safe, let us know, okay? We'll be careful, I promise."

She nodded mutely. Marty went to the arch and called across the dining room to the kitchen, "Melva? Thanks. Come on back now if you want, we're done." She turned back into the living room, glancing idly at the sound system next to the arch, the rows of CDs on the shelves. Classic rock, lots of jazz.

And Lily Pistols.

It couldn't mean anything. Marty picked up the CD and asked, "Laurie, are you the Lily Pistols fan?"

"Must be Gordon's. I didn't know we had that."

"Laurie, did Gordon know Hoyt Heller?"

"You mean that rock star the tornado killed? No, he never

mentioned him. Of course just about anybody could be his client and I'd never know. Gordon just worked and worked." Laurie dissolved into tears once more, half bitter anger and half bitter guilt.

Marty asked, "He liked their music?"

"I don't know. I thought he liked John Coltrane," she sobbed. Melva bustled to her side, murmuring soothing words as Marty let herself out and got back into the cruiser.

Two people dead of carbon monoxide. And lots of questions. Steffie and Gordon were lawyer and client, maybe more than that. They worked in the same building. And they died in the same office, Marty was ready to put money on that. Steffie had been in the office (why?) and had been overcome by the gas (and had it come from a faulty heating system, or from something else?) Someone, probably Gordon, had been with her, or had come to the office that night and found her sick or comatose, had tried to revive her as she lay on Gordon's sofa and, failing, had moved her to the lobby, called the manager for emergency help, and disappeared. Why hadn't he wanted to talk to the police? Because he was hiding something. Because he and Steffie were having an affair. Or because he'd murdered her. Was that it? Maybe Steffie was demanding marriage, or money to keep quiet about an affair. So Gordon filled his office with carbon monoxide, telling her he'd be right back, disappearing for a while, returning to carry her downstairs so she wouldn't be found in his office. Laurie had said he was distracted and depressed the past two days. So his death might be a guilt-suicide a few days later.

Or had Gordon seen Steffie's killer and feared to talk to the police because of what the killer might do to him? But if he'd seen the killer at the bank, why would he return alone to the lethal office?

Anyway, who else would want Steffie dead?

Her ex. Big blond Clay Stollnitz. Okay. And if she and Gordon had been having an affair, Clay would want Gordon dead too.

And Gordon might not have known he was in danger. In that scenario, he wouldn't know why she died, or that she'd died of carbon monoxide poisoning. Even Doc hadn't figured it out for a while.

It was midnight already, too late to rouse people for questioning, especially for deaths that could still turn out to be due to a malfunctioning heat system. But first thing tomorrow she'd get Debra to show her the records of what Gordon had been doing after hours.

* * *

Len Abbott sidled along the shadowy side wall of Clyde's Bar. He could hear country music blaring, and through the window could just make out Clay Stollnitz's blond head near this end of the bar. As he watched, Stollnitz signalled for another drink.

He had a few minutes, then. Len looked at the younger man's blue Tempo a few cars away. What the hell, he'd take a look.

Len returned to his T-bird, removed his spare jacket from the wire coat hanger, and straightened the hanger as he walked across to the Tempo. It took a few minutes of jabbing carefully at the lock before he got it open, but luckily no one came out of Clyde's to notice. After a wary glance around, Len got into the Tempo and started looking.

The car was a pigsty. Old burger wrappers, empty beer cans and a fresh six-pack, three dirty towels, empty oil cans. The plastic grocery sacks in the backseat held snack foods, a new *Hustler* magazine, candy bars. A heavy-duty canvas bowling bag also held a pair of swim trunks in addition to the bowling ball. In the glove compartment were a pack of Camels, Tylenol, cough drops. No strange medications or narrow knives for killing someone's beautiful daughter. There were registration papers, an NFL record book, a couple of unpaid parking tickets from Muncie, a single black winter glove, and a freestanding nameplate, black letters on golden-tan plastic. Len stared at it a long time. Small letters in the corner read "Montgomery State Bank." The larger letters spelled out "Stephanie Stollnitz."

Len's vision went misty and he had to blink. Damn murdering bastard didn't have a right to this. Len put it in his breast pocket.

Under the seats there were two pencils, more old greasy wrappers, forty-one cents in change, a pair of smelly sneakers, and a badly maintained .38 revolver. Jesus. Len broke it open and found it loaded with three rounds and some rust. He stuck it in his belt.

There were maps on the dashboard, along with a half-eaten candy bar and an empty Burger King cup. Behind the sunshade was a three-by-four photo of Steffie in her cheerleader's sweater. Len took that too.

But that was all.

How the hell had he killed her? Bullets left traces that even the dumbest country coroners would notice.

Twelve minutes had gone by. Suddenly nervous, Len got out quickly, relocked the door, and walked around the edge of the lot to peer through the window into the bar again.

Stollnitz was still there, still drinking. He'd apparently made friends with a little dark-haired guy.

A couple of patrons left the bar, and Len crossed the street to the service station to use the phone. But the sheriff was out somewhere, and Len was told to leave a message. "I'll call back later," he said, and returned to his car.

It was close to one o'clock when Stollnitz finally came out of Clyde's. He wasn't alone. Two others were helping him, the little dark-haired guy and a larger man that Len recognized as the bartender. Stollnitz was singing, sort of, and Len's fists clenched when he recognized lines from his high-school victory song. Len had heard it a million times when Steffie was a cheerleader. Stollnitz's drunken voice was an insult to her memory. "Victory!" he shouted to the black sky, thrusting his fist toward the heavens. "Victory, victory is ours!"

The other two men helped Stollnitz into a light-colored Escort. He balked for a moment, saying "Where's my car?" But the others soothed him, and finally he got into the Escort. The bartender fastened a seatbelt around Stollnitz, and the smaller guy got in the driver's side, waved good-bye to the bartender, and drove off. "Victory! Victory!" yelled Stollnitz, punching his arm out the window.

The little guy turned out to be some sort of good Samaritan. He took Stollnitz to a small frame house on the fringes of Dunning, helped him inside, sat him on a couch, and turned on the TV for him. Len stood in the bushes by the window and watched a couple of minutes, but when Stollnitz sank sideways on the couch, clearly asleep, he decided he'd better get some shut-eye himself. He'd stay nearby.

He tried the sheriff's office again, but the sheriff was not available for anything. The dispatcher said he'd give Len's message to the deputy on the case—Len figured it was the girl deputy who'd taken notes. She was working another case, the dispatcher said, but could call him back later.

"This was murder, dammit!" Len said.

"So's the case she's working on, sir," said the dispatcher.

Len slammed down the receiver. The hell with them anyway. He got a Coke before he left the service station, and drove back to his post.

"At least your heart's doing fine," Wes's wife Shirley said soothingly.

Shirley was right, of course. Ever since that terrifying heart attack three years ago in an abandoned limestone quarry, Wes's constant anxiety was not about the bad guys out there but about the sneaky destruction of his heart from within. He hated to admit the relief he'd felt just now when Doc Hendricks had told him that the old ticker was still slogging along pretty well even after its brush with carbon monoxide. But he groused, "All I got out of this was a nap."

Shirley's smile was dimpled, twinkly, and as familiar as his soul. "Listen, Champ, a nap is worth a whole lot right now."

"Yeah. Well, let's get out of here." Mercy Hospital, overcrowded still with the injured from the tornado, had checked him out quickly, almost eagerly. It wasn't even one A.M. yet. But as he shrugged into his jacket he had a thought. "No, wait, seeing as how we're here, I have a question for my buddy Jake."

He and Shirley made their way to Jake's room. The night nurse in the hall was vigorous, fortyish, with blue eyes and brunette hair that looked younger than her weathered skin. Some sort of cousin of Deputy Mason's, Wes remembered. "Hi, Miz Kinser. Can I ask Jake a question before I leave?"

"Oh, dear. The poor man is so uncomfortable. He only just got to sleep an hour ago."

"We don't need to wake him if you can help. We're trying to locate his Pacers cap. It may be missing."

"Let's look." Nurse Kinser opened a narrow locker-like door next to the bathroom. Jake's clothing was hung on hooks inside. She reached up to the shelf above. "Is this it?"

Wes took it. So the bad guy hadn't stolen it after all. Had Jake meant the guy had a similar hat? Or had he meant something else? Probably he was so spaced out on painkillers he didn't know what he meant. Wes sighed and started to hand the cap back to the nurse. His thumb brushed something stiff inside it. He turned it upside down.

A small cardboard slip from the photo place next to Denny's was stuck in the inner band.

"Son of a gun!" Wes pulled it out and scribbled a receipt. "Miz Kinser, I'm going to take this and pick up Jake's photos for him, okay?"

"Sure thing."

Outside the night was cool and humid. They had to run a gantlet of security men who were keeping a bevy of reporters at bay. Under the parking-lot lights, puddles from the afternoon's rain glittered against the black night. Shirley took out her keys and asked, "Are Jake's photos so important?"

"Maybe not. But Jake was trying to tell me something about a

Pacers cap. And maybe this is it." He glanced at the card and slid it into his breast pocket. "They don't open until seven. Let me go cheer up the troops before we go home."

Shirley rolled her eyes at his foolishness but she followed his directions through a section of tornado damage where weary men guarded the rubble of the shopping center. "Any action?" he asked.

"Not much, sir," replied a National Guardsman. "Couple of dogs." He played his light across the piles of debris that had been roofs and walls. The shifting inky shadows gave the landscape a science-fiction feel, as though the aliens had just won a battle. Well, they had, Wes thought.

Two rangy animals, looked like coonhound crosses, were exploring a heap near the Country Griddle. They'd probably found a treasure trove of breakfast sausage or chicken legs. What a waste. "Well, there's that much less to rot. Hang in there," Wes told the guardsman. He turned to Shirley. "I better pick up my cruiser. Let's go on to the Montgomery State Bank."

Twenty-Nine

At the Friday morning roll-call, Marty inspected the sheriff surreptitiously. He looked okay, none the worse for his collapse last night. He read off the assignments—her job was to follow up on Gordon Yeager's death—and told the assembled deputies about the government disaster-relief application center that would open Monday. "They'll set up at the White River School cafeteria, so tell folks to go there. Let's see." He picked up a note. "On the Heller death. Crime Scene tells us they got a couple of interesting things at the Matthews farm where he died. One was an empty greenhouse back in the woods behind the barn."

Marty remembered the pink glint of sunset on glass that she'd glimpsed through the trees as she watched over Hoyt Heller's body.

The sheriff continued, "What's interesting is it was clean. Real clean. Like it'd been scrubbed. No one's farmed that place for four years but the greenhouse is scrubbed."

No one answered. He said, "Hopkins, ask the Turley kid about it when you get a chance. And ask about this too. It's the tape from the answering machine at the Matthews farmhouse." He punched the recorder button and a male voice said, "Hoyt! Things are getting tense. Get your girlfriend over to the farm real soon."

Marty tried to place the familiar voice. Something must have showed in her face, because the sheriff said, "Hopkins? Ring a bell?"

"No bells, sir. But I've heard the voice."

"Good. Work on it. One last thing." He squinted at them. "Doc Altman called a couple minutes ago. He says that both of the people who died in the Montgomery State Bank building were victims of carbon monoxide poisoning. We're cooperating with the investigation of the bank's heating system. But if anyone has any other ideas about it, let me know."

"Sir," Marty asked, "did Doc give any kind of timetable for the deaths?"

"Yeager died about one or two hours before I found him at eleven fifteen. Exposure to the gas would have been maybe for half an hour before his death. The Stollnitz woman's case is more complicated. Apparently her exposure was about the same time of night, nine P.M. or thereabouts. But she didn't die immediately, only went into a coma. Then for some reason the air got better. She was moved, or something held over her mouth was removed. Doc says she went on breathing a long time before she finally died. That's what confused things—even though she was already basically brain-dead around nine P.M., her system kept on cleaning out the poisons and by the time she died officially at three thirty A.M., her blood level was close to normal."

Marty nodded. That fit with her idea of Gordon or someone carrying her down from the contaminated office upstairs to the airy bank lobby.

"No more questions? All right, troops, let's move!" said the sheriff.

The morning was clear and cool. Marty drove first to the Montgomery State Bank. A group of investigators was peering into the air vents of the lobby. Upstairs in the Hansen and Yeager office she found Debra at the reception desk bundled up in a lilac-colored mohair jacket, the window behind her opened wide to the cool air. Marty said, "Hey, I thought they gave the all-clear hours ago."

Debra shrugged. "I don't care. I'm not going to breathe this air until they figure out what went wrong and fix it."

"Don't blame you. I was kind of holding my breath too. Listen,

182

we're trying to find out what Gordon was doing here last night. Can you give me some help?"

"I've been wondering too," Debra said.

"First, could you give a look around his office and tell me if anything seems out of place?" Marty broke the police seal and opened the door. "Here, just stand in the door and look around. Anything odd?"

"See, the problem is, he's not a real neat person. Gets all the work done and then some, but not real neat." Debra wrinkled her nose at the thought of Gordon's lack of neatness.

"Well, just do your best," Marty said.

Debra looked around the office carefully. "No, looks fine," she began. "Except for papers being in different stacks. But those are different every morning."

"Anything else around the office seem different?"

"No, except there were lots of footprints in the carpet today. Looked like boots. But I figured it was you guys."

"Yeah, you figured right." Marty hoped Kev had gotten photos of the carpet before the firemen had arrived. She turned back to the main office. "What's your guess about what Gordon was working on?"

"Like I said, I don't really know much. Just the billings."

"Can I see a list of those?"

"Oh, Marty, you know everything here is confidential. I'll check with Chip, but, you know—"

"I know." Too bad this was a law office. Marty laid her Stetson on Debra's desk and ran her fingers through her curls. "Look, Debra, we're thinking that there's a possibility that it wasn't the heating system. That it wasn't an accidental malfunction."

"You mean someone meant to do it?"

"It's possible."

Alarm flared in Debra's eyes. "And might do it again?"

"We just don't know. That's why I'm interested in what Gordon was doing. But I don't have probable cause for a search warrant yet. So while we're trying to find a lead somewhere else, if you happen across a list of the people he was working with after hours, you might think about who might have had it in for Gordon." Marty watched Debra glance nervously toward Gordon's office and added, "I have to use the bathroom. Be out in a minute."

Hoping that Debra would take the hint, she took her time, applying her lipstick carefully, rubbing at a spot on her brown uniform shirt, shifting her gunbelt to a more comfortable position. In a moment she was pleased to hear the whine of a printer outside. She inspected the bags under her eyes and decided the only thing that would fix them was a good night's sleep. She adjusted her stud earrings and emerged. Debra, standing in front of her desk, announced, "I gotta go too," and disappeared into the bathroom.

Marty picked up her Stetson from the desk. Under it now was a printout.

Marty read it carefully. Most of the names were individuals. She recognized a lot of them. There were some pretty important local folks, several doctors and a County Commissioner. Stephanie Stollnitz's name was there, sitting innocently among the S's. The dozen businesses included Dunning Stone Company, three real estate offices, and some bigger fish. Gordon had done work for Burger King, Arby's, even the giant Indiana drug company Eli Lilly—although it must have been for branch offices, because all three had Bloomington addresses.

Debra had pencilled question marks by four of the names. "Don't recognize these," she'd scribbled beside them. They were R. A. Anders, Matt Joseph, Wally Peters, Olaf Whitney. Marty didn't recognize them either. She stared at the whole list a moment. There was something missing. What? But it wouldn't come. She folded the paper and slid it into her notebook as Debra came out.

"Thanks, Debra. I'll be back officially when I've got something."

The door opened and Chip came in, blond, tousled and worried-looking. "Marty! Are you here about Gordon? Do you know what happened?"

"Not yet. They're working on it now. Uh . . . Chip, you'll have his clients now, right? Because if we find out it wasn't an accidental malfunction, we'll have to look more closely at what Gordon was working on."

"What do you mean, not an accidental malfunction?"

"If it looks like it was done on purpose, it could've been directed toward Gordon."

"Oh, God, that couldn't be!" Chip rubbed his forehead. "Gordon was salt of the earth. It's just a terrible accident, I'm sure. Listen, is Sheriff Cochran okay?"

"Yes, he's doing fine."

"Good, good. I spoke to Ed at the bank. He swears he'll get to the bottom of this."

"Meanwhile I'm keeping the windows open," Debra announced firmly.

Marty asked, "Chip, could you give a look around Gordon's office? See if anything looks unusual, or out of place?"

184

Chip looked around. "God, I don't know. I never paid much attention to his office. Looks about the same."

"What about Gordon? Did he seem to be under extra pressure or anything?"

Chip looked at her oddly. "What do you expect? One of his clients died downstairs Tuesday night, and there was a tornado Wednesday. We're all under pressure. Look, Marty, it's got to be the bank heating system. Nothing else makes sense."

"Okay. But if you think of anything, let me know. Oh . . . one other thing." She pushed a curl aside on her forehead. "Since I'm here, I should tell you that Brad and I decided to try a divorce mediator."

Chip frowned. "Are you sure you want to go that route?"

"I want to at least try it."

Chip shook his head. "Okay by me, but I have to warn you it could be dangerous. Make sure you aren't pressured into giving up what you really need. Your husband's a persuasive type, you know."

"I sure do." She wavered an instant, thinking of Brad's earnest dark eyes and agile words building oh-so-beautiful castles in the air. Chip was much better than she was at cutting through those pretty words to expose what Brad was really saying. But Chrissie's sad little face was more powerful than her fear of Brad's eloquence. Marty said, "If it doesn't work I'll be back, Chip. But I want to try it."

"You'll let me look over the agreement, if you get to that?"

"God, yes! I'd never sign anything without your okay."

"All right. Good luck."

She left him shaking his head.

Even with the help of officers from nearby counties, Wes knew it would be hard to control the reporters, all scrambling for a new angle on the Hoyt Heller case. A lot of them had settled for tornado-site coverage, but as he approached Mercy Hospital, where Heller's body still lay, he saw a woman tucking her press card into her pocketbook. By the time he'd parked and approached the deputy at the door, she was deep into a discussion of her tornado-injured aunt who lay within, she said. The deputy turned her away politely. Wes grinned and said, "Whatsa matter? You think reporters don't have relatives?"

"Well, if they do, they better be able to remember their last name. That gal tried four names, none on my list. Said her aunt had remarried."

"Yeah, if she hasn't done her homework any better than that, she doesn't deserve to get in." Wes entered the hospital and found his way to Jake's room.

"Hey there, Jake," he said cheerily. "You still look like something the vultures left behind. You feel that way too?"

"Uh-huh." Jake's unbandaged eye regarded him dully.

"Yesterday you were going on and on about your Pacers cap. So I had a look-see, and decided you just couldn't wait to see how your photos came out."

The eye was suddenly alert. "Uh-huh!"

"Well, I'll show them to you. Some are tornado damage. You're not interested in those, are you?" He fanned out the set of photos.

Jake said, "Unh-unh."

Wes held up the next half-dozen. "And here's a bunch of Miss Coral Turley dressed in her show-biz clothes. Are these the ones?" He fanned them out, hoping Jake could focus.

But Jake said, "Unh-unh."

"Not those? The only other is one lonely photo of a guy in a parking lot—"

"Uh-huh! Uh-huh!"

"Yeah, I figured this might be it. Caucasian, about five-ten, one-sixty, age around forty, brown hair and a mustache—looks a whole lot like the description you gave me yesterday."

"Uh-huh!"

"So for reasons we'll figure out later, you took his picture. And from the way he's looking at you, he noticed you doing it. And a little later he ran you off the road and stole your camera and left you for dead. Right so far?"

"Uh-huh." Jake's eye stared at Wes eagerly.

"This gray Lincoln he's got his hand on, is that what he drives?"

"Uh-huh."

Wes squinted at the photo. "Can't see the license plate. Are they Indiana plates?"

"Unh-unh."

"You sound real definite, buddy. Do you know the plate number?"

"Unh-unh." Jake managed to put a lot of regret into his grunt.

Wes said, "Okay, let's work on the state. Not Indiana. We'll start with our neighbors. How about Illinois?"

"Unh-unh."

"Kentucky?"

"Unh-unh."

"Ohio?"

"Uh-huh! Uh-huh!"

"Good work. I'm gonna do two things for you, Jake. Number one, I'll send out an APB to watch for this guy and for his gray Lincoln with Ohio plates. So we'll catch him soon. Number two, Mercy Hospital is already under guard because we've got a celebrity corpse here. Did you know that?"

"Uh-huh." Sorrow in the grunt.

Wes looked at Jake sharply. "Jake Shaw, if you didn't have a doctor swearing to all those broken bones, I'd think you were just trying to finagle your way into this hospital. I saw a reporter outside inventing an injured relative to try to get in. Well, I'll believe you for now. So I'm going to show this photo to our guys at the gate, 'cause it occurs to me that if this fella's got your camera, and finds out that this picture he's so nervous about ain't in it, he may think about coming here to look for it. And we kinda want to discourage that."

"Uh-huh!" Jake exclaimed fervently.

"Okay. Anything else you want to say to me about this guy?"

"Unh-unh."

"Your doc tells me in a couple of days you'll be sitting up and he can set up a typewriter for you. He say's you've got two good fingers. So I'm gonna want the whole story then. But meanwhile, don't you think I'm the smartest sheriff you ever saw?"

"Uuunh—" said the bandaged head dubiously.

Wes cocked his fist at Jake. "Now I know why people like to make you a punching bag! See you later, you old buzzard."

Thirty

It was time to take a fresh look at the facts, whatever the facts were in this three-way tangle of death and confusion. As she left the bank building, Marty thought about glancing over the reports in the files at the station.

But Hopkins, you already know the facts, she thought as she turned the ignition. The problem is you need more. And not just about Gordon Yeager's death. The tornado rescue effort hadn't given her much chance to think about Steffie's or Hoyt's deaths either, and she sure didn't see any logic to this. Shoot, she didn't even know if they were accidents as they appeared or murders as she feared. She turned east and pulled out her sunglasses to fend off the glittering morning light and wondered what she was missing.

Okay, Hopkins, if there's no logic, go with your gut. What feels wrong?

Coral's story, for one. Her passion for music and performing rang true, and her closeness to her mother. Her account of running her car into a ditch sounded okay, might even be true. But something was wrong with part of her story, the crucial part that involved Hoyt Heller.

Marty noticed she was driving toward White Oak Farm. Okay.

What was Coral hiding? Some involvement with drugs, maybe? For one so young she seemed very savvy about music, about the music business, about getting media attention. Coral would know that on one level drug use was not a problem, was expected by fans. Even jail wouldn't hurt rock singers, might even help, as long as it was brief. On the other hand, Coral would want to avoid the hassle of arrest, especially right now, when her career was getting a jump-start.

And if there was something to cover up, her parents would not help the cops. They'd try to protect her. Dee, good citizen though she was, was definitely batty about her daughter. And Tom would go along with Dee.

Marty tried to imagine Chrissie in bad trouble. How much would she do to protect her daughter? Would she lie? Obstruct justice?

Surely there would be ways to do the right thing for the girl within the law.

But rising through the logical thought came the scream of the wild and woolly Marty beneath: No way! Don't touch my kid!

She didn't know what she'd do until she had to face it.

Marty shook her head, impatient with herself. Time to forget the what-ifs and figure out what else to ask Coral.

Okay. What about Steffie's death? Or Gordon's death? Any links with Hoyt Heller there? Marty was willing to bet that the night she died, Steffie had been in Gordon's office, for business or pleasure. She could believe that the ex-husband might kill her as he tried to regain control over her. He'd kill Gordon too, if he thought Gordon was her new lover, maybe if he thought Gordon had encouraged the divorce. But carbon monoxide seemed the wrong weapon for

Clay Stollnitz. He was more a knife or blunt instrument type, she thought. And why would he kill Hoyt Heller?

Maybe Coral could tell her why.

White Oak Farm looked refreshed this morning in the cool September air. As Marty rounded the curve, she noted how the drought-worn fields were greening already, how the White Oak Farm sign on the new wing of the store gleamed in the sun, how the glass of the greenhouses sparkled. There were half a dozen vehicles including a TV van in the store parking lot. She'd guessed right. Coral was on the premises. The two Lily Pistols security men in their black military-cut uniforms stood guard on the farmhouse porch. Marty approached and told Gary or Rocky, she still didn't know which was which, that she had to see Coral about Hoyt's death. "That's what they all say," he scowled, but let her pass. "Go ahead, she's up already."

Tom Turley opened the door. Good, she could ask him what he'd seen when he cleaned the bank last night. Maybe he was more observant than his fellow janitor Jumbo Jim. But right now he looked like a shorter, grouchier version of the guards outside with his dark navy shirt and his frown. "Yes?" he barked.

"Hey, Tom, it's just me," Marty said. "I have a couple more questions for you and Coral, then I'll be out of your way."

"Hi, Marty, honey," Dee called from the door at the end of the hall. "C'mon back here to the kitchen."

Dee was in jeans and a T-shirt the color of ripe apples. Her corn-blond hair shone in its usual braided circlet. She added, "Don't mind Tom. We're just suffering from all these long hours."

"Suffering from all this celebrity too," Tom grumbled. "Sorry, Marty."

Marty said, "It's been a real tough couple days." She and Tom followed Dee into the kitchen. A familiar kitchen of warm oak with views of the hills, baskets of bright vegetables and fruits. She hadn't been in here since she was twelve, and there were brand-new white floors and countertops, but it still felt like home to Marty.

Coral, scrubbed and still damp from a shower, sat at the oak kitchen table behind baskets of muffins and tangerines. She wore a pink T-shirt and black jeans, and her wet curly hair was slicked down into flat zig-zags against her perfect skull. She wiggled her fingers at Marty in greeting. "Hi, Deputy Hopkins. I thought you guys were finished with me."

"Yeah. I thought so too, but something came up."

"Sit down," Dee commanded. "I'm going to pour us all some more coffee."

"Thanks." Marty took the chair across from Coral. Tom hung back by the door, but when Dee handed him a mug of coffee, he sat too, rocking his chair back away from the table. Dee handed around the other mugs, nudged the muffin basket in Marty's direction, and sat down with them. The coffee was strong and hot and very welcome.

"Okay. So what came up that you have to ask about?" Coral sounded wary.

Marty put down her mug and explained, "Basically I'm supposed to find out about Hoyt's local connections here."

"Basically, the connection was me," Coral said. "This was only the third time he's been in Indiana, and he never stayed more than two or three days before."

"Who arranged for him to come this time?"

"The whole band decided to do the racetrack videos. You mean who made the travel arrangements?"

"Yeah, and who got other things lined up. Advance men or whatever. And anything else you can think of."

"Sure. Rafael and Duke. I'll give you the numbers."

"Did anyone else have an Indiana connection?"

"Not that I ever heard of."

Marty sipped more coffee and studied the girl. "Coral, you said you didn't tell your parents you were coming this time."

Coral shrugged, too casually. "Yeah. I'm sorry, Ma. But I figured I was disowned or something." Dee started to shake her head and Coral added impatiently, "Okay, I know now. But that's what I thought."

"But you did call to say you were okay, right?" Marty asked. "Because Tom and Dee said we could quit looking."

"Sure. I called a few weeks after Hoyt . . . after I joined Hoyt," Coral said.

"You must have known your mother was worried."

Tom said, "Look, it's okay now. Don't blame the girl."

"I'm just asking. Coral, why'd you wait so long? And why didn't you get in touch again till now?" Marty said.

"Listen, it wasn't easy! I did it as soon as I could!" Coral's big eyes were suddenly full of pain, and Marty went on alert. Time to push a little, Hopkins. We're getting close to something.

Dee was saying gently, "Honey, I know you did, it was—"

Marty cut off the soothing words. "Coral, what kind of excuse is that? It was just a phone call! Why couldn't you just pick up the phone and put your mother's mind at ease?"

190

"Because they wouldn't let me!" Coral blurted.

Tom's fist crashed on the table. "Leave the kid alone!"

Dee reached anxiously for her daughter's hand and crooned, "Coral, honey, we know it was hard for—"

Marty broke in again. "Dee, Tom, I want to hear Coral's side right now. Why wouldn't they let you?"

Coral leaned back, retreating from Marty and her mother both. "I just meant, you know, there was always so much going on."

"That's not what you said. You said they wouldn't let you."

"So I didn't say it very well. Anyway, I thought you wanted to know about Hoyt," Coral protested.

"Was Hoyt the one who wouldn't let you call?" Marty said.

"I said I didn't mean that! I was just busy!"

"You said Hoyt saw you at Asphodel Springs Resort, and liked your music, and a couple days later sent for you. What did you mean, sent for you?"

"He told me he wanted me to come. So I did. It was my big chance. Anyway, I did call after a while."

"But why didn't you tell your mother right away?"

Coral swallowed some coffee, gripping the mug with both hands as though trying to hide behind it. She said defiantly, "Because I'm a selfish bitchy teenager!"

"I don't believe you, kiddo. I've known you all too long for that. What really happened?"

Coral rolled her eyes up. "That's what really happened. Is it so damn hard to understand? I want to be a singer, I get my big chance, I don't think about my mother for a while, and then when I do, a few weeks have gone by. I mean, go ahead and scold me, but it's not against the law to forget to call!"

"Okay. Let's go on to another question," Marty said, and Coral looked surprised at her change of direction. "When your band rented Joe Matthews' farm, your parents obviously weren't involved because they didn't know you were here. So who made the arrangements?"

"Duke. Hoyt's gofer."

"That's one of the phone numbers you're going to give me, right? Okay. So Duke knows enough about this area to find a farmhouse for rent in Nichols County?"

"No, he probably just called up some real-estate dude. What's so strange about that?"

"Nothing." Marty made a mental note to ask Joe Matthews who the real-estate dude was. She went after another point. "But you

191

were raised in this county. Why didn't they ask you to ask Dee to make arrangements?"

"We thought Dee and Tom would fuss a lot. And anyway I wanted to just show up and play it by ear."

"She thought if we had any warning we'd start throwing things," Dee said with a smile.

Marty pushed on. "Okay, but Duke must have asked you about the farm. You had to be the expert on this county."

"I told them the county was halfway between Indy and Louisville, and I told them which roads were off the beaten track, that kind of thing. But I'd never rented a farm myself, so I couldn't help with that."

"When you say 'they,' who do you mean?"

"Duke and Hoyt and . . ." Coral swirled the coffee in her mug, frowning. "Duke said something about getting in touch with their Indiana man."

"Good," Marty said. "Did he say who the Indiana man was?"

"No. Like I say, probably someone in real estate. Why don't you ask Duke?"

"I will, soon as you tell me how to reach him."

Coral fumbled in her waist pack, pulled out a little book, and pointed at an entry. Marty said, "Peter Wallis?"

"Yeah, that's Duke's real name."

Marty wrote it down and said, "Now, let me ask you about a couple of specific people. Did Hoyt, or you, or anyone else know Stephanie Stollnitz? Or mention her?" She focused on Coral, but was aware of puzzled stares from Dee and Tom both.

Coral shook her head. "Never heard of her."

"How about Gordon Yeager? The lawyer?"

"I met him a couple of times when I was younger, like at Dee's charity cookouts. I never heard Hoyt mention him. Why would he know him?"

Tom was leaning forward, his dark eyes intense. "Why are you hassling Coral about Gordon Yeager? Is Yeager okay?"

He'd hear soon anyway, he worked in the bank building. Marty sighed. "Yeager died last night in his office."

"Oh, no!" Dee exclaimed. "What happened?"

"That's what we're trying to find out."

Tom was still staring at her. "In his office? Last night?"

"Yeah. That was the other thing I was going to ask about. Did you clean the bank last night?"

"Yeah." Tom, suddenly the center of attention, leaned back self-consciously in his chair.

192

"Did you see anything unusual?"

He shook his head slowly. "Everything seemed normal."

"What time did you leave?"

"Usual time. Eight or eight thirty."

"Was Gordon Yeager there?"

Tom rubbed his forehead. "Yeah. Yeah, I even spoke to him, briefly. Would have been when I first got to that floor, seven thirty or thereabouts. He was working and he told me not to bother doing his office, so I vacuumed the other three rooms and went away. God, what happened to him?"

"Did he seem nervous or anything?"

"Not that I noticed. But we only said a couple of words. Like I say, he was busy."

"Who else was around last night?"

"The accountant was working late too. But no one else. Except—" He frowned at the muffin basket. "As I was leaving, I saw a big blond guy approaching from the Burger King parking lot. I wondered about him because the bank is the only reasonable place he'd be going."

"Good." Marty made a note. "What did he look like?"

"About thirty. Six-two, six-three, lots of muscle. Had on a foot-ball sweatshirt and jeans."

"Did you see his vehicle?"

Tom shrugged. "There were about twenty in the Burger King lot."

"Okay. Coral, do you know this six-two blond guy?"

The girl looked up, startled. "I don't think so."

"Do you know a guy named Clay Stollnitz? Either of you?"

Both shook their heads. Coral asked, "Is he some relative of the woman who died in the bank?"

"It's a possible connection, if that's who it was. Did Hoyt, or anyone else, ever mention the name?"

Coral shrugged. "I don't remember. Hoyt knew about four million people."

Tom burst out, "What's going on here, Marty? Hoyt didn't die in the bank. He got killed by that tornado. So why are you bugging Coral if there's no connection?"

Marty said, "Maybe there isn't. But I have to check it out."

Tom said, "Well, I think you should quit hassling her!"

It was hard sometimes to interview people you'd grown up with. Marty stood up slowly and leaned into the table, one hand on her nightstick. She said mildly, "Tom, I know you want to help your

193

family. But this isn't a social call. It's a police investigation and I need to know about Hoyt."

He jumped up too, not big but tough and wiry, mouth tight, eyes furious. Then he lurched to the door and slammed out of the kitchen.

Coral looked frightened now. Marty sat down again and ran her hand through her curls. Sometimes she hated her job. She said, "Coral, do you want your mom to leave too? You can talk to me privately."

Dee moved her chair closer to her daughter's. "Honey, you don't have to say anything."

Coral leaned back wearily. "She'll just keep after me, Ma. Might as well get it over with." She squared her shoulders and glanced sourly at Marty. "So. You want to know about Hoyt."

Thirty-One

Wes hoped that the experts would figure out where the carbon monoxide had come from, but when he met with them Friday morning in the maze of ducts and pipes in the Montgomery State Bank sub-basement, he was disappointed. They had run every test they could devise on the heating plant. "It's new, it's well maintained, it's innocent," said Leahy, the head technician from the gas company, and the crime scene technicians and fire department experts all nodded soberly.

Wes glanced at the snarl of elbowed tubes that surrounded him. "So if it didn't come from here, where did it come from?"

"Whatever it was, it's not in the bank any more," Leahy declared. "If it ever was."

"We're going to check the exterior too, see if there's any way they could access from there," explained one of the state crime scene boys. Wes nodded.

Leahy went on, "Another reason we think it's not the building system is that the flippers on the vent in that one office were in the closed position, so it was getting a minimum of air from the system."

"Interesting."

"Yeah. In my opinion, you're looking for something portable. Maybe someone brought in a space heater. Or for some reason they might have been running some other combustion machine. I've seen carbon monoxide victims from all kinds of motors—lawn mowers, power washers, snowblowers, cars of course. Motel over in Terre Haute had a problem with their swimming pool heater. Some of the exhaust leaked into the nearby rooms and sent a couple guests to meet their maker."

Wes flashed on his own drowsy headache last night and snapped, "Not many swimming pools around this bank. Did you find anything in the office?"

The crime scene technician shrugged. "Nothing obvious. We vacuumed up lots of dust and fibers to analyze."

"Okay, let me know. Thanks."

Wes ducked a four-inch pipe near the door and stomped out, frustrated. Shouldn't let it bug him, but goddamn, the gas had pretty near knocked him out too. That made it personal.

He tried to remember what it had smelled like, but whatever it was had been too faint to register. That's how it had blindsided him. Probably not auto exhaust, then. Exhaust smoke smelled strong enough to make you cough, even if it was the odorless ingredient that killed you.

He hiked across the parking lot to pick up a cup of coffee at the Burger King.

"Hey there, Mandy, how about one to go?" he said to the waitress. Forty if she was a day, but still as dimpled and pony-tailed as she'd been in high school.

She set a foam cup on the counter and filled it for him. "Hi, Sheriff. You doing better?"

Word spread fast. He said, "Yeah, no big problem. But we want to figure out what went wrong with the air over there."

"That's terrible, that lawyer dying. From what Debra tells me, it'll probably be the furnace, don't you think?"

"Could be, but the experts are looking for something portable. Somebody's space heater, maybe. You didn't notice anything like that, did you?" Wes leaned against the counter and took a sip of his coffee. "Do you know if anyone there complains about it being cold?"

"Not to me, they don't." She fetched him a plastic lid for his foam cup and added, "You know, I saw that guy go in last night. That lawyer."

"Gordon Yeager?"

"Yeah. He never used to come in here but Debra pointed him out once, said he was one of her bosses. So I knew him."

"What time did you see him?"

"About six o'clock yesterday. We were real busy here. The tornado's brought in a lot of customers. But I saw his car drive in."

"Was he alone?"

"Yeah, went into the building alone."

Wes started to fit the lid on to his foam cup. "Any other cars there?"

"I remember a big gray one. I didn't see it leave, but it was gone maybe half an hour after I saw Mr. Yeager's car drive in."

Wes looked up. "Gray? You remember what make car it was?"

"Something posh. Reminded me of a guy's car I saw earlier this week. Out-of-town guy."

"What'd he look like?"

"Middle-aged, glasses, mustache. Casual clothes but not cheap ones, you know? A few days ago he was in here asking where to stay around here. I said Knight's Inn but Jake suggested Asphodel Springs Resort and he must've been right because the guy left a big tip."

"Jake was there too? The reporter?"

"Yeah."

Well, well. Wes asked, "What was this other guy's name?"

Mandy shrugged a plump shoulder. "He never said."

He pulled out the photo Jake had taken. "Look familiar?"

"That's the guy. That's the car," Mandy said. "What's going on here, Sheriff?"

"That's what I'm trying to figure out. Look, this is important. If he comes back here, don't cross him, okay? Just act normal and get someone to call us real quiet." Wes put money on the counter. "And you call us if you remember anything else, okay? About Yeager or about this stranger with the gray car."

He ran for the cruiser. Had Jake somehow blundered across Gordon Yeager's killer? And practically been killed himself? Wes switched on the pulsar lights and turned toward Asphodel Springs.

Coral was having second thoughts. She didn't really want to tell Deputy Hopkins what had happened. She didn't even want to think about it anymore. But Dee hugged her and urged, "Come on, honey, it's better if you tell Marty. She wants to find out what happened to Hoyt so we can get on with our lives."

"What difference does it make? I won't testify about any of it. And Dee, if you try to do anything I'll never speak to you again!"

Dee shivered. "I won't. I want what's best for you."

Deputy Hopkins said, "Nobody has to testify. I just want to know what happened so I can understand the guy better. Understand his death."

"I don't know where to start."

The deputy said gently, "Start with meeting them."

What the hell, get it over with. Coral said, "I already told you all that. They came through Asphodel Springs and we clowned around together and then they went away."

"And then they sent for you. How?"

The memory came back in a rush, as though she'd been flipped into another world, laughing with her girlfriends who also had summer jobs at the resort, the potted palms and flowers giving a softness and fragrance and lustful innocence to the air. Coral said slowly, "You know the Palm Court, that's the café area at Asphodel Springs? We were singing at lunchtime, and here came Duke, the band's gofer, all of a sudden. He's this middle-aged guy, looks real respectable."

"Is this the guy I saw standing in the corner in Bloomington?"

"Yeah. He's in charge of security and stuff. Anyway, he said Hoyt wanted a date. I didn't believe him at first, but he finally convinced me, and I was like, my God, this is Lily Pistols, this is big time! I bet half the girls in the USA want a date with Hoyt Heller. So I asked Duke if I could be back here at the farm by eleven, and he said no problem. God, I was such a dummy!" She hit her forehead with the heel of her hand.

"Honey, it wasn't your fault," Dee said.

"Yeah, well, I must've known even then, 'cause I lied to you, right? I called you and said I was going out with Mark."

"Doesn't make you the villain," Dee said tartly.

Her mother's vehemence brought a lump to Coral's throat as she explained to the deputy, "See, I knew she and Tom would say no. And . . . it sounds stupid now, but I didn't want them to worry."

"Yeah. I understand," Deputy Hopkins said. "It was Lily Pistols. You couldn't say no."

Coral was pleased. Maybe this deputy would get it. She said, "Right. I'm a singer. Do you have any idea how hard it is to get started in this business? This was the chance of a lifetime. So I went with Duke. He drove me to Evansville, and sure enough, there was Hoyt, and Skell, and Brian, and two women they'd picked up at the University of Evansville. They were groupies, really crazy about Lily Pistols. And everybody was doing coke and acting stupid." She stared at Dee's bowl of tangerines, not meeting anyone's eyes.

197

"So anyway, it wasn't like I thought it would be. It wasn't romantic or anything. Hoyt just wanted me to take off my clothes in front of everybody, but I was like, no way! So he was pissed and sort of held me down, and I fought back, and Duke got a big golf club—" Damn, something was clogging her throat. Coral coughed and tried not to remember Hoyt's bruising hands on her arms, the cold touch of the club against her temple. "And he asked Hoyt if he should knock my head into the rough. So I quit fighting, and Hoyt, you know—" Coral saw that tears were dropping on her jeans. She rubbed her wet cheek with her free hand. Get it over with. "Hurt like hell. And then Hoyt wanted Duke to take a turn, and he did, and then . . . see, Skell said I was bleeding and that turned him off, and besides the Evansville groupies were complaining. Anyway, they let me alone, and I just lay there curled up, staring at the wall. The motel had these dumb botanic prints on the wall, still life, and I pretty well memorized the one with pomegranates." Her mother was silent, tears on her face too, strength and love in the warm pressure of her hand on Coral's.

The deputy said gently, "What happened next?"

Coral cleared her throat again. "Well, it got later and later. Hoyt was asleep and I tried to leave but Duke was outside on the balcony smoking. At first he was nice, like he'd been at Asphodel Springs, and he said sure, he'd give me the keys to a rental car they had if I'd return it. But when I took him seriously and said no, I couldn't drive, I just wanted to call my parents, he grabbed me and looked through my bag, and then he started swearing. Maybe he was still teasing, you know, Jekyll–Hyde stuff, but I was really scared. And he pushed me back in the room and tore out the phone."

"What'd you have in your bag?" the deputy asked.

"Nothing special. Makeup, high-school ID, my tip money, an address book."

"Same address book you just showed me?"

"Yeah, but there are lots of new addresses now."

"Let me see the bag."

Coral handed it to her and the deputy skimmed through the book, then shook her head and started looking at the rest. "So then what?"

"It went on that way for two weeks, almost. I tried to sneak out a couple times but they caught me, and Duke has lots of guns, and there was no way out. When Hoyt got coked up, the best thing to do was get it over with. But he was nice most of the time. He got kind of obsessed with me, maybe 'cause I cried a lot and he wanted to make me happy. Duke kept telling me to be nice, there was a

198

lot of money in this for me if I'd cooperate, but I told him I didn't want his damn money and cried some more. We were traveling in that bus they have, and when they did gigs Duke would keep me company in the dressing rooms to keep me away from the phones."

The deputy's gray eyes had gone steely. She was holding Coral's California driver's license. "Coral, you said you couldn't drive. How old were you when this happened?"

"Fifteen."

"Jesus. Look, we've got them on rape, child molesting, criminal confinement, drug counts—"

"No!" said Coral. "You don't get it!"

"Marty, honey, let her finish the story," Dee said.

The deputy looked hard at Dee, then sighed. "Okay. Finish the story."

"Well, I kept wondering why I'd agreed to go with Duke, why I'd been so dumb. Then—I remember it was the ninth day—I thought, hell, I know why I came, it's because of the music. It was like a message from God, you know? Saying here's your goddamn big chance and you're snivelling in the corner. So I decided, okay, they keep me away from phones and bus stations, but they can't keep me away from the music! So I went to Duke, and I was like, you want me to cooperate? Okay, forget paying me. Make me famous. And he was like, oh no, not another wannabe! But all these songs were suddenly in my head, like they wanted to be written, and Hoyt was going through a dry spell, kept making false starts and giving up. So Duke came through. Told Hoyt to listen to one of my songs and he said why not? I sang 'Deathwind' and Hoyt loved it. And I sang one of the pieces he'd been having trouble with and kind of fixed it, and he loved that too."

Dee said, "Of course he loved it. Even bastards love it."

Coral squeezed her mother's hand. "Anyway, Hoyt and Skell and I worked on 'Deathwind' a while, and they decided to use it on the album. And Skell—well, he's an asshole about everything but music, but he's a genius there. And he liked my stuff, and started sticking up for me and got me into the backup group, and things got easier. That's when I got away from Duke long enough to call home from backstage."

Dee said sadly, "And her mother was so depressed she wasn't answering the phone."

Coral said, "I thought Dee was mad because I'd run away. So I thought the hell with this, Hoyt's a bastard but he's got what I want, so I'll get it from him. I mean, the guy owed me, right? And he knew he owed me except when he was on coke. And Duke knew he owed me. So I decided to collect."

"You're a tough kid, Coral," the deputy said with sympathy. "Um, who got you the drugs?"

"Duke. But I didn't use them often 'cause I saw what it did to Hoyt. You going to arrest me?"

"Not unless I see you selling or using. I'm just trying to get the picture."

"It was like a cafeteria. If Hoyt got ugly sometimes I'd take a downer. But not often. I wanted to stay in control."

"Good." But the deputy's gray eyes were troubled, and Coral suddenly realized what she must be thinking.

"Look, I didn't have anything to do with Hoyt dying!" she exclaimed. "I'm telling you the whole story. He loved me, yeah, but to me it wasn't love or hate, it was music. The music is all that matters. That's the only way they can ever make it up to me. And in that tornado I really was trying to get back to make sure he was okay!"

"That's true," Dee said. "She'd just barely said hello to me and then she forced me into the tornado shelter and drove off like a madwoman."

"Yeah. Drove right into the goddamn ditch," Coral said bitterly.

"Okay," said Deputy Hopkins, her gray eyes sharp on Coral. "But I'm just trying to understand. I mean, it looks like you're getting a big boost for your personal career right now. I don't see how Hoyt Heller being alive could help you any more."

"That's 'cause you don't know the business," Coral said. "See, Hoyt was a sure thing. And he was starting to introduce me to people in the business, but they don't really know me yet. I needed more time. Now it's really iffy. We're a headless band, and if we blow it we'll be forgotten in two months. What I'm trying to do is get some momentum while everybody still cares about Hoyt."

"And you don't even want to bring charges against Duke?"

Coral said, "Look, Deputy Hopkins, I'd be lying if I said I haven't had fantasies about nailing Duke someday, and Hoyt too. But as long as I don't file charges, these guys are giving me a chance at what I want most of all. Right now revenge and garbage like that will just slow me down. So forget it. I'm going for the gold."

The deputy looked at Dee. "How about you? It's not that long ago you would've thrown the book at them."

"You're right. But see, Marty honey, in a different way I was trapped too, thinking this terrible thing was the end of everything.

200

It was terrible, yes. My child was stolen, raped, dead to me. No child, no mother could suffer more."

Dee paused, swallowed. Coral said, "Yeah. It was hell, I guess for her too. But it wasn't the end."

"It wasn't the end," her mother echoed. "I understand that now. Coral was dragged down to the depths, but she believes there's treasure there. I want to help her find it." Dee's eyes flashed. "I won't allow those evil men to go on controlling us. They're irrelevant now. What's important is Coral going forward with her life, the way she chooses to go on with it."

"And you going on with your life," Coral said softly.

"Yeah. Maybe there's treasure for everyone," Dee said.

Thirty-Two

Wes radioed Foley on his way to Asphodel Springs, and was surprised when his dispatcher told him to phone in. Standing at the pay phone in front of the Mobil station on Highway 817, Wes learned that the bulletin they'd sent out with the photo Jake had taken was bearing fruit. "Columbus Ohio says this bad guy's from California," Foley told him. "Does odd jobs for rich people on any side of the law. Wanted for questioning in homicide cases, major drug trafficking, racketeering. Word is he'll do anything for a price. Most recently linked to the Lily Pistols rock band."

"How 'bout that. What's his name?"

"Peter Wallis, but they call him Duke. Let's see. He loves golf and sometimes uses the game to cozy up to his victims before he kneecaps them."

"Upscale heavy hitter," Wes said, thinking of Jake and then of Mandy. He hoped she'd stay cool if this character showed up again at Burger King.

"Yup," Foley said. "Columbus doesn't have anything on him, but the LAPD got a tip he was in Ohio, that's how come they're up to date."

"But now he's here. I've got a witness says he was asking about Asphodel Springs Resort, so I'm heading out there to see if he's sleeping in today. Tell the other units to stand by. I may need extra beef." The tornado work had stretched them too thin to pull them from their work before he even knew the guy was there.

Wes started to get into the cruiser, then hesitated and opened his trunk instead. It only took a minute to put on the bulletproof vest. He made sure the shotgun in his front-seat rack was ready to go, then turned the ignition.

Funny how adrenaline could wipe out exhaustion. He roared down the highway toward Asphodel Springs.

Len Abbott had awakened as creaky as an old gate and full of panic. Had Stollnitz escaped him? But once he'd focused his bleary eyes he saw that it was the smaller man, the good Samaritan, who was stirring, slamming the door, waking Len up. The man got into his car, alone, and drove off.

Len, still parked off the road in a thicket of bushes, had waited a few minutes and then tiptoed to the house. It was six thirty A.M. The morning was already bright and sparkling, and he'd felt very exposed and much more foolish than he'd felt last night, peeking into this same window. But Stollnitz had still been there, sprawled on the couch, his blond hair tousled and his face cherubic.

No, the sheriff wouldn't want to arrest such a pretty boy. He'd probably been taken in, just like the Samaritan, just like Steffie.

Len had hurried away from the window and gotten back into his car. Did he dare get breakfast? The county highway was only a block away. He'd driven there hastily and turned toward the intersection with 37. That had turned out to be a mistake—that direction was where the tornado had been, and he'd soon been caught in a tangle of traffic and detours. Finally he'd been able to reverse direction. He'd found a convenience store that had coffee and packaged doughnuts, and hurried back to his hiding place.

No need to worry, as it turned out. Stollnitz was still asleep.

Len resumed his vigil.

Marty paused as she nosed the cruiser out of the White Oak Farm driveway, then turned toward Dunning, though she wasn't real sure where to go next. She believed Coral's story. The girl's ambivalence toward Hoyt made sense now. Rapist and mentor—what a combination! Marty wanted to lock up the whole band, starting with that sadistic guy with the golf club, Duke. But Coral seemed to be getting even—no, more than that, getting what she wanted from them. Marty just hoped she wasn't overestimating what they'd let her do.

The problem was, there was still no sign of what she was looking for: a connection between Hoyt and Steffie, or Hoyt and Gordon, except that they'd all died the same way, in the same county, in the same three-day period.

So Coral's story is another dead end for now, Hopkins. Move on.

What were those names on Gordon's client list that Debra hadn't recognized? Marty pulled out the printout, setting it on top of the radio to read it. R. A. Anders, Wally Peters, Matt Joseph, Olaf Whitney. Nope. She didn't know who they were either.

After hours, Gordon had done business with California, Debra had said. Okay, so maybe these were Californians. And of course after hours he'd met with Steffie too, and with . . . who was it he'd met late Monday? Debra had said the name. Andy Ragg, that's who it was. Marty knew Andy and his wife Ruth. They ran a trucking company on County 405.

But he wasn't on Gordon's client list at all. She scanned it again to be sure. No Andy Ragg, no Ragg Trucking Inc.

She'd known something was missing from that printout! Marty yanked the wheel around in a hard U-turn and sped past the Three Bears Restaurant to the Ragg place. Andy was in the parking lot in front of the long garage building, peering into a fourteen-footer's engine. He straightened up when her cruiser skidded to a stop beside him and Marty hopped out.

"Howdy, Marty. What's up?" He wiped his hands on a grimy towel.

"Got a question, Andy. Did Gordon Yeager ever do any work for you?"

Andy took off his grease-stained baseball cap and rubbed his hair, still brown around a small bald spot. "Yeah, he did. I just heard he died. That's a shame."

"Yeah. What did he do for you?"

"Handled our mortgage on the property here and on the big rig, plus he helped when that guy in Terre Haute tried to sue us."

"Did you see him Monday night?"

He replaced his cap. "Yeah, maybe five minutes. I had to sign some papers about the truck loan."

"What time?"

"Six o'clock. How come you're asking?"

"Just clearing up some details. Did you see anyone else there? Maybe as you were leaving?"

"Nobody in the office. There were some people around in the bank still."

Marty had pulled out her notebook. "Did you see him yesterday?"

"Yesterday? God, no, ever since the tornado I've been real busy here. Everyone needs trucks. Plus a couple of friends had their vehicles damaged in the wind, and I'm trying to get them to run right."

"Okay. Thanks, Andy." She climbed back in the cruiser. Debra was right, then, Andy was a client. Was he really not on Gordon's list?

He really wasn't.

She glanced again at the four mysterious names.

The first was R. A. Anders, then came . . .

Jesus. Could Andy be on the list after all? Some kind of code, first and last names transposed? But why?

She stared at the other names. Wally Peters. If R. A. Anders was Andy Ragg, Wally Peters could be Peter something. Wall, Waller, Walter? Or Wallis.

Peter Wallis was the name Coral had given her. Peter Wallis, better known as Duke. Hoyt's security man who made travel arrangements and threatened fifteen-year-old girls with golf clubs.

Hey, Hopkins, there it is, the link you need between Hoyt and Gordon Yeager! What about the other names? But she couldn't figure out Olaf Whitney. William, Whit, Walter? Oliver, Olson, O'Leary? None of the combinations made sense.

Matt Joseph, on the other hand, was a piece of cake: Joe Matthews, who owned the farm that Peter Wallis—Duke—had rented for Hoyt.

Another link. She had to talk to this Duke.

Marty glanced out the window. Andy Ragg was staring at her uneasily. She realized she'd been sitting here quite a few minutes. And she realized that Andy probably could tell her more.

She rolled down the glass. "Andy, listen, do you know a guy named Peter Wallis? Nickname Duke."

He shook his head. "Nope."

"How about Joe Matthews?"

"Yeah, he used to raise hogs over on Gate Road. But he moved away three, four years ago."

"Was Gordon Yeager always on the up-and-up with you?"

"Yeah, sure." He licked his lips. She pushed a little.

"Gordon's dead, Andy. No need to protect him."

"The deal was, I kept quiet," Andy said uncertainly.

"Deal's off now. He's dead. Look, whatever it is, we're going

204

to find it now. We'll be checking his files, and we'll know soon if you're cooperating with us or not."

Andy glanced around his parking-lot but apparently saw no way out. He cleared his throat. "Look, Marty, you know I'm running a business, right? Problem was, Gordon's bill for the Terre Haute thing was bigger than I expected. So I did a couple of off-the-books runs for him." He held up a hand as Marty started to ask. "It was in crates. Furniture from the Matthews farm, Gordon said. I picked them up at the farm, took them to a warehouse in Indy, brought back an envelope of papers for Gordon."

"When did you do this? Recently?"

"Earlier in the summer, both runs. Maybe first week in July."

"None since?"

"None. Gordon said we were square."

"I'll need the Indianapolis address."

She noted down his answer. "Okay, Andy, thanks. You got anything else you want to tell me?"

"Told you everything I know. So what's all this about?"

"We don't know yet. But thanks for your cooperation. I'll remember it."

So Gordon Yeager had been a busy man, she thought as she turned the ignition. Busy with Steffie. Busy scrambling for money to pay off Laurie's gambling debt. Busy with Duke Wallis, who arranged things for Lily Pistols. And busy moving stuff to the state capital from an abandoned farm on the back roads of Nichols County. He'd kept it quiet, off the books, off the beaten path. Sounded a whole lot like drugs.

Coral was still wrung out from reliving those terrible days for Deputy Hopkins and was relieved when Dee steered the conversation to business. "You said Hoyt's last album would get attention but after that it would be hard to keep media attention," Dee mused. "How about a big benefit concert for somebody? That could get good press."

Coral pulled up one knee from under the table and hugged it. "Media might like it, but Lily Pistols has never done goody-goody stuff like that."

"You know your audience," Dee answered. "But people like to help. You saw the response to the volunteer center, just overnight. And a benefit performance for disaster victims like Hoyt would get lots of attention. With a song like 'Deathwind'—"

Pride was shining in her mother's eyes. Coral said, "I don't want people to think we're just using Hoyt."

"Of course you're using Hoyt. He used you," Dee snapped, and polished off the last of her coffee.

Coral laughed. "Of course, Ma. But I don't want people to think it."

"They won't. You'll say it's in his memory, you invite other name bands, you give the profits to help storm victims worldwide—no problem."

It could work. Coral said, "Yeah. I'll check with the label. We'll help people, get publicity, get a showcase for the new band, all at once."

"There's another thing. Your fans are all of a sudden having to deal with a real death. That makes it a new Lily Pistols, like it or not." Dee touched her hand. "Honey, what about you? Are you dealing with it? Not just the death, everything?"

Coral felt her lip trembling again. She pressed her mouth against her denim-clad knee and mumbled her answer. "I get nightmares, Ma. Yeah, and depressions, and some days I want to cut off their hands and feet and balls. But I don't, because I'm stronger than they are. They stole my life, yeah, but I'm going to make them give me a whole new one."

"You've made a good start."

"Yep. Anyway, ol' Hoyt wouldn't want to be left out, the bastard." Coral found herself smiling almost fondly. "I guess he'll always be with us. Maybe we can get an Elvis thing going later. People will sight him, I know they will, and we can go to where the sightings are and do videos—" A song was stirring in her brain, *Across the chasm I call to you, come back, come back* . . . Everyone would think it meant Hoyt, they wouldn't know it was herself, Dee's youthful innocent daughter, that she missed.

Dee was smiling too. "You've turned into such a businesswoman all of a sudden!"

"Hey, not all of a sudden. I've been watching you all these years. Listen, do me a favor, Ma?"

"Sure."

"I want to go back to the Matthews farm to pick up some clothes before I go to Bloomington. But I can't get past the reporters out there. Could you bring the van up for me? Then I can drive it out and maybe they'll think I'm you and won't follow."

"Okay. But didn't Marty say there was a police roadblock?"

"Yeah, on Gate Road. But I bet I can avoid it if I take the tractor lane from Vine."

"Honey—don't do anything suspicious."

206

"I know. Marty thinks maybe I killed him somehow. But I've got to have something besides my leather and this pink T-shirt to wear."

"Be careful." Dee put on her sunglasses and got her straw hat and an oatmeal-colored cardigan from the rack next to the back door. "I'll tell them I'm taking stuff to the volunteer center. I'll be at the back door in a minute."

She rolled up a moment later in the Jeep, not the van, and threw some boxes into the backseat. "Here, take my sweater and hat," she said with an impish glint in her eyes. "That'll fool them."

"Hey, all right!" Coral followed directions. With the straw hat pulled low over her sunglasses, she made a K-turn and rolled nonchalantly down the driveway and on to the road. None of the reporters in the parking lot followed. Even Gary and Rocky looked after her, bored.

Free at last. Or was she trapped forever?

She used to chase butterflies in these meadows, pick blackberries in the hedgerows, run between rows of corn until lost in a rustling, dusty, sweet-scented, green and growing world.

Across the chasm I call to you . . .

The Eagle slammed down the receiver of the pay phone. Damn snooty bastard! Guy had no respect. "Yeah, you could be in bad trouble from the law, buddy boy," he'd said cheerfully. "But I've got some important business calls to make now. Talk to you later." And he'd hung up.

Important business! He didn't know how important business with the Eagle could be.

But at least he'd let slip that trouble from the law was looming. The Eagle thought that over. Must be Sheriff Cochran's little pet, Deputy Marty Hopkins. She'd been sniffing around a little too close, and didn't seem to be in any mood to back off. Women were so stubborn, so unreasonable. They made demands that could kill a guy, and then magically turned on the smiles and soft words that could revive him again. But they were unpredictable. He'd better not tell her yet what he was doing for her. He could remember what that one fighter pilot had told him over beer one night. "Yeah, my wife is divorcing me. Says I've gotten mean, hard-hearted. Stupid bitches. They send you out to do the dirty work for them, and then when you've done it and come back dirty, they get offended. Jesus, what do they want us to do? Do they think if we ask politely the enemy will put down his

207

guns? Do they think we can get rid of the killers without killing? Stupid bitches."

Yeah, thought the Eagle, stupid.

All the same, he'd better add Deputy Hopkins to his list. And soon, before she figured anything out. She was getting too close for comfort.

The Thunderbolt was still in the back this morning. The Eagle got in the driver's seat and tried to figure out where Deputy Hopkins might go next.

Marty radioed dispatch. "Unless you want me somewhere else, I'm going to the Gate Road location, ETA eight minutes."

"Nah, don't need you. National Guard's taken over tornado duty. You still on this morning's assignment?"

"That's right."

"Ten-four."

She turned the nose of the cruiser toward the Matthews farm, still trying to figure it out.

If Gordon Yeager was running drugs, where did they come from? The farm? And why would he rent out the house on the same farm? Of course if Lily Pistols were the renters, they might not care. Might even be a selling point.

One of the roadblocks that prevented anything but emergency vehicles from going into the tornado-damaged areas had been set up on Gate Road. The sleepy deputy, on loan from French Lick, moved the barrier so she could get by and asked, "Are you part of the search crew?"

"No, they'll be here around noon," Marty told him.

The Matthews farm was a mile farther along the winding road. The main tornado path was a quarter mile to the right, but there was scattered damage here from the strong peripheral winds and from debris that the whirling cone had sucked up and then dropped. The roadside was littered with small branches, papers, shingles, bits of siding like the one that had cut Hoyt Heller's neck. Looked like the park the day after the Fourth of July picnics.

She had to get out to move the police tape stretched across the deserted asphalt driveway of the pig farm. Despite the sparkle of the morning, Wednesday night returned in a rush: the stinking tornado, the miles of devastation afterward, the sprinkle of rain as the daylight dimmed, the body on the lawn, the aching hour trying to revive him.

Get hold of yourself, Hopkins. You're looking for facts.

Marty climbed out briskly, slammed the cruiser door, and looked around. No clues jumped out at her, but the sunshine erased some of the fuzziness in her memory. The asphalt driveway ended by an open gate to the old cement pig barn, but a rutted lane for tractors and wagons led on back along the barnyard fence until it disappeared into a grove of aspens and poplars, and eventually joined a similar lane that came out on Vine. The woods stretched alongside the house too, on the far side of the lawn. Marty turned full circle. The road along the front was partially blocked by bushes and trees, that's why she hadn't seen Coral approaching until she was almost here. On the side of the drive away from the house, a weedy field led down to a pond.

She didn't know what she was looking for, exactly. She walked up to the pig barn and looked inside. Big cement area, basically vacant, although rats and birds had moved in. Turning back, she saw the sun glitter on the greenhouse hidden in the woods. The first quick search had found nothing, but the technicians coming at noon might find something. She'd check it in a minute.

The lawn where Hoyt's body had been was greener, though there were still worn patches. She remembered shallow muddy footprints, but there were none here now. Two rains had erased them. She'd have to look at Kev's photos to check, but she thought the long scrapes leading to the body could have been drag marks, not the scuffs of a man crawling. If so, someone had dragged Hoyt from the shelter, dumped him on the lawn, and sliced his dead neck with that piece of metal siding.

The siding was gone. Doc had mentioned it in his report. She hoped he had it.

Marty squatted on the driveway behind the cruiser, near the tornado shelter door in the lawn. There were still blurry traces of tire prints in the dirt between the driveway and the door, but she couldn't see the footprints that had been there, or those light parallel grooves that had been pressed into the grass. What was nagging her about those grooves? A little over a foot apart. Maybe sled marks? The weather had been summery, steamy. But was that why the grooves looked so familiar, because they reminded her of Chrissie's sled?

No. They were familiar because she'd seen similar grooves in the carpet of the closet at Hansen and Yeager. The closet that opened to the outer office, but butted against Gordon Yeager's wall.

Hot damn!

But don't congratulate yourself yet, Hopkins. You still don't know

209

why there should be sled marks, or why these three people were gassed to death, or who did it.

She tugged the shelter door open and fitted the simple brace over its steel hook. Propped upright like this, the three-quarter-inch thick plank door might withstand a strong wind, but not a tornado. Marty left it braced open and climbed down into the seven-by-ten room. The steps were planks too, bolted to a framework of steel tubing.

There sat the kerosene lamp, plump and innocent-looking on its shelf, matches beside it. There was the bench Coral had mentioned. Weird place to want to have sex if you were as rich as Hoyt Heller. Marty's outdoor fantasies featured starlit swimming holes or camp-fires in the mountains, not cinder-block bunkers in the ground. But Hoyt Heller was a rapist, probably weird even with consensual sex. He made his money being weird.

Could that be what happened? Coral and Hoyt here together in the shelter as the storm roared by outside, not realizing that some-thing was poisoning the air? Then Hoyt collapsing, Coral helping him up the steps, dragging him out onto the lawn? Was she strong enough? She would have been breathing carbon monoxide too. At best she'd have a headache and the drowsiness Sheriff Cochran had experienced. Didn't seem likely.

There was a rumble in the background, and a crunch. It took Marty a moment to identify it as a car coming down the driveway. Not up from the road, down from the outbuildings. Who the hell would be back there? She started up the steps to meet the visitor.

But instead of stopping, the engine suddenly roared and the car slammed into the shelter door. The sturdy brace buckled and the plank door snapped closed like a mousetrap, smacking Marty hard on the skull and knocking her off the steps. For a moment she sat dazed in the darkness, her hand on her head.

The throb of the engine above her suddenly cut out. In the black silence Marty lurched dizzily to her feet, steadied herself against the wall, and yelled, "Hey, watch it! Someone's down here!"

There was no answer, but the planks above her creaked.

Thirty-Three

At Asphodel Springs a U-shaped drive curved around a flower-bordered lawn to the wide front steps, and on each side of the U a big parking lot fanned out, landscaped with trees that flowered in the spring. Wes ignored the signs and drove right up to the steps. He pulled his twelve-gauge from the rack and glanced at the building. Three stories of turn-of-the-century yellow brick were shaded by gingerbread balconies running the length of the building. The panes of French windows glittered from the shadows. Wes climbed the front steps and entered the spacious lobby. The young woman at the desk of the resort reminded Wes of an airline stewardess, slim, uniformed, competent, and always smiling, although she did blink when she saw the shotgun. He said, "Hi, Arlene, how's your dad doing?"

"Real well, thanks, Sheriff," she beamed. "All he lost was a barn and a couple pigs, and he says the insurance ought to cover that. What can I do for you?"

Wes turned sideways so he could talk to her while keeping an eye on the main door and the two corridors that fed into the entry area. This lobby was at the center of the rambling E-shaped building and opened into a big glass-covered patio full of potted plants. Young white-shirted waiters served coffee and iced tea to people sitting at the wicker tables. A Victorian fountain in the middle sported a man-sized black marble statue of a smiling horned devil who held up a jug that spilled water into the white marble pool below. The people didn't seem devilish, Wes thought. In their pastel polo shirts they looked a lot like your average Methodist picnic. If Duke the golfer was there, he blended right in.

Wes pushed the photo Jake had taken toward the smiling Arlene. "Is this guy staying here?"

"Yeah, that's Mr. Norton," she said readily. "He checked in Tuesday."

"What's he doing here?"

"Vacation. He wanted a place with a golf course."

211

Bingo. "Do you have his license plate number?"

"Sure, we get that from all our guests." Smiling a little nervously now, she read off the Ohio plate number.

Wes glanced at the staircase again. "What room is he in?"

"Two-fourteen, second floor front. It's funny, I offered him one with a view of the golf course and woods, but he picked one in the front. What's all this about?"

"We have a few questions for him." Wes remembered all the French windows that overlooked the parking lot. Duke's room must have been among them. He asked, "Is he there now?"

Arlene shrugged. "He had breakfast sent up an hour ago. But there are a million exits in this place so I can't promise anything."

He'd need backup. Rule one was, don't take on California organized crime all by your lonesome. Wes thanked Arlene and started for his cruiser to radio Foley for assistance, but at the top of the steps he glimpsed movement across the vast parking lot.

Shit. A gray Lincoln was sliding out of the lot.

The shelter door over Marty's head would not budge. She shone her flashlight around the edges but whatever the problem was, it wasn't visible from down here. She tried her portable radio, but this far from the station, and underground to boot, she got nothing but static, even when she held it close to the plank door above her. The Indiana limestone that surrounded her did a real good job of blocking radio waves.

There was a thump and what sounded like footsteps on the door above her. Marty yelled, "Hey, up there! Can you get this door open for me?"

There was no answer, except for more thumps and the sound of a car door closing. Marty yelled hopelessly, "Hey!"

Who the hell was up there? What were they doing? Why had they trapped her? They knew she was law enforcement. The cruiser was in full view on the driveway. Were they doing something they didn't want her to see?

The daylight from the knothole blacked out and a low whirring sound began.

Something in her knew, even before the first warm, faintly musty puff of air reached her nostrils.

Someone was pumping carbon monoxide into the shelter.

Wes stayed well behind the gray Lincoln. Don't panic, Duke ol' buddy, sure it's a cruiser back here, just happens to be going your

212

direction, just by chance. Can't be the first time that's happened to you in the last few months. Just coincidence. We'll just mosey along, nobody getting excited, nobody getting hurt.

Meanwhile he was calling in a ten seventy-eight for assistance. He gave the dispatcher the license number, the description of the vehicle, the description of the bad guy. None of the other units were nearby, but Culp, Hopkins, and Sims should be able to get to this part of the county in fifteen or twenty minutes. Outside, the midmorning sun lit the peaceful hills. The trees beside the road looked scrubbed, rejuvenated, as though the storm had given them a second wind after the long summer drought. Second wind, ha! Tell that to the folks whose houses and barns were flattened.

The Lincoln turned onto the Paoli road. Wes followed.

He'd gotten a second wind too. He'd just about ODed on the multiple tragedies of hurt people, lost homes, injured animals and devastated fields that the tornado had left behind, and on the insoluble puzzle of three unrelated people suddenly dead of carbon monoxide. Frustrating as hell, all of it, no good answers for anyone. And he was sick of the media questions, bad enough when they were about the tornado, infuriating when they were concerned only with Mr. Celebrity Heller.

Now, suddenly, he was back in the saddle, chasing a bad guy, smelling danger sharp in the air, getting his team in place. Simple, clean. Made him remember why he'd wanted to be sheriff in the first place.

The gray Lincoln turned south on a side road. Testing him. Shit, the backup units weren't yet in place. But the road Dukie Boy had chosen, Starr Road, was narrow and twisting, and he wouldn't make good time. Wes decided to stay on the Paoli road two more miles and then turn south on County 822 on the other side of the Haines farm. It'd be easy to head him off near the Sanders Creek bridge. Wes informed the dispatcher that the subject was headed south on Starr, and with only a glance he drove past the intersection, the very image of a clueless country sheriff. Jist off to catch a varmint, suh, cain't keep up with you slick California-type criminals. In his rearview mirror he could see the gray Lincoln beginning the first of the twists and turns that eventually would bring Starr Road through the limestone hills to County 822 near the Sanders Creek bridge. His own way was longer but a hell of a lot straighter, and he'd easy get to the bridge first.

Even so, as soon as the Lincoln was out of sight, Wes notched up the speed. Wouldn't want to miss this rendezvous.

*   *   *

213

Marty's first impulse was to scream and pound on the door overhead. But Doc's words about how Hoyt Heller's death might have been hastened by exertion came back to her.

Calm down, Hopkins. Assess the situation.

But the air is being poisoned!

Okay, okay. How?

Probably pumping it in through the knothole. Probably some kind of pipe or hose on the other side.

Can you poke it out?

Her pencil jabbed through the knothole but wouldn't move the encircling hose. Her nightstick wouldn't fit. Marty drew her service Glock and fired three rounds. She was rewarded by a hissed "Shit!" from above. And there was a glimmer of light through the knothole. She'd punctured the hose.

Then the knothole brightened. She saw a speck of blue sky. The hose was gone!

Don't kid yourself, Hopkins, it's not over.

She fired again through the overhead door, this time at the other end of the shelter. The bullet ripped a small ragged hole in the planks.

From above came a hoarse whisper, maybe a man. "Calm down. I'll let you out in an hour or so. But no more shooting."

His words were cool, businesslike. He didn't realize that she knew about the carbon monoxide. Keep that advantage, Hopkins! She asked, "Why don't you let me out? Then I won't have to shoot."

"I can shoot too, you know. Besides, you'll stop shooting now, if you care about your daughter."

No. He hadn't said that. He hadn't. But the numbing fear that surged through her body ignored her mind's protests. She holstered her gun with trembling fingers and said, "Okay. She's just a kid, she's no danger to you. I don't talk about work at home anyway. But it would be real dangerous for you to try to hurt her."

The hoarse whisper said, "Just be quiet, now, and she'll be fine."

Marty could hear a scraping sound as he worked on something. Probably fixing the hose. She said, "Okay, good. I won't shoot anymore."

"Don't worry, you'll be out of here in an hour. Just be patient."

An hour was way too long. The sheriff had been in trouble after twenty minutes.

In a moment the knothole blacked out again, and the deadly air began to steal past her cheeks.

She would have preferred the blast of the tornado.

Thirty-Four

Rolling east on the Paoli Road, Wes reached the intersection with County 822 within a few minutes. No word yet from Hopkins, but two of his deputies had checked in. Sims was already in the southern part of the county, so Wes told him to get on 822 immediately and come north toward the Sanders Creek bridge. Wes would go south on the same road toward the bridge and meet him. Culp, meanwhile, was to stay on the Paoli Road near Starr Road, where Wes had last seen Duke's gray Lincoln, just in case he changed his mind and came back.

Wes turned right on 822 toward the bridge, taking the easy turns at a good clip. The day was clear and fresh, as though the recent storms and tornados had never occurred. Fall was here at last. Wes could remember going to school on days like this, anticipation fizzing within him, knowing that stupendous things would happen, a kid eager to test himself against the entire world.

Shirley would say he was still that kid. Maybe he was.

Sims's cruiser, he figured, was by now coming toward him from somewhere on the far side of the Sanders Creek bridge, and their quarry, the gray Lincoln, was winding its way toward the same bridge on Starr, a twisty and badly paved road that served four hardscrabble farms.

There weren't many cars on 822. He passed two, met four. Most of the traffic in the county was near Dunning where the tornado had hit.

As Wes went around the next turn, he saw Sanders Creek at last to the left of the road. Now 822 was paralleling the creek, which was still muddy from the recent rain, glossy tan in the sunshine. On his right, the Starr Road side, the eroded limestone was too rough to farm, and trees and scrawny brush covered the knobby hills.

There were sinkholes in this kind of country, but none next to the road. Too bad. Meant they couldn't force Duke into one, the way he'd forced poor old Jake.

215

The highway curved left through a six-foot-high roadcut that was topped by a cedar thicket. The dark foliage brooded over the blond exposed limestone of the cut.

In another quarter mile he saw the crossroads. The road he was travelling, County 822, continued along this bank of Sanders Creek for miles. From the right, Starr Road descended from the rough limestone knobs, crossed this road, and continued east over rickety Sanders Creek bridge. The crossroads wasn't square, because Starr's twisting route brought it in at a sharp angle.

No gray Lincolns in sight yet.

But here came Sims, heading toward him on 822. Wes stopped and Sims pulled up so the two drivers' windows were next to each other. Sims's bony face under his Stetson was tense, excited. Wes said, "The angle Starr Road comes in, he won't want to make that tight turn to go south. So my guess is he'll either cross the bridge or go north on this road. I'll go across the bridge, head him off there. You continue north around the bend, wait for him. There's a roadcut there that'll make it harder for him to get around us. Block him, but be ready to chase him. And Sims, put on your flak jacket."

"Yes sir." Sims was off instantly. Good man.

Wes turned left, crossed the bridge, then U-turned and edged over to the side of the road where he was shielded by a tangle of vine-infested maples. He cut the motor. Far away, the purr of Sims' motor faded.

The sounds of the fall day were clear in the sudden silence. Cicadas strummed in the foliage, telling of the change of season. An Indianapolis-bound jet crossed the blue sky above him. The creek lapped at its limestone banks. The engine of his cruiser ticked slowly as it cooled. He heard the whistle of a red-winged black-bird.

And then what he was waiting for, the purr of a car from across the creek, getting louder. Now the crunch of tires on gravel. Now a glint of gray metal through the brush that lined Starr Road, a puff of dust. Now at last the nose of the gray Lincoln coming around the last bend. Wes's right hand was on the ignition, his left on the mike as he murmured, "Subject eastbound on Starr, approaching intersection with County 822. He's pausing, looking it over. Now he's moving into the intersection toward Sanders Creek bridge." Wes had his cruiser moving now too, rolling out into the traffic lane, where Duke in the Lincoln could see him. He saw the man's fist hit the steering wheel in frustration, and felt a ferocious joy.

Hey, Duke buddy, thought you'd lost me, right? Thought you'd lost the old sheriff in his own backyard.

Then Duke was twisting his steering wheel, gunning the motor. "Subject heading north on 822," Wes barked as the powerful Lincoln charged up the road Wes had just come down. He jammed down the accelerator and his cruiser catapulted across the bridge in pursuit.

Don't panic, Hopkins, Marty told herself. Think. Just take a deep breath and— No! Don't take a deep breath!

Don't breathe at all.

But think.

As long as he's up there he can't get Chrissie. And if you can last until he leaves, you can get out and stop him. Hang on to that. Hang on for Chrissie.

And turn on the flashlight. Don't die in the dark.

Don't die at all! Think!

The poison was coming in the knothole. But there was a second hole. Her bullet hole. Ragged, only a half inch wide if that, but a hole. She pulled the bench underneath and tried to get her nose next to it. Couldn't, really, even when she craned her neck way back and mashed her nose against the splintery plank of the overhead door. But the air had to be better here than in the rest of the shelter. She stayed.

God, what she wouldn't give for one of those fire department gas masks!

Should she shoot again? Make the hole larger? She pulled her gun out, but hesitated. Three problems with that plan. One, he might decide to shoot at her, as he'd threatened, and she was a sitting duck down here. Two, he'd notice the hole for sure and seal it. Three, he'd probably realize that she was onto the game—and that was her only slim advantage, that she knew what was happening and he didn't know she knew.

There was a number four too. Even though she knew his promise was worth zero, he'd said if she stopped shooting he wouldn't harm Chrissie, and that weighed in a mother's heart.

For now, she'd save her ammunition.

But what if this bullet hole acted as a sort of chimney, attracting a stream of poisoned air? What if the air she was craning her neck to breathe was just as bad as the rest?

Maybe she wasn't going to make it.

And if she didn't, Marty decided suddenly, she wanted to be sure that the sheriff and Doc and the rest knew everything she knew.

She pulled out her notepad, propped her flashlight between her shoulder and her cheek so she could see, took a breath at her bullet hole, and tried to think of what she knew that the sheriff didn't already know.

There was the information about Gordon Yeager's possible drug dealings. There were the coded names on Yeager's list. There was Coral's story.

She took another breath. It still smelled musty, overheated. Dammit, she wished she could tell if it was good air or contaminated.

To hell with Yeager. She had to write to Chrissie, to tell her to be brave, to tell her that she loved her, would love her for ever. She remembered Chrissie at the church supper hurling herself after her, trying to stop her from going out into the storm, the childish arms tight around her. She remembered Chrissie at the volunteer center, the accusing tone: "You always run off when I need you!" Marty wiped the dampness from her eyes. She'd responded to the kid's anguish by blowing a straw at her, and had been rewarded by that grudging giggle.

A straw.

Could it work?

Marty tore a page from her notepad, rolled it into a tube, and stuck one end into the bullet hole and the other into her mouth. Yes!

She sucked in air. Cool, fresh air, with the taste of cedar and of mint. Glory be!

It was damned uncomfortable to balance on the bench, head tilted back awkwardly, breathing through a paper tube.

But shoot, comfort wasn't the point, was it?

Wes flipped on the siren as he careened on to 822 after the big Lincoln. A blue pickup approaching from the south slowed to let him on. Wise move. Wes left it far behind.

As the road curved through the roadcut topped by the cedar thicket, Wes caught sight of the gray Lincoln, brakelights bright, skidding to a stop in the middle of the cut. Sims' cruiser blocked the road ahead. Wes stomped on the brakes and his cruiser fishtailed to a screeching stop across both lanes, rear end near the cedars. Then he was out, shotgun in hand, sheltering behind his vehicle and screaming, "Outta the car! Lemme see your hands! Now!"

Sims, farther around the curve on Wes's right, had jumped out too and, shielded by the driver's door, was positioning his own twelve-gauge. If Duke was in the center of a clockface with Wes at six o'clock, Sims was at two o'clock. The limestone roadcut blocked eleven to seven, the cedars three to five. Good positions, but not perfect. Duke might still get past Sims by using the narrow shoulder on the left side of the curve. Still, it'd be a squeeze between Sims's cruiser and the limestone.

He could see Duke sizing things up, toting up his chances. He definitely wasn't showing his hands. He was reaching for something on the seat beside him.

"Outta the car! Now! Lemme see your hands!" Wes yelled again. He could hear the fear and fury in his own scream.

Then Deputy Culp's cruiser roared around the bend and past Sims on the shoulder, kicking gravel as it skidded to a halt, its siren wailing. Now Duke's one escape route was neatly blocked.

And a worse problem loomed. Wes shouted, "Move, dammit, Culp!" But the excited rookie hadn't yet figured out the problem, maybe couldn't hear Wes's shouts what with three sirens going. Culp scrambled behind his cruiser. He was directly on the other side of the Lincoln, the idiot, at twelve o'clock to Wes's six o'clock position, where he'd be hit for sure if Wes fired his shotgun.

And where a shot from his semiautomatic, aimed at Duke, might hit Wes.

Wes could see that Duke had figured it all out instantly, that he knew Wes wouldn't fire, and neither would Culp once he realized his bullets could hit his boss. Duke stayed in his Lincoln but suddenly an ugly Uzi nosed out of the passenger window.

Sims, an old hand, saw it was up to him and fired.

Shot spattered the hood of the Lincoln. The Uzi turned to fire at Sims, spitting out shells. Wes took advantage of the distraction to dive behind his cruiser into the roadside bushes and the cedar thicket. He belly-crawled through the prickly brush to the top of the roadcut, four o'clock position, where he could see them again.

Three sirens still yowled.

Culp, who didn't yet realize that Wes was no longer in his line of fire, was not shooting. Not that his semiautomatic was any match for the Uzi.

In the Lincoln's half-open passenger window, the Uzi had swung back and was now firing at Wes's cruiser.

Sims was down. Shit. He'd fallen into his vehicle and lay crumpled across the driver's seat, only his gangly legs extending out the open door.

In icy fury, Wes squinted down into the Lincoln's passenger window. Duke was leaning low across the seat from the driver's side, making a difficult target for the underarmed Culp, and was firing out the half-opened passenger window toward Wes's cruiser. He paused, maybe wondering if he'd won already, if he'd taken out the sheriff as well as Sims.

Not yet you haven't, buddy. Wes sighted carefully and pulled the trigger.

The blast wiped out his hearing for a second. In the ringing silence he saw rather than heard the Uzi fall to the asphalt next to the suddenly splintered passenger window of the Lincoln.

For a moment, nothing happened. As his ears kicked in again, three sirens still screamed, three pulsar lights flashed. Only the Uzi was silent.

Culp moved then, coming out from behind his cruiser. Wes yelled, "Careful! Could be a trick! Come in slow, Culp, I'm watching him! And for God's sake stay out of my line of fire!"

Culp looked across at the roadcut, saw Wes, and did a good job of staying clear as he came in, gun extended before him, yelling "Lemme see your hands! Do it now!"

There was no answer, no movement. Culp circled to the rear of the Lincoln, then darted to the passenger door and opened it.

Duke's head drooped out and one arm fell down toward the asphalt. Culp kicked the Uzi out of reach. Blood was dribbling on to the pavement.

Wes skidded down the stone cliff of the roadcut to the Lincoln. The side of Duke's head and his shoulder were chewed up like hamburger by the shotgun pellets and the splintered glass. They cuffed him anyway and searched him quickly. Three automatics, and behind the seat a rifle. "Unload them, Culp, then see if he's alive," Wes instructed, and ran to Sims.

His deputy had been hit in the neck right above his bulletproof vest and was bleeding profusely. Not an artery. Wes pulled out his handkerchief and pressed it against the wound. Sims was lying on his back across the driver's seat, legs outside, head lolling against his radio. Wes used his left hand to call for an ambulance, then felt for a pulse.

"Hey, outstanding, you're still with us," he told Sims. "Help's coming. Hang in there." He glanced across at Culp, who was pulling the first-aid kit from his trunk, and yelled, "Over here first. If that SOB's still breathing, shackle him to something."

"Already did," Culp yelled back and came running to help Sims.

Wes turned off Sims's siren but not the pulsar light. Now he could hear horns blaring. Looking up 822, he could see that Sims had placed orange safety cones across both lanes to stop traffic from that direction. The drivers of the first cars were craning their necks to see what had happened, but on around the curve out of sight, the civilians were getting impatient. Tough.

They could sure use some extra hands here. Where the hell was Hopkins? She'd better have a damn good excuse.

Thirty-Five

Through the mouth, Hopkins, not the nose, Marty reminded herself, and sucked air through her home-made straw.

Every few minutes he'd hiss down at her, "Just a few more minutes. How're you doing?" She soon stopped answering, so he'd think she'd gone under.

Who the hell was it up there? And why had she been trapped? What was there to discover here that the crime scene technicians hadn't already discovered?

No way to answer that, 'cause she hadn't found it.

She breathed in through her tube.

Maybe it was personal. The guy up there knew who she was, that she had a daughter. She went clammy again, had to remind herself that she hadn't heard him leave, and as long as he was keeping her trapped here, he couldn't hurt Chrissie. You're okay, Hopkins, just stay quiet, just stay alive, and when he thinks you're good and dead he'll check on you, and then he'll get a surprise. You're okay. Just keep snorkeling in the limestone.

She focused again. Suppose it was personal. Suppose it was something she already knew, not something she might learn on this farm. That might be the reason. But what did she know?

She knew Laurie was in debt to organized crime. Maybe Laurie had told someone that she'd told Marty.

But Laurie wouldn't know the back way onto this farm. She hadn't been a kid in these hills, had never lived on a farm here.

Gordon had grown up here, though. Had he told Laurie? And of

221

course Marty had just talked to Andy Ragg, who'd done trucking for Gordon. Andy had grown up here too, he'd know the back ways.

She thought suddenly of the too-clean greenhouse back in the woods of this farm. What if it had been used to grow flats full of marijuana plants, maybe even of poppies? That'd make an abandoned backwoods farm profitable.

Profitable, and dangerous to law enforcement officers.

Was it Andy up there? Or someone Andy had called? He might have reported that she was sniffing about. And when they saw her headed for this farm, they went for her.

Who? Who could Andy call, now that Gordon was dead?

Well, Andy Ragg was on Gordon's coded client list. So was Peter Wallis, "Duke." And Joe Matthews, who owned this farm. Could be Duke or Joe up there.

She took another breath.

The name she hadn't figured out was Whitney. Olaf Whitney. Who was it? Marty tried out more combinations: William Osborn, Walter Oliver, Winifred Owens. Nope. Nobody around here with a name like that. Who the hell did she know with the initials W.O. ?

She sucked air through her paper tube, and a sign swam into her head, bright letters sparkling in the sun. White Oak Farm Store. White Oak?

Nah, wrong track. Duke and Joe made more sense.

But might as well play with the idea, Hopkins. What else you got to do, besides breathe?

So say it's White Oak on Gordon Yeager's secret list. White Oak, where Coral Turley grew up. And Duke was on the list, the gofer in Coral's band. And Joe Matthews was on the list, the guy who owned the farm where Coral was living.

Was Coral doing business with Gordon Yeager?

No, Coral was so damn young!

Marty thought about the girl for a moment. Remembered her telling about the rape, the young hands white-knuckled, gripping the coffee mug. Harder to make you hands lie than your words. It had happened, all right, or something damn close.

Marty sucked in a deep breath. Her tired neck and shoulders hurt, and her head where the door had slammed down on it, and she'd better roll a fresh piece of notebook paper because this one was wet and collapsing.

Okay. Suppose Coral was telling the truth. How would things fit together then?

222

Coral's story was simple. Big star got the hots for a young singer. He sent his gofer, Duke, to pick her up, probably thinking she would be no different from any other coked-up groupie. But things went wrong, they raped her.

Then Duke learned she was underage.

Bad news, that. Drug busts, okay, their fans could understand that, even respect it in a funny way. Ordinary rape you might beat. But child abuse, no. So what could they do?

Same thing the rich generally do when they're in trouble: buy them off.

It took Duke and Hoyt a while to figure out how to buy off Coral, because she didn't want money. They kept her captive, didn't let her call home. But once they learned that what she wanted was a chance in the music business, and that she actually had some talent, they were home free.

Marty wriggled her weary shoulders.

So Duke's big problem was the parents. He wouldn't want to blunder in blind. He needed someone who knew the territory to approach them. Preferably someone who was in debt to his contacts in the drug world, someone willing to organize something illegal. He needed Gordon Yeager.

Watch out, Hopkins, don't get too excited! You almost took a breath through your nose!

Okay. So Duke said to Gordon, fix this up, buy off the hillbillies, price is no object.

What would Gordon do? He knew Dee. He knew there was no hope she could be bought off. She doted on her kid, and she was a tough businesswoman who didn't need anybody else's money. So Gordon knew there was no deal possible there. That left Tom.

Tom, who'd had money to expand the store—even in a drought year, even with Dee depressed and useless.

Tom, who'd written down the wrong number so Dee couldn't return that first call when Coral briefly escaped to phone.

Tom, who'd tried to keep Marty from hearing Coral's story.

And oh yeah, Tom, who knew about things like faulty greenhouse heaters. Faulty greenhouse heaters that gave off too much carbon monoxide, and that sat on metal skids that looked like sled runners.

Tom.

Coral drove along the rutted overgrown tractor lane, bumping up and down to the scratchy accompaniment of the Joe Pye weed and stickerbushes clawing at the car. She was feeling smug. She'd outwitted the cops with their silly roadblocks. It wasn't fair for them to keep her stuff so long. She hadn't caused the problem, had she?

Plus she needed her clothes for the interviews that were coming up soon. Duke had scheduled three for this afternoon. Everyone had seen her leather last night, and she couldn't do interviews in this geeky pink T-shirt. Might as well show up in a choir robe.

The lane bent to the left and she saw the big greenhouse tucked into the woods. She'd always wondered why Joe Matthews had put it in such an odd place. Back there in the trees, the sun only came down through the roof. You lost the morning and evening rays. Well, nobody said Matthews was a smart farmer. No wonder he'd gone out of business and moved to Seymour.

She was approaching the back of the cement pig barn. Beyond it she could see the rear of the house, and—

Shit! Was that a sheriff's cruiser parked in the driveway?

Maybe she should wait and go later.

But hell, what could a deputy do to her besides say no? And Deputy Hopkins had said they'd soon unseal the place. Maybe they'd say it was okay.

She drove a little nearer. As the lawn came into view she was astonished to see a familiar van parked on the grass at right angles to the driveway, its rear wheels on the tornado shelter door near the asphalt. Her mother? No, Dee couldn't have gotten here first without passing Coral. Tom, then.

Coral stopped in the driveway just above the cruiser and jumped out. Tom came around the front of the van, looking just as surprised as she was. "What're you doing here?" he called.

"I live here, remember? Came to get my clothes," Coral said. She could hear a faint whining, maybe a car or something down on the road. She jerked her thumb toward the cruiser as she approached the van. "Is the sheriff's department here? What's going on?"

Tom shrugged stiffly. "Don't know where they are. Haven't seen them."

"Think they're in the house?" She looked at the pulled blinds, the police tape still in place. Not unsealed yet.

"Maybe," said Tom. "Or in the woods."

"Didn't see anyone back there," Coral said dubiously. She started toward the house, angling past the nose of his van toward the porch, looking for the deputy. Almost as an afterthought she asked, "So how come you're here?"

224

He shrugged. "No reason."

She paused. She'd thought he'd say "Curiosity," or "I wanted to see where Hoyt died," or some such thing. "No reason" was odd. And why was he so tense, so unsmiling? Coral frowned at him and realized that the whining sound was not on the road below, but behind the van. She took a quick step toward the van, trying to see past Tom.

"How come you're parked on the lawn?" Coral asked. She could almost see something now, a machine with a hose like a vacuum cleaner or something, sitting on the tornado shelter door next to the van's rear tire. "What are you doing, Tom?"

But he looked past her toward the house and said, "Hello, Deputy, what's going on?"

Coral turned quickly. "Where—"

Shards of brightness lanced across her vision an instant before the glaring pain. Then all went black.

For an instant Marty's hopes soared. He'd said deputy! Was there another deputy there? But she hadn't heard another car.

Then she heard Coral say "Where—" and then a little moan. And then nothing.

What had happened? Was there someone else up there who'd come on foot and attacked both Coral and Tom?

Marty sucked another breath through her scrolled paper tube.

Tom wouldn't hurt Coral, would he? He was her father. He'd killed for her. He'd killed her rapist and her rapist's local helper. He'd be a danger to Duke, yes, but surely not to Coral!

But he'd taken their money to remodel his store. Maybe he didn't give a damn about Coral.

Now Marty heard Tom grunting, and the van door opening and closing.

Then the whine of the machine stopped, and light beamed through the knothole.

More grunting. Something heavy dragged across the door above her. He must be moving the heater.

There was definitely no other deputy up there.

The van door opened again, slammed again, and its engine started to rumble. It must be driving away. A sag in the plank door above Marty suddenly straightened. She hadn't noticed it before but it made sense. The reason she couldn't push up the door was that the van had been parked on it.

Now it wasn't.

Marty bounded from her bench to the stairs and up two steps to push the door open. Then she became aware of two things. First, she'd stupidly started breathing the air, as though the van had taken all the poison with it when it left. Bad move, Hopkins.

Second, the van had stopped again.

He hadn't left yet. He was coming back.

Her best chance was if he thought he'd succeeded. She blew out everything in her lungs and leaped back to the bench and her breathing tube. The handle of the door above her rattled. She sucked in a huge breath and collapsed on to the floor.

When the door rose and light flooded in, she lay absolutely relaxed and still. She was on her side, head toward the stairs, eyes half closed.

Footsteps descended.

Through her eyelashes she could see his legs, and the double barrels of a shotgun.

Stay cool, Hopkins, he doesn't want to shoot you, he doesn't know you're alive, he wants you to be another mysterious death, not a shotgun victim.

He nudged her with the toe of his shoe. She didn't resist, allowed the nudged arm to flop behind her.

He picked up her arm and for a second she feared he'd check her pulse. She had a pulse, all right, pounding at double time. But he seemed in a hurry, satisfied with the floppiness of her hand. He dropped it and started up the stairs.

He didn't want to breathe this stuff either, she realized. He must be going up to take another breath.

He'd reached the third step when Marty tackled him, ramming him in the knees and grabbing the shotgun with both hands, twisting it away, throwing it out the shelter door as he thrashed for balance. He fell backwards. His head cracked against the cement wall but not hard enough. She turned, pulling out her handcuffs and reaching for her gun, but he was tough and fast and lunged at her. She caught him in the knees again and brought him down but he twisted toward her, now grabbing for her gun. It was too close. If she pulled it out of the holster he'd have it in a minute. Instead Marty concentrated on his reaching arm and snapped a handcuff around the wrist. She hung on desperately to keep his hand away from her gun. He was upright again, punching her with his other fist, kicking at her. No hope of getting his other arm behind him. He had too much speed and wiry strength. She'd be lucky to keep him away from her Glock.

She tried to trip him, pushing against the metal stair rail tubing for traction, but he knocked her back and her right knee hit the stair and twisted. For a second she couldn't move her leg at all, she could only blink back the pain. But she hung on to his cuffed wrist.

He lunged for her gun again and Marty saw her chance. Quicker than thought, she used his momentum to pull his reaching arm past her holster and down next to the tubular steel stair support. She snapped the second handcuff bracelet to the tubing. He'd grabbed her holster and it took all her strength to pry off his grasping fingers. She jerked away and scuttled backwards up the stairs. He snatched at her ankles but she pulled free.

He was hollering now, "Get me out!" But Marty kept moving, lurching out of the shelter and halfway across the lawn, where she flopped flat and lay gulping great lungfuls of air.

"You got to get me out of here!" he yelled.

Marty stood up shakily, tried her leg. Pain shrieked from her knee but it held weight, didn't buckle. She looked around. He'd moved the van only a few feet toward the house. Where was Coral? The greenhouse heater still sat on its skids beside the shelter door. She hobbled back to the opening and looked down. Tom was struggling with the handcuffs, trying to get them off. She said, "Tom, throw me the keys to your van."

"Get me out first!"

Marty limped back beside the heater and began to close the shelter door.

"No, please, wait!" he screamed.

"Van keys," she said curtly.

He tossed them onto the lawn. She left the shelter door open and retrieved them, then stumbled painfully across the lawn to the van.

Coral was locked in the back, lying on a thin cotton blanket and moaning.

"Coral, you okay?" Marty asked.

Coral blinked at her and asked in a thick voice, "Did you hit me? How come?"

"Not me, honey. Let me look."

The girl struggled a moment and said, "My hands got tangled up somehow. Oh, God, my head hurts!"

He'd tied her hands with a corner of the blanket. Marty freed her, brought her to the sunlit door of the van, and took a careful look at her pupils. "You'll do," she said. "Just take it easy for a few minutes."

Coral's pretty brow furrowed. "But what happened? Why did you hit me? Hey, who's yelling? Is that Tom?"

"Yeah."

"Shouldn't we help him?" Coral jumped down to the ground, then winced, hand to her head. Marty sympathized. She was feeling a bit beat up herself.

"No, don't help him yet, Coral. I've got to call this in."

The radio in her cruiser was crackling with messages. Something big had gone down a few minutes earlier near Sanders Creek. There were casualties. When she finally got through and identified herself Foley said, "Where the hell you been? Sheriff needed you. You're in bad trouble."

Shit. Marty cleared her throat and said, "I've got a suspect in custody here at the Matthews farm, and I need backup. Okay?"

"Ten-four. But it'll be a while."

Coral had ignored instructions and walked to the shelter opening. "What's going on? He's handcuffed to that rail!" she yelled at Marty. "Come help!" She started down the steps.

"Get back, Coral!" Marty ignored her knee and sprinted the few yards to the shelter. She grabbed the girl's arm and wrenched her up and out of the shelter. They both fell onto the lawn.

"What's wrong? What the hell are you doing?" Coral cried.

"Look, Coral. Number one, you've had a bump on your head and there's probably still carbon monoxide in that shelter. Don't mess with your brain. Number two, we don't need a hostage situation."

"Hostage?"

"He'll grab you and threaten to hurt you."

Coral wasn't buying it. "Tom wouldn't do that! He's my father!"

"Honey, he hit you on the head and locked you in the van. And you don't know it, but he helped them keep you hostage for months." She limped over to the shelter. "Tom! Shut up for a minute. We'll talk about getting you up into the air, but first I have something to say to you. You have the right to remain silent . . ."

Thirty-Six

Len had dozed off again, and it was eleven thirty when he jerked awake for the second time. A door had slammed. Stollnitz? Yes, there went the bastard, rubbing his temples and frowning at the bright daylight. He was walking toward the highway. Probably headed for Clyde's Bar to pick up his car.

Len had had enough. If the sheriff ever came down off his high horse and listened, Len could tell him how Stollnitz had gotten into the bank to kill Steffie, and he could tell him that Stollnitz knew exactly where Steffie's apartment was. He couldn't yet tell them exactly how Stollnitz had killed her without leaving a trace, but Len's suspicion was that he had left a trace and the incompetent law enforcement here just hadn't found it.

The clumsy sheriff had had his chance. Len grabbed Stollnitz's revolver and got out.

Clay Stollnitz glanced around at the slam of the car door. He blinked stupidly at Len for a second, then his blue eyes shifted to the revolver and he held up both hands, palms out. "Mr. Abbott, listen, I didn't do it! I swear!"

"Quit lying," Len yelled. They were thirty yards apart. "My only question is, how did you do it? You always left her bruised and bloody before!"

"Jesus!" said Stollnitz, and took off like a rabbit toward the highway, dodging into and out of the roadside brush.

Len raced after. I'll get him, Steffie, he swore. I'll get him this time.

Marty got a second pair of handcuffs from the trunk of her cruiser. "Okay, Tom, if you want to get your head above ground, reach your left arm up along the stair railing as far as you can. I'll cuff you to the top brace, then unlock your right hand so you can move up a few steps and stick your head out."

Tom stretched out his arms, Christ-like, and she locked his left wrist to the upper stair support. The carbon monoxide in the shelter

229

was probably diluted by now, but she held her breath anyway as she hobbled down the stairs beside him to unlock his right hand. The instant his lower wrist was free he snatched at the handcuff key. She jerked back, threw the key out on to the lawn, and pulled her gun to keep him from grabbing at her injured leg as she limped up the stairs.

She couldn't see her keys. She scrutinized the lawn a moment, then noticed Coral, hand in pocket, sidling toward the shelter door. Hell. Marty stayed out of Tom's reach but stood between him and his daughter. "Let me have the keys, Coral."

"Look, that's my dad!"

"I know, honey, but—"

Tom said, "She's made a mistake, Coral. Unlock me so I can show her."

Coral looked Marty in the eye, and Marty recognized the girl's determination, the strength that had enabled her to turn a hideous kidnapping and rape into a personal victory. Coral said confidently, "You won't shoot me," and started toward her father.

Tom said, "That's right, honey, you're right."

Marty leveled the gun at Tom and answered Coral. "But if you let him go, I'll shoot him."

"What?" Coral paused.

"He killed Hoyt, Coral. Trapped him in that shelter and filled it full of carbon monoxide. And he just tried to do the same to me."

"To you? You were in there?"

"That's where I was when you arrived. And that heater over there was on, pumping in carbon monoxide through that hose. Same as it did when Hoyt was in there."

"Jeez." Coral frowned. "Yeah, I heard the heater working. But I didn't know what was happening. Before I could look close, something hit me."

"Tom hit you," said Marty.

"She's making it up, Coral! Don't listen to her," Tom said.

"But that heater was running when I came, she's right," Coral said.

He shook his head. "Look, I can show you it wasn't me. Just let me go."

Coral turned to Marty again. "I can't believe it! Tom? Why would he hit me?"

"He didn't want you to see he was murdering me," Marty explained.

"Tom, was she in there or not?"

Tom's cuffed arm stretched back behind him to the stair support rail as he leaned out from the opening of the shelter, trying to get as far from the deadly air as he could. "Coral, don't get dragged into this. Just unlock me and I'll take care of it."

Marty said, "I was in the shelter, figuring out how Hoyt had died, and Tom trapped me in there. Parked the van on top of the door, you saw that. And he hooked up the heater and the hose. You saw that too."

"Yeah." The girl's intelligent face was troubled. "And you say he did it to Hoyt too."

"It was revenge for you," Tom said, suddenly shifting ground. "That guy ran off with you, wrecked your life and your mother's life. I had to fix it."

"But I don't want it fixed that way!" Coral said. "Yeah, Hoyt wrecked things, but I was making him pay it back, and then some!"

"A man can't let that happen to his family," Tom said.

Marty broke in. "Sure he can. You let it happen. You even helped."

There was a flash of alarm in Tom's face but he said, "Coral, you see that woman's crazy. Unlock me and I'll show you."

Marty said again, "Coral, he's a killer. If you unlock him and he tries to escape I'll have to shoot him."

Coral ran her fingers through her blond hair. It had dried curly, bouncy as little flames. "What do you mean, he helped?"

"A few days after you disappeared, Tom called off the police search. And a few days after that, you tried to call your mother and you got Tom instead."

"Yes," Coral said. "And he said Dee was mad at me but he'd tell her to call back. But she didn't."

"Why didn't she?" Marty pursued.

Tom said, "I made a mistake! I wrote down the number wrong!"

"That's what Dee said too," Coral agreed.

"And does Dee say she was mad at you?"

"No." Coral pointed her finger at Tom. "You were wrong, Tom. She wasn't mad. She was sad. Crazy with grief, she says."

"Right!" Marty said. "Because Tom was telling her you didn't want to come back. And he was telling you she was angry. And he was giving her the wrong number, making sure you couldn't talk."

"Tom, why? Why did you do that?" Coral demanded.

"I thought it would make it easier for her," Tom said. "Look, honey, the truth is, I was real worried about what was going to happen to Dee when you grew up. She encouraged your singing and I could see you getting wilder about it. I knew you were going

231

to be leaving soon, and I knew she'd be hurt whenever it happened. You would've been off chasing your dream in another year anyway. You didn't want to hang around this county, you wanted to go be a singer. And so that's what I told Dee. I thought it would make it easier for her if she thought you were happy."

"Happy! That first two weeks? Jesus!" Coral rolled her eyes.

Tom said nervously, "You wanted to be a star, right? I figured this was the best chance you'd get. At least these guys were rich. On your own you would've starved."

"So you let her be raped for her own good?" Marty snapped. "Come on! You had a better reason to keep Dee quiet, didn't you, Tom? Why don't you tell us about your remodeled White Oak Farm store and your new kitchen?"

"I wanted to make Dee happy! She said last year she wished we had enough money for those things, we should save up for them—"

"Yeah, and it was real lucky you suddenly had that much to spend in a drought year, wasn't it?" Marty said. "A drought year, and a year when Dee wasn't able to contribute any work at all, because she was so depressed about Coral."

"Yeah," said Coral. "Where did you get that money, Tom? Last year wasn't all that good. This year must've been terrible."

Tom was silent.

"Tell her where, Tom," Marty said.

"Look, I don't have to answer."

"Of course you don't. But it'll really make us wonder about what you've been growing in that greenhouse back in the woods."

"There's nothing in that greenhouse!"

"Yeah, it's real clean now. But the technicians who are coming at noon will find traces. Opium poppies, right? Or just pot?"

"You're crazy!" he said.

"Those guys had you in the palm of their hand, didn't they?" Marty said. He shook his head angrily, and she realized this was his tender spot and bored in. "You'd do anything for them. Grow dope. Hand over your daughter. Throw your wife into a depression. They must've paid real well. They jerked the strings, you jumped."

"No! I was getting out of it! I was!"

"But it wasn't easy, was it? Because you'd already spent their money."

"We weren't making anything this year," Tom said. "I had to do something. I'm the head of the family."

"So Coral runs off for a date and they imprison her. And when

232

they call you about it they offer you money to keep quiet, to call off the search. And you accept without even talking to Coral."

"They said she was fine. Anyway, that guy Duke—you don't cross him, they said."

"Why the hell didn't you tell us? We know how to deal with kidnappers. Were they offering you that much money, Tom?"

"Money?" Coral yelped. "You took money from them and left me with Duke?"

"They said you were fine," Tom repeated.

Coral stared at him with shocked eyes. "Jesus. You sold me!"

"It wasn't like that! They said you wanted to be with them!"

Coral was standing very stiffly, her face pale. "What about Dee?" she demanded. "Did she sell me too?"

Tom laughed harshly. "I never told Dee. She was always nutty when it came to you, you know that. Always Coral this, Coral that. Those first days she looked for you everywhere, like nothing else existed. I kept saying you didn't want to come back but she refused to listen. Her own husband!"

There was pain in Tom's voice. Marty realized suddenly that he was jealous of Coral, and almost pitied the little man. Coral and Dee, wrapped up in each other, leaving Tom out, unnecessary, beside the point. He had struggled for years to become significant in the eyes of his beautiful wife, head of the family, lord and provider, but had never been able to break into the magic circle that enclosed Dee and Coral.

Marty said, "Okay. You were taking money from them, and in exchange you kept quiet and kept Dee from learning anything, and you supplied them with drugs. You gave Dee the wrong number so she couldn't return Coral's call."

"But after that she got depressed," Tom said. "She'd been running around, looking for clues, talking to people, keeping up the farm . . . she was worried but I figured she'd get over it once she knew Coral was okay and didn't want to come home. But instead she just crashed. The doctors couldn't help. I tried to comfort her, but nothing helped. Not the new kitchen, nothing. She was wasting away. So I told them to send Coral back, the deal was off if they didn't. But it took a real long time."

Coral was still staring at him, horror written on her lovely face. Marty thought of Chrissie and prayed that her daughter would never hear of a betrayal like this.

Tom squirmed under Coral's eyes and protested, "You told me yourself you didn't want to come back!"

"Yeah, I said that! When you told me Dee was mad and didn't want to talk to me, well, it's true, I didn't want to come back!" She threw the handcuff keys to Marty and sat down miserably on the lawn.

"But I tried!" Tom insisted. "When I saw how sick Dee was, I tried to get you back! And they refused. They tightened the screws. Said they could send me to jail for years."

"For what?" Coral looked confused.

Marty had pocketed her keys and holstered her gun. She sat down near Coral and said, "If they had proof that he knew what was going on and accepted money to go along with it, yeah, they could get him for child selling, plus conspiracy to commit every felony they'd be charged with. Rape, assault, criminal confinement, child molesting—they were right, it could add up to a lot of years. Plus they had him on drug charges too. Tom, who made these threats? Was it Duke?"

"Not directly. They were local calls. For a long time I didn't recognize the voice. See, that was the problem, that was why I couldn't get out of it at first. And Dee was getting sicker—"

Marty said, "But you finally figured it out, right? You figured out who it was."

"Two weeks ago," Tom said. "It was when he called to say Coral was coming to the county, he'd try to get her to see Dee if I could guarantee nobody would say anything. And I finally recognized the voice, because I'd just cleaned the bank the night before, and I'd heard him talking to someone on the phone."

"Gordon Yeager," said Marty.

"Yes. And by then, with Dee so sick, I was ready to firebomb them all," Tom said. "But I decided to wait a few days until Coral showed up. And that week the heater went bad, and I had it in the van and the whole plan just came to me."

"I see," Marty said. "And you chose a night when Jumbo Jim would be cleaning instead of you."

"Yeah." Tom shrugged his free shoulder. "Seemed like a good idea. Soon as he left I parked in the same place he'd been and rushed in to set up. Nobody ever notices you if you're in uniform, but I still didn't want to stay long. That was the problem, I was in a hurry. I saw the light on in Yeager's office but I didn't open the door to see who it was. I didn't want to be seen."

Marty thought of a photo of cheerleaders, a lovingly arranged apartment with dormer windows, a father's grieving brown eyes, and felt deeply sad. "So poor Steffie was just a mistake. She was in the wrong place at the wrong time."

"Why was she in his office anyway? And how was I supposed to know? He worked late a lot. It should've been him."

"And Hoyt?" Coral demanded, tears still streaking her young cheeks. "How did you know— Oh my God. I told you where he was, didn't I? I came into the store and told you! And while I was talking to Dee you ran right over here and killed him!"

"Look, it was the only way to get us away from them!" Tom shouted. "I'm the head of the family! I'm supposed to solve your problems!"

"You asshole! You pitiful deluded little crumb!" Coral cried and buried her face in her hands.

Marty saw Tom cringe as though he'd been kicked.

Wes was still wired from the excitement of the shootout and the worry about Grady Sims. The ambulance had taken Sims away, Duke Wallis too, but it would probably be hours before the doctors could report. Once Wes got the technicians launched on the crime scene, picking up cartridges and directing traffic, he called dispatch. "Where the hell is Three twenty-one?" he asked.

"She's at the Matthews farm. Says she's got a suspect in custody and wants backup. That's all I know."

"I'll swing by on my way to check on Sims at the hospital," Wes said. He was still burned that she hadn't responded to his call for backup.

Something was going on at the Matthews farm, all right. As he pulled past the police tape into the asphalt driveway, he saw Hopkins' cruiser parked near the tornado shelter door, and beyond it a Jeep. The White Oak Farm van was on the lawn, and Hopkins, rubbing her knee, was sitting on the grass nearby. So was Coral Turley. Tom Turley was at the tornado shelter, leaning out, his arm apparently stuck on something. Wes climbed out of his cruiser and slammed the door. No, Tom wasn't stuck, he was handcuffed to the stairs.

Hopkins was scrambling to her feet. Wes saw her wince as she straightened the leg she'd been rubbing. She had some cuts on her face and a puffy eye too. He said gruffly, "Hopkins, can you explain all this?"

"Uh, yes sir. See, I was investigating—"

"So was I. We were taking a bad guy with an Uzi off the streets. So why didn't you even acknowledge my ten seventy-eight call?"

"Because Mr. Turley, uh, detained me in the shelter by parking his van on top of it and blowing in carbon monoxide. And, uh, my portable radio won't work through bedrock, sir."

Jesus. Wes cleared his throat and said, "Well, Hopkins, don't let it happen again."

"You can absolutely depend on that, sir."

Next to the shelter there was a greenhouse heater. Wes said, "Are you going to tell me that thing is our murder weapon?"

"Yes sir. Three times, going on four."

"Goddamn." Wes walked over for a better look. A smallish blue and chrome job, the brand name "Thunderbolt" emblazoned across it. Looked innocent as hell. "Lot of paperwork coming up. Let's book him and get started. And Hopkins, one more thing."

"Yes sir?"

"Gimme five!"

They slapped hands, grinning as though they'd just won the NBA championship.

Thirty-Seven

Nurse Kinser brought Jake his so-called lunch: strained cream of chicken soup, vegetable juice, milkshake. Everything came with straws. In the distant past, hidden by the mists of time or maybe by the damn painkillers, he thought he remembered eating hamburgers, home fries, pumpkin pie. The present reality made such meals seem like exotic fairy-tale foods.

"If I put the tray right here you can move everything with your right hand, and reach what you need," the nurse chirped.

"Uh-huh." Of course the cast on his arm immobilized the fingers sticking out the end, and his ribs hurt when he moved his right arm. But painful or not, it was good to have a tiny bit of control. He adjusted the placement of the soup cup with his mitt and got the straw between his lips with his left fingers.

"You're doing great, honey!" The nurse was rearranging the medications on his table and throwing away the old cups and straws. She added, "Sheriff Cochran just called. Said to tell you the guy with the gray Lincoln is at Dunning South hospital in a lot worse shape than you are. May not make it, and if he does he's under arrest. Said you'd know who he meant."

236

Hallelujah! Jake felt a bit of the tension leaving his muscles. The thought of that guy coming in to finish the job had weighed heavily on him. He saw Nurse Kinser looking at him curiously, so he said, "Uh-huh."

"You're going to have a good story to tell when you can talk, I bet." She straightened the blanket at the foot of his bed. "Well, I'll be back in a few minutes. Enjoy your lunch."

Fiscarelli stopped by as he was tackling the amazingly bland strawberry milkshake. Jake was embarrassed to have his editor see him this way, but pleased when he said, "Well, Jake, guess I'll have to approve some sick leave after all. Say, can you talk at all?"

"Uh-huh. Unh-unh."

"I see. Okay, I'll talk. We'll want a first-person account soon as they let you out of here. WCTV in Chicago has been calling, that guy Stu. Says they've gotten hundreds of calls about the tornado and the Lily Pistols thing. Gave us a nice credit, by the way. I've put Betty Burke on the story—" Jake groaned and Fiscarelli added quickly, "—she knows it's your story, but we've got to follow up now, you know that. Really put this paper on the map. You'll probably be up for an award this year, I bet. Well, guess I'm off, and—"

"Uhhh!" said Jake. He made poking motions with his left forefinger.

Fiscarelli's face lit up. "You've got it! One laptop coming up! I'll send it over this afternoon. See you soon, buddy." And he was gone.

Jake sipped his milkshake, happily composing his lead in his head.

Marty got into the cruiser, wincing at the pang in her knee. Time to leave this scene where Hoyt Heller had died and she almost had. Tom had been taken to jail in Mason's cruiser, and she had to follow to do the paperwork. Walker would do guard duty until the forensic guys arrived. Coral Turley, dazed and still wrestling with this second cataclysm in her universe, had said to Marty, "It's so hard to believe! He was always so quiet! If he got angry, he'd just go away. You know, keep it inside, not hurt anybody. And then— God, he sold me, the bastard!"

"Yeah. It's tough, Coral." Marty too would have had more sympathy for Tom if he'd never cooperated with his daughter's abductors and rapists, if he'd struck in pure revenge. She asked, "Are you okay for now? Want me to drive you somewhere?"

"No, I'll take the jeep back." And with the resilience of the young, she tossed her head and added, "I'm not going to ask you guys for my clothes after all. I've got to do those interviews in Bloomington, and I can get black Spandex and chains there."

"Yeah. We'll get another statement tonight. You'll be back at White Oak?"

"Yeah, but it may be late."

"See you soon."

Marty started back to the station, almost looking forward to a quiet hour of paperwork. As she approached the intersection with Corydon Road, the dispatcher's excited voice came on. "Ten-ten in progress, shots fired—Corydon, near 2120!"

Shit, Marty thought, she'd seen enough guys with guns for one day. But she was nearest so she responded. "Three twenty-one. I'm turning on to Corydon right now, proceeding east, passing 2208, 2180, 2166—subject in sight, 2140 Corydon, north side of the road. We've got a white male about 50, curly hair—oh, I've got an ID, it's Mr. Abbott!" She was out of the cruiser now, shielded by the driver's door, her Glock trained on Abbott fifteen feet away. "Mr. Abbott! Drop the gun!"

Abbot was staring down at a blond man lying in the weeds at his feet. At Marty's shout Abbott glanced around and suddenly the man came to life, lunging up for the gun, jerking it from Abbott's hand. It went off and the blond man screamed.

"Mr. Abbott! Mr. Stollnitz! Drop the gun!"

Abbott complied, but Stollnitz was grabbing for it again. Marty lurched across, her knee aflame with pain again, and managed to kick it out of reach. She backed away from them. Couple of jerks. She yelled, "Both of you! Sit down with your hands on your heads and let's get this straightened out!"

Stollnitz grunted and did so. Abbott looked surprised. "Me too?"

"You too. Now! No, sit out of reach of Mr. Stollnitz. That's better. Okay, now, what's going on here?"

Clay Stollnitz said, "This crazy idiot just came out of the blue waving a gun at me! And of course I ran, but I stumbled and he shot at me! My God, I've got blood all over!"

"Keep your hands on top of your head, Mr. Stollnitz. We'll get the medics here to check you out. Mr. Abbott, what's your side of the story?"

Abbott was sitting with spine erect, hands interlaced on the little bald spot at the center of his waving graying hair. He said, "I've been following this bastard for two days. Your sheriff as good as told me he didn't have time to investigate Steffie's murder, but I didn't want this guy to get away, and now I've got proof!"

"Proof of what?" Marty asked sharply.

Stollnitz exclaimed, "I told you, he's crazy! I haven't done a thing! I just wanted to hang around long enough to find out how Steffie had been these last few months, because nobody ever told me a thing! And God, my leg hurts, and I'm bleeding, and—"

"I've got proof that he killed her." Abbott answered Marty calmly, as though the younger man hadn't spoken. "He knew where she lived. And he got into the bank last night."

"He what?"

"Went right into the bank where she worked, and—"

Marty could hear sirens in the background, her backup coming. "What time are you talking about?"

"About nine o'clock at night."

"But the bank was closed!"

"That's what I'm telling you! The cleaning guy came out to put some sort of vacuum cleaner into his van, and this bastard stuck something in the hinge so the door didn't close. And then a few minutes later he went sneaking in."

"I just wanted something of hers!" Clay Stollnitz burst out. "That little name plate, that's all, the bank didn't need it!" He closed his eyes tight but a tear squeezed out anyway.

"Mr. Stollnitz, do you want to press charges?"

His eyes opened, eager now. "Yeah! I'll press charges! I'll sue him for all he's got! First he breaks up my marriage, then he shoots me!"

Abbott said in disbelief, "He can do that? He can sue me?"

"Yeah." Marty wished her knee would stop throbbing. "He can sue you, but he better have a real good lawyer, because when the jury sees Steffie's hospital records and the orders of protection and so forth they'll sympathize with you, not him."

"But he shot me!" Stollnitz wailed. "That's against the law!"

"Just a minute, Mr. Stollnitz. You think about what you want to do while I ask Mr. Abbott a couple more questions. Did you see exactly what the cleaning service man was doing?"

"Just putting away a funny vacuum cleaner, skinny hose on it. The point is, this bastard—"

"Did you see what color the machine was?" Marty asked.

"Blue and white. Look, don't you understand what I'm telling you?"

"Sure, Mr. Abbott. Actually we have some news about what happened to Steffie."

"You do? The coroner's report? What happened? How did he do it?"

"He didn't. Mr. Stollnitz didn't do it."

"I've been telling you!" Stollnitz exclaimed.

"What do you mean, he didn't do it? He broke her bones and then he killed her in that bank!"

"No, sir. The thing is, we've caught the guy who killed your daughter."

"Yeah, you've got him right here! Stollnitz!"

"No sir. Another man has confessed."

"Somebody else confessed? But that's impossible!" Abbott looked thunderstruck, as though his carefully constructed universe had just broken to bits. Maybe it had.

The medics rolled up and began to fuss over Stollnitz. Marty said to Abbott, "I have to handcuff you, sir, and take you in. The judge'll let you out pretty quick, I'm sure."

Dazed and compliant, he let her cuff him and lead him to her cruiser. He asked, "I don't understand. Why would someone else confess?"

"The coroner's report says she died of carbon monoxide poisoning. And the man we've got confessed to killing three people with carbon monoxide."

"But why?"

"He was a father," Marty said gently. "He was trying to get back at the people who'd hurt his daughter, and he took justice into his own hands. But he got the wrong person. He got Steffie."

Len Abbott bowed his head, and she closed the door.

Wes sat by Grady Sims's bedside, waiting for his deputy to wake up. They'd been through a lot together, he and Sims. Basketball, Nam—different tours but still a bond, occasional fishing trips, and fifteen years in the sheriff's department. Once, over beers, Sims had confessed that he loved law enforcement, and that the only other job he'd ever had, selling home appliances for Sears, had left him feeling like a failure. "I knew the products, but I've got no sales skills," he'd said. True enough. Sims was gawky-looking and quiet, but in this job he always sized up situations shrewdly, always followed orders, always was there when he was needed.

Now the docs said he'd lost the use of his left arm. The bullet in his neck had hit a spinal nerve. Better than being dead, but to an active outdoor guy like Sims it was a major loss.

Sims stirred and Wes said, "How you doing, buddy?"

"Okay," he answered thickly.

"Need a drink? All I have is water. They don't sell beer in this dumb joint."

"Okay."

Wes raised the head of the bed and placed a sissy hospital cup of water in Sims's right hand. Sims gulped it and asked, "Is Culp okay?"

"Not a scratch, except for the chewing out I gave him for getting in my line of fire."

"He's a rookie," Sims said. "He'll do better."

"Yeah." Wes refilled the flimsy cup.

Sims said, "The doctor says my left arm's no good."

"Yeah, we'll see. We've got time. Foley's retiring in a couple months, and I'll need you on dispatch for a while. So don't go taking any sales jobs."

"Yes sir." Sims took another swallow and asked, "How's the bad guy?"

"Hell of a lot worse off than you. They're still digging shot out of him. Lost an eye, an arm, part of his brain—he'll be lucky if he can talk. May have some problems with the rougher types in jail."

Sims couldn't nod, but he didn't seem sorry to hear it.

Wes pushed back his chair and said. "Well, I'll let you get some sleep. See you soon."

On his way out he paused by Jake Shaw's door, but the reporter was sitting up in his bed, pecking industriously at a laptop computer, so he didn't bother him.

It was late when Coral got back to White Oak Farm, and Dee, her hair loose in amber waves, was wearing a royal-blue nightgown. Coral, of course, was still in the black bike shorts and Tibetan bone necklace she'd bought for her Bloomington interviews. She and Dee hugged each other and had a good cry. "Probably I should have divorced him," Dee sobbed. "But he was always so quiet and helpful, had me on this silly pedestal, even when we weren't communicating at all. I just let it slide. There were so many other things that needed doing . . ."

Coral stroked her mother's pretty hair. "I think he just snapped, Dee. Marty Hopkins got him talking somehow. I never heard him talk so much. And it sounded like he thought he wasn't a real man if he wasn't in charge, if he wasn't making money, if he wasn't ruling over all of us."

"Yeah, I used to be able to buck him up, give him credit for the

241

good work he did. But when I thought you were gone for ever—well, it was all I could do to get myself through a day."

Coral nodded and leaned back in the wheat-colored sofa. "I talked to the label, Dee. They've put this young hotshot named Eddie St. John in charge of Lily Pistols. He'll do our publicity and also all the stuff that Duke used to do." She took another swallow of tea, and Dee patted her shoulder encouragingly.

"Duke's out of your life now, honey."

"Yeah. I talked to Deputy Hopkins, Ma. She said he probably won't be able to speak, and his arm and eye and ear are gone, and he'll go to jail a long time." Her mother looked blurry to her and she realized she was crying again. "Ma, do you think my nightmares will stop now?" she asked in a small voice.

"Probably not completely, honey. They're part of how we deal with loss."

Coral nodded, drank more tea, and took a deep breath. "Okay. And Eddie St. John says the label will pay for a lawyer for Tom, so we can get the best spin on the case."

"God." Dee shook her head. "I still can't believe it was Tom!"

"Me either. Anyway, there's more. Eddie says the label wants to remix 'Deathwind' on the new album because of the response to my version. They'll keep Hoyt's vocal, of course, but add mine. And they're setting up a six-month tour starting when the album comes out, and I'll sing duets with Hoyt's recorded voice. Skell is real excited about the new arrangements. It'll be neat."

Dee smiled. "It'll be wonderful, except you'll be away again."

"But this time I won't be afraid to phone you."

Dee hugged her. "I know. It'll be a wonderful tour."

"Yeah. You'll be okay, Ma?" Coral asked anxiously.

"Honey, you and I have both been to hell and back. We can take anything now. Yeah, I'll be okay, and so will you."

Dee's smile seemed to flood Coral with joy and sorrow and strength, and maybe her smile did the same for Dee. She said, "Okay, Ma. And anyway, I'll be back to see you in the spring."

Thirty-Eight

The gloomy December day had produced a sprinkle of snow across southern Indiana. Up in Nichols County, it dusted the highway as Jake, one leg still in a light cast, cautiously drove his newly purchased used Toyota to the office. On a wooded hillside not far away, the snow floated through the framing beams of the cabin that Romey Dennis was building, with tornado-proof basement and a view from the soon-to-be deck that Marty loved, a glimpse through trees of the shining river. It fell on the stubbly drowsing fields of Dee's White Oak Farm, on the new roof of the Prince of Pizza, on the cleared but still naked site that had been the Country Griddle, and on the jagged stumps and scarred trees that marked the path of the great wind.

A few miles away, down in Vanderburgh County near Evansville, it fell on the shopping strip where Joel Mitchum had his office, whitening the roofs of a red Mazda with Tennessee plates and a Nichols County Sheriff's Department cruiser parked outside.

Inside the office, the atmosphere was turbulent. "Swear to God, Joel, all I want is what's fair! She's the one who wants a divorce, not me. So why should I have to make it easy for her?" Brad pushed aside the dark hair that flopped into his earnest, sorrowing eyes.

This'll never work, Marty thought, fists clenched. She looked out the office window. Dark snowclouds frowned back as though confirming her view. It had been hard to agree on dates for meetings, hard as hell to agree on general goals the first time they'd met. How could they ever agree on the all-important specifics?

The mediator was a tall, scrawny-necked, beak-nosed man in his forties with unkempt blond hair, close-set brown eyes and a gentle manner. It was like putting her future in the hands of Big Bird, Marty thought in despair. He said, "In your position I might feel that way too, Brad. One of the things you have to decide is if you want to participate in a process that'll probably lead to the end of the marriage. If you don't want to do that, better not continue with the mediation."

243

Brad said, "Yeah, but the lawyers tell me I can't stop her, and they'll have to charge a lot of money, and the judge'll make all the decisions, not me."

Joel's bird-like head nodded. "It's true that if you can agree on the terms here, it won't be as expensive as working them out through the courts. Another thing is, the two of you will be more in control. But remember that either one of you can quit whenever you want."

"She's just got to know that she won't get everything her way. She wants to take my kid and my car and all I've put into that house and even my Elvis records. Well, that's just not fair!"

Damn, it was scary how convincing he sounded, especially with those tragic eyes. He'd probably win over Joel and she'd lose everything. Marty wished Chip was here to answer for her. She said lamely, "I'm not trying to be unfair, Brad!"

"Well, what do you call it when you run off with a hundred percent of everything?" Brad glared at her. She could only shake her head.

Joel said, "It sounds like fairness is a high priority for you, Brad."

"It sure is!"

The mediator's gaze shifted to Marty. "What about you? Is fairness your highest priority?"

"Well, yeah, it's important, but for me the main thing is Chrissie. I want to—"

"See, Joel? I told you she wanted to take my kid!"

Marty's fists clenched again. But Joel said mildly, "In our first session one of the goals we agreed on was to try to find a solution that meets everyone's needs. So it's important to let Marty explain her priorities, or the process won't work. Marty, what do you mean when you say Chrissie is your highest priority?"

"I mean she's already hurting and I think we should protect her as much as we can. Right now she needs stability. She needs to stay in the house she knows and in the school she knows and with the friends she knows. And she should see both of us a lot."

Joel asked, "What did you hear Marty say, Brad?"

"I heard her say Chrissie should be with her. Well, there's a lot more to life than this stability crap! There's music and dancing and advice about things. A girl needs a father, dammit! So I'm not going to let Marty lock me out of my daughter's life! She should be with me!" He banged his fist on the table.

Joel said, "I'm beginning to understand what it's like to be Chrissie, caught between what her mother wants and what her father wants."

Tears sprang to Marty's eyes. She blurted, "I don't want that! She loves both of us, Brad!" Then a wave of panic hit. Would Brad bore in on this sign of weakness?

But Brad's voice sounded husky too when he said, "I don't want Chrissie caught in the middle either. That's not fair." And for an instant hope blossomed in Marty's chest.

Joel nodded his tousled blond head. "So we have a major shared concern about Chrissie. Brad, what do you think we should do about this?"

"Well, I want her with me eventually. But meanwhile I don't see what's wrong with the way it's been. She comes to Tennessee on a lot of her vacations, and I come visit when I can. But this vicious woman wants a goddamn divorce just to close me out of Chrissie's life!"

Dammit, that was so unfair! She'd never, ever asked to close him out! Marty opened her mouth to protest but Joel's gentle voice headed her off. "It must be very upsetting to think of being closed out of your daughter's life. Marty, with regards to Chrissie, how do you feel about that plan? Chrissie spending some vacations in Tennessee and Brad coming here to visit her sometimes, for the time being?"

Oh, God, she'd almost blown it, almost responded to Brad's angry words instead of to the reasonable suggestion he'd hidden behind them. She was so frightened and angry she was having trouble hearing him.

But if Joel was right, if Brad was truly afraid she'd take Chrissie from him, it would explain why he was having trouble hearing her. Dee's words hummed in the back of her mind, *I'm learning to deal with how much of motherhood is loss.* Of fatherhood too, it seemed.

Marty took a deep breath. "Maybe that plan could work," she said, and though it broke her heart she added, "I think in a year or two we can review the arrangements, and she'll be old enough then to help us decide which place is better for her to be."

Brad looked at her with surprise. "You mean that? Really? I can live with that!"

There'd be a thousand details to battle out and a thousand tears to shed, but at that moment Marty knew they could work together for Chrissie.

Outside the winter clouds, chilly and repressive, muscled their way across the sky. Yet under the shadowed snowfields roots and seeds, only half asleep, were counting the days of cold, the hours of dark. They knew the solstice was near. The faraway feeble

245

sun would soon stay longer and smile more warmly, encouraging the tropical air masses to stream northward with their welcome troublesome gifts of heat and moisture. Seeds would sprout, leaves unfold, blossoms open upon a world of clashing sun and rain, blue skies and clouds, warm breezes and angry storms. And when the tropical air was warm and moist enough, and the northern air cold enough, and the winds aloft energetic enough, titanic thunderheads would again boil up and spew out lightning, rain, hail, even tornadoes.

But for now, the snow lay on the fields as gently as a mother's hand.